Memories
of Old E.T.

Silver Leos Writers Guild

ISBN: 1453744797

ISBN-13: 9781453744796

FOREWARD

THE SILVER LEOS WRITERS GUILD

PRESENTS

Memories
of Old E.T.

During the Texas A&M University-Commerce Homecoming of 2009, at the behest of our advisor, Fred Tarpley, Ph.D., the membership of the Silver Leos Writers Guild chose to embark on the production of an anthology of memories from alumni who attended Old E.T. The organization requested submissions by reaching out to the public through the alumni newsletter, news releases, and gatherings. Over one hundred anecdotes arrived for inclusion. In addition, several short memories from the fifty-year anniversaries of classes from 1938 through 1946 found their way into this book.

We are justifiably proud of both our E.T. heritage and our current affiliation as a member of the Texas A&M System.

These stories clearly demonstrate the extent to which we former students of Old E.T. appreciated our teachers, administrative leadership, and the learning environment provided by the State of Texas for our higher education. They reflect the pride, hard work, and pure enjoyment we experienced during our journey through those precious years.

Acknowledgments

We, the members of the Silver Leos Writers Guild, provide these anecdotes for the enjoyment of the readers and deny responsibility for the accuracy of any of the contents. Errors of a technical nature belong to the SLWG.

Without the efforts of our caring contributors, our hard-working anthology staff, and a supportive TAMU-C, we could not have recorded these precious memories.

All proceeds from "Memories of Old E.T." go to a TAMU-C scholarship fund to be determined. For additional copies contact:

Silver Leos Writers Guild
P.O. Box 1123
Commerce, Texas 75429
silverleoswritersguild@gmail.com

Since 1889

Dear Reader,

As a journalist and scholar, I have a deep love and appreciation for the printed word. As I read the thoughtfully composed "Memories of Old E.T.," I felt a profound sense of gratitude for the effort and generosity of spirit the Silver Leos invested in this project. The stories they have grafted are priceless nuggets from our past that will enrich the university's promising future.

As you enjoy reading the pages that follow, I hope you take time to do more than skim the stories of former classmates. I hope you find something that sparks memories of your experiences and that helps you recall what made your time at "Old E.T." or A&M-Commerce special. Maybe it was a professor who uttered profound words after class that altered your path in life. Perhaps it was a fellow student who later became your best friend. Whatever your memory, I invite you to examine these pages with an open heart and mind, and allow yourself the privilege of reminiscing and remembering the journey that brought you to where you stand today.

Like many of the great things that have shaped our university, the Silver Leos began as a simple idea that, thanks to the ambition and pride of our alumni, evolved into something much greater. Published separately, each story would be worthy of remembrance. Bound together, the stories become a great tribute to the legacy Professor Mayo bequeathed to us 121 years ago. Collectively, these stories are more than fond memories; they are a bridge to the future. For only by looking back can we see how far we've come, and the Silver Leos have done a superb job in illuminating our path.

Professor Mayo said, "No industrious, ambitious youth shall be denied an education if I can prevent it." Through the development of this book, the Silver Leos have proven that they represent the kinds of students Mayo so eagerly wished to serve. Both industrious and ambitious in their pursuit, these proud Lions for Life tell stories that are a testament to the legacy of talent and creativity that has been nurtured on this campus. Numerous authors have found their tools for success here, and gone on to develop their talents into marketable skills. As a university community, we are blessed beyond measure to enjoy these stories. Some are memories of humorous episodes, others speak of challenges overcome, all awaken within us a sense of pride in the way that this university inspires greatness.

"Memories of Old E.T." serves as a reminder that while Texas A&M University-Commerce has changed in name, our rich heritage of transforming lives through higher education remains strong, and lives on in the hearts of our alumni and the students we touch daily. The stories that follow and the stories yet to be written are important reminders to us all that we are the inheritors of Professor Mayo's injunction to follow our dreams and persist in "ceaseless industry, fearless investigation, unfettered thought and unselfish service to others."

Sincerely,

Dan R. Jones, Ph.D.
President

Office of the President
P.O. Box 3011 • Commerce, TX 75429-3011 • Phone; 903.886.5014
Fax: 903.886.5010 • www.tamu-commerce.edu
A Member of The Texas A&M University System
**

DEDICATION

The members of the Silver Leos Writers Guild wish to dedicate this work to Fred Tarpley, Ph.D. for his understanding of the writing process, his organizational skills in structuring writing instruction and activities, his comprehension of our individual desires to relate personal experiences in meaningful ways, his recognition of the creative nature of writing, his gentle motivation and encouragement of each of us as we attempt to express our own meanings, and his memories of his own participation in many events at Old E.T. Dr. Tarpley provided a safe environment where we could translate the written responses to our own complicated life events at a crucial period of our lives.

We appreciate the details of his considerable thoughtfulness. Not only did he devote countless hours conducting writing skill seminars, edit at least one paper for each student every week, critique our compositions with skill and kindness, find established writers to conduct seminars for the group, and direct writing tutorials in his home; he found ways to support participants in the cost of the process by arranging for tuition-free status at Texas A&M University-Commerce, free campus parking passes, free copy service for many documents, and university credit for successful completion of the course.

Fred Tarpley continues to serve as an excellent role model for students and associates, just as he did when we were undergraduates in the 50s and 60s. He is acclaimed in literary circles in the academic arena of higher education for his research and publication on dialect and place names in Northeast Texas. He has expressed his ideas about his beloved Texas in books, plays, and multi-media scripts. He is hailed as the "favorite professor" by thousands of college students. While we are proud of his public image, we are most grateful for our personal relationships with Dr. Tarpley. He remains our teacher, our mentor, our neighbor, and our friend, providing guidance, inspiration, and celebration for our lives.

SILVER LEOS WRITERS GUILD

The Silver Leos Writers Guild evolved from a TAMU-C graduate school memoir writing class taught during the spring of 2009 by Fred Tarpley, Ph.D. Rather than abandon the progress made and fellowship enjoyed during the classroom experience, members of the group mobilized a writing club. Monthly meetings improved our skills in the areas of writing, editing, and publishing to a greater degree. Active SLWG members at the time of this production include:

Membership

Lewis Allen	Betty Montgomery
Peggy Bedingfield	Shirley Moore-Secretary
Dane Bethea	Arlan Purdy
Nelma Dodd	Bobbie Purdy
Vivian Freeman	DeLois Stolusky
Bobby Harper	Earl Stubbs-Vice-president
Jerry Hyde	Fred Tarpley-Advisor
Barbara Kersey-Treasurer	Mary Beth Tuck
Betty Lancaster	Lavonne Wells-President

Anthology Committee

Lewis Allen-Selections	Bobbie Purdy-Editor
Dane Bethea-Selections	DeLois Stolusky-Editor
Bobby Harper-Co-chair	Earl Stubbs-Co-chair
Barbara Kersey-Editor	Mary Beth Tuck-Selections
Shirley Moore-Editor	Vivian Freeman-Marketing

CONTENTS

Prologue

Chapter 1

THEY CAME

Earl Stubbs—Class of 1957—Naples

In 1889, a visionary, William Leonidas Mayo, founded a college in Cooper, Texas, for the expressed purpose of training teachers. Awakened by the prospect of a fuller, more productive life, many hard-working people and their family members sacrificed to take advantage of the opportunity. Attending college and enjoying the attendant advantages no longer loomed beyond their dreams, and they found a way to get there.

Higher education was already available to the wealthy, but those who came to the Cooper school, and after 1894 to Commerce, were often from hardscrabble farms where a good brace of mules, a successful crop, food for the table, and plenty of wood for the fireplace and cook stove required most of their attention.

Additionally, those early students came from the working class in the cities and small, vibrant towns in pursuit of an affordable profession. They came to fulfill a need for scholarly interaction with those of their own ilk.

At first, individuals came, and later their siblings, their kin, their acquaintances, and the numbers grew. After World War II and the demise of the Great Depression, they arrived at East Texas State Teachers College by the thousands. To fulfill the needs of this burgeoning student population, the curriculum expanded and expands still.

What those educational pioneers experienced was far more than they could have anticipated or imagined. Over the decades, these scholars found remarkable leaders and teachers at E.T. who took them under the cloak of their wisdom and guided them to academic and social achievements. They found organizations of intra- and extra-curricular activities that formed memories enduring for a lifetime. They increased their knowledge at the feet of learned and impressive individuals whom they would always remember. They found friends, husbands, and wives around which they built lives. When they moved on, they left behind a base from which they could return for sustenance.

Special faculty members and administrators opened up the curiosity of the students and sent them out to perform good works. Graduates of the school of education taught and improved the lives of hundreds of thousands of our youth over the decades.

Not all former students became teachers. Some became captains of industry; some renowned musicians; many became agriculturists of the highest order in an area still dominated by the cattle industry. Thousands became part of the technological industry that germinated in the Metroplex and spread over the world. Some went away to war, never to return to the fruits of their academic labors. Some pursued the military and represented Old E.T. with remarkable achievements. Some gained international fame in the world of politics, and others remained in the academic community where they made significant contributions to future generations.

While Old E.T. no longer exists, its ghosts may still walk the campus discussing a touchdown scored fifty years ago or a class taught by a gifted professor who made the subject matter leap from the chalk boards into the minds and lives of students. So many derived so much from the time spent at this school that it is no small wonder the acronym E.T. lies imbedded in our souls.

Aulton D. Mullendore—Class of 1938

When I entered E.T. in September 1931, times were hard. I earned a tuition scholarship but needed more. I took a cow to Commerce, milked her, and gave milk to a boarding house in exchange for board and room. I had to drop out of school after two years. I worked, taught school, and returned to graduate with the class of 1938. The Honorable Sam Rayburn of Bonham, Speaker of the House of Representatives, was awarded an honorary doctorate with this class. Judge Sarah T. Hughes delivered the commencement address.

Chapter 2

GIANT

Michael Johnson—Class of 1971—New Boston

Remember that old movie from 1956? Rock Hudson, James Dean, Elizabeth Taylor, Carroll Baker, Chill Wills, Dennis Hopper, Sal Mineo, Earl Holliman, and a host of others brought Edna Ferber's novel to life. Filmed in and around the West Texas sprawl of Marfa, the film was a giant. The bible says they walked the earth at one time—giants, I mean. Did you ever know one? Ever know a real giant? I did. I even walked with one for a time. His name was Sam Cochran.

I arrived at East Texas State University in 1969—the runt of the litter if there ever was one—a rodeo bum with an old truck, a one-horse Miley trailer, two pairs of jeans, couple of sweatshirts, and one good little filly who could run like the wind in a spring storm. I also brought something else with me . . . thirteen consecutive F's in my college career. Thirteen.

Then, I sought to change my ways. My father recently dead, my mother devastated by grief, I was bound and determined to make up for my past failures. Oh, and I forgot to mention . . . I was scared to death.

My fears grew unmanageable when the counselor casually mentioned, "You need to go find Dr. Sam Cochran and ask him a question." I've long forgotten what the question was, but I remember the gut-twisting apprehension I felt.

"*Ask Sam Cochran a question?*" I thought to myself. "*Are you crazy, ma'am? I can't do that. You can't just walk up to a giant and ask him something.*"

And a giant he was. Here was a man who did not live on the earth with the rest of us. The pilot and only survivor of a B-26 shot down over France, Sam Cochran was captured by German soldiers and hospitalized in France. He escaped and survived by eating pigeons until rescued. Eventually, he made his way home, graduating from Ohio State with his Ph.D. Now he was my major adviser . . . and I'm supposed to ask him a question?

Cold fall day. Wind blowing across the campus, and then I saw him. He was walking—I can see him now—him with his long, purposeful strides. Walking with his topcoat on—striding, reaching with his long legs. I followed behind, shaking in my boots. Young farm boy with a stammer so bad I could hardly finish a sentence. And, I know you won't believe this, but as he covered that ground . . . *the leaves were parting!* The leaves were actually getting out of his way, so as not to impede the progress of this great man. Almost forty years now—I still remember the words as if I spoke them a moment ago . . .

"D-d-dr. Ch-ch-ch-ocran? C-c-an I b-b-other you for a m-m-oment?"

He stopped in mid-stride. In the slowest of motions, he began to turn toward me. Then his hawk eyes locked on mine, and my brain said, *"Warning, warning, Will Robinson—we are going down, we are going down."* And, he said . . . .

"Bother me? OF COURSE, you can bother me, young man! Don't you know that's what I'm for?"

Almost forty years later, I still remember. And, the giant became my friend.

Oh, he wasn't my syrupy, best buddy. As a matter of fact, he constantly prodded, pushed, fretted, and sometimes scolded me, always obsessing about the same thing. "You can do this. You have no idea the things you can do. Don't tell me you can't. I already know that you can. Come on, I'll show you how—and the awesome thing about it is it's not that hard to do!"

An obsessive bike rider, he frequently rode out to the old farmhouse I lived in eight miles from town. "Just to see how you're doing," he would say. During one of his early visits, he taught me how to study . . . .

"Let's take one single fact from the book," he began, sitting at my old kitchen table. "And let's write that down." I did as he asked. " Now write that same fact ten more times." Again, I did as instructed. " Now read and repeat that fact twenty times." After doing so, I realized we had spent almost twenty minutes on this one item. " Now I'm going to ask you a question," he said. "Tell me about this item we have been studying. Tell me all about it—when it happened, who did it, why they did it, what their background was, etc." I did so. Then he said, "Excellent! Now all you have to do is repeat this procedure with *all* of the items in these chapters you have been assigned to study . . . and you can make straight A's!"

I thought for a moment about how long we had worked on this one question and said, "All of the items? My goodness, Dr. Cochran, that will take all night." He stood up and at the top of his voice thundered, "OF COURSE IT WILL! THAT'S HOW YOU MAKE A'S!"

Shakespeare said, "The evil that men do lives after them. The good is oft interred with their bones." Sorry, Willie. That's wrong. While the evil some people do may well live on, the good that others do does too. Even though he's been gone for some time, the good that Dr. Sam did for me lives on. Because of the way he lived his life and the way he treated not only me but also everyone he encountered, the good he did lives on. Where would I be without him? Where would any of us be without the people who helped us?

Dr. Sam Cochran died June 5, 2003. He was eighty-one. He's buried in a little cemetery in Wayne County, Mississippi. I wasn't the best student he ever had, but I am the proudest to have been his student. I plan on going to that cemetery before I die. Don't know exactly what I'll do once I'm there. Might plant a flower on his grave. I'll probably cry a little, and I'll still wonder why someone like him ever gave someone like me the time of day. Don't know what I'll do for sure—except for one thing. Before I approach that place where he's resting . . . I'll take my boots off.

-- In memory of Sam Cochran

Aug. 1, 1921 – June 5, 2003

Clatie C. Hurt—Class of 1938

When my advisor checked my graduation plans, she found I needed a three-hour non-related course. That summer the only course offered at the time I could take one was a 300 course in statistics. Since I had no Math courses, I begged the instructor for permission to take the course. He agreed. My project was to measure 1,000 leaves of a campus shrub to arrive at the general width and length. I did the statistics and passed the course with flying colors, thanks to an understanding professor.

Chapter 3

HOW I GOT OUT
OF THE COTTON PATCH
AND
LIVED HAPPILY EVER AFTER

Mary Cimarolli—Class of 1972—Sulphur Springs

" I don't want to go to East Texas State Teachers College! I don't want to be a teacher!"

I was seventeen in 1948 when I graduated from Sulphur Springs High School and pretty cheeky considering the fact that I would be darn lucky to go to any college anywhere, anytime.

You have to understand that the war was still fresh in my mind. Not fresh as in the mind of someone who had been directly involved in that war but rather as an observer on its periphery. Glimpses of the possibilities opening for women during and after World War II were awesome, to borrow an already worn-out word from this new century. I might be something more than a farm wife, a dime store clerk, a secretary, or a nurse. I might be a foreign correspondent and get to travel the world! I might be a pilot! I might meet President Roosevelt, or even Joe Louis. How thrilling it would be to see what might lie outside the boundaries of Hopkins and Wood counties.

I didn't have a real quarrel with teaching. I was quite fond of my aunt and uncle who were teachers. I had studied under the watchful eye of Miss Annie Mae Whisenant at Seymore grade school, and I was greatly encouraged in my writing endeavors by Mrs. Jessie Featherstone of Sulphur Springs High School.

Neither did I have anything but respect for the college in Commerce. Certainly, I was proud of my mother, who had attended sub-college ever so briefly in 1920 when dear old E.T. was known as East Texas State Normal College. I was proud of my older sister who had attended East Texas State Teachers College in the early forties and who had even served as editor of *The East Texan* when the male editor went away to war.

So, you see it was the war I blame for my rotten attitude about the teaching profession and East Texas State Teachers College. Not even the revival of Sadie Hawkins Day after the war changed my mind. On a high school field trip to the ETSTC campus in 1945, I admit to being thrilled to see college girls "got up" like Al Capp's comic strip Daisy Mae, each prowling the campus for her own "Li'l Abner" who would take her to the dance that evening. I can still see how fetching Toby McDowell appeared that day in her little black and white polka dot blouse and short skirt. How wonderful it would be if a girl did not have to stand around waiting for an invitation to dance.

I found another college with a co-op program that would permit me to work a certain number of hours per week in exchange for reduced room and board costs. It didn't have *teacher* in its title. When my great-uncle agreed to lend me the first semester's tuition, I was off on the yellow brick road.

Suffice it to say, I wasn't prepared for college, but I managed to graduate in three years by attending every summer session. I didn't learn very much during July and August scorches, but college did keep me out of the cotton patch. Marriage followed graduation, and I went to Chicago to live.

Fast forward now, about eighteen years. I have returned to Sulphur Springs, a different person. I find myself a young, widowed mother with no job and no prospects for a job.

Suddenly East Texas State University looks like a great place to be.

When I enrolled in late 1969, I expected to see more dissent on campus. After all, I had come from Chicago, where all hell had broken loose in 1968, and dissent had become a way of life for many. There were still a few rebels around campus, but chiefly they expressed their rebelliousness in hairstyle and manner of dress, not in locking themselves in department offices until they could persuade administrators and professors to see things their way.

There were no special classes at E.T. for women returning to school in 1970, but the professors, with very few exceptions, were extremely helpful. Several of the other graduate students were a little older, like me. I remember meeting Dr. Paul Barrus on registration day. He was so helpful and courteous that I decided to enroll in his History of the English Language class. Mid-way into that first period of my first course at E.T., I recognized that I was about to be challenged as never before. (Notebooks from my various Paul Barrus classes are now prized possessions.) On the first day of class, he told us that there were 2,796 languages in the world. Thank God, he didn't expect us to learn all of them, but he did want us to learn that these languages made up twelve categories: Altaic, Uralic, Semitic, Chinese, Japanese, Indo-European, and . . . and . . . Well, you can't expect me to remember them all! I do remember (because he told us *nota bene*, and I thought that was probably code for "This will be on the test") that Sanskrit *tri,* Persian *thri*, German *drei*, Latin *tres*, and English *three* came from one root.

As I drove back and forth between Sulphur Springs and Commerce that first semester, I practiced saying aloud "The Lord's Prayer" in Old English (a Dr. Barrus assignment) and in East Texas English. I asked the Lord to have pity on me and help me pass the course. After that first experience with a real master teacher, I took all the Barrus courses I possibly could and fell in love with writers I would not have given a second glance if left to my own devices: John Milton, Ralph Waldo Emerson, Henry David Thoreau, Herman Melville, Mark Twain, and, of course, Flannery O'Connor.

Dr. Mary Beth Malone taught the undergraduate class I took that first semester. Dear Mary Beth was so busy corralling some of her more rambunctious students that she let me go my own way, and when I had time, I would secretly be conjugating, pre-fixing, and inflecting for the Barrus class.

Learning about early Greek drama from Dr. Bill Jack and studying research techniques with Dr. Charles Linck were other eye-opening experiences. Dr. Fred Tarpley gave imaginative assignments. Once he had each of us to interview an illiterate acquaintance in order to understand how that person learned. I fell in love with the little old lady I interviewed because of her phenomenal memory. She had never been to school, but she was very intelligent and her memory was crystal clear.

A Shakespeare class with Dr. Lawrence McNamee afforded us the chance to see wonderful plays by the great bard transformed into movies. I kept on the good side of Dr. McNamee by bringing him cans of sauerkraut juice, which he couldn't buy in Commerce. Did he actually drink that stuff? He was a boxer once; maybe he dreamed of becoming a boxer again. He was a great gardener; perhaps the sour kraut juice gave new life to his garden soil. Known as a good gardener, maybe he fed it to his plants.

Mademoiselle Eusibia Lutz saved many an older graduate student struggling with beginning French. She also pampered us with chocolates she had bought on her last trip to Paris (France, that is!) Once she told our fortunes by tracing the lines in our palms.

An audio-visual course taught by Dr. Bea Murphy presented many of us with a once-in-a-lifetime chance of writing, directing, and acting in front of TV cameras, as well as the opportunity to learn more practical skills needed when we became classroom teachers.

Yes, classroom teachers! That's the profession I was headed for, after all the earlier fuss about not wanting to be a teacher. And, it's the profession I followed all the way from teaching freshmen as a graduate student at E.T. to becoming a professor emeritus in retirement from Richland College. Teaching was the profession I loved and still love.

Thanks, E.T. I love you, too.

Roberta Frances (Knight) Edmondson—Class of 1939

My entire formal education from kindergarten through eighth grade, and four years of college was on the campus of East Texas State. I lived in the dormitory with the exception of six weeks that I lived in the Home Management House. It was while I was living in the HHH that the incident occurred. It seems that someone took the fire hose down and turned it on although there was no fire. Water ran down to the first floor.

Another thing happened in the old dorm. A gopher got in our room. I awakened half of the dorm with my screams. It was caught later. I was a member of the college choir. We made many trips on Sunday. One, I remember, was to Fort Worth. I sang my first solo and was scared to death. We put on an operetta, "HMS Pinafore," and had a wonderful time doing it.

Chapter 4

REVERBERATIONS
IN
LEGISLATIVE HALLS

Fred Tarpley—Class of 1951—Hooks

"Where Will World War III Begin?" "Can the United Nations Control Communism?" and "Overseas Teaching Adventures" were some of the programs that shook undergraduates from their Northeast Texas provincialism each Thursday night at East Texas State Teachers College. The sponsors of the International Relations Club, Dr. Nannie M. Tilley of History and Miss Adelle Rogers Clark of English, guided our international perspectives with an array of stimulating programs that broadened our Bible Belt views.

My travel had been limited to a radius of three hundred miles of Leonard, my birthplace. I had been transported through the magic of mind travel on a fantastic frigate enabling me "to visit lands away" through the images of literature and the landscapes of movies. IRC was a life-altering experience as I met natives of countries I knew little about.

During the fall semester of 1949, I went as a delegate with Dr. Tilley and other members of IRC to a southwestern regional meeting at Centenary College in Shreveport, Louisiana. My horizons expanded as we encircled the globe from one presentation to the next at the conference. Dr. Tilley could add some extra insights to every talk we heard.

In addition to the excitement of getting to know students from other regional colleges, I was sitting in a lecture hall for the first time with Negro students. Texas in 1949 was still segregated, and my only contact with Negroes had been with those who did occasional housework for people I knew or with a few Negro boys who gathered at the gin pool in Hooks to go swimming.

The Negro delegates to the IRC gathering were different from any I had ever met before. They ate with us, swapped college yarns, and matched every story we reported about our IRC speakers and activities. As the sessions progressed, discussion turned to choosing a chapter to host the next regional conference. "Oh, please, Dr. Tilley, could we make a bid for IRC on our campus?" some of the E.T. delegation pleaded. "We.. ll ah think we would do a tha..uht," Dr. Tilley drawled in her beguiling South Carolina dialect. But ah will need to telephone Dean Young," she added.

An hour later she called us together, reporting that Dean Frank Young hesitated for a time after she told him that the conference would require accommodation of the Negro students for lodging, meals, and on-campus sessions. "Go ahead and make your bid, and I will inform President Gee of the result," Dean Young told our sponsor.

With this news, we huddled to plan our strategies. In our presentation we impressed delegates with descriptions of the "South's Most Democratic College," our growing campus, our friendly student body, and our tasty cafeteria food. Other campuses made bids, but when the vote was taken, East Texas State Teachers College was the victor.

Back on campus, IRC basked in the glory of its triumph at the regional conference. Attendance increased, enthusiasm soared, planning began. The host chapter had the honor of naming the regional president and vice president. The president would attend the national meeting in the spring, this time in Kalamazoo, Michigan. I was elected president, with John Bemis as the vice president.

The national meeting would convene in Michigan in April 1950, and I prepared for my first venture into the land of the Yankees and the home of the automobile industry. With a train ticket from Commerce, I could make connections through Dallas and Chicago, right into Kalamazoo.

The week before departure for Kalamazoo, my picture appeared in the *East Texan*. There I stood, dressed in convention attire and pointing to the convention site on a wall map. Wardrobe assembled, bag packed, and tickets reserved, I was ready for the trip of my life. Then a telephone call came from the president's office. "Fred, President Gee would like for you and John Bemis to come to his office anytime this afternoon between 2 and 3 for a short conference," the administrator's secretary told me.

I had never been summoned to the president's office before, but class-mates had told me about their audiences with the president. None of their experiences had ever been anything I desired for myself. John and I arrived in the executive office at the south end of the Education Building. Jimmy Gee, as his wife and a few brash faculty members called him, was a retired U.S. Army colonel, a former assistant to Gen. George Patton during World War II, and a native of South Carolina although that geographical kinship cut no favor for Dr. Tilley. President Gee had taught agriculture and served as an administrator at Sam Houston State Teachers College before his selection as ETSTC president in 1947.

Ushered into the president's office, John Bemis and I were invited to be seated in the austere room by the commander of the college campus. With broad shoulders, a heroically-chiseled face, and an expensively tailored busi-ness suit, Dr. Gee gave us a baritone greeting. "Good afternoon, gentlemen. I understand that you have never been called to this office before and that both of you have good reputations on the campus. However, I have learned that without my approval, Dean Young gave permission to the sponsor of your International Relations Club to hold a regional conference at our college next fall. I have also discovered recently that the conference will be attended by persons of the Negro race."

Relief and concern swept over me at the same time. I hadn't done anything wrong, but I was in big trouble nevertheless. John and I exchanged helpless glances. The president continued, but his words tested my vocabulary, and his phrasing and his dramatic tone reminded me of Oscar-winning actors I had seen in important movies in Hooks. He repeated those statements in a letter he sent to both of us. As best as I can remember, my college president intoned, "Because both of you are so supportive of this institution, I firmly believe that neither of you would ever want to be part of an event that would send negative reverberations through legislative halls, violate social mores, and bring wrath upon this institution." He concluded in plain English, "I wish Dean Young had consulted me before approving your conference. It will not be held here." Neither John nor I remembered our cordial dismissal that preceded our immediate exit.

Trying to regain the composure of a college junior, I went to the library to do a vocabulary check on Dr. Gee's vocabulary in the Merriam-Webster unabridged.

Then in complete control of *reverberations* and *mores*—words that I did not use in my everyday conversations—I got the picture. Dr. Gee was telling us that if Negroes came to the IRC conference, the state government in Austin might scold our college or cut its funding, and everyone would suffer. Why didn't he say that?

While I didn't want to offend the legislature or society or see our funding cut at our college where fees and tuition were only $44 per semester with textbooks furnished free, I still wondered why ETSTC could not offer students the same experience as Centenary College. Eventually I got over the disappointment and having to explain to everyone why I had not gone to Kalamazoo.

President Gee remains in my memory as a visionary leader at East Texas State who raised the stature of the college while simultaneously raising the blood pressure of some of the faculty members who objected to his military style. Lest he be given the label of a racist administrator, I should point out that although ETSU was one of the last public colleges in Texas to integrate in 1962, it was one of the smoothest operations. As a good soldier, President Gee knew that he would have to eventually obey the order of his superior (the Texas governor) and integrate the campus. Despite his Southern upbringing and personal views, President Gee had assembled a top secret faculty committee to formulate a plan that would provide total integration of the institution. The tactical strategies were waiting to be executed when the integration order came from the governor several years later. When the governor gave his command, the college family assembled to hear the integration plan, and it was clear that Jimmy Gee had planned the operation as expertly as he had managed logistics for General Patton during World War II.

The IRC continued to bring world awareness to the campus, but our members did not attend another regional conference. After writing a letter to the national office, an embarrassed Dr. Tilley later learned that the fall conference we had been chosen to host was held at an Oklahoma state park. No other college could be found to invite IRC for an integrated campus meeting in 1950.

My interest in international relations continued, with an addiction for foreign travel, a passion for teaching English as a second language, friendships with many international students, and other side effects. But I never got to Kalamazoo.

Chapter 5

WHAT A DIFFERENCE TWENTY-FIVE YEARS MAKE

Bobbie Fleming Purdy—Class of 1967—Bonham

The year was 1963, and I was at the same time both thrilled and terrified. I was a freshman at East Texas State College . . . having come all the way from Bonham. My parents, accompanied by my younger sister, Reba, had driven those thirty-five miles that Sunday to bring me to Commerce where I would stay . . . away from home for an entire week for the first time in my life. With all necessities packed in one suitcase, a box or two containing pictures, books and other supplies, and a few items on hangers, I arrived that September day to check in at East Hall. Butterflies in my stomach and knees knocking, I ascended the stairs to meet my two roommates, both total strangers to me and to each other. One, Sue Bass Camplen, became a life-long friend; the other moved on to other interests after the first semester, and I lost contact with her.

Move in was rather easy back then. You hung your dresses in the closet, put your toiletries and underwear in the built-in drawers, set out a desk lamp and a photo or two, placed a few books on the shelf, rolled out a small area rug, made your bed with a spread that hopefully didn't clash with the one your roommate brought—and the decorating was done. The biggest decisions were who got what closet and which towel rod did you want. Desks, beds, and chairs were moveable, and occasionally we did rearrange the room. The walls were institutional white, and whatever was hung there had to magically stay without aid of a nail or tape that might mar the paint when removed. Each room was equipped with a phone, and blinds were standard window treatment. We could have curtains but only if using spring rods to hang them. Heaven help the girl who put a nail hole in the window facing or wall! Electrical appliances like irons, hot plates, pop corn poppers, coffee pots, and toasters were forbidden in individual rooms. A laundry room with ironing boards was located on each wing, so each time we needed to press something we toted our iron down the hall and back again. For the most part, even our alarm clocks were the wind-up kind. As far as keeping cool, each room had two large windows that could be conveniently raised or lowered, but electric fans were not allowed. Yes, we did have a television, but only one very small black and white model on the sun porch for our entire floor's use. I recall all the second floor girls crowding around it to watch the funeral of President John F. Kennedy. We had to cut class to do so, as the administration made no plans to close the school or excuse class absence. However, nearly everyone had lenient professors who kindly overlooked our skipping class on this, one of the most dreadful days in U.S. history.

Most of us had entered college at the ripe old age of eighteen, and it was believed that we, naive young women all, had been entrusted to the care of the college by our parents and should be unreservedly protected. We were allowed to date, but men got no farther than the lobby to call for us under the vigilant supervision and ever-attentive eyes of dorm mothers Helen Crader and Lucille Perkins. Departure times and destinations were logged in the dorm office before leaving, and we were required to sign in upon return. Curfew was 10:30 p.m., and God help the girl who came in late and had to ring the bell to gain admittance. If the chilling greeting by either Mrs. Crader or Mrs. Perkins wasn't enough, too many late arrivals earned a fear-provoking interview with Dean of Women Coye Bass Allen.

And, yes, we did have a dress code. No matter how frigid the weather, neither slacks nor jeans could be worn by co-eds before 6 p.m. . . . and then only if departing campus. The one exception to this rule was during Western Week, when girls were permitted to dress in western attire, jeans included. Shorts were allowed on the tennis court only, and then a knee-length skirt must be worn to cover them until arrival at the courts.

Having grown up in Commerce, my daughter, Meredyth, was familiar with the campus, knew many of the instructors when she entered ETSU in 1989, and could pop in at home anytime she desired to do so—a frequent occurrence. When she moved to the Kappa Delta house, we hauled a pickup truckload of her belongings across town where rooms were outfitted, at parents' expense, with refrigerators, microwaves, answering machines, computers, printers, carpeting cut-to-fit on move-in day, pictures hung on the walls using nails and hangers, and walls and furniture painted any color of the rainbow. Some co-eds decorated with wallpaper or paper borders, and drapery rods were affixed to the wall. Electric fans, irons, ironing boards, televisions, and stereos were considered necessities for each room. Beds were elevated on blocks to allow for extra storage, or even bunked with the aid of frames most often built by someone's dad. And, Meredyth had a key that not only opened the door to her room but also the door to the sorority house. At no time in her entire college life was she required to tell anyone on campus where she was going, or when she planned to return. When she spent time at home, I never quite got used to her dressing to go out while I was getting ready for bed, usually in the 10 p.m. to 11 p.m. range. Most Greek activities seemed to begin at what was the "bewitching hour" in the 1960s. Men still called for their dates in the living room on the first floor of the sorority house, but often there were open houses when men could visit upstairs in the girls' rooms. As far as dress codes were concerned, about the only thing a student wasn't allowed to attend class or college activities in was "the nude."

Meredyth graduated from East Texas State University in 1992. I had done so twenty-five years earlier in 1967. What a difference the twenty-five years made in privileges permitted to the younger co-eds. One thing that the quarter of century didn't change, though, is the host of friends each of us acquired during this, one of the best times of our lives.

Annie B. (Spivey) Raley—Class of 1940

My father borrowed $225 that was to pay for nine months in sub-college. He transferred the money to a bank in Commerce from the First National Bank in Winnsboro. The bank in Commerce went under, carrying $75 with it. He went back to the bank in Winnsboro and borrowed $75 more. I taught my first school beginning in the fall of 1928 following graduation from sub-college in the spring of the same year. I paid this note off, which was a total of $302, including what we lost plus interest.

I was fortunate, however. I did have four dresses, one pair of shoes, one coat, and one hood to wear on my head.

Chapter 6

A Confusing Day

Bobby Harper—Class of 1962—Caddo Mills

Joy fills some events, and you are happy that you were a part of them. Others make you wish they had never happened. There have been a few events in my life that bring back memories that confuse me. They make me wonder if they belong in the good memories or bad. The experience may be joyful at the time, and then later you are sorry that it occurred while the opposite can also be true. One such confusing event occurred during my senior year at E.T. Even today, I struggle with the bittersweet nature of this event. As it happens, it is even more disturbing as I write this paper.

On December 14, 1961, four of the local orphanages—Goodland Indian Home, Boles Home, Buckner's Orphan's Home, and the Oddfellows Home—brought several busloads of children to the E.T. campus to enjoy a fun-packed day in celebration of Christmas. There were 284 children and a similar number of couples from E.T. selected to be parents-for-the-day. I did not have a steady girlfriend at the time but wanted to participate. As it happened, a similarly unattached female student was also interested in participating in this annual event. For now, let's call her Judy. The college paired us to be one of the couples to serve as parents. Of course, we had no idea which child would be our adoptee for the day, but, as it happened, our youngster for the day was a beautiful little three-year-old boy. Let's call him Danny.

All sorts of planned activities awaited the children. There were pony rides, fireworks, games, a Christmas party, and a big Christmas dinner. The best part of all, for me, was the free time Judy and I had with Danny. We wandered around campus, had cokes at the Student Union Building, and just let this little boy run and play. Danny had started a little guarded, but by the end of the day, it felt as if he belonged to us, and he had us wrapped around his little finger.

Finally, late that cold December day it came time to put Danny back on the bus. His little hands clutched at my jacket as he tried to hold on to me—'to hold on to that day filled with love, laughter, and fun. His tears ran down his cheeks and splashed against my neck as I reluctantly handed him off for placement back on the bus that had delivered him to Judy and me. It had been a good day for all three of us, but it was difficult for us when the day had to end.

It did not hit me as hard then as it does today. I have mellowed with age, and raised a son and grandson of my own. I now have a deeper understanding of attachment feelings. For that day he had volunteer parents who devoted their every minute to his happiness. I will always wonder if he had ever experienced such love and affection during his life at the orphanage. He may have had a wonderful life at the home, and great parents may have adopted him. I don't know how life unfolded for little Danny and that may be for the best. However, down deep in my heart, I would love to know the story of how his life turned out. There will always be that little bit of sadness, and wondering. Maybe this is another of those events that could go either way. If I knew his story, would it be one of joy or sorrow? If his life has been a tragic one, would I feel sad, and wonder if I could have done more?

When I look at the old January 1962, *Locust Special* and see Danny on page fourteen, I will always feel a bit of a tug at my heart.

It was a happy event, but I suppose I am still confused.

Frances L. Reasonover—Class of 1938

I helped my mother can food all summer to go to college. Betty and I had two rooms with bath privileges at Mrs. Neal's. We had to put some of our food in a "smokehouse," and someone stole a box of our good peaches. We didn't think too much of it. We suspected they needed them worse than we did.

E.T. was very serious business to this depression gal, so I can't find much amusing to write about, but these are some of the things I loved: Miss Lomond's art classes, Mr. Lutz's chemistry classes, and just being with the "kids" in general. It was a great day when we had enough money to go to the movies and buy a Fudgesicle on the way home!

Chapter 7

MORE THAN A DEGREE

DeLois Bethea Stolusky—Class of 1957—Caddo Mills

I left home in the summer of 1953 and immediately fell in love. Not with a good-looking boy—I had already done that—but with the very air that I was breathing. I was seventeen, twenty-five miles from home, and living the good life on a real college campus, East Texas State Teachers College . . . the best. My professors called me Miss Bethea. Wow—that was a deviation from the past.

A constant flurry of change danced around in my head. Things like sipping a coke between classes with music in the background, buying my own books that were not "Issued by the State of Texas," and studying in a separate library building with tall, paned windows. I was having the time of my life, yet, on the other hand, I had a sense of purpose that I couldn't explain. I might as well have been at Princeton. Naïve, yes, but it worked for me.

I recall my first teacher, Miss Mary Lou Whitley, the daughter of a former E.T. president. She was dramatic, flashy, and reputed to have flown an undergarment from the flagpole in front of the Education Building. My newly found English classmates from Commerce High School passed that on to me the first week. That little tidbit of gossip interfered with my ability to concentrate every day, but I had to overcome. Our next day's assignment depended on what we could remember from Miss Whitley's oral summaries of Shakespeare's plays. I conjured up a mental image of the flagpole thing every time she started the class. She was precise, articulate, and somewhat demanding, but in spite of my juvenile mindset, I still consider her as one of my best professors.

Miss Effie Taylor probably was the person who first popped me out of my cocoon of security woven snugly around me in tiny, little, family-filled

Caddo Mills. After realizing I had failed to turn in one page of my final English exam, I thought nothing of leaving my next class to turn in the missing page without incident. She was appalled and said, "Miss Bethea, this is the oldest trick in the book. You students from little country towns are so pampered you expect us to continue coddling you. I'll take your paper, but you will not pass the test. I was stunned; my nose burned, and tears formed. No one had ever questioned my integrity. Well, she did, and I woke up in a new world right then and there at the age of eighteen. I made a D in the course. My major. Guess what? It's still there.

As the summer waned, I moved into the freshman dorm, decorated my room, met girls from all over Northeast Texas, and began to take part in campus activities. We settled into small groups and formed lasting friendships. We ate together in one cafeteria using the meal ticket that Mom and Dad bought. I learned to eat everything I didn't like because there was no extra money for hamburgers. I also felt the need to improve my table manners, so, with the help of my new Marpessa sisters, I solved that little problem.

After my roommate, Carol Harper, left to marry Tommy Felmet, I took her place working in Mr. George Kibler's office in the Industrial Arts Building. What a rich sidebar that was. As he lectured to his architectural drawing class, I listened from my glassed-in office space that opened into the classroom and learned these facts: First, it cost $10.00 a square foot to build a new house in 1955. Second, the classic picture windows of the 50s do not belong in houses without a view. This was his pet peeve next to seeing a lamp perched on a table obstructing the view from the inside. I still think of him when I see inappropriate plate glass windows.

Next, I quickly found out that the world renown architect, Frank Lloyd Wright, was Mr. Kibler's favorite architect—so much his favorite that he influenced me to appreciate his works and technique. Now, was I likely to become a fan of Frank Lloyd Wright's in my English classes?

Last, but most important, Mr. Kibler was wise. Lately, I've thought of him and the little classroom office where I used to sit. I smiled as my mind drifted off to some unsolicited advice he gave me one afternoon. He must have known something was brewing. "Miss DeLois, when you decide to marry, just remember this: Of all the obstacles and troubles you might have, the most damaging ones will center around finances." I didn't have a clue why he chose to tell me that, but you can bet I do now. He was sooo wise.

Ah, but I have learned so much since those days. I've done graduate work, taught English, Spanish, art and reading for thirty-two years, married my college sweetheart, raised two children, experienced devastating illnesses in my family, served on too many committees, shopped 'til I dropped, and enjoyed friendships from all over the U.S. I owe my ability to manage these experiences with grace and confidence to my parents and to my alma mater.

When I talk with old friends from E.T., we reminisce about our good times on the campus; then we mention that we don't think our children had the rich, warm, bonding experiences that we experienced.

Recently, I have returned to E.T. for a writing class with Dr. Fred Tarpley. I drive one hour each way. As I turn from Interstate 30 onto Highway 50 that leads to Commerce, nostalgia creeps in "on little cats' feet." I feel an overwhelming rush of gratitude to my mother and dad for sacrificing to send my brothers, Dane and Dex, and me to college and for how proud they were of us. Then, as I see the outline of the buildings in the distance and begin to hunt a parking place, I am actually overcome with love and warmth for the friends, professors, and great times I had there. When I detect an older building still doing its duty nestled low among the new, I feel warm and give it a thumbs up as I turn off my ignition..

My purpose in writing this memoir is simple. I hope I've imparted to you how much I love and respect old E.T., and how lucky I was to have inched twenty-five miles east out of the Blackland Prairie into the sand, pines, and oaks. It was the best time of my life and a springboard into what lay ahead of me after graduation in 1957. I repeat, "My E.T. was more than a degree, and it certainly worked for me."

Delbert G. Tarter—Class of 1943
When I started to E.T. in 1940, I took P.E. for the first four semesters in order to fulfill that graduation requirement. World War II began and the school built an obstacle course behind Whitley Gym. Then every boy in college was required to take P.E. every semester he was in college.

I lived across Monroe Street from the East Dormitory, and the shortest route to class was through the dormitory lobby. That's where I met Margaret Watkins, my future wife.

Chapter 8

BABY STEPS

Shirley H. Moore—Class of 1973—Ft. Worth

I felt like a *hippy* as I sat there on the concrete steps on the incline near the library. I held my four-month-old daughter on my lap as I fed her cereal and fruit from a plastic container. It was almost time for my class to begin, and I wanted to make sure she would be full, happy, and quiet before we went into the classroom. "Happy and quiet"—that was part of the deal I had struck with Dr. Harold Murphy. Out of desperation, I inquired if I could bring my baby girl with me to the next couple of class meetings. I surprised myself when I gathered up enough courage to ask him because as much as I liked him as a professor, Dr. Murphy still intimidated me with his crooked little smile—close to a smirk—and the way he ruffled those heavy eyebrows as he drew his head back and squinted at you. There was never a guarantee as to what comment would follow *that look*, but it was nearly always a memorable example of his wry humor and colorful vocabulary. This time he said that Shelly would be welcome as long as—and I paraphrase here—he didn't have to compete with any interruptions from her. As I remember it, she slept soundly through both of the classes she attended. It must have been all that cereal that I fed her while perched on those concrete steps because I was never aware of anyone else who dared to sleep in one of Dr. Murphy's classes.

When I signed up for guidance and counseling classes at East Texas State University in the fall of 1972, I didn't know what to expect. My second child, Shelly, was two months old, and my oldest, Stacey, was almost three. I had been teaching in the Dallas ISD for nine years, having graduated with my B.A. from Baylor University in 1961. A lot of time had passed since I had been a student in a college classroom. My husband, Jerold, graduated from E.T. in

1963 and was supportive of my returning to school at his alma mater, and his voice joined with that of my friend and teaching colleague, Sherry Durrett, persuading me to take the step. As it turned out, Sherry and I kept almost identical schedules as we worked on our master's degrees in guidance/counseling, and that made it convenient for us to make the commute from Dallas to Commerce together. I remember many study sessions when the speedometer indicated seventy-five miles per hour—sometimes even eighty—as we zipped along I-30. It was an absolute miracle that we made all of those trips without accident or ticket.

I completed my coursework and received my Master of Education degree in December 1973. By then, East Texas State University seemed like home. In the following years, I found myself taking course after course designed to enhance and expand my educational career in the areas of counseling, special education, and administration.

But—to tell the truth—no other professor at Old E.T. had quite the same effect on me as Dr. Harold Murphy. I learned very quickly, whether sitting in his class or simply passing him on campus, that when I saw that look—those ruffled eyebrows, twinkling eyes, and crooked grin—he was getting ready to give forth an interesting comment in his own unique and colorful way. His classes were stimulating and lively, known for both a high level of entertainment and a heavy dose of pragmatic ideas about guidance/counseling. For this reason, I never wanted to miss one of his classes. I'm glad that this warmhearted professor is a part of my memories of Old E.T.

I will also always remember sitting on those concrete steps beside the library spooning cereal into the mouth of my baby girl so that she would be happy and quiet, allowing me to attend Dr. Murphy's class. By the way, that baby girl came back to the campus as an adult to earn a B.A. in business in 2002. She doesn't remember her days in Dr. Murphy's class at *Old E.T.*, but I suspect that, as a student, she would have enjoyed his classes as much as her mother did.

Chapter 9

FIRST SUMMER

Mary Beth Rabb Tuck—Class of 1951—Point

My dad drove me to Commerce early on a Saturday morning in June 1948. It was a beautiful sunny day as we drove into the parking lot behind the East Dormitory on the East Texas State Teachers College campus. Daddy and I went to the dorm office where we met Mrs. Ruth Gant, the dorm director. She directed us to the stairs going up to my room. Here, Daddy told me goodbye and drove away.

I settled into my corner room on the third floor where my roommate, Doris Hunter, was waiting. My sister, Bobbie, who had just graduated, was a member of the Les Choisites Club. The Lacy members welcomed Bobbie's sister onto the north wing of the dorm and took me right in. They began prepping me for college and for membership of this social club. All day Saturday, we visited, ate in the dining room, and toured the small campus in the afternoon to see where everything was located. First, we went past the Education Building on the north side of the campus where I would eventually take courses. Then we walked east on the sidewalk that passed in front of the library, where we would go on Monday to check out our textbooks for the semester. Near the library steps, we paused by the old leaning tree as the Lacy's told me about the many couples who had lingered there.

I felt festive in the new sundress my mother made for me, and it was perfect on this warm, sunny day. As we walked, we stayed on sidewalks, because the Lacys told me that walking on the grass was taboo with both the student body and the faculty. If you walked on the grass and another student caught you, a scolding resulted. From then on, I was very careful not to traverse the campus on the grass. Our next stop was the new student union building (SUB) for a soda and a short rest in one of the booths. The long building had a ballroom where dances and other large events occurred. A second floor wrapped around and overlooked the ballroom, where students played cards and dominoes or studied. The other end of the Student Union Building was Arthurs where students could buy books and school supplies. It also had a fountain for sodas, coffee, and other beverages and 'burgers. With comfortable booths, it was a favorite hangout for students between classes and after dates.

Soon we left the SUB and continued our walk. We crossed over to the parking lot behind East Dorm and continued to Old Main on the left. Old Main held the Music Department. At forty-years-old, it was the oldest building on campus, but was still beautiful and loved by the students.

We began to walk faster, across the street to Whitley gym, where we would register for our classes on Monday morning. At this point, I knew where to register and get my books. I also saw the new Science and Industrial Arts building. One of the Lacys who was a Home Economics major told me that Home Economics, Chemistry, and Biology, were all housed in that attractive new building. It suddenly dawned on me that I would be in this building most of the time during my college education! Whew! Later I would find a long hall with stairs going up three flights. My Home Economics classes would be on the third floor. *Maybe this will trim me down as I climb the steps several times a day*, I thought, as we started back down the steps. I would be on all three floors of this building most of the time while completing my bachelor's degree in Home Economics. All the courses I needed to take in this building also had laboratories. I could imagine me being ensconced in this building for four years. Luckily, as it turned out, I loved the Home Economics courses with Miss Mary Booth, Department Head, Miss Orpa Dennis and Miss Anna Maxwell.

We left the Science building and headed for East Dorm. It was getting close to six o'clock, dinnertime, and we couldn't be late. Dinner at East Dorm was so different from dinner at my home or at my high school, where we now had the school lunch program. I joined the Lacy's table with seven more coeds all attired neatly in summer dresses. Only women were in East Dorm as well as the dining room, except for President Jimmy Gee. Nearly every Sunday, President and Mrs. Gee came to lunch at East Dorm. Mrs. Gee was always dressed up to the nines and wore a fancy hat. Sunday was a day we were all supposed to be dressed up in nice dresses with heels and hose. Today was Saturday, so we wore our everyday dresses in the East Dorm dining room.

I followed my friends to a long table and stood behind the chair. Not until all the ladies were behind each chair at the table did anyone sit.

After the eight of us seated ourselves at our dining table, a student worker brought our food in serving dishes on a cart with enough for eight people. Then she placed each bowl and platter of food on the table for each of the diners to serve themselves. We expected to enjoy one another with soft, pleasant talk. We always had a well-balanced meal with dessert served separately. I did my very best to mind my manners at the table. This is where we ate three times a day as long as we were in East Dorm, and I didn't mind at all. Soon, we would not have this elegance.

On Monday, we all scattered to register for our classes, purchase our pens, paper, and other things we would need for our class work, and check out the books we needed from the library. First, we went to Whitley gym where lines of tables stretched around the gym floor and signs announced the department where you would sign up for a course. Since I was taking only two courses, a swimming class and an English class, it didn't take me long to register. Soon, I went to the bookstore at the SUB, bought what I needed for my one class, and got a cup of coffee with a friend. Then I strolled over to the library to check out one book for my English class. There was no textbook for the swimming class, so I headed back to the dorm.

Classes began the next week, and I arose early to join my friends in the dining room for breakfast and a bit of talk about yesterday's events and plans for today. After breakfast, I collected what I needed for swimming class and left the dorm to walk to the municipal pool. Several of my new friends were also taking swimming class, and we walked to the swimming pool together. After arriving, I went to the dressing room to put on my bathing suit, and then went to the pool. Swimming class was great as our teacher, Miss Gertrude Warmack, taught us safety and different swimming strokes.

Often the Lacy's on my floor and I would walk to the pool just to sun, pose, and maybe swim. Occasionally, someone from the college newspaper, The "East Texan," would snap our pictures and print them . . . beautiful young ladies in skimpy bathing suits with great legs! This was a fine summer with many memories of my first semester at "Old E.T."

Chapter 10

G. I. VILLAGE

Lavonne Verner Wells—Class of 1950—Commerce

The year was 1954. My husband was a second term freshman at East Texas State College. This was after the Korean War, and there were many veterans returning to go to school on the G. I. Bill.

The college had moved military barracks onto campus to house G. I. married couples such as us. These units consisted of four apartments in one long unit, and there were five rows of them. We quickly added our name to the list of prospective tenants because they were located near the campus, about where the south parking lots are now. Maybe one or two couples had a car, but no one in our unit did.

We lived in the second row of apartments—the second unit from the west end. To the left of us lived a couple named George and Louann Fisher and their daughter Lynn. From Kansas City, George played on the football team. To the right of us was a couple I had known all my life because we all grew up in Commerce, Texas. They were James and Mary Jeffcoat and their daughter, Rosalind. James also played football. Our daughter Karen had two playmates.

We were stay-at-home moms. I had my teaching certification and degree but did not want to teach that year. We ladies had time to form great friendships while the children played and we did laundry. We did grocery shopping once a week.

From early spring to the first real frost, we could sit out on our steps and visit our neighbors. Usually the moms took the children outside so the dads could study.

We managed to go to all the school activities that we had time for, and we took the kids along unless one of our neighbors would baby sit. We walked to town to the Palace Theater every Saturday to watch the latest movie, which cost a quarter. Our kids went right along with us, and I do not recall that being a problem.

My husband's G. I. Bill paid for his tuition and books, and he had $130 left. We paid rent with another $30, so that left us $100 for groceries, incidentals, and entertainment.

By the end of the month, all the couples seemed to be in the same boat. Being creative, I organized our four units to have potluck dinners. This worked just great. My uncle, who was a route salesman for Tastee Bread Company, brought me the day old brown and serve rolls. Mom furnished the butter and jelly; someone else the peanut butter; and another brought bologna and veggies. None of us ever went hungry. We always had fresh milk and eggs because I had uncles who lived in the country. I should write a book, *A Thousand Ways to Fix Bologna*.

None of the units had TVs, and it was before the days of the microwave. We didn't have washers or dryers, so we washed our clothes in the kitchen sinks. We did our washing by hand and hung it on the clothesline outside to dry. We didn't think we were underprivileged. We just did what we had to do to get by. There was rarely a day that diapers were not hanging on the line.

Now, I think the quote "It was the best of times. It was the worst of times." could have applied to us. We actually enjoyed our three semesters in G. I. Village.

I do not know the year the Village was torn down, but I do know that East Texas State College provided a quality education for many returning veterans who otherwise would not have had the opportunity.

I thank Old E.T. for the thousands of hours of learning from instructors who knew you by name and cared if you succeeded.

I taught in Texas and California. My husband was a teacher as well. It was a wonderful time in my life.

E.T., thanks for the memories.

Chapter 11
COLLEGE FOR A COUNTRY KID

Jim H. Ainsworth—Class of 1965—Campbell

I overheard Mother and Daddy fretting about how to pay for my college tuition. Only a few weeks away from high school graduation in 1962, I was angry that they were taking away my euphoria before I had a chance to enjoy it—before I walked across the stage. I had never said I was going to college, anyway. I sure didn't want to.

Problem was, I didn't know what to do if I didn't go to college. It was time to go out in the world, and I had no marketable skills, no natural abilities. East Texas State College was only eight miles from our front porch, but it seemed like a foreign country. My parents expected me to go, even though nobody else in the family had.

I knew money would be tight, knew about the medical expenses and the drought that had wiped us out. How could I add college expenses to their burdens? I searched through the college catalog of courses and majors. Nothing there for me. Why waste hard-earned money? When I told them of my decision, Daddy stared at the floor for a long time. He always had a habit of drifting off, staring into space. I hadn't inherited his ability with his hands, but I had inherited that drifting off. He stood and motioned for me to follow him outside.

The tone of the discussion that followed surprised me. No longer man-to-boy, but man-to-man. Daddy believed that praise and affection drew value from their scarcity.

"Sounds like you're backing out on college because of money."

"I know we can't afford it. I don't know what good a degree would do me, anyway. I got no idea what to do with one."

"That's the point of going, Jim. They put that college over there in Commerce for kids just like you. Go a year. Give it a chance. You'll find something that suits."

"How are we gonna come up with tuition and books?"

"You always had a job of some sort. You help out with gas and spending money, your mama and me will take care of the rest." He started back to the house, then turned and came back. He put a calloused hand on my arm. "You make the grades; keep out of trouble, money won't ever be mentioned again."

I was surprised at the intensity of his expression and his words. A little tenderness crept into a selfish boy's heart. But I did not answer.

He focused his one good eye on me. "Take the chance I never had."

I nodded. Daddy has been gone for forty years now, and that last sentence returns to my mind often.

I found a job at City Pharmacy in downtown Commerce jerking sodas, mopping floors, and delivering prescriptions. No skills required. Mother cosigned a note for a '54 Ford so that I could get back and forth to school and work. I delayed college for the summer, dreading it every day.

In the fall, I stood in the Field House, staring at a sea of tables, kids, and professors. Everybody in that gym looked smarter, more experienced, and worldlier. Some well-dressed young man asked if I was a freshman. I said I guessed I was about to be, and he handed me a beanie. I stuck it in the back pocket of my Levis, hoping that wearing it was not mandatory.

I had dog-eared the pages of my catalog devising a plan to get through one semester. I decided on the general studies courses and an easy elective. Dr. Clyde Arnspiger, they said, was nationally known as the father of general studies, and he required everyone to attend Forum Arts and take Personality Foundations.

My job started at one, so I had to get all my courses in before noon. I was making progress before I stopped at Dr. Elton Johnson's table. The morning session of Business Math was full, he said, and I would just have to take it in the afternoon. I meekly protested that I had to work in the afternoon. He removed his cigar and pointed it in my direction. "Work or school. You need to decide, boy." I hid behind the bleachers and waited until he took a lunch break. The graduate assistant who replaced him took pity on me. Little did I know that I was destined to cross paths with Dr. Johnson many more times. I even grew to like him.

In freshman English, Dr. Fred Tarpley wrote a nice note on one of my first college papers. He asked me to consider English as a major. He doesn't remember either of these, but his words made me think I might just be able to do this college thing.

I learned more about literature from Bill Jack and Bob Dowell and was privileged to meet and listen in on a discussion with Flannery O'Connor, though I am ashamed to admit I did not appreciate the significance of the event and the effort it must have taken to bring a legend of literature to Commerce.

Dr. Lawrence McNamee joked with me in German class and made me feel collegiate. E. W. Roland seated us alphabetically and separated the boys from the girls. He made showing up late a humiliating experience, but he and Dr. Joe Saylor taught me things about politics and government that I still use today. Hugh I. Shott asked me to join the honors program, but I declined, still not sure how I would ever make it to graduation, much less with honors.

When Accounting and Finance chose me (I did not choose them), I started to feel a part of a small circle of new friends. I met Carroll Kennemer, another small-town boy, and we have remained friends for almost five decades. Ken McCord and Emmett McAnally convinced me that I could actually get a degree. In Office Machines class, Weldon King told me I had excellent hand-eye coordination. Too bad it had to be with a ten-key adding machine instead of a baseball bat or the reins of a good cow horse.

Some students went to SMU in the summer to avoid Dr. Carroll Adams' classes in economics, but that was impossible for me. He made me sweat, but taught me lessons that continue to serve me well.

Dr. Perry Broom's statistics class featured tiny mechanical calculators with knobs that had to be rung backward and forward with ears pressed close until a bell sounded. Distinguishing my bell from twenty others was impossible. He taught from a book he had written instead of the text listed in the catalog. His book was long out of print, but I managed to procure a worn copy.

A tennis player in the class challenged the three-hundred-pound-plus Dr. Broom to a tennis match. The whole class watched as Broom beat him three sets without moving more than ten feet.

When graduation moved from dream to reality, and E.T. changed from college to university, the school arranged interviews for prospective graduates. Dr. Graham Johnson took me aside and counseled against a job I wanted. "You'll be bored in a month."

I told him it paid twenty bucks more per month than the second best offer. He looked down at the shoes I had bought for job interviews and asked how much they cost. I said seven bucks. He looked down at his. "These cost twenty. You'll get used to quality." With that analogy, he tried to convey the naiveté of a career decision based on the price of a pair of good shoes. I missed his point and took the job anyway. What matters is that he cared enough to take the time.

E.T. provided an opportunity that changed my life for the better. I have one of the last ETSC rings and one of the first ETSU diplomas. I was a student when the first doctoral programs were added and when the Memorial Student Center was constructed. I parked on campus a few weeks ago and watched them tear it down.

The Four Lads performed on campus when I was a student, singing "Moments to Remember," the chosen song of my high school class. I was so disassociated with campus social life and so short of funds that I did not attend. I regret missing that event and many others like it, but in retrospect, I appreciate the university more because the institution, the professors, and fellow students pulled a green country kid along paths for his own good, even when he resisted. The student center of my day may be gone and the campus changed forever, but I can still walk across it, imagine President Gee carrying his swagger stick, and have those "moments to remember."

T. C. Newsom—Class of 1938

An amusing incident in my college life happened this way. We were all country, green, and timid. One day we moved between classes in the Education Building. At our door, History 221, we entered and took our seats. Then I noticed one boy there who did not belong. Our teacher was Dr. C. T. Neu, and he had been lecturing thirty-five or forty minutes when this boy raised up and asked in a high squeaky voice, "Dr Neu, what class is this?"

Dr. Neu answered, "History 221."

"Oh, hell," said the boy, "I'm supposed to be in English."

Chapter 12
As the Good Times Rolled

Dewayne Bethea—Class of 1961—Caddo Mills

After finishing my summer job as a house mover on Friday, I played around over the weekend, and moved into E.T.'s East Dorm the following Sunday afternoon. It was early September 1956. My first college roommate was Tommy Kelly, T.K. for short. We grew up together and graduated from Caddo Mills High School. Our room was located on the west side with a window overlooking what soon became my favorite haunt, the Student Union Building. The SUB, as it was called, was the hub of the campus; here we enjoyed fifties music, dancing, sipping cokes, smoking, and every kind of conversation imaginable. During my first semester at East Texas State Teachers College, I ate in the cafeteria, walked or hitched rides, attended most classes, spent time at the library, played intramural sports, and met many new friends. At this point, I was a typical college freshman, just happy to be there. I was one of the 2,160 students enrolled in East Texas State Teachers College during the fall semester of 1956.

Having met many members of the Tejas Club while I was in high school, my choice of a social club was easy. T.K. and I met many great guys that fall while pledging; little did we dream we would all become life long friends. My future brother-in-law, Robert *Stoz* Stolusky, was one of them. The typical Tejas member was either a veteran or an athlete or both. Dr. Fred Tarpley was our faithful sponsor and friend.

Beanie-clad, bright-eyed, cute, freshman girls around every corner constantly reminded me of the endless possibilities. However, since I did not have a car, dating college coeds was limited to special occasions, so those endless possibilities had to wait.

Settling into my first college semester, I found myself pledging Tejas, attending classes, hanging out in the SUB while listening to Jimmy Reed or the Clovers, and playing intramural sports. The Christmas holidays arrived, the semester ended, and I returned to Caddo Mills, rejoining the house moving crew.

The year 1956 was a memorable one for me; my sports hero, Rocky Marciano, retired undefeated as the world's heavyweight boxing champion, I graduated from high school, and my favorite rock and roll song, *Let the Good Times Roll*, hit the charts in August. Another interesting occurrence happened that year. The *Andrea Doria*, the ill-fated Italian ocean liner, sank after colliding with the *Stockholm* off Nantucket Island. Miraculously Sarkees Kaprielian, a passenger on the *Andrea Doria,* survived. He found his way down a long and winding road to good old E.T. and became a Tejas. When the Soviet Union invaded the small country of Armenia, Sarkees and his family fled to Beirut, Lebanon and on to Latakia, Syria. His family pooled their money and sent him to Ellis Island where he arrived wearing only his boxer shorts and a borrowed shirt. I am delighted to say he spent several happy holidays with the Bethea family in Caddo Mills during his college years. Almost too soon, the fall semester of 1956 ended, but I was hooked; E.T. was where I belonged.

Working through the Christmas holidays, I pocketed some extra cash and pronounced myself ready for the spring semester and the challenges of 1957. I said good-bye to East Dorm and the school cafeteria and moved due east down Greenville Street past the sycamore trees to 1911 Washington Street. On the corner of Greenville and Washington sat a small, one-room bungalow. It was just large enough for beds, a kitchen, and a bathroom. For six or seven years, only Caddo Mills boys were invited to lodge in the bungalow. We shared cooking, dishwashing, and house cleaning duties. Our front yard was large enough for playing touch football, parking a few old cars, and hanging out. The rent was $15.00 per month divided by the number of renters. Joe Johnson was the original person to find and rent the bungalow. One spring day, Burley Denton and Joe Blackwood drove into the yard in a 1946 Ford convertible. Seizing the opportunity to show out in front of a group of Hosses, Burley popped the clutch and gassed the convertible. The door flew open and he fell out, but Blackwood was so preoccupied with the dog and pony show, he didn't know the car was driverless until it hit the bungalow, doing extensive damage to both the car and the house. Tommy Gavin, Rex Lytle, Bobby

Harper, Burley Denton, Joe Johnson, Tony Gavin, Roy Lee Rogers, and I at one time or the other lived in the legendary bungalow.

My newfound freedom, as a college freshman, presented me with many new eye-opening experiences. I learned what a two keg beer bust, in an oak thicket on the banks of the South Sulphur River, was. How many ways can unbridled Texas youth get into trouble by crossing the Red River into Oklahoma? More than I have time or space to write in this sitting. I eventually found that English classes and wild oats are not compatible bedfellows, and the list goes on.

Robert Stolusky and my sister, DeLois Bethea, married on January 25, 1957. Their college careers were winding down as mine was starting. Robert was a running back on the Lions football team and a member of the Tejas club. My sister was a Marpessa, a Locust beauty, and a member of the AFROTC Angel Flight. They were my friends, family, and allies, and to them I owe much.

Left jab—left jab—fake right cross—and a left hook to the jaw—**bam!** I had done it again; he was finished. It was my favorite combination and it usually worked. I had just completed my forty-fourth boxing bout and won the1957 Greenville Annual Golden Gloves middleweight championship. I was lucky; I had not worked out a single day as a boxer for one full year. That was very risky business, but at eighteen, I was bullet proof, so once again I walked on the edge and got away with it.

The hot shower knocked the smell of blood, sweat, and wintergreen off my young body; it felt almost as good as the satisfaction of winning another tournament. I stepped out of the locker room into the raucous crowd, and Bobby Harper, an E.T. and Caddo Mills buddy, met me near the door. He said, "We have a group of friends from E.T. here, but that's not all." With an awestruck look on his face tempered with a slight grin, he told me a cute little chick named Frances would like to see me at the north door. I knew she was Frances McNatt, but I had never met her.

Sporting my beige leather jacket and my dirty white bucks, I picked my way through the rowdy crowd and arrived at the designated north entrance. We spoke, smiled, flirted, and worked our way through small talk, but more than anything else, I tried to be cool. The next thing I knew we were breezing through the February night in her 1957 red Oldsmobile convertible listening to old time rock and roll. I drove back to the bungalow late that night in my dad's borrowed 1954 Chevrolet work truck. I quietly caressed my boxing trophy, while thinking of the cute blue-eyed girl and thought, *Oh what a night!* and smiled contently in the dark. Ultimately succumbing to wanderlust, our four months of steady teenage romance came to a halt because I left town for the summer with three E.T. friends for Kentucky to work on the pipeline. At this point in my life I was running, jumping, and prancing much like a young buck, while throwing caution to the wind.

I returned from Kentucky after Labor Day to begin the fall semester of 1957. I left the bungalow and moved into the Tejas house at 1322 Chestnut Street rejoining my former roommate, T.K. My two-year tenure at the Hoss House, as it was sometimes called, was a blast, but my grade point average suffered. This legendary house was occupied at one time or the other by the likes of Earl Stubbs, Bud Smith, Robert Clements, Jerry Flemmons, Burley Denton, Eddie Griggs, Red Payne, Damon McDonald, Rip Templeton, Robert Stolusky, Bryson Ponder, Red Carroll, Red Elliott, Buddy White, Tommy Kelly, and me. A small one-eyed street dog named Gotch Eye lived among this rowdy crew. Her puppy, Chantilly Lace, named after a rock and roll song by the Big Bopper, was born in Jerry Flemmon's closet.

I listened as Mac Navarro described a fine looking, well-dressed new freshman girl with dark brown, sporty, duck-tailed hair, brown eyes, slender build, with a friendly smile. Mac had the gift for describing the anatomy of a female female student to perfection. I immediately became curious as one might expect an eighteen-year-old male to be. I met the pretty freshman girl with the sporty duck-tailed haircut a few days later in the SUB by accident. We met face to face in the pen, pencil, and paper aisle of all places. Little did I know, standing there in the school supply aisle, how Earlene "Pepper" Granger would affect my life for the next fifty-three years.

Lorena C. Carroll Sanders—Class of 1940

The greatest thrill was walking on campus and through the old buildings that my mother had walked when Professor Mayo founded the school. She lived in the Mayo home and cared for their children. My professors were great! I left E.T. more determined to teach than when I entered.

Chapter 13

MY LONGEST JOURNEY

Nelma Dodd—Class of 1970—Commerce

I t was 5 a.m. on a cold January day in December of 1966, when out of no-where, an almost scary thought appeared before me. A little voice said, *it has been sixteen years since you graduated from high school. Are you going to continue to live your entire life for your husband and children? Is it time for you to do something for yourself? Is it time for you to get your piece of pie?* After thinking about this a few minutes, I began to understand. For sixteen years I had given most my time to others; and, even though I was only thirty-two years old, I realized I was getting older, not younger. I had never before considered pursuing a college education. Again, I made a decision that greatly changed my life. I decided to get a college education. I was going to become a student at East Texas State University.

It is amazing how excitement can build within a person. I became so excited I could hardly stand myself. I knew I would be entering a new phase of my life; and, I knew it would be hard work. However, I was willing to do what it would take to go those extra miles.

There was one little thing I had not even considered—"who would pay for this venture"? My husband was the sole supporter for our family, and we lived from paycheck to paycheck every week. He was making thirty-five dollars a week, feeding a family of five, and supporting three children in school. This almost made me change my mind. Then I had another thought. One of my best friends, Jerry Lytle, was serving as the head of financial aid at the university. I immediately called Jerry and told him my plans; he told me to come by his office on Friday, and we would work it out.

With my financial plans solved, Jerry directed me to the registrar's office for additional instructions. I was given a stack of papers and told to fill them out and bring them back on Monday morning. At 8 a.m. Monday, I was the first person in line at the registrar's office. I gave the young lady the stack of papers. She sent me down the hall to take a test so she would know which English course I needed to take. I returned after taking the test and was informed I would know the results on Tuesday. The young woman asked if I had taken the ACT. When I asked her what an ACT was, she looked at me with a big question mark in her eyes. "You don't know what the ACT is?" she asked. When I explained I had not been in school for the last sixteen years, she smiled and sent me down the hall.

There were five people in the room, four young people and a lady who appeared to be close to my age. A young man distributed the test and told us there was no time limit. "You have all day if you need it," he said. Thirty minutes later, the first test taker went to the front with his test. Within the next thirty minutes, three others delivered their tests to the "tester." The only people left in the room were the other woman and me. We looked at each other, smiled, shrugged our shoulders, and kept working. About two hours later, we both completed our test and turned them in. As we left the room, another lady stopped us. She told us there would be a meeting of all new female students on Tuesday morning in Binnion Hall. We thanked her for the information and continued on our way.

We arrived at Binnion Hall at 8:45 a.m. Tuesday. The room was already full of young women. As we entered the room, my friend and I felt as though all eyes were on us asking, *Why are you two old ladies here?* At that time, I was thirty-two years old, and my new friend was thirty-four; there were not many our age beginning a college career at that time. We assumed the young women in the room were looking at us as *beyond old.* We smiled and found a place to sit down.

Everyone was dressed as if we were going to church. You must remember this was in 1967, before the surge of blue jeans and flip flops; everyone always dressed nicely. I will never forget the content of this meeting. A very distinguished lady, whom I assumed was the Dean of Women at East Texas State University, walked to the front of the room. She welcomed us and thanked us for being prompt for this meeting. Her first comments were aimed at those students who would be living in the dorms. She laid out rules pertaining to dress, dorm hours, and curfews.

Pants unacceptable anywhere on campus. Dresses, skirts, sweaters or blouses worn when outside of the dorm.

All females wore closed-in shoes with either socks or hose.

All females in their rooms no later than 11 p.m.

Doors locked at 11:05 p.m. and not unlocked until 7 a.m. the next morning.

The rules applied to those of us who did not stay in the dorms also. None of us could be on campus past 11 p.m. My mind began to twirl, and once again, I thought, *"Am I too old to go on with this?"* I could not understand how these rules could ever be monitored. *Oh, well,* I said to myself, *I will soon find out.* This meeting lasted until noon and every one in attendance went across the street to the college cafeteria to eat lunch; and as well as I can remember, it was very good.

Following lunch, I returned to the Registrar's office to see about my financial-aid check. I had to arrange to pay $105.00, which covered the twelve class hours I had registered for. I understood my books would cost approximately fifty dollars. While in the registrar's office, Mrs. Sue Sefzik, a woman whom I had known for some time, asked if I had received my ACT scores yet and I replied, "No." She said, "I will get them; I am so proud of you." This statement really placed me on the mountain top. I could see myself making, perhaps, a score of eighty or ninety. When she returned, my thoughts of a high score plummeted. "You made a score of thirteen on your first big college test," she said. My feathers fell. I looked at Sue and boldly said, "thirteen?" Seeing that I had signs of disappointment in my voice, she quickly explained that this was a good score for anyone, especially for someone who had been out of school a long time. She proceeded to give me the score sheet to give to the person who was helping me register. Excitement was back. I was now a college student ready for my first class on Monday.

We had only one car, which my husband drove to work. This left me without transportation to and from school. However, I did not worry about such a small problem. My mother or my father-in-law could take me to class and pick me up when I was ready to go home. There were no cell phones at this time in my life, so, I did it the hard way. I made a time schedule, and I never missed a ride home.

SILVER LEOS WRITERS GUILD

Again, I thought I was ready to begin my new venture. But no, I still had one more stop. Someone had made an appointment for me to visit with my counselor, Dr. Ruth Ann White. She quickly became the one person with whom I had always a direct line. During our first visit, I confided in her that I had become a little frightened and wondered if I had made the correct choice. She said to me, "Yes, I think you made right choice; you will do much better in your new role as a student than some of those who have recently graduated from high school. You know why you're here; and, you also know how much work will be needed to reach your goal." This visit, and especially her last statement, gave me the strength to "keep on trucking."

Everyday I thank God for leading me in this direction. He gave me thirty-five years in the field of education working with some of the greatest people in the world. I have never forgotten those times when I had to do a lot of praying to make it through "just one more day."

Earl Stubbs—Class of 1957

The most impressive theatrical performance during my time in E.T. drama came from Ralph Marcom who played Lackie in the "Hasty Heart." The part required not only a superb actor but mastery of a difficult Scottish dialect. Ralph nailed them both.

Ralph and I were both married and in our senior years. We lived across the hall from each other in Mrs. Rhu's apartments.

Ralph became a medical doctor—a loss to the acting profession. I joined the pharmaceutical industry in later years and came in contact with Ralph on a professional level.

Chapter 14
PLEDGING TEJAS

Dick Rothwell—1957/1959—Talco

I enrolled at E.T. in the fall of 1957. Don Eberts and I graduated from high school at Talco and were roommates. During the first semester of campus life, we decided we wanted to join a social club. We noticed that girls usually surrounded a group of guys in booths and around tables at the Student Union Building. This looked good to Don and me. We learned those guys were Tejas and referred to themselves as "Hosses." We knew John Clemmons, Eddie Griggs, and Larry Horton from Talco were Tejas, and Tommy Neugent from Talco was pledging Tejas, so we started talking to them about pledging. Don and I were "green" about social clubs. They could have told us the word gullible wasn't in the dictionary.

Don and I met Buffer Bethea, Jace Carrington, Robert Clements, Burley Denton, Paul Galvan, Tom Kelly, Gerald Whitesides, and John Williamson to mention a few of the "Hosses" who showered us with their brilliance and worldly ways. We learned the "Hosses" were campus leaders because they told us they were. Academics were a high priority to them as evidenced by their bleary red eyes from long hours of studying. For these reasons, and the fact that no other club invited us, Don and I accepted the invitation to pledge the Tejas in the spring of 1958. Some of the other pledges that I keep in touch with were Richard Roberts, Chuck Shultz, and Jerry Norman.

By the first club meeting, Don, I, and the other pledges learned things weren't going to be quite as pleasant as we had initially thought. Apparently, the members' opinion of the pledges had declined since we had accepted the invitation to pledge. We were no longer on a first name basis. Pledges addressed members as mister. Members addressed pledges as meatheads when they were in a good mood. The pledge captain was Bryson Ponder. Bry . . . um . . . Mr. Ponder was having withdrawal pains after leaving the Navy, and we pledges provided his therapy. We were, of course, delighted we could be of help to Mr. Ponder.

One of our responsibilities as pledges was to visit members and perform a chore to get their signature. This allowed us to spend time with the members and get to know them. A brilliant plan! Don and I went to Kel...um... Mr. Robinson and Mr. Bearden's apartment one evening to get their signature. Mr. Robinson, who was an Ag major, assigned us the task of cleaning his cowboy boots. I don't know what courses Mr. Robinson was taking, but his place of study had to be close behind cows, sheep, and/or goats. Manure layered his boots. This led to speculation by Don and me about Mr. Robinson's class work. We took the boots to the bathroom to clean them and decided they needed to soak. Don proposed we soak the boots in the toilet, and while they were soaking, urinate on them. I objected and pointed out it was unsanitary and might cause Mr. Robinson to have foot fungus. Don countered that he would buy the beer. I withdrew my objection. We cleaned the boots using our special technique, returned them to Mr. Robinson, and got his and Mr. Bearden's signature.

During a club meeting about mid semester, Mr. Ponder was having a more difficult time than usual with his withdrawal pains. After the meeting, Don and I discussed ways we could further assist him in his therapy. Don proposed we relocate Mr. Ponder's car to a no parking zone on campus. I objected and pointed out this might result in Mr. Ponder's car being towed and impounded. He would be without his car for a time, and it would be costly to retrieve his car from the impounding yard. Don countered he would buy the beer. I withdrew my objection. We had the plan; now we had to execute.

There was a light rain that evening—just enough to provide cover while Don and I relocated Mr. Ponder's car. He lived in barracks south of the Journalism Building, so we only needed to push his car a short distance to the no parking zone. In those days, people didn't lock their cars and most had manual transmissions. I opened the door and put his car in neutral, and we started pushing the car. We had pushed his car a short distance when his neighbor turned on his porch light and came running out of his house shouting, "Leave that car alone!"

This alerted Mr. Ponder, who turned on his porch light and came running out of his house. We immediately started running away from Mr. Ponder's house with me in the lead. We had two problems: first, the shouting by all parties other than Don and me caused porch lights to turn on all along the street, and second, we ran north and our apartment was two blocks to the south. I turned between two barracks, ran to the backyard, and turned south with Don close behind. After a short distance, something or someone grabbed my head. My body continued forward and became airborne until I was horizontal with the ground three or four feet in the air. As I fell, Don ran under me, and we both crashed to the ground. I felt a sharp pain in my face, and I put my hands to my face, which was wet and hot. I told Don I was bleeding. He felt my face and agreed. We got up and discovered a clothesline had grabbed me.

We rushed to our apartment, and I quickly went to the bathroom mirror to see my face. Mud and water covered my face, and a small trickle of blood came from the bridge of my nose. Thinking I had been seriously injured, we started laughing at the small size of the wound. To this day, I carry a huge one-quarter inch scar across the bridge of my nose.

The Tejas mascot at the time we pledged was a pedigreed dog named "Sir Royal Gotch-Eye of Tejas" affectionately known as Gotch-Eye. I don't recall why Don and I felt a measure of revenge was necessary against Jer . . . um . . . Mr. Flemmons, but we did. Don proposed we tie Gotch-Eye in Mr. Flemmons' bed during the day so he would relieve himself in the bed. I objected, pointing out that would be inhumane to Gotch-Eye. Don countered he would buy the beer. I withdrew my objection.

We went to the Tejas House one morning after Mr. Flemmons had left for class and tied Gotch-Eye to the four corners of his bed. Gotch-Eye performed as predicted. Unfortunately, other Tejas members spotted us and squealed. Mr. Flemmons and others visited us that evening and took us to the Tejas House for a work detail. We lost ground on that venture.

After many threats to the contrary, the Tejas Club accepted us as members near the end of the semester. We formed relationships with existing and future members that are still active after fifty years.

The above recollections of pledging the Tejas Social Club are true; except those that aren't.

Chapter 15

SCHOOL DAYS

Jean Cranford Appleton—Class of 1956—Commerce

My memories of East Texas State Teachers College begin much earlier than recollections of my college days. I began kindergarten at the age of four in 1941 at East Texas State Teachers College Training School. My recollections begin in what we called the Education Building, now called the Ferguson Social Science Building.

The building seemed enormous to me. The second floor housed classes for kindergarten through third grade. Fourth grade through Sixth grade were on the first floor. Our playground was on the south side of the building where we had swings, seesaws, and parallel bars. During recess when we weren't jumping off the seesaw so that the person on the other end hit the ground, or dangling from the parallel bars, the girls were chasing the boys or vice versa. There was an area for small animals. Rabbits and guinea pigs are all I remember, but on one occasion, a boy named Joel brought his white rat to school. My whole class, all of about ten students, expressed our amazement by squealing and giggling.

Most of the students went home for lunch, but on rainy days, my mother brought paper bag lunches to school for my brother, Jerry, who was two years ahead of me, and for me. We loved eating lunch at school in what we called the basement, a recessed area on the first floor. Our classes were small, our teachers memorable, and our education wonderful.

The Association of Early Childhood Education held an annual tea at the president's home for the elementary school children. We dressed up in our Sunday school finery on that day, and the pretty student teachers entertained us as we sat on the floor eating cookies, drinking punch, and listening to stories.

I remember the names of all of my teachers from kindergarten through sixth grade: Miss Pledger, Miss Pickering, Mrs. Doty, Miss Clemmer, Mrs. Shepherd, Miss Sanders, and Miss Quinby. Our principal was Mr. Watson. For music, we had Miss Patton, for art Miss Neal, for Spanish Miss Clark, and for P.E. Miss Branom and Miss Huggins—inspiring teachers all. Miss Quinby left the most lasting impression. Her hair tint ranged from henna red to orange to pink. She often wore a colorful purple dress with her ample bosom buttressed by a corset. However, while her appearance mesmerized our class, her travels were of the utmost interest to us. She had been to China, Europe, and the South Seas. What wonderful stories she had to tell. We adored her.

In the spring, Miss Clark would begin to teach us the hat dance and the words to Linda Piñata. On Cinco de Mayo we presented a program in Spanish. The boys wore sombreros and serapes. The girls wore peasant blouses and full skirts. We were sure we looked authentically Mexican. Although we had Spanish classes from third grade to sixth grade, every year we had to relearn the song and the dance. One year, we wore flower costumes with the petals circling our faces. This was less than successful as we had trouble seeing the people on either side of us. We kept bumping into each other during the dance.

At the end of my sixth grade year, the Training School ended. What a sad time that was. My mother had attended and graduated from Training School, as had many residents of Commerce. My brother and I finished our middle school and high school years in the Commerce Public Schools. I was well prepared at Training School to join a new system, and my education in the public schools continued to prepare me for college.

When I entered East Texas State Teachers College as a freshman in 1953, I was following the tradition set by my grandmother, mother, and brother, and once again, most of my classes were in the Education Building. It didn't seem quite so large to me then, but once again, I had outstanding teachers. Miss Clark, Miss Branom, Miss Huggins, and Miss Neal were still on the faculty. Among faculty members with whom I had classes were Dr. Paul Barrus, Mr. James Lacy, Dr. James Byrd, Miss Eusibia Lutz, Mr. Vincent Miller, Mr. Lawrence McNamee (my faculty adviser who came to meetings through the window instead of the door), Dr. Arthur Pullen, Dr. Margaret Wiley, Miss Mary Bowman, Miss Elizabeth Huggins, Miss Lorena Brannom, Dr. Everettt Shepherd, and many, many more. Dr. James G. Gee was the president of the college, and I cannot imagine a more dignified and courtly president. Miss Margaret Berry was Dean of Women. She was strict and firm, yet kind, as she controlled the campus lives of the female students.

We had to wear raincoats over our shorts when we were going to P.E. The only time we could wear jeans was during Western Week.

During the fall semester of my freshman year in 1953, Duaine and I married. With permission from Dean Berry and my instructors, I missed two weeks of school and pledged a social club a week later than the rest of the pledge class. Duaine left for Korea, and I returned to my classes and pledged Tooanoowe. Duaine returned from Korea in 1955, resumed his education, and graduated with me in 1956. Those were different times, but the understanding of Dean Berry and our teachers made it possible for us to continue our paths in college and finish our degrees.

My years as an elementary student and as a college student at ETSTC were so important to me in both my educational and social growth. The experience challenged, encouraged, and most of all, educated me. The administration, the faculty, and the student body communicated and interacted with each other with respect on all sides. What a wonderful time and place to be a student. I am proud to have a Bachelor of Arts degree from East Texas State Teachers College.

Evelyn Underwood Click—Class of 1943

Perhaps my most memorable experience was the big move we made from the new East Dorm to the ancient West Dorm when the WACS came to our campus for training during World War II. Rather than move to the Les Choisites House, I chose to move with Miss Frances Potts and many others to the old West Dorm, and there I met many new friends and loved living in that needed-to-be-condemned building until graduation.

Chapter 16
HELP FOR CLASSES

Peggy Bedingfield—Class of 1983—Quinlan

We are writing stories about memories from college. ETSU, as I knew it. What to write about? Dr. Lawrence McNamee, perhaps? Or maybe Dr. Jack Lamb and his jokes in class, or his love of science and math rolled together into one obsession? How about the Baptist Student Union, as it was called then? R.O.T.C.? Old roomies? New adventures? How does one choose? Not much really stands out from that time. (What was that time?) Well, there might be one or two memories.

I was a junior and trying to get it together in time to pay for classes, but the Financial Aid Office lost my paperwork for the grant and student financial aid.

I had two days to pay for classes and no money. I was devastated. I had some of my books and my class schedule but no money to pay for those classes. I went to talk to one of my best friends about what to do, but she was busy. Then I went to the BSU and plopped down on one of the couches placed beside a large plate glass window.

I sat there feeling sorry for myself, sighing and moping about when the BSU Secretary, Linda Edwards, came out and asked why I had such a long face. I shrugged, not really wanting to talk to an *ADULT* member of the staff about my problems. For some reason I didn't think of myself as an adult. After all, I was only nineteen.

She finally got me to tell her my problem, and all she said was "Hmm. Let me talk to someone."

I smiled at her and shrugged it off, deciding I had better get packed and ready to head home with my "tail between my legs." My parents would roll their eyes and do the "I told you so" thing when I got there, but at the time,

I didn't think I had any other choice. Much to my surprise, I was proven wrong the next day.

Linda called me into her office and closed the door. "*Oh, boy,*" I thought, "*I did SOMETHING wrong!*"

Linda's husband, Wendell, who taught accounting, was there, looking very stern and stoic. He started talking about responsibility of paying back loans and signing papers at the bank, and other things I couldn't wrap my poor brain around. I had NO idea what he was talking about.

Finally, Linda explained that she and Wyndell were willing to co-sign a student loan for me for that semester. I nearly fainted. My own parents hadn't offered that.

We went to the local branch of what was then Banc One, and Wendell told the financial officer what they wanted to do. He tried to discourage them, but in the end, Wendell and Linda signed the note.

I paid for classes and finished buying books and other supplies. Then I started working even harder to get the paperwork found and filed. After two months, and about three days before the loan was due, my paperwork came through, and the money became available.

I rushed to the bank and paid off the loan, feeling proud of myself and highly relieved. I went to the BSU and told Linda the loan was paid back, along with the interest. She just smiled and said, "Good." and left it at that.

A month later she gave me the paperwork the bank had sent them showing the loan was paid.

I honestly feel that if it had not been for Linda and Wendell, I would never have finished college or met the many wonderful people who have passed through my life. Some of whom are still around.

Elizabeth S. White—Class of 1940

Because W. T.'s (Dub's) only sister was killed in a car wreck in December of our senior year, we were married in March and moved in with his family. Married students in college were the exception to the rule in 1940, and I remember at the graduation exercises President Sam Whitley announced my name and then said, "And this young lady made four As and one B and got married all in the same semester."

Chapter 17

MAM'SELLE

Jane Harper—Class of 1963—Paris

If you are going to teach French, they will always expect you to be a bit eccentric; don't ever disappoint them. Eusibia Lutz, 1961

The rustle of the repeated reference was everywhere: "Mam'selle said . . . ; Mam'selle always . . . ; Mam'selle never . . . ; Mam'selle would have . . . ." Each "Mam'selle" was spoken with respect, with a touch of reverence, with fond remembrance, with gratitude, with wonder, with awe as well as with a hint of magnolias in the pronunciation, as she had taught us herself. The house of the Texas A&M University-Commerce president was filled with former students and faculty friends dressed in black and white, sporting pins and broaches and bracelets and necklaces and earrings and cuff links and tie tacks in the form of a fleur de lys, the symbol of the French monarchy. We were celebrating what would have been the one hundredth birthday of our honoree, professor/scholar/friend Mlle Eusibia Lutz. As we had always done, we fell into perfect step with her preferences, her ideals, her image, our shared memory of her elegance and dignity.

Celebration of the significance of her life on each of ours was our primary reason for gathering back on campus that day. The other celebration was secondary, but still important to those of us who had waited eagerly to hear each new chapter of the novel that she had written (and re-written) through the years. After decades of crafting and redesigning the details of the story and adding increasingly tantalizing snippets to enhance the chances of publication, Mam'selle had given up on getting the story of her fictional Denise to press and to the public. So we, her students and friends, had finally taken matters into our own hands. *Strangers in Babylon* was edited, proofread, and published by our admiring group of devotees. Our birthday celebration doubled as the coming-out party for her long-anticipated manuscript.

Such long-term devotion to a professor by decades of students at any university must be rare, but it seems totally natural for those of us who spent years of study under her careful direction. Such devotion was birthed and nourished by the dedication of Eusibia Lutz to her students.

Mam'selle was the teacher-scholar who guided us to the understanding and acceptance that the humanities function as a system, as a whole. Everything works together and influences everything else. There are no separate boxes where music and art and literature and languages and history and politics and sociology and psychology reside and work independently of all the rest. Whatever is discovered in one discipline has immediate and irrefutable application to all other intellectual realms. Therefore, the study of French encompasses the study of ballet and theatre and mime, of art songs and orchestra and opera and folk tunes, of military and political and intellectual and cultural and monetary history, of sculpture and painting and fashion and cuisine and garden design, of poetry and prose and drama and essays and children's riddles, in addition to expected topics of grammar and vocabulary and tense and dialect and register. Mam'selle flooded us with information, ideas, theories, suppositions, and possibilities and helped us to discover the possible connections and relationships among them all.

She referred to her teaching style as "audio—visual—edible" education. (As I write this essay, I keep having visions of "babas au rhum" served at French Club, where I never wanted my rum-soaked cake to touch the napkin for obvious reasons.) We were to experience French with all our senses all the time. Perhaps this total immersion in all things French was the secret that allowed teenagers from East Texas to acquire understandable speech patterns and writing skills and international interests that would permit us to develop lifelong friendships with native speakers of French from various parts of the world.

Merci mille fois, Mam'selle. You have made possible this academic life of wonder that I experience on a daily basis.

Chapter 18

HITCH HIKE, "LEAVE THE DRIVING TO US," OR CAR POOL

Jerry Hyde—Class of 1954—Greenville

In September 1950, I began an adventure that would last four years—commuting to East Texas State Teachers College. I was sixteen, and though I had been kissed, I was still green, green as the Johnson grass that grew on my father's farm. Earlier that year my father had sold our farm located close to Wagner, and we moved to Greenville. I had secured a job at White's Department Store as a sales person working from 1 to 5 p.m. on weekdays, and 7 to 9 p.m. on Saturdays. With such lucrative employment in Greenville, I could not stay on the campus of Old E.T. as the college town was fifteen miles from the Hunt County seat. Therefore, I was forced to commute.

My first year as a commuter was fun; I rode to school with comrades, even though the driver was eccentric. The driver, Vic, had a 1939 Chevrolet sedan that he kept immaculately clean. Vic's apparel was nearly always the same—blue jeans, white tee shirt with the sleeves rolled up, and a package of Lucky Strike cigarettes neatly inserted in the sleeve of his left arm (Sound like The Fonz?). He placed that arm out the left window with bicep flexed. This was all right, but in the winter, it got kind of cold for Howard and me in the back. The fourth passenger, Bill, always rode in the front passenger seat, for the driver assigned seating in the '39 Chevrolet. Bill, his best friend, got the prize seat; Howard, his classmate, got the second best seat, the one behind the driver. My seat was the "rotten apple" of the basket—the right hand rear seat. For in the winter with the driver's front window glass rolled down, the occupant of this seat was apt to freeze to death.

The second year of commuting was a little different. Vic, my driver, dropped out of college, sold his '39 Chevrolet, and joined the Air Force. Since none of Vic's passengers had access to a car, and Howard could not even drive, we had to find other means of transportation. So "leave the driving to us" became the three's motto. The Greyhound bus left the county seat at 6:15 a.m. and arrived at the college town about 7 a.m., thus giving the bus riders thirty minutes to walk the half mile to their first class.

The bus ride was not bad. The seats were comfortable, and at least you did not freeze in the winter. The problem was that the big Greyhound did not go from Commerce to Greenville in the early afternoon, so to get home; the carless commuters had to catch a ride.

Hitch hiking was normally non-eventful. But, there were a few adventures that my fellow hikers and I had. There were several incidents where we caught rides with people who were intoxicated. It is not easy do your home work when the vehicle you're riding in is on the wrong side of the road, or when the drivers have to stop numerous times to relieve themselves.

To the best of my knowledge, no commuter was ever hurt in an accident but several had to change their garments when they reached their designation. On one occasion a sexual advance was reported, but knowing the hiker, I took no stock in this report.

Between classes, off-time for the commuter was different from the live-in Commerce students. The live-ins would go to the dorm, "club," or home to study, visit, or fool around. Much of the commuter's off-time was spent in old autos. Commuters with money could go to the Student Union Building for a little refreshment. The talented ones could practice the two-step with a member of the opposite sex, or the athletic ones could play ping pong for hour on hour. Those without funds, talent, or athletic ability holed up in those old cars, summer, winter, spring, and fall, attempting to out-do each other telling yarns of our adventures, bragging about conquests made, and describing ventures planned . . . and perhaps, just once in a while, resorting to cracking the books.

Of the four commuters from my first year, Vic joined the Air Force, Bill got drafted, I graduated, and Howard just disappeared.

Chapter 19

DR. HUMFELD, THE RUBBER CHICKEN, AND THE OVERTURE OF 1812

B. A. Montgomery—Class of 1972—Dallas

I rarely speak or write of my time as an undergrad at E.T. for the simple reason that it is a very hazy and vague place in my mind. I never was very good at history in school because I had no memory at all for dates. The names of acquaintances or historical characters would often flee from my mind soon after introduction. I had to say the name of a person a number of times before I could remember and must speak to them often to connect a name to a face. This is sad, socially embarrassing, but all too true.

Given the above, there are a number of stories that I could tell that others might find interesting because of who they were. However, I can't remember the folks' names!

I do remember Dr. Neil Humfeld quite well as I was a loyal and proud member of Humfy's Heroes from the fall of 1968 to the December graduation of 1972. The group was also known as the Lion Marching Band.

That man amazed me. At my first band practice my freshman year, he greeted each of us, and after we were seated in our sections with instruments at ready, he started at the back of the Band Hall with the always rowdy drum section and started naming names. When he got to a freshman, he introduced us as a new member giving our hometown and high school as he had with all the others. He did all of this from memory. There was no cheat sheet in evidence, and I can tell you that he performed the same feat every new marching season that I was in the band.

Another incident with the band that everyone enjoyed, even Dr. Humfeld, involved a rubber chicken. The predictable kind of rubber chicken that looks dead and totally plucked.

We were practicing for a concert, and one of the numbers just happened to be the Overture of 1812. The drum section had wanted real cannon of course, but that idea had been vetoed quickly. Then someone suggested a shotgun shooting blanks into a barrel. This was vetoed as well. Dr. Humfeld's solution and, thus, the one used, involved the bass drum and the tympani struck in unison. This solution was much to the disappointment of the drum sections. The idea of the shotgun blasting into a drum was by far the most popular solution within the drum section.

Dr. Humfeld told us of various odd ways other bands emulated the sound effect of cannons. One of the tales he told was of an outside performance where a shotgun actually had been used. Unfortunately the drummer in charge of it had forgotten to replace the real bullets with blanks resulting in a dead duck falling out of the sky during the concert.

Thus during one practice session in the band hall, just after the boom of the drums emulating the cannons of that famous battle, a rubber chicken came sailing over everyone's heads. It just happened to narrowly miss Dr. Humfeld's head causing him to duck wildly and everyone to gasp at the close call. Then, as we realized no harm was done, we all cracked up. Dr. Humfeld was chuckling as he stepped from his director's podium to pick up the fake, denuded chicken.

From somewhere back in the drum section, a voice called, "Sorry sir! I didn't mean to get that close!"

As I remember, Dr. Humfeld's reply was, while holding up the scraggly looking rubber chicken and grinning, "Well, now at least you know why I vetoed the shotgun!"

Chapter 20
CALL ME *MISTER* ADAMS

Arlan Purdy—Class of 1967—Bonham

In the fall of 1964, my classes included "Introduction to Economics." Numerous students had told me that they hoped I *did not* get Dr. Carroll Adams, warning me that he was somewhat demanding and his courses quite challenging. On the first class day, the professor walked into the room and wrote his name on the board. Lo and behold, there it was: "W. C. Adams."

"My name is William Carroll Adams. I have an earned doctorate but prefer to be called *Mister*," he stated. Continuing, he outlined his class expectations, "#1 Be to class on time. I will lock the door. #2 Always wear socks. I will buy you a pair if you do not have any and can't afford them. Socks are normal business attire. #3 No chewing gum in class. If caught, you will be asked to leave. #4 No studying or reading in class unless it is a study session for this class. If work for this class is complete, then you may study for another course."

In this brief introduction, Carroll Adams earned my respect and admiration. He continues to own it.

As a whole, *we were on time, socked, gumless, and adhered to studying only economics during class time.* We also complied with his wishes that he be addressed as *Mister*.

Mr. Adams also told us that at one time he had been a high school English teacher. From all the red marks on some of my papers, I believe it. However, he seldom deducted points for spelling and grammatical errors unless they were critical to the answer.

I had Mr. Adams for four courses: the intro course, the second economics course, money and banking course, and a graduate economics course. Try as I might, I was never able to make an "A" in the classes but never made less than a "B." His courses were tough, but I left each knowing I had received a wealth of knowledge from a very well-educated man committed to educating any willing to stay the course.

On one occasion, Mr. Adams was away from campus, and someone else gave an exam to our class. It consisted of five essay questions. I filled the better part of a Blue Book, turned it in, and left the room. As I stepped over the threshold, I realized that I had taken the wrong side of the fence on one question.

"Oh, well. I'll essentially be starting at 80 points," I thought.

When we got our papers back, much to my surprise, I had received a grade of eighty-six. He asked each of us to come to his office to discuss the exam with him. Like most of my papers, this one had an awfully lot of red ink for grammatical errors and misspelled words.

"I expected to make less than eighty because I knew I missed that one question," I told him.

"Even though the answer was wrong, you supported it well. That's why you lost only ten points rather than the whole twenty," he explained.

Mister Adams, as always, was demanding, exacting, and often somewhat taxing but ever dedicated to his profession, open-minded, just, and fair.

Wilson E. (Pat) Speir—Class of 1940

I entered E.T. in the fall of 1935 and graduated in the summer of 1940. One of my fondest and respectful memories of my days at E.T. was the understanding, support, and helpfulness extended by the faculty and staff to the students. I think this is what made E.T. GREAT and continues to do just that.

The severe Depression of the thirties had lingered in East Texas, and this situation caused many of us to work just to make it.

Along with others, it is easy to recall that there were hundreds of good-looking girls on campus and social time blending with work and study time made life interesting indeed.

I enjoyed sports, and we did have some good ball clubs in those days. I was proud of E.T. in 1935, and I am still proud of my Alma Mater.

Chapter 21

MARGARET BERRY
LEGENDARY DEAN OF WOMEN

Fred Tarpley—Class of 1951—Hooks

S tudents who attended E.T. between 1950 and 1961 have stories to spare about the lady called "the lean dean," or even "the mean dean," depending upon their experiences with Margaret Berry. She was the counterpart of J. W. "Dough" Rollins, dean of men.

As a male student during Dean Berry's early tenure and later as a colleague, I had no fear of discipline from her for violating the campus code for hair rollers, shorts or slacks, or visits to buildings where men resided. There are many tales about Dean Berry patrolling the streets to arrest coeds who transgressed boundaries of feminine conduct and ignored the disciplines decreed in her office. I never experienced any of the episodes my female classmates often discussed with long-suffering agony.

Dean Berry approved the arrangement sheets for organizations planning campus or off-campus activities requiring signatures by authorized chaperones, details of what would transpire at the event, and assurances that the sponsors accepted responsibility for the behavior and safety of the students. Male students knew that failure to live up to E.T. standards at the approved functions would result in discipline from Dean Rollins.

Dean Berry, who had taught history at Navarro College before coming to E.T., knew all of the students living on campus in those days when the total enrollment was zooming upward from 2,400, and her knowledge of their behavior was omniscient. She knew their grade point averages, whom they were dating, which girls missed dormitory curfews, and all sorts of other information. While Dean Berry attempted to convince the ladies that they should conform to the ritziest finishing school decorum, she devoted much energy to creating nurturing opportunities for every student on campus as well.

As editor of the *East Texan* in 1950-1951, I wrote an editorial questioning what I considered an "undemocratic" administrative action. At one of the home football games, the fabulous world famous Rangerettes from Kilgore College came to give a high-kicking halftime performance. The smiling, curvaceous, prancing members of the drill team arrived on our campus in white boots, short red skirts, white blouses, and Western hats to make their choreographed moves on our football field. Dean Berry assigned a quota to each male social club for escorts to meet their bus, offer an arm, and guide the bewitching Rangerettes safely into the stadium. "Why," my editorial asked, "couldn't the independents be a part of this privileged assignment?"

Some students, myself included, who were not members of social clubs had their own "independent clubs" but were not affiliated with any social organization. The departmental and service organizations kept us busy. Somehow the quota of escorts to social clubs seemed to contradict our claim to be "The South's Most Democratic College." After all, the independents appreciated gorgeous women and precision formations just as much as the socialites.

The next time I saw Dean Berry, she discussed the editorial with me, not with any resentful attitude but with a desire for my advice on how democratic allotments could guide quotas in the future. I always found her to be cordial and reasonable when we discussed any subject. The well-groomed, fashionably dressed dean, who supported many campus activities and wrote notes of support to student achievers, was a model for sophistication and humanity.

As my graduation approached, she asked what career plans I had. When I told her that Ball High School in Galveston had invited me to interview to teach journalism, she beamed and told me that she had taught history at Ball High. She immediately sent a telegram to Superintendent Hill. It stated, "I enthusiastically endorse Fred Tarpley as Ball High School journalism teacher. He's tops." After the interview the Galveston school board hired me to begin teaching at age nineteen. The superintendent asked me to take his warmest regards to Margaret Berry. Her office was the first place I visited after I returned to the campus.

Dean Berry left E.T. in 1961 to become a dean of students at UT-Austin and to begin doctoral studies at Columbia University. A few years later I went to New York during a summer vacation, and I called Dean Berry to arrange a visit. I went to her residence hall on the Columbia campus, where she was completing her doctorate. We had dinner together, and when I left to board a bus to Broadway to see a performance of the new musical "Camelot" with Richard Burton and Julie Andrews, the dean said she would like to ride with me to the theatre. "I've seen 'Camelot' twice, or I would go with you," she said. "I just love to ride the bus and absorb all the energy of New York," the dean said with exuberance.

Through the years I heard reports of her success as a dean in Austin. She was in the vanguard of integrating dormitories with male and female students under the same roof. I learned that she never cruised the streets of Austin looking for coeds in hair rollers. Dean Berry and society had moved far beyond the mores she enforced at E.T.

When the University of Texas Press published my *1001 Place Names*, she called to invite me to lunch at the UT faculty club. She also invited Dr. Edith Parker, a former E.T. history professor who lived in Austin at the time. By then Dean Berry had written the centennial history of the University of Texas and a book on UT traditions. She was a well-known personality in Austin.

During a later visit, I asked the former E.T. dean if she had created the code of conduct for E.T. coeds or if she was following orders from President James G. Gee. She explained that the rules were part of social expectations at that time but that President Gee, ever the Southern gentleman, made it clear that the dean of women owned responsibility for maintaining high standards among the young female scholars.

When I became chair of the E.T. centennial committee in 1989, I asked Dean Berry for advice, knowing that she had been a key person in the celebration of the UT centennial a few years earlier. She shared many great ideas.

Dean Berry returned to the E.T. campus in the spring of 1989 to give the commencement address at the centennial graduation. During our visit before graduation, she asked me if the university had maces that were carried in the academic processions at commencement and other campus ceremonial events. "I just love the maces that the various departments and colleges use in processions at UT and that are permanently displayed in the main library," she said. She added that she thought E.T. should look into acquiring a mace.

At the end of the graduation ceremonies, Dean Berry returned her speaker's stipend to President Jerry Morris, expressing the wish that it be used for E.T.'s first mace. Our centennial committee asked Gordon Thomas to design it. Gordon was director of creative services and later sculptor of campus statues of W. L. Mayo, the founding president, and of Sam Rayburn, the most famous alumnus. Dr. Grady Tice, a retired professor of Secondary and Higher Education, turned the walnut wood that became the staff of the mace. The committee had hoped for bois d'arc since Commerce had become the bois d'arc capital of Texas, but that wood would always split during the lathing. Dr. Tice selected a handsome specimen of walnut. The committee commissioned a Fort Worth sculptor to create a lion's head for the top of the staff. That mace is still borne in academic processions at Texas A&M University-Commerce.

The woman who became my steadfast friend maintained her loyalty to the institution. I hope others had the opportunity, as I did, to appreciate her as a unique, caring, multi-dimensional personality.

J. D. McKeown—Class of 1940

A recent ice storm brought to mind the kind of entertainment we enjoyed at E.T. way back then. One icy day a group went to the creek off the campus. The boys were swinging across the water on a grapevine they found hanging in a tree. One young lady, who was a little larger than most, wanted to join in the fun. By the time we fished her out of the water and got her back to the dorm, her clothes were frozen to her body. Fortunately, no one suffered any permanent damage.

Chapter 22

DIGGING OUT OF A HOLE

Sherman K. Burns—Class of 1976—Mesquite

College was always in the back of my mind, but way back. Having grown up in a blue collar family, it was encouraged but not required.

It was late summer of 1972 after my graduation from North Mesquite High School. I was working with my older brother as I had done for the last couple of summers in the excavation business. My job was what is known as an "oiler" or "swamper" or just a "helper" on a piece of heavy earth moving equipment called a "Gradall."

One day on the job, my brother and I met up with an older gentleman off State Highway 183 in Irving and followed him for what seemed like hours and miles to a field in the middle of nowhere. The field was barren, and all I saw was a wooden stake with a pink plastic ribbon wrapped around it.

The man explained that we needed to find a fifteen-inch pipe buried about twelve feet down. The pipe was to supply jet fuel to the new Dallas-Fort Worth International Airport that was just beginning construction. "It is important that you do NOT hit the pipe or damage it in anyway," he explained. "Take your time and do not damage the pipe."

That was just the first challenge. My brother and I had already been working on a job that morning that we had been on for several days. We had gotten out of the habit of replenishing our water cooler every morning because that job site had water. On this new project, there was no water in sight.

So by 2 p.m., late July and about 105 in the shade—of which there was none—my brother and I were parched. My brother explained to the man that we had forgotten water. He acknowledged the concern and promised to return in about half an hour.

He left and we started digging.

It wasn't an easy task. As we got close to the depth of the pipe, my brother would lift me down into the hole on the bucket of the Gradall with a shovel in my hands. I would dig around for a few minutes. He would lift me out, take out another scoop of dirt, and then lift me back down.

This went on for over an hour until we successfully found the pipe without damaging it. But it didn't go unnoticed that the old man didn't return for over two hours. Meanwhile my brother and I started suffering from dehydration warning signs like severe headaches.

Needless to say, this experience was a learning lesson. I didn't know how I wanted to make a living, but I knew my future profession wouldn't be in the evacuation business! When I returned home that evening, I dug out my application for East Texas State University. I finished filling it out and promptly mailed it for the fall semester of 1972.

The rest is poetry. I was accepted into the university. I had been in choir my high school years and really enjoyed music. So being a music major originally sounded like a good idea. After my first semester at ETSU I quickly realized that music was not for me. I think it had something to do with the fact that it was more fun to party with my fraternity brothers (Delta Chi) in the evenings than sit in a practice room.

There were several older fraternity brothers who had graduated with liberal arts degrees but were returning to school to work on masters degrees. The economy was weak, and they could not find jobs. So they encouraged me to get a business degree. I decided not to officially change my major for a while and to just get caught up with general studies classes while I gave it more thought.

Registration was a royal pain. We had assigned times to go through the Sam Rayburn Student Center. What a nightmare! You showed up, waited for hours, then went around to the various departmental tables that were set up on the third floor begging for a computer card with your class assignment on it. Then you had to stand in another line (which seemed to take hours) to pay.

During my second semester when I was at a registration table trying to get a history class at 9 a.m. that was supposedly closed, I mentioned to the professor that I was a music major. He said, "Oh a music major. Why didn't you say so to begin with . . . here you go."

WOW! Did light bulbs go off in my head! So for the next several semesters when I really wanted a certain general studies class at a certain time, not too early, not too late, I would simply say, "But you don't understand. I'm a music major, and I have to have that class at that time." Worked every time—without exception. It was amazing. I could not really use that with my upper level business classes, but I really never needed it.

I graduated in August of 1976 with a BBA in General Business. I never really figured out what I wanted to do, hence the General Business Degree. But it served me well as I was lucky enough to get into the securities industry. I am now a managing director of Green Street Advisors, managing the equity trading desk.

I not only have ETSU to thank but that old man that wanted me and my brother to find that jet fuel pipe as well.

Dorothy Willis Pound—Class of 1938
I shall always remember such outstanding teachers as C. V. Hall, C. W. LaGrone, Mary Nelson, Vera English, J. G. Smith, and Maude Noyes. During my freshman year, I was in Stanley Pugh's typing class when the students "walked classes" before the big North Texas football game. Mr. Pugh always locked his door during class. When the students came to the room, they took the pins out of the door hinges so that we could "walk" too.

Chapter 23

THE STORMING OF
A SANCTUARY

Earl Stubbs—Class of 1957—Naples

During the ETSTC school year of 1955-56, several East Coast universities staged and executed campus events known as panty raids. Most such institutions severely segregated the sexes during those times, and males had virtually no access to female domiciles. The daring young men of that era, in a fit of rebellion, gained clandestine entrance to the female dorms and ran throughout the buildings in search of women's undergarments. These episodes made national news, horrified the country, and prompted two members of the Tejas Social Club to create an evening of fun that has withstood the test of time fifty-five years later. Here's what happened.

After wearing out my welcome at E.T. during the fall of 1954, I retreated to the peace and quiet of Kilgore Junior College campus for the spring semester. Even a quiet, studious person such as myself soon met most of the students on the campus of that small college including several Rangerettes and even a couple of guys. One was a Navy veteran named Bud Smith. Ironically, he had shared time in the shore patrol with a former Artema from E.T. named Joe Terrell, who was my brother-in-law at the time. At 5' 5", Bud must have struck terror into the hearts of wayward sailors.

After an uneventful spring at K.J.C., I went back for another crack at East Texas the following fall. As it turned out, several members of the Rangerettes, along with Bud Smith, joined me there. I liked Bud, and it was only natural that I would invite him to join the Tejas Club, a men's social organization of which I was already a member. Bud joined and pledged during the fall of

1955. Due to a shared love for prose and poetry, we became roommates at the Tejas House on Chestnut Street, which served as a cultural center for campus activities.

I had never lived in a frat house before. Due to the unruly study habits of the members, it was not always easy to find sleep, especially since a group of rowdy Delta County boys were in the next room. That bunch included "El Presidente," Damon McDonald, and his erstwhile roomy, Billy Van "Rip" Templeton.

One night, following a lengthy session of studying, Bud and I attempted to chat ourselves to sleep. Our thoughts and conversation moved to a discussion of those daring young men in the Northeast who gained national attention by staging panty raids. To be brutally honest, we were a bit jealous of their inventive notoriety.

It is impossible to remember who made the statement "We could do that." However, history proves that one of us did. At first, we were not completely serious. Then we started discussing logistics, and matters got serious in a hurry. We decided to explore the possibilities by contacting the leadership of the other men's social clubs and get their take on the idea. They were usually a bit more conventional than the Tejas, and most Tejas were more conservative than Bud and me. It was likely that they would respond by turning up their collective noses at the plan, and we could get on with our lives.

I recall that I spoke with Richard Stevenson, the Artema president. To my great surprise, he thought it was a grand idea and agreed to have Artema reps at the planned meeting behind the stadium that night. The Cavaliers, Friars, Ogimas, and Paragons also readily joined the cause. A nice-sized crowd gathered behind the stadium to make plans and receive instructions.

Bud Smith got up in the bed of a pickup and laid out the big night according to our prepared guidelines. The plan was simplicity itself. Binnion Hall closed and locked down at 10:30 p.m., under the watchful eye of Mrs. Gant, the queen of population control. However, a close and personal friend of mine, a Kalir with a winsome spirit named Alice Kaiser, agreed to unlock the northwest door at 11 p.m. so that the troops could enter the building and pillage at will. To conceal our identity, we would all wear raincoats and women's stockings over our heads. We all swore, that if caught, we would deny any knowledge or participation. Yeah right!

The night arrived. We all gathered in groups behind Binnion Hall and waited for zero hour. At the stroke of 11 p.m., I tried the door. To my great surprise, it opened, and a horde of social clubbers began pouring through the door and running up the stairs. Of course, the girls all knew we were coming

For the next five minutes, every participant gained memories that will last a lifetime. We all snapped mental pictures of the transpiring scenes. Mine include charging up to the third floor and looking for a friendly face. I found one, took the offered panties, visited for a few moments, and then I headed for the exit. On the way I glanced down the hall and witnessed the huge Clyde "Red" Carroll, with a sheer stocking over his face, walking along chatting with the dorm mother, Mrs. Gant.

The dorm filled and cleared in short order with our mission accomplished. We all retired to various venues of celebration and recounted our experiences. We had enjoyed our fun, and now the only thing remaining was to avoid expulsion. We heard stories that the school president left his campus home and charged to Binnion Hall, waving a pearled-handled .45 Colt. One would expect such behavior from a former member of General Patton's World War II staff.

The dean of men, J. W. "Dough" Rollins, went to work early the next day. He called in social club members and offered them a deal. Give him names and stay in school. It didn't take long before a Paragon spilled his guts, and the dean went to work. He invited all of us to spend time with him on an individual basis. When my time came, I looked into his kindly face and asked with all the sincerity I could muster, "What panty raid?"

He countered with a letter to my father stating that there had been a panty raid, I had feigned innocence, but that he considered me a prime suspect. My father asked me, "What is a Binnion?"

To my knowledge, the dean chose not to severely punish any student involved since the cream of the campus was involved. I still feel bad about lying to the dean, but after all, it was a matter of our verbal contract. I had no choice. Did I?

I attended my fiftieth class reunion at what is now Texas A&M University-Commerce in 2007. One of the current professors took us on a tour of the campus. When we reached Binnion Hall, he told us all about one of the historic panty raids. I said nothing.

Chapter 24
. . . EVERY WORD IS TRUE

Jerry Biggs—Class of 1972—McKinney

The first time I came to ETSU was in 1966. I came with some friends to attend a track meet. I had already heard of E.T., because one of my cousins, John Kent Bozman, had attended the school and was on the Dean's List.

When I was a senior at McKinney High School, I took a speech course for two reasons. One was to avoid homework; the other was that the teacher was cool. The teacher, an E.T. graduate, was quite a revolutionary at MHS. His name was Jerry Phillips, now Dr. Jerry Phillips. He changed the course of my life.

After I gave a few speeches, he said, "Biggs, I need to see you after class."

"I didn't do it!" I said.

"No, no no. I just need to see you." After class he said, "I'm casting my first play of the year, and I want you to read for it."

"No way," said I.

"Why?" he inquired.

Being seventeen and knowing all things, I said, "Because only sissies and snobs do that kind of stuff."

"Read for it, and I think you'll find it a little different from that," he said.

Well, I read for it, got in, and did all three plays that year. That was 1967, and I graduated in 1968. Mr. Phillips was going back to E.T. to finish work on his master's degree and told me I should go there and major in theater. He said E.T. was one of the best theater schools around.

Later at MHS, he took our class on a field trip to E.T. to see a production of *Look Homeward, Angel* by Thomas Wolfe. I still remember how mesmerized

I was by the experience, especially by the performance of Dave Cook. He later became head of the Theater Department at the University of Tulsa.

I came to E.T. in the fall of 1968 and had to dropout because of financial and other reasons. I was able to come back in 1972. The Drama Department had just won the American College Theatre Festival. E.T. was the place to be to study theater in this part of the world.

Dr. Curtis L. Pope was the department head. On the staff were Mr. Nathan Wilson, Dr. Anthony Buckley, and others, all of whom had high standards.

My first university play was *The Great Cross Country Race*. I played Mr. Spiney, a hedgehog. It is the story of the tortoise and the hare. All the animals had to sing songs. During the first rehearsal of singing, Nathan Wilson stopped the singing, saying, "Stop! Stop! Stop! Somebody is way off key!" Well, of course, I was incensed! That was, after all, a university production, and how dare someone not be prepared to sing on key? We all had to stand in a straight line, and Mr. Wilson went to the first woodland creature, who sang a few notes. "Next," he said, and so on. He got to me, and I uttered some noise, and he said, "You! You! Don't sing. Just mouth the words." I was the only woodland creature who wasn't allowed to sing. It was a great lesson in humility. To this day, I'm still not allowed to sing on stage.

Dr. Pope directed *Philadelphia, Here I Come* by Bryan Friel. Cast as the canon, the character didn't appear until the third act, the script called for the canon to laugh, "Hee, hee, hee." Dr. Pope would stop me and say, "No, Biggs, it's 'Hee, hee, hee'."

I would go, "Hee, hee, hee."

Again, Dr. Pope would say, "It's 'Hee, hee, hee.'"

The play advanced in the American Theater Festival, and we performed in the Scott Theater in Fort Worth. I vaguely remember the performance because I came down with the flu, but the critics singled me out and gave me a positive review.

The next year I was taking an acting class that had mainly graduate students in it. One of them was Carolyn Andrews Doyle. For an assignment, I chose a monologue from Mark Twain's book *Roughing It*, one of my favorites. Carolyn, preparing to get her master's degree with an emphasis on folklore, worked with J. Mason Brewer, the distinguished folklorist teaching in the E. T. English department.

Part of her thesis was to write a play. She wrote, *A Musical Mark Twain*. Done as a university production, it sold out every night of its scheduled run. Held over for two nights, the additional productions sold out as well. We would have done it a third night to an almost sold out audience except I came down with the flu. *A Musical Mark Twin* toured in various cities over the next three years. It was a great experience for me as an actor.

One day I was in Jerry Phillips' office in the old theater building, and his phone rang. The caller was a fellow E.T. student, Jim Bowden, calling to see if Jerry Phillips would consider taking a summer job at Six Flags Over Texas in the gunfight show, where yet another E.T. student, Steve Huey, was working and had to quit. Unavailable for the job, Jerry Phillips sent me to Jim Bowden, and he hired me. I worked for Six Flags for three years. It was a great learning experience for me. I also did my first commercial for Six Flags. With Jim Bowden's theatrical training from E.T., he, I, and the rest of our talented crew became the biggest attraction at Six Flags, and management wanted to design their advertising campaign around our show. Jim Bowden used a talent agent named Peggy Taylor. She was one of the first talent representatives in Dallas and was highly respected. Jim introduced me to her, and she put me under contract. That is how I started working in films and television.

"Had I not had an E.T. alum for a high school teacher, had I not studied under Dr. Curtis L. Pope, had I not gotten my first break with the help of Jim Bowden, another E.T. alum, I would not have had a career in films and television. But there I was in front of the cameras, acting my heart out beside Kevin Costner and Kevin Klein in *Silverado*; Tommy Lee Jones and Danny Glover in *Lonesome Dove*, and Robert Duval in *Tender Mercies*. I was in three films written by the masterful Horton Foote: *Tender Mercies*, *1918*, and *Convicts*.

That's my story, and I'm sticking to it.

Chapter 25

1990 Homecoming with the Rams

Jan Vowell—Coach's Wife—Beaver, OK

Anticipation mounted. The nationally ranked ETSU Lions were playing the Angelo State University Rams for the conference championship. The Rams were 4-1 in conference, and the Lions were 5-0. That meant we had to win, or we'd both be 5-1 and tied for the conference championship. The Lions were not going to let that happen; besides, it was homecoming, and we had to win our homecoming game.

There were many Homecoming festivities. On Friday, we had hotdogs and hamburgers on the east lawn in front of the Student Union Building and enjoyed a twilight parade to the bonfire. The band's stirring music and the cheerleaders' rousing cheers whipped up the boisterous crowd. President Jerry Morris, athletic director Margo Harbison, and head coach Eddie Vowell gave speeches. The captains of the football team, Bobby Bounds, Terry Bagsby, and Gary Compton, told the cheering crowd that the Lions would be the winners in the Homecoming game against the Rams. As the hot, crackling fire died down, the band led us in the alma mater, and we all looked forward to the game the next day.

Saturday morning dawned with the sun shining, and everything was right with the world. The Homecoming parade snaked through the streets of the ETSU campus, ending at the downtown square. Coach Vowell, I, and our grandson, Jarrett, rode with Harry and Rheba Icenhower in their 1931 Tudor Sedan Model A Ford. Jarrett was five at the time and loved waving to the crowd. That was the first time he'd been in a parade, and he felt very important.

Rheba Icenhower had a busy morning. Not only was she a co-chair of the Homecoming festivities, she was presented the Gold Blazer Award at the East Texas State University Alumni Recognition Luncheon. Her husband, Harry, kept her from seeing the printed program, so she had no idea that she was going to be a recipient. It was such fun to see her surprise. Earl Stubbs, an ETSTC graduate of 1957, was also honored with the Gold Blazer Award.

After all of the festivities, it was time to turn our attention to the game. The coaches were nervous about the loss of most of our ball carriers. Ankle injuries sidelined Jarrod Owens and Willie Mozeke. Various other injuries made David Chapman, Jarred Harrison, and Greg Pearson questionable. "We're getting to the point of the season where we're pretty banged up," said Coach Vowell. The Lions did have two healthy tailbacks, Gary "Air" Perry and James Anderson, and they both had game experience.

The Lions' defense was awesome. Linebacker Terry Bagsby was all over the Rams' quarterback, Greg Stephens. Stephens was sacked four times with Bagsby's pass rush, and Bagsby had numerous hurries and hits just after the pass. The only touchdown the Rams made was due to a fumble in an exchange between quarterback Bob Bounds and tailback Gary Perry.

They both made up for the fumble with outstanding play. Bounds led the scoring with drives of 80, 99, 15, 74, and 45 yards. He was perfect in his play, as the Lions amassed 462 yards against a Rams' defense that had been the best in the conference. Gary "Air" Perry had 34 rushes for 198 yards. He had this big night in spite of hurting his hand, again.

Before coming to E.T., Gary broke his hand while riding a rodeo bull. His hand was repaired by inserting a plate with screws in the back of his hand. During the game, he came to the sideline with his hand bleeding. A screw was coming out, and he wanted Dr. Sandy Bahm to take it out, but Dr. Bahm didn't want to. Coach Vowell said he looked over, and Gary was taking the screw out himself with a Phillips screwdriver. He went back in and didn't miss a play.

His first score was a 1-yard spurt into the end zone, after an 80-yard drive. His awesome 36-yard run was followed by an incredible leap from the Rams' seven to the one-foot line. He said that if he'd known where the goal line was, he'd have gotten higher instead of level, so he could have made the touchdown with his leap. Amazing.

The kicking team was flawless. Punter Shane Summers kicked a career best of 78 yards, and kicker Billy Watkins made six extra point kicks.

He broke Mark Regian's 1971 school record of kick scoring in a season. Watkins had 65 kicking points and a string of 24 consecutive extra points.

The score was 14-7 in the first quarter, and with a 99-yard drive in the second, the halftime score was 21-7. The halftime show included the crowning of the Homecoming queen, Tisha Lynn May from Rockwall, and king, Spencer Reamy of Sugarland, Texas.

The Lions had the wind in the third quarter and proceeded to score three touchdowns in the first nine minutes. Everything that could go wrong with the Rams did in the third quarter. The Lions had a 42-7 lead with 5:08 left in the third quarter. The Lions coasted in the fourth and had no scoring.

When the final whistle blew, pandemonium broke out. The players carried Coach Vowell off the field, and when KETR interviewed Coach Vowell, he was visibly emotional. "Boy, I tell you, I'm so happy I'm trying to keep from crying." He attributed the success of the 1990 Lions to "a lot of great kids, a lot of hard work, and a super staff." He also credited former head coach Earnest Hawkins and his long-time assistant C.W. "Boley" Crawford for any success that he'd had.

What a nice ending to a great Homecoming.

Dorelle Clark McAfee—Class of 1942

A most vivid memory centered on summer school and the course in educational instruction I took with Miss Eusibia Lutz. I was to observe her French class. She was bitten by a black widow spider, and to my horror, I had to teach the class. I went by daily to confer as she lay up properly in bed. The semester went by in a blur as I attended other classes, entertained out-of-town guests, interviewed for teaching positions, and graduated. I'm not sure how, but I went off to teach at White Oak.

Chapter 26
THE INGRAM LEGACY
1946-1949

Dorothy Ingram—Class of 1955—Commerce

I t was 1946, and the Big War was over. Things were settling down to a more
normal routine. There was no more war news on radio; rationing was not a
major part of family life; grieving mothers no longer placed gold stars in the
windows. On the East Texas State Teachers College campus, the basketball
team was creating quite a stir, primarily due to a group of Quitman players
from a family named Ingram. There were two sets of brothers, Troy and Robert
Earl "Bill" Ingram and two other brothers, Truitt and Gayle Ingram, plus a
nephew, Travis Gilbreath, the son of Troy and Robert Earl's sister. Bill, older
than the other family members, had gone to college one year before serving
in the Army, and he returned to join the team in 1946.

In addition to the Ingram family, other dedicated, talented players comprised the team. They included Jake Carter, Dick Carpenter, Jimmy Littlejohn,
Benny Kelly, Caddo Matthews, Jack Routt, Harry and David Miller, J.T.
Odom, Gerald "Precious" Pinkham, DeWitt Alexander, Orvel Hurley, and
others.

In reviewing the basketball scorebooks for 1947, sports fans will find that
four of the Ingrams played in all the games and scored more than half the points
in almost every game. For example, on December 4, 1947, in a game with
Centenary College, the Ingrams scored forty-three of the final fifty points.

At the time the Ingrams began playing together on the team, Dennis
Vinzant was head coach. Then in 1947, Tulane University hired Mr. Vinzant
as head coach at the New Orleans university. Darrell Tulley, a former All

American football player, and at that time the assistant football coach, was elevated to head basketball coach. Mr Tulley was not an experienced basketball player or coach, but he wisely sought the advice of his great players. The collaboration resulted in a winning team which tied for the Lone Star Conference that year. They lost in the first round of the NAIB district playoffs.

Coach Tulley was also superstitious—frequently wearing the same tie to games the team had won. He would place his good luck "buckeye" on the bench and point it at the opponents' baskets in an effort to jinx the opponents' shot attempts.

During this time, the team traveled by private cars since the school did not have vans or a bus at its disposal. In addition to the coach and other volunteers, a frequent driver was J.W. "Dough" Rollins, dean of men, As the story goes, when the team traveled through Quitman to a game, Mr. Rollins would say to the occupants of his car, "Gentlemen, please remove your hats. This town is keeping Mr. Tulley's job safe by sending these Ingram players to Commerce."

Playing on the East Texas basketball team must have instilled the sport into the hearts of all the Ingrams. With the exception of Gayle, they all became coaches after they left college to start careers of their own.

Bill and wife, Mary, moved to LaPoynor, where Bill coached basketball for several years. During their stay there, Bill's team won the Class B state championship. After that they moved to Jacksonville, where Mary taught in the elementary school. Bill finished his highly successful coaching career there, climaxed by another state championship. The story goes that at the game in which his team clinched the district championship, he was wearing a new shirt. Just a mite superstitious, he bought a new shirt for every game that followed, including the state finals. He and Mary lived in Jacksonville until Bill's death in 1999 at the age of eighty-eight.

Troy, the first four-year letterman in E.T. history, married Dorothy Dunn in May of 1948, and the couple moved HOME to Quitman, where Troy coached basketball for five years. During those years, his teams won four district championships and advanced to the regional finals in Class A all four years. When Lockney High School called, the couple moved west where Troy coached girls' and boys' teams for two years, while Dorothy taught business subjects and coached the girls' tennis team. A fatal illness cut short Troy's career at age thirty-two.

Truitt, an outstanding center for the team for three years, was named to the NAIB All American team during his senior year. Later, he was inducted into the ETSU Athletic Hall of Fame for his outstanding career as a Lion basketball player. He and his wife, Gwen, moved to Paul Pewitt High School where he was basketball coach. Soon, however, school administration came calling, and they moved to Commerce where Truitt was high school principal. He held several superintendent positions including superintendent of Marshall Independent School District until he retired. He and Gwen retired to HOME in Quitman for the remainder of his life.

Gayle Ingram, youngest of the clan, played point guard for three years. The social chairman of the group, he kept basketball at a joyous level. Following graduation, he and his wife, Dorothy, moved HOME to Quitman and established a successful cattle ranch. Dorothy taught English at Quitman High School. Gayle was a nationally certified auctioneer for many years, selling everything from jewelry to cattle, sheep, and goats. He once held the record for selling the highest priced goat in the USA.

Travis Gilbreath was a very talented player, winning a place on two Lone Star Conference teams. Basketball coaching was also in his blood, so following graduation, he moved his family to Mt. Pleasant where he was highly successful for a number of years. Another career was cut short when cancer took his life in his early forties.

John D. "Jake" Carter, an outstanding center, was chosen an NAIB All American.

Although not a member of the Ingram family, he was an important part of the team and basketball continued to be an integral part of his life. He was a basketball coach for many years at Dallas Adamson. Jake is also a member of the ETSU Athletic Hall of Fame.

The Ingrams called Quitman home during their young lives and as they retired, they went back home—to Quitman. The Ingram legacy will always hold a special place in East Texas basketball history.

Chapter 27

THE SCHOLARSHIP

Jace Carrington—Class of 1961—Enloe

In the fall of 1954 and fresh out of Enloe High School, I arrived on the campus of East Texas State Teachers College. At that time, I joined roughly 2,000 students on campus which amounted to about half of the total Delta County population.

I was like a fish out of water since I was twenty-one miles from my hometown and my own family. However, my brother Bob was already there, and I had heard a multitude of stories about life on the E.T. campus where Bob's nickname was "Country." I soon gained the nickname "Little Country" and that fit my personality and limited experience. I pledged the Tejas Club, and it became my new family.

With two sons in college, my parents were proud but financially strapped. Bob and Earl "The Ghost" Stubbs informed a group of us that the G.I. Bill would expire on January 1, 1955. If we joined the U.S. Army for three years, we would receive a four-year paid education at the government's expense. At the time that sounded great to eleven young, unprepared men, so we signed on the dotted line without our parents' knowledge or consent.

We left college for basic training so quickly that we could not take final exams that semester. Many years later, Bob informed me that he received all As on his final grades that semester because he told his professors of his plan of valor to receive the G.I. Bill for military service. He surely had someone whisper that plan in his ear, such as Brenda Cain, who soon became his wife. I, on the other hand, vanished from the scholastic environment with my transcript flawed with either a W (withdrawal) or F (failure) for my first semester at Old E.T.

Five of the eleven guys who joined that day were from our hometown of Enloe, and when we left, the community population had a significant reduction. Our parents were in shock but had no choice but to drive us to our new destination.

I still recall all eleven enlisted men as if it were yesterday. Originally, five of the young men were Tejas, but our cheerleader, Earl Stubbs, remained behind due to family health issues.

Three years later, nine of the eleven experienced young solders returned to ETSU and completed their education. They received degrees with the financial support of the G.I. Bill. Most of us thought of it as a scholarship of $120 a month in payment for our military service in the USA and Europe. We felt privileged to receive this support at a time when funds for our education were not otherwise available to us. With this educational opportunity, we moved forward to successful careers, reaching goals that would not have been possible without this support. Over the years, I have not forgotten that financial aid received over fifty-five years ago. It gave me the desire to give back to the university, helping other students with their own opportunities.

C. W. Romans—Class of 1939

I well remember the marble tiled stairway in the Education Building leading from the ground floor upward to the hallway entrances to the auditorium. One particular day I had on a new pair of shoes with leather heels and soles. My class had ended, and I had proceeded to the head of the stairway on my way to my next class. As I took my first step downward, my feet slipped out from under me, my books flew out of my arms, and I went scooting down the stairway on my rear. When I landed at the bottom, I looked up and there stood a man watching me.

The man asked, "Are you hurt?"

"No, but my pride is," I replied.

Chapter 28

Uptown Girls

Ann Oglesby Julian—Class of 1956—Commerce

My very best friends haven't returned their memory notes, so I will give you a glimpse of these fantastic people. We lived at home throughout our college days. Our curfews and other rules were as strict or more so than those for the dormitory students.

Betty Ann Cates was another sixteen-year-old graduate of Commerce High School. She graduated on Friday night and started college on Monday. Betty had her eye set on SMU, but the proximity of E.T. had a stronger calling. She was very studious and always kept a high grade point average. This achievement is not to say that she was a bookworm. She joined Kaidishan social club, did her pledge work, and went on to excel in all ventures connected with the club and other areas.

Betty met her husband, Charles A. Robertson at E.T. A native of Frisco, Texas, he was an agriculture major, class president, president of the Rodeo Club and an ROTC member. Charlie, as he was called then, earned his B.S. and M.S. After college, he entered the Air Force as a first lieutenant, and they traveled to many countries. Charlie retired a lieutenant colonel and base commander of Carswell Air Force Base in Fort Worth. He then went immediately to work at the Los Alamos Laboratory. They were married for over fifty years.

Nita Follis was so anxious to attend college that she took college classes during her senior year of high school. This talented art major illustrated a book for Miss Adelle Clark, an E.T. Spanish teacher. She was a member of the Angel Flight, an auxiliary of the AFROTC Nita and Mary Cates did the photography for the *Locust,* our yearbook, in their junior year. Nita was also one of the first girls to join the Rodeo Club.

Nita met her husband, David Ivie, a Bonham high school graduate, at E.T. David was a studious young man with a flair for the dance. He and Nita danced their way through a courtship and over fifty years of marriage. David was an agriculture student and another Rodeo Club member. David retired as Pest Control Director for the state of Texas. They now live in Elgin, Texas.

Nita and David received their degrees on the same day. Nita's mother, Aryless Bundren Follis, received her degree on that day also. That was truly a family event.

Mary Nell Cates was another Commerce graduate who joined the college life right after graduation. Another summer freshman was on her way. As an art student, Mary was involved in many projects. Mary and Nita Follis made and selected illustrations and photos for the yearbook in their junior year. As a devoted Kaidishan member, Mary helped design and do some of the creative work of the club floats. Many boxes of Kleenex and white paper napkins were used for the fluffy effect needed on the floats.

Mary met her husband, Larry Cooper at E.T. Larry was from Whitewright and earned course credits in the summer but returned to A&M in college station. Their long distance romance continued. Both received their degrees from their respective schools and joined the work force. After establishing ground work for their careers, they met up again and tied the knot. They have been married for over fifty years. E.T. holds special memories because that is where they met. It was a square dance session on a Monday night that brought them together. They are still dancing.

Chapter 29

HAZING AS AN ART FORM

Buddy Kinamon—Class of 1964—Blue Ridge

I entered E.T. in the fall of 1958—a seventeen-year-old freshman from Blue Ridge High School. I was a member of a graduating class of eighteen.

I had never seen so many people in my life. I figured joining a social club (national fraternities and sororities were not yet acceptable on campus) might help me adapt to this new environment. Because of my academic and work responsibilities, coupled with an inherent proclivity toward introversion, I had not made many acquaintances in the world of social clubs.

If you recall the opening scene of the movie *Animal House*, you will get a good picture of my roommate and me going to rush parties. We got bids from two or three (Didn't everybody?) but wanted to pledge Paragon Club, from which we did not receive a bid. We trekked over to the Paragon House, announced our intention, and were told to wait until they discussed the matter. Perhaps because no one really knew us, they pinned us, and we became pledges.

Pledges met in a different room from active members, and we received instructions from the Pledge Trainer. Each Monday night he assigned us projects for the upcoming week. The usual tasks included some mixture of the following:

Getting signatures of each member, his major, hometown, etc., which we were expected to know by the next Monday night.
Cleaning members' rooms.
Getting our paddle boards signed by each of the fifty members in one week, each member providing as many "licks" as he felt appropriate.

<u>Having a coke date</u> with a girl at the Student Union Building. (This was sometimes harder than other tasks.)

<u>Going on lengthy walks</u>.

<u>Building a shoeshine box</u>.

<u>Completing fireplug assignments</u>. Members painted numbers on ten fireplugs around town. We had one week to locate and document each one. Some of them were in the most obscure locations.

<u>Sleeping on members' floors</u>—as required.

<u>Sleeping in the bathtub</u> at the Paragon House. Once only.

<u>Executing diabolical tasks</u> dreamed up by members.

<u>Enjoying Pledge Day</u> during which pledges took some measure of revenge on actives; remembering the next event immediately following Pledge Day.

<u>Mock Initiation</u>, a volume in itself but abridged to fit.

<u>Formal Initiation</u>, the big day when the active members initiated the pledges into the mysteries of the club, and when initiates earned the right to wreak vengeance on the next pledge class.

Here are explanations of some of the items from above:

Walks: A euphemism to describe an event in which active members drove pledges to the edge of civilization and left them with nothing but a dime each.

One pledge brother and I found ourselves in a place with no visible lights in any direction. Since we did not know which way to go, we started walking. Fortunately, we had walked less than a mile before coming upon a house. We could see a light in the window, so we knocked on the door. The folks were quite understanding and allowed us to use their phone. We called a mutual friend in Greenville who commuted to ET. He picked us up. We spent the night at his house. His mom fixed us a nice breakfast. He drove us to within a couple of blocks of the Paragon House. We walked to the House, signed in at 7:15 a.m., and insisted that we had walked the entire way. Everyone seemed to feel sorry for our ordeal. This is the first time I have admitted otherwise. I hope this does not affect my membership.

One walk was unique. Told to report to the Paragon House at 10:30 p.m. (as always), we began a group walk when members drove us to the courthouse square in Greenville and released us. We wore nothing but our underwear and shoes. We had to get back to Commerce the best way we could.

By this time, we were a finely tuned machine. We had developed a foolproof plan. We loaded three cars with extra clothes and drove them to Greenville to be ready when the members dropped us off. We chuckled to ourselves over our ingenuity.

When we arrived at the House at 10:30 p.m., they loaded us into cars and drove in the opposite direction to Ladonia and dropped us with no recovery plan. We walked down Main Street hooping and hollering when the sheriff arrived in his pickup truck. He tried to arrest all thirteen of us. He was so nervous that he dropped his pistol. We explained the situation to him, and he agreed to drive us to the city limits, clearly pointing out that we were not to return.

After we were deposited at the city limits, some of us hitched a ride on a semi loaded with bales of hay. A few got inside, and others rode on the gas tanks. Upon arriving back in Commerce, we got enough cars and went back for the others. We discovered that hitchhiking is more difficult when one is wearing only underwear and shoes, especially in December.

Shoeshine Box—Pledges were required to build a shoeshine box and use it to make $6.00 in a week for donation to the Paragon Club. Members paid $0.10 per shine; whereas, others paid whatever the traffic would bear.

My favorite story involving a shoeshine box came later when the fellow who was to become my longest tenured roommate was a pledge and I was the Pledge Trainer. When I told them to bring their boxes for inspection, he brought a box that looked exactly like my Kiwi box that I received for high school graduation except it was painted red and contained the Paragon letters. I looked him in the eye and asked, "Pledge, did you make this box yourself?" (Remember Rodney Dangerfield in the movie *Back to School*?) He looked at me and said (a la Rodney.), "Yes, I did." Whereupon, I opened the box lid and praised his attention to detail including the Kiwi label and logo. I never mentioned it again, except to him every chance I get, even now.

Mock Initiation—This final step came just before formal initiation. The club conducted mock under a bridge on the Campbell highway. After divesting each pledge of all clothing and blindfolding him, the initiation involved eating and drinking all sorts of disgusting things such as a mouthful of Crisco, an ample quantity of castor oil, a cracker-and-Vicks-Salve sandwich sprinkled with snuff, raw oysters, and a few other items all washed down with "Paragon

Punch," a highly volatile liquid that could etch glass. We were highly motivated by the initial admonition that if, at any stage of the process, one threw up the contents, he would be allowed to start over at the beginning. It is amazing what a motivational speech can do for one's performance. There were, uh, other activities much too sacred and mystical to reveal.

The final step was getting painted with red enamel covering 100% of the body except for eyes. Again, we had made preparations. We stocked up my dorm room with supplies for removing the paint, old towels for cleaning up, and fresh clothes. Just before leaving us under the bridge without transportation, we were told that we could not clean up in the dorm. Some other pledges had cleaned up there a few nights earlier and brought down the wrath of the administration.

We convinced the dragline operator to donate enough diesel fuel to wash off. So there we were in late December, gathered around the fire, cleaning off paint with diesel and washing the diesel off in the creek. For the next two weeks, the inside of my T-shirts turned red each day from the residual paint. It is a wonder we did not all die from lead poisoning.

Trying to make sense of all this in today's environment is difficult. Laws now forbid hazing, mental or physical. Too many injuries and deaths have resulted from reckless behavior involving hazing. But, in those kindlier, gentler days, this practice was considered good bull. It helped to cement the pledges as a unit and was mostly fun, even at the time. One thing that prevented injuries and risky situations was that no alcohol was involved. Not only were pledges not forced to drink (as has happened in recent times), everyone, including members, were forbidden to consume alcohol at any function, including mock initiation.

Chapter 30

A FAMILY AFFAIR

George B. Cox—Class of1955—Commerce

My family's connections to E.T. go back to the 1920s. My mother, Zelma Bartlett, attended East Texas Normal College and later got her first degree in 1926 from ETSTC. My dad, Homer Cox, graduated from Bonham High School in l923 at the age of twenty-two and from ETSTC in 1927. I once had copies of the 1923-1927 editions of the *Locust,* and one of these had several pages of jokes in the back. One of the jokes was as follows:

Homer: "Can you take a joke?"

Zelma: "Is this a proposal?"

This couple had to be my parents. Where else could you find a Homer/Zelma?

My brother, Bill, and my sister, Tweet (Ellen to some), graduated in l949 and l950 respectively, both at age nineteen. My brother later brought shame to the family by earning the Masters and Ph.D. degrees from Texas A&M. Tweet and I avoided institutions of higher learning after our graduation from ET.

I began kindergarten in 1939 at the ETSTC Training School, located in the old Education Building. I got a spanking the first day for pulling Billy Weaver's sock off during naptime. I can also remember being as mad as a hornet when the teacher tried to tell me that Bill's name was William and Tweet's name was Ellen. Never did like school!

With four years of ROTC or the infantry ahead of me, I took my sweet time and received my BS degree and USAF 2nd Lt. commission on May 22, 1955, in the same old education building. The joy of being through with school is still fresh in my memory.

Most of the new second lieutenants in my graduating class went on to USAF pilot training. We were assigned to Class 57A along with students from Texas Tech, Texas A&M, North Texas, West Point, Naval Academy, and the USAF Officer Candidate School. The USAF trained this class at a time when it had determined that it had too many pilots. We lost a few students for various reasons, mostly physical problems, before beginning to fly. Only forty-one percent of the 70-80 students that began jet school at Webb AFB actually completed the school. Not one of these losses was an ET graduate. We were not more skilled or smarter than the other folks were; we were just more desperate. On one occasion in jet school, I was handed a "pink slip" (meaning a failing grade on the flight) by an instructor I had never seen before and told, "Lt. Cox, everyone in pilot training gets at least one pink slip, and this one is yours." Three pink slips and a flight student had to meet with the evaluation board, and almost every one came away from one of those meetings washed out.

Many of my ET classmates went on to distinguished military careers. I chose a civilian life. After a brief time as a high school math teacher at Bellaire High School in Houston. I had a career with the FAA. I worked as an air traffic controller (Fort Worth ARTCC) and a budget analyst in the Southwest Region headquarters. I retired as regional budget officer in 1994.

Ford W. Hall—Class of 1940

During most of our college years, Raymond Cameron and I owned a 1935 Chevrolet named "Jezebel." We each paid $5 for her, fixed her up in running condition, and painted her a silver paint. We improvised a canvas top and a propeller carved out of a pine 2x4, which would whirl in the wind as we achieved fantastic speeds of 25-30 miles per hour. We drove her to the Texas Centennial Exhibition in Dallas and pulled into a parking lot outside the fair grounds. It wasn't a self-parking lot, but when the attendant saw us turn the ignition on and off by twisting and untwisting two copper wires, he asked us to park it ourselves.

Jezebel afforded us a lot of great moments, particularly in dating. We used to like to pick up coeds and take them riding down a steep hill north of town with a railroad crossing at the bottom. We would pretend that we had no brakes and would holler, "There's a train coming!" and most of the girls would hold on to us for dear life. During most of our college life, Jezebel was a familiar sight at pep rallies and other campus events.

Chapter 31

MY FARM BOY EXPERIENCE

Carrol Wade Adams—Class of 1955—Linden

I arrived at the E. T. college farm in the fall of 1951. My first assignment was to work on the farm garbage truck. Every afternoon two men would take an old army surplus stake bed International truck to the college cafeteria and pick up cans of garbage. These were loaded onto the back of the flat bed truck. We then made our way to the hog farm to empty the cans.

Often times one or more of those garbage cans would turn over on the way to the farm. The spill had to be cleaned up before the empty cans were returned to the cafeteria. This truck was the same one used by farm boys to travel from the college farm to the cafeteria for breakfast and dinner.

We learned to turn off the ignition switch and turn it back on quickly and the truck would backfire. The sound was loud and could be heard all over campus. Everyone knew when we were around.

I served on the garbage run all of my freshman year. In June of 1952, I went to the hog farm. We kept the breeding stock there. We had several registered breeds. The fences were always in poor condition and in need of repair.

There were always 50-100 head of hogs on the farm lot. When these hogs reached 200-250 pounds, we slaughtered them. The college cafeteria used the meat for meals. The college farm also supplied much of the milk, pork, beef, eggs, and poultry used in the cafeteria.

The farm boy hog manager had to go to the hog farm every morning at 5 a.m. to feed the hogs and check everything out. Then go to breakfast and report to a 7:30 a.m. class. Some farm boys were known to sleep through Dr. Louis Harlan's first period American History class. He sometimes threw pieces of chalk at sleeping students.

I lived in the Old Barracks on the college farm, where the high rise dorm is now located.

The normal schedule for a farm boy was:

5 a.m.—Up for chores at the farm. Shower, shave, and dress; then go to the cafeteria for breakfast.

7:30 a.m.—Attend first period class and other classes until lunch.

12 p.m.—Lunch in the cafeteria.

1 p.m.—Work at the farm, building fences, bailing hay, cutting silage, and other assigned chores

5 p.m.—Evening chores.

7 p.m.—Cafeteria for supper, then go to the Library or to their study activities.

The average bedtime was after 10:30 p.m.

The program permitted farm boy labs during one afternoon each week. For the work performed on the college farm, we received room, board, tuition, and $5.00 per month. We bought our own books, clothing, and laundry. We had one week-end a month off duty and others had to do our chores.

After graduation, I taught Vocational Agriculture at Norton High School near Ballinger for eighteen months. After my teaching career ended, the USDA Soil Conservation Service employed me for thirty-seven years, where I advanced to assistant manager of Programs for GS 10 with state wide leadership.

I had an outstanding professional career made possible by my years on the college farm and my education at East Texas State Teachers College. This continues with the second and third generation in my family. My wife and I have three sons and all are college graduates with excellent careers.

The majority of the farm boys became outstanding professional men, businessmen, and educators. Most became leaders in their field of service and communities. Many of them met and married young women who were graduates of the university, as was my wife of fifty-five years, who has a degree in Home Economics and taught for twenty-nine years.

The Farm Boy experience improved my life, and I am forever grateful.

Chapter 32

COUNTRY COMES TO COMMERCE

Jim Hammock—Class of 1964—Hubbard

I graduated from a small high school in Hubbard, Texas, in 1960 as a good football quarterback but with an injured right shoulder that kept me from throwing a football more than about thirty yards. To my disappointment, only Tarleton State in Stephenville offered a four-year-scholarship and that was to play halfback.

There I was, down and out in Hubbard, Texas, with the college enrollment deadline approaching in a couple of weeks. A discussion at the local Magnolia Gasoline Station led to my reluctant decision to join a friend named Morris Lee Dewberry in attending East Texas State College in Commerce.

I mounted the road in my '56 Oldsmobile, hung up my clothes across the back seat, and drove the 120 miles to Commerce, arriving in time to find out that the brand, spanking new West Dorms were not completed. University officials told us not to worry because they had put Morris Lee and me in the East Dorm. East—West. Who cares? However, as it turned out, the East Dorm was a girl's dorm, and the housing people made special arrangements for about thirty guys to stay in the lounge. I thought I had died and gone to heaven. Upon completion of the West Dorms, the administration threatened Morris and me with expulsion if we did not leave the lounge.

Morris Lee and I were quick to join in all the intramural sports, found the Student Union Building (the SUB), and discovered those amazing parties where something called fraternities had pretty girls hand out free cigarettes. These "smokers" as it turned out, like most free and seemingly wonderful things, had a hook to them. The fraternity people notified Morris and me that we needed to select the organization that we wanted to pledge. Not able to compare one fraternity from the next, much less remember their odd names, I headed to the Student Union Building for guidance on the night before our decision was due. I sought out the cutest girls I could find and asked about the fraternities. They gave me expert advice. A very cute blonde said that I should pledge the Tejas Club, soon to be Sigma Phi Epsilon, because one of their members was the cutest boy in school. His name was Jerry (Jace) Carrington. This is how I became a charter and lifetime member of the E.T. Sig Eps, and Jace Carrington became, and remains, a close friend until this day. He is still somewhat cute.

My long studied and committed goal in life was to be a football coach, which led to my major in Physical Education. When I was asked to choose a minor, I fell back on the recommendation of my high school superintendent, who said that my aptitude tested out well to enter the computer field, which was in its infancy in 1961. Since there was no Computer Science curriculum or even a single computer installed at E.T., I selected a second major in Mathematics.

Graduating in January of 1964, I taught math and coached in Tyler for four months before joining IBM. I married my one and only wife while in my second year at E.T., and we have two great sons and six wonderful grandchildren. My career led me to serve as chief executive officer for several high technology "start-up" companies in the Silicon Valley area of California.

God has blessed me in many ways including nudging me into my two mature and well thought out decisions to attend what is now Texas A&M University-Commerce and join my Sig Ep family. The caring and dedicated academic staff at E.T. guided me through an excellent curriculum while teach-ing me a life-long lesson: that I could lead a life seeking intellectual growth without giving up in any way the wisdom and "down to earth lifestyle" attained from growing up in a small and loving town in Central Texas.

God Bless E.T. and the Hubbard City Café.

Chapter 33

CLARK'S STORY

Glenn Ann Hunt—1959/1962—Commerce

In February of 1975, I interviewed my grandfather, Clark Regan James, about his life. Born in 1890, he attended Mayo Normal College in 1908. Grandfather James stayed in Commerce attending class for two weeks and then walked to his home in Pecan Gap for a day or two to get his laundry done. By the road, it was about fIfteen miles from Commerce to Pecan Gap, but, since he was a country boy, he cut across country making the one-way trip about ten miles. Some of the items he was required to bring to college were a well rope and a lantern.

Grandfather James went to college for two-and-a-half years. He remembered that at the time, Professor Mayo had two children, a son called "Doc" and a daughter named Gladys. According to him, Gladys was pretty and talented musically.

After leaving college, Grandfather James rode with Dr. E. H. Starks as he made his rounds. One time, when they were called to the Covington home in Dial to deliver a baby, the doctor went out to see about his horse, leaving Clark to deliver the baby.

Old Man "Blank" Blankenship lived on the Ben Franklin Road east of Pecan Gap. Usually, Dr. Starks charged $10 to deliver a baby, but he had recently raised his price to $15. When Dr. Starks delivered the Blankenship baby, "Old Blank" cussed the doctor for going up on his price. Dr. Starks said, "I charge for what I know, not what I do." Later, the doctor received two boar pigs as payment from another patient. He asked Clark and Blank to castrate the pigs. They did, and the doctor inquired, "How much do I owe you?" "Thirty-dollars," Blank replied. Dr. Starks raised a fuss, thinking this was too much, but "Blank" told him that he, too, got paid for what he knew, not what he did. After that, Dr. Starks never again took boar pigs as payment for services.

Glenn Ann's Story: I went to E.T. directly out of high school, beginning college two weeks after I graduated from Commerce in May of 1959. Back then, the summer semesters were six weeks long, and there were two each summer. As a freshman, I wore a little billed blue beanie hat with blue and gold letters. In a short time I made several special friends, a girl named Barbara from Linden, Texas; Sandra Kelly, Jerry Don Smith, and Macklyn Erwin from Ladonia; and Gale Jones (her parents ran the funeral home) and Glenda Carr from Commerce.

One of my favorite teachers was Miss Pauline Rogers, who taught literature. We had class in the old Library Building. I also enjoyed my government class very much.

Between classes, we hung out in the Student Union Building, better known as the SUB. Here we could also buy food or visit the bookstore to purchase text books.

At Christmas time, for a day we would "adopt" a child from Boles Orphanage. The children would come to campus on busses. One year, Gale Jones and I adopted a little girl whose name was Bettie Christmas.

In the winter when it snowed, it was fun to go sledding in the sloping bowl area. Buildings now fill most of that bowl.

I lived in the little community of Jardin and drove to school each day. One of my friends from Klondike lived in an apartment in town that was owned by Lois Hineman, who had been our high school typing teacher. My friend, Barbara, lived in another apartment near Jones Funeral Home. It was fun to visit both of them in their apartments.

I recall Rush Week activities with the sororities. Declining the invitation, I did not pledge; however, I really don't know why I didn't.

My classes in the summer began at 6:30 in the morning. In the spring and fall, there were A days (Monday, Wednesday, and Friday) and B days (Tuesday and Thursday). One attended two or three classes on A days and two or three different classes on B Days. My major was elementary education. I got married in 1961 and went back to school for one semester in 1962. Shortly after that I had a child and never returned to finish my degree. I lacked forty hours completing it when I quit. I have always regretted not finishing.

Chapter 34

REGISTRATION DAY

Jennie Jennings DeGenaro—Class of 1957—Avery

I believe I should justify some of my ridiculous behavior at East Texas State Teachers College. I was seventeen and had never been away from home before. My parents didn't believe in too much freedom for their children, so I can also use this as an excuse for immature behavior.

Registration at ETSTC was the worst experience in my life. Today registration is a joy and runs smoothly, but not in those days. I look back on the day I registered in September 1939. It must have been 104 degrees in the shade.

Students were lined up around the registration building. My sister and our friend from Avery had read in a magazine that girls in college should not wear cottons in September, but woolen skirts and sweaters were appropriate. There were no transitionals in those days, so not to be "out of it," we wore woolens. This information must have been directed to girls going to school in the East. We were sweltering while trying to look "cool." I felt I was going to faint, so I asked my sophomore sister to register me for whatever she was taking, and that's how I became an Elementary Education major.

One of the first social affairs I attended was a "Goulash Dance" and open only to freshmen. I didn't know what a "Goulash Dance" was, but I decided to go. When we got there, someone explained the rules. Boys and girls could ask someone to dance, and if they decided the partner wasn't for them, they said "Goulash" and were free to choose another partner. This sounded fine to me until a boy said "Goulash," and I was left on the dance floor stunned. Some other boy saved me from total embarrassment. I thought I'd never go to another one; it was just too humiliating. I needn't have worried because this was the first and last of the "Goulash" dances.

The first class my sister had signed me up for was a Middle Eastern geography class. The instructor started by discussing Arabs. I was completely thrown because I had never heard of "Air-ubs." I thought I must be the dumbest freshman at East Texas. In Avery, we had A–rabs (pronounced with a long "a"), but not Air-ubs. After class, the instructor explained these were the same people, just different pronunciations. I was somewhat relieved.

I joined the Tooanoowe Social Club and enjoyed the affairs that the club sponsored. When a member mentioned that one of our directors was in the hospital, I asked what was wrong with her, and an upper classman said, "Didn't you even notice, Freshman? She is pregnant and having a baby?" I just thought she was fat.

My other memories are happy and not traumatic. After getting married and having a daughter, I still lacked one semester. One summer while my husband was on duty in the Air Force elsewhere, I went back to East Texas and got my degree.

When my husband went to Indiana University for his Master's degree, I decided to get my M.S. as well. Had they known me in my undergraduate days, no one would have believed that I would be an honor graduate at I.U. in my great passion—reading.

It is with the greatest of pleasure that I look back on my years at East Texas, now Texas A&M University-Commerce. It was a joy to have a college so near and one that my father could afford as two of my three sisters were in college at the same time I was. In fact, two of my sisters and I graduated from East Texas State University, as well as two brothers-in-law, a nephew, and his wife. I feel very close to my "old" university even though it has a "new" name.

Chapter 35

JOURNEY

Pat Turner—Class of 1971—Vernon

At thirty-three years of age, I awoke from a coma and realized I was in a hospital room. The situation came about as the result of a collision with a federal vehicle. After several months of recovering from amnesia and a broken body, my mind and emotions slowly improved. Physicians recommended that I enroll in school to rejuvenate my mind and to allow time to heal the rest.

I did as suggested and enrolled in Henderson County Junior College even though I was still emotionally and physically spent. To be quite honest, I was horrified at the prospect. I wondered how I could succeed realizing I would need counseling and changes in the curriculum delivery systems. After finishing the community college curriculum, my doctors told me to continue studying.

I knew I had a long way to go if I was to properly function in a four-year institution even though I was an A student in the community college. After much counseling with Dr. Graham Johnson, Dr. Trezzie Presley, and others, they assured me that if I worked hard, I could master the curriculum and compete with the younger, healthier students. My decision was to enroll in East Texas State University.

My major became Business Administration. At the end of the first semester, my grades were lower than I had earned from the community college. However, I was not discouraged.

In 1969, I was a thirty-five year old junior majoring in Business Administration. I wore hose and high heels to class. You would have thought I would have learned the dress code in the community college, but that was not to be. After all, I had worked in Dallas as a professional in the banking and tobacco business. GEEZ.

Now classified as a second semester junior, I convinced Dr. Dorries to allow me to enroll in an independent study of economics. WOW! My assignment was to prepare a detailed outline and summary of each chapter. You've not done anything until you have outlined an Econ book. During the summer registration, I handed the enormous stack of papers (my outline) to Dr. Dorries. Dr Graham Johnson, Dean of College Administration, stood behind the registration table and appeared interested in the discussion between the faculty member and student. He asked Dr. Dorries, "What is this?" Dr. Dorries proceeded to explain. Dr. Johnson, looking at Dr. Dorries, said, "Maybe we need to talk."

I left saying under my breath, "Thank God, this is my last economics course." Later, when I worked on my master's and doctoral degrees, I had two more economics courses under Dr. Dorries. This little tale will be amusing only if you had economics under the dedicated Dr. Dorries, who I am sure thought all of his students were going to be economists.

During my senior year Dr. Bob Steelman entered my academic life. He was the Dean of Continuing Education. He approached me on a campus parking lot and offered me a graduate assistantship in the Continuing Education Department. After graduation, I became a full time employee as program coordinator in the department. My responsibilities were to organize, develop, staff, and produce seminars, conferences, institutes and off campus credit courses. THIS WAS THE BEGINNING OF MY LIFE'S CAREER JOURNEY. I learned to organize, develop, multi-task, and most of all, work with people. I fell in love with this work.

In 1971, I felt great. My chute was packed. I had my BBA, a fulltime job, and was working on my MBA. With the assistance and encouragement from the faculty and administration and acceptance from the younger students, my emotional and physical health was healing. By this time I had learned to blend in with the student body. In fact I had gained their respect. I was ready for the next tour in my journey.

I moved to Dallas and became employed with two Dallas Community College District institutions. During this time I commuted to Commerce to study for the MBA. After I graduated from ETSU with the degree, I moved to San Angelo to develop and organize Angelo State University's Adult and Continuing Education Department, thus remaining true to my career goals instilled in me at ETSU.

In 1978, ETSU called with an interesting job offer, which I accepted. I again took a new route on my career journey. Named Director of Student Development, the department was in the university's Student Affairs Department reporting to the Vice President for Student Affairs. Oh, I wish I had time to share some hair-raising experiences. My responsibilities included student organizations (excluding Social Greeks), cheerleaders, freshman leadership class, homecoming, beauty pageants, Sam Rayburn Symposium, student government, Bi-Centennial parade, staff retreats, and any other duties assigned. The any other duties assigned can kill you especially in student activities. Two major events stand out in my mind: one was the Bi-Centennial Parade and the second was the homecoming bonfire. I just have to tell you about the bonfire.

I do not have to tell you how important bonfires are to students at Homecoming—something like a "Rite of Passage." The Friday of the week or two before Homecoming, a student organization was responsible for the preparation. This group of students cut wood from local farms to build the structure, and the university maintenance department moved the wood from the local farms to the campus. That Friday the students came in and requested permission to move the wood to campus the next Saturday. I called maintenance and they said no. They had planned to move the wood the next week. I informed the students—who were sitting in my office—of the decision. You can imagine the shock I got when I was coming to work Monday and saw a gigantic stack of wood. When I got to my office, these same students were waiting for me. My question was, "HOW DID YOU MOVE THAT WOOD?" After much dialogue—they confessed. There was a construction site across the street so they took it upon themselves to borrow (their terms) the equipment and move the lumber across the highway from west to east to the campus. What really happened was that they hot wired/stole the state equipment and moved the load across state Highway 50 to a state-owned university. By this time I could have choked them, but they were "oh so proud" of themselves. I called the construction supervisor and explained to him what had happened. He told me he would not press charges if the university would take care of the matter.

I really wanted to lock them in my office. I left, and by the time I got to the construction site, the students were sitting on his door steps. By then, choking them would be a treat compared to the way I felt because I did not really know what we had on our hands except some students who had stolen state property and were excited about Homecoming. I immediately sent them back to my office. When I returned to my office, these same students were sitting with arms loaded with red roses. I did not know whether to laugh or cry. Instead, I sent the students with the roses to the nursing home and then straight to the office of the Vice President for Student Affairs.

I must share with you a trip with the football team. It was Thanksgiving season, and the Lions were to play in the Orange bowl. The cheerleaders and their sponsors traveled with the team to all out-of-town games. Since this was Thanksgiving, our hosts treated the East Texas group to a luncheon before the game. In a very short time, a commotion started. People were banging on toilet doors, not knocking—yelling, "Open up—I gotta go—Hurry—Hurry up, open up." We had a bunch of sick football players (including the quarterback) cheerleaders, and some sponsors. So the bucket brigade began. There were not enough toilets, so away we went to the hospital. We borrowed containers of any kind. Cars transported the sick to the emergency room. They had food poisoning. The game was scheduled for late afternoon. We got though the adventure. I do not remember if we won or lost, but as far as I am concerned, we won. We all lived.

The Bi-Centennial Homecoming Parade was one of those "as any other duties as assigned." This was my BABY. I decided bi-centennial matters.

No cars were allowed except antiques and a convertible for President F. H. "Bub" McDowell and his wife, Martha Jo. I wanted color guards representing all branches of the U.S. Military including the Confederate Army. We had eighty entries.

The most hilarious episode occurred because I had asked Jerry Morris, Dean Truax, and Harold Murphy to be clowns in the parade. Their job was to hand out American flags. I went to Dallas to a costume shop to choose their costumes. I selected HUGE bird feather costumes of red, white, and blue. From the waist down, they wore tights. Their bodies were feathers, and their beaks were flashlights—flashing flashlights.

When I arrived at the parade area to give Harold, Jerry, and Truax the flags, Harold started yelling. He was holding his tights. He yelled, "Pat Turner, these sons of bitches are too big. I need a safety pin." I did not have one. He was having a good time running up and down the parade route yelling his famous phrase. While I was there, no one gave him a pin. He handed out very few flags, but I know he had a good time. The highlight of the parade was the three big birds.

Early one morning I put those costumes in a room in the Sam Rayburn Student Center, locked the door, and left. Most of the committee had not been to bed including this one. We worked all night as people were coming in at all hours. We had a committee including Ron Robinson, Frank Barchard, Sam McCord, students Janice King, Mary Wheeler, and others. They were great to work with, and we had a wonderful time. This event is probably my fondest memory except graduating with the doctoral degree. The angels wept as I composed this.

However, the big birds paid me back.. The next summer I enrolled in the summer statistics class required for my doctoral degree. No one would take a stat course unless it was required. Dr. Harold Murphy was the professor, and he taught it in an elementary school. The chalk board was located a few feet from the floor. Murphy taught on his knees. I cannot repeat Murphy's remarks. We should have given him knee pads, but we did not do so.

I ended my career after twenty-eight years with The Texas A&M University System. For an East Texas girl, being the first family member to attend a four-year institution of higher education, my career was successful.

My job duties were heavy STUFF. If I had not had the educational journey through East Texas State University, I could not make this statement. My passion for this university and its people is indescribable. I love and always have loved East Texas State University. Its gift prepared me to accomplish what most people dream of. The phrase "Dreams are made of this" is appropriate. My wish is that this wonderful institution will do for its students and community what it has done for me. East Texas State University opened its door to me—Pat Turner—broken—and brought me back. Oh, I forgot to tell you, I sued the United States of America over the car wreck and won while getting these degrees.

Chapter 36
THE MYSTERY OF 1959

Earlene Bethea—Class of 1961—Mesquite

In 1957 1 enrolled in East Texas State College, having worked for one year at the Relief and Annuity Board for the Southern Baptist Convention as a file clerk. My family had no money to send me to college, so I saved everything I made and entered the wonderful world of college life.

Our curfew in Binnion Hall was 10:30 p.m., and we loved it because party time started after we came in from our dates. We trotted down the halls with towels draped around us, wearing flip-flops, and carrying a washcloth and a bar of soap to take a quick shower. Next, we slid into our pajamas, got out the cards, and proceeded to play mean games of Canasta. It was a shame that there was no class in Canasta. We would have been A students. It was rowdy and fun, and we loved it.

At some point, someone would end the revelry by asking, "Don't we have a test in McNamee's class tomorrow?" Or, maybe it was an important paper due for Dr. Bill Dunn. Then it was, *Oh, woe is me.* We would get busy throwing something together that we could turn in. That was always when my stomach started to churn, because I was always running late. That was our system.

In March 1959 something occurred that almost ended our college careers. It was the dumbest thing we ever did. I was on a date with some gorgeous guy at the Dairy Queen. In walked my buddies Anita Rhodes, Sonja Graves, Virginia Mosely, and Shelby Craig. I should have run and hid in the restroom. They had this wonderful plan to do something really fun. The weather was perfect, and it would be such fun to spend the night outside the dorm. I thought they had lost their minds. There was no way I would spend the night outside. I was afraid a serial killer, a snake, or maybe a bug would get on me. Their argument was that I had to go because they had already signed me in. If I had had any sense, I would have returned to the dorm and pretended that someone had written on my line. However, I crawled into the car which began what would be quite an adventure in more ways than one.

First off, Shelby Craig had secretly married Benny Bickers. So, we were in his car. The bad news was that she had not asked if she could use it. We had to have that car in front of the Artema House by 6:30 the next morning. I don't know why she took it without asking, but for all practical purposes, we were in a stolen car.

We headed for Greenville without one idea of what to do. They had a little dinky motel with Sunrise or some such in its name. We didn't dare stay there because they would suspect college girls and call the Dreaded Feared Dean Margaret Berry. So on we drove, and drove, and drove.

We finally found ourselves in the Oak Cliff section of Dallas. We spotted a cheap hotel and decided to try it. Shelby and Sonja went in to register for the two of them. The other three sneaked in too. So here we were, five girls in one room with one double bed. This makes three in the bed and two on the floor in a dinky dump. By this time, we were tired, grumpy, and eager to conclude the night.

We had no liquor, no boys, and certainly no drugs. Suddenly someone said, "Get up, it's four in the morning, so out we dragged ourselves to the car. We were dirty, tired, and disgusted, but Nita Lou could always make you think you were having fun because she is such a comedian. We finally made it back to Commerce to the Artema House. All was quiet. We got out of the car but did not have enough sense to be quiet or split up. Oh no, we went down the street and giggled our way to the back door of our wing in Binnion Hall. Somebody saw us and snitched to Mrs. Gant, our precious dorm mother. One by one, she called us in the next day. We had no plan or collaboration prepared, so each of us gave a different story. Now this was not good. As we began to realize what was happening, we finally got together to make up another lie.

Our cover was Nita Lou's mother. Our lie was that we went to Sulphur Springs to watch the Academy Awards and spent the night. However, it was not over, not by a long shot. Mrs. Rhodes backed our story when Dean Berry called numerous times.

The East Texas State Supreme Court convened in the administration building. They sat in a long line opposite us in chairs. There was Dean Berry, the Big Demon, whom we feared greatly. Dean Rollins and a whole host of department chairmen attended as well. It was akin to facing a parole board. They knew we were lying, but they couldn't figure out what horrible sin we had committed. The height of the interrogation came when Dean Berry said, "Why do you not want to be expelled from college, Virginia?" She burst out into a loud howl and cried, "It will ruin my career." I don't think I ever said a word. I was petrified and felt like a criminal facing justice. I didn't know how I would face my mother after expulsion. Her hard earned dollars had kept me in school.

The authorities finally sentenced us to be "campused" for six weeks. We were so relieved that we weren't kicked out of school. We told Nita Lou that we would kill her if she came up with any more nutty ideas.

So now you have the truth. One little addendum; they put in the margin of our transcripts, *See Disciplinary Case X59-2d*. During all of those thirty years I spent in the classroom of the public school system, nobody ever asked me about it, but it is still a thorn in my side.

Kids do ridiculous things. We can never apply rules from one generation to another. But considering all that goes on now on college campuses and in college dorms, our case would never have caused the sensation that it did. I made sure that I was in the dorm on time after that.

Jimmy T. Rice—Class of 1940
In the fall of 1938, a friend of mine named "Red" and I were dating two lovely coeds, whose names shall remain anonymous. On Saturday night the four of us decided to go to a dance in Terrell, Texas. My friend, who evidently had money, owned a Model A 1930 Ford, so for that night we were "big time."

On our return to E.T. about midnight, Red decided to park awhile. He knew a roadside park near Quinlan. As he turned into the park, he did not realize how close the road was to the Sabine River. Into the river we went; fortunately, there was a big old stump right there in the bend of the river. We hit the dead tree, and all of us climbed safely out of the overturned car, wet and bewildered but unhurt. It was about dawn when we finally got back to E.T., thanks to some kind farmer who pulled us out.

Chapter 37
THE AMERICAN DREAM

Linda Ward Osmundson—Class of 1963—Mesquite

College? How could I even consider going to college? After my parents' divorce, we were three—my mother, my eight-month-old brother and nine-year-old me. We moved to Mesquite from Dallas. My senior year in high school, Mother worked nights in a factory, and I took care of my third grade brother. We squeaked by on her small income. My father owned a body and fender shop in a Chicago suburb. He acted like he had lots of money although I'd never seen any of it. Maybe he'd help.

I asked to visit the summer between my junior and senior years of high school. He sent me a plane ticket. I went with the sole purpose of asking him to finance some of my college expenses. I wasted my time. He explained how he'd set himself up in business with only an eighth grade education and reiterated his belief that girls need not go to college. Besides, he now had five other children to support, including a son who would certainly need a college degree. I learned where my brother and I fit in—I was on my own. Ranked third in my class of sixty-seven, I felt, girl or not, I had what it took to debunk his old-fashioned ideas.

Determined, I applied and received a $200 scholarship from Future Homemakers of America. I worked and saved during two summers and accepted whatever money my mother could spare. A little late, I requested admittance to East Texas State College for the fall of 1957.

Mother convinced me to study business. I preferred English. She asked, "What can you do with an English degree?" So I majored in business.

Binnion Hall had already filled by the time I received acceptance. They opened up one first floor wing of Mayo Hall, the men's dorm. I donned my freshman beanie and moved in with a few other women students and a house mother. One night my roommate and I watched in dismay as the guys staged a panty raid on Binnion. One of the boys came to our window and assured us it was all in fun.

Dean of Women, Margaret Berry, required all women to wear hats and gloves to the football games. I pledged Tooanoowe my second semester. After Monday meetings everyone headed to the Student Union Building to mingle and dance.

My classes included dance with Gertrude Warmack, English under Dr. Byrd, Eusibia Lutz's French, Dr. Graham Johnson's accounting and a much loved art appreciation class. Although not the straight "A" student as in high school, I encountered few problems my first year.

My sophomore year I acquired a job in the cafeteria amidst warnings of the dietitian's irritable disposition. However, we got along great.

Not all grades came easily, especially accounting. Dr. Graham Johnson welcomed a woman student in his second level class, which tendered more of a challenge for me. The third level class proved to be my downfall. Another Dr. Johnson handed us the book and workbook. He left the answer sheets on his desk for our use and expected us to figure out what fit between on our own. Even a male friend couldn't pull me through the class with a decent grade.

Besides accounting, my typing stunk. After subtracting for errors, my scores fell in the minus column. The teacher let me take roll everyday so I could pass the class. Wish he could see me now. In comparison to then, my fingers fly over the computer keys making few errors. And, even if I make mistakes, spell check solves the problems.

After two years, the decision to quit E.T. came because of a lack of funds and poor grades in a major I despised. I gave up a student senate seat and withdrew.

I approached Proctor and Gamble, not for the office that paid little, but the factory which paid more. They hired me. I sold my new car and bought a clunker. In eight months I saved enough money to go back to E.T. as long as I obtained a campus job. I enrolled for spring classes in 1962 and continued through the summer session. Summer found me living at home and commuting until the clunker gave out. To finish classes, I shared gas expenses with another commuter student.

Now I knew what I wanted to do—teach. I changed my major to elementary education and breezed through most classes. With maturity and a major I desired, my grades improved. Maturity may have helped in class but not in social arenas. Since I had few dates, I worked and studied.

When I graduated the summer of 1963, a teaching position awaited me at Jefferson County Schools in Denver, Colorado. My dad's sister and my mother attended graduation. I was the first in either of my parents' families to receive a college degree.

In my second year of teaching, I met my future husband—an accountant, if you'll believe that, with a major oil company. I taught another year after our marriage. Upon expecting our first child, we decided I'd be a stay-at-home mom.

I gave interactive tours in four art museums as my husband's job descriptions changed and transfers moved us throughout the west. I finally put my love of English to work. A freelancer, I write for magazines, newspapers, and Chicken Soup books. I've taught classes on writing personal stories.

My degree took longer than normal, but thanks to East Texas State College, I found my niche, a comfortable home and lifestyle, three sons and seven grandchildren including two sets of twins ages twelve and one in 2010. How much more of the American Dream could I possibly want?

For the record, Texas A&M University-Commerce will always be E.T. to me.

Chapter 38

FROM COLLEGE TO
UNIVERSITY

Rob Whitener—Class of 1964—Texarkana

In the fall of 1964, Mr. F.H. "Bub" McDowell, the university business manager, contacted me (President of the Student Senate) and Sam Chenault
(Attorney General of the Student Senate) to help draft a strategy for changing
the name of East Texas State College to East Texas State University. It was the
feeling that our institution had the proper recognition and scholastic programs
to qualify as a university.

By the spring semester, we had met with Mr. McDowell and President
James G. Gee many times to formulate a plan. Sam and I also had numerous
conferences with Senator Ralph Hall of Rockwall and Representative A.M.
Aiken of Paris to gain guidance as to whom to contact at the state legislative
level.

We gathered a huge amount of information for distribution to state leaders
on the various education and higher education agencies. All the committees
asked us to be student witnesses before each group meeting, and we agreed.
However, we only had a onetime appearance even though we were present
on the floor of the capital almost every Monday through Thursday from mid-
January to the middle of March.

With a nod here, a wink, or a finger point there, Senator Ralph Hall and
Representative A. M. Aiken worked their magic behind the scenes. It was
truly an artistic presentation to behold. The approval came out of committee
with a favorable recommendation and proceeded to the House and Senate for a

vote. The bill passed. The state authorities notified Dr. Gee on the birthday of our institution's founding that the name was now East Texas State University.

Thanks for the opportunity to present this tidbit of ETSU history. It was a fun time and great feeling to have contributed to the permanent record of our Alma Mater.

Editor's note: Rob Whitener attended Maud High School from 1955-1958 after which he transferred to Texarkana Arkansas High School. He graduated from the latter in the spring of 1959. He attended E.T. from 1961-1965 where he played on the Lion basketball team. Rob was a member of the team that won the Lone Star Conference Championship in 1964. Whitener obtained his B.S. degree in 1964 and his M.Ed. degree in 1965.

Whitener was both vice-president and president of Sigma Chi Fraternity. Active in student affairs, he served as Vice-President of the United Students Association, President of the Student Senate, and President of the West Halls Council.

Whitener pioneered alumni affairs when he became the first full-time director and served in that capacity from 1966-1974. Additionally, he served as a member of the Alumni Association Board, the University Foundation Board, and the Athletic Association Board.

Whitener received a Gold Blazer Award for his decades of service to alumni affairs.

Chapter 39

HOW E.T. OPENED THE WORLD FOR ME

Mark Busby—Class of 1967—Ennis

On November 22, 1963, as I walked from the Hall of Languages at East Texas State University toward the Education Building, someone driving by yelled that President Kennedy had been shot in Dallas. A seventeen-year-old freshman who had grown up in an uneducated family in the small town of Ennis twenty miles south of Dallas, I reacted with ambivalence—shocked by the news that our President had been attacked. Tempered by the conventional reactionary political attitudes with which I had been raised, attitudes that helped create the poisonous atmosphere of hate that made Dallas a city that has lived in infamy, I walked to my Personality Foundations class, and my teacher led the class in expressing our feelings about the news as we waited to find out the President's condition, only to learn that President Kennedy was dead. That was the first of many formative experiences for me over the next six years, as I finished a B.A. and then an M.A. in English.

There in the pugilist Dr. Lawrence McNamee's Shakespeare class I met Linda Whitehouse, journalism major and editor of the *ETSU Special*, who became (and still is) my wife but then a master's candidate in Student Personnel and Guidance.

Linda typed my thesis on Marxist literary theory that I finished with Dr. Thomas Perry. She completed the last page the day I received my draft notice in January 1969, which led to the first major adult experience away from Commerce—the U.S. Army in Fort Polk, Louisiana, and then Officer Candidate School at Fort Benning, Georgia. After the army I received my

Ph.D. from the University of Colorado in Boulder, where I went at the suggestion of Dr. Roger Brooks, then dean of Arts and Sciences at E.T. and professor of English. Besides Dr. Brooks and Dr. McNamee, I took classes from the now legendary English faculty during the 1960s and '70s—Dr. (Father) Paul Barrus, Dr. Jim Byrd, Dr. Bill Jack, and Dr. Fred Tarpley.

From Dr. Barrus, I learned to love the etymology of words, recalling how he would explain a word like *obsequious* as he acted out the meaning: "Obsequious, literally means bowing walking backward" by bowing down walking backward. As I discussed the inherent value of poetry one day in a class, I commented on the rhythmical nature of language, and I again recalled Paul Barrus. "Think of a little girl on a swing at the park singing out in rhythm with the swing, 'I like to go high, I like to go high, I like to go high in the sky.'" He would next mention the rhythmical, if ungrammatical, response he once heard: "If I'd a knowed, I coulda rode, I woulda went." When the last day of my own classes arrive, I tell my students the date and time of the final exam, and I ask the class if anyone can tell me what St. Peter said before he died, again becoming Paul Barrus. "'I have fought the good fight,'" I quote for my class, "'and I have finished the course.' After the exam you can say the same thing."

From Dr. Thomas Perry, I learned that hard work and an enthusiasm for teaching can overcome physical difficulties. Dr. Perry suffered from a condition that caused him to shake his head and shoulders vigorously from side to side, a visually distracting condition. But when Dr. Perry began to teach, he either stopped the movements or perhaps led us so deeply into the literature that we no longer noticed them.

From Dr. Byrd, I discovered that my own home territory was worthy of literary and academic study. Dr. Byrd taught folklore with a seeming insouciance for some of the details of teaching but with a genuine enthusiasm for the folklore of Texas and beyond. Byrd also introduced me to Ralph Ellison's work, about whom I wrote one of my first books. And his emphasis on knowing one's region had an effect on my current position as the Jerome H. and Catherine E. Supple Professor of Southwestern Studies and Director of the Southwest Regional Humanities Center and Center for the Study of the Southwest at Texas State University in San Marcos.

From Dr. Bill Jack, I learned how a wry, sometimes biting humor can build a strong learning environment. Dr. Jack taught American drama with a biting sarcasm through which he mocked the ideas that limited people's ability to exercise the kind of freedom of thought that he led his students to believe was necessary to cast off the fetters of small-mindedness—something with which many of my classmates from small Texas towns and I and were burdened.

From Dr. Fred Tarpley, I learned that a good teacher sets standards and leads his students to attend to details. Dr. Tarpley taught the classes required of teaching assistants, essentially an introduction to teaching. He demonstrated how good teaching results not only from sarcasm, enthusiasm, humor, or stage presence, but that careful preparation and organization are essential as well.

Drs. Paul Barrus, Lawrence McNamee, Thomas Perry, James Byrd, Bill Jack, Fred Tarpley, Roger Brooks, and others (Oscar Santucho, Charles Linck) with whom I studied during my formative years at Commerce taught me that an effective teacher creates a powerful legacy. They required and encouraged me to participate in the varied Forum Arts presentations that included such major writers as Malcolm Cowley, Flannery O'Connor, and Shelby Foote. I especially remember a powerful presentation on the violence that racism produces by *Black Like Me* author John Howard Griffin, who grew up in Mansfield not far from my hometown of Ennis, and I knew that the people of whom he spoke were my family, friends, and neighbors. And I was completely entranced by the memorable one-man show for which Hal Holbrook has won many awards in *Mark Twain Tonight!*. It was actually in mid-morning in the Education Building auditorium, where Holbrook walked in smoking a cigar. As he stood several minutes without speaking, watching the smoke waft up in sunlight streaming in from the skylights, he became Mark Twain, and Linda and I have tried to see Holbrook as Twain each decade since.

From my fellow students, some of whom became lifelong friends, I learned to accept and embrace the diversity of American life but also to question much. It was in Commerce that I woke up late one night to hear that Martin Luther King had been shot and not long after to learn the same fate that met Robert Kennedy. And it was at E.T. that we watched television as American Olympic athletes, including E.T. sprinter John Carlos, raised the black power salute in protest on the award stand. And it was there that we watched the nightly reports on Vietnam, including the surprising 1968 TET attack in Vietnam that overturned our government's position that we were moving forward in Vietnam.

As a boy from a small Texas town who spent six years at a not particularly well-known college, I left East Texas and entered the wider world with not a small amount of trepidation. Could I compete with the graduates of Harvard, Yale, and the storied universities of America? In miniature steps I began to realize that the experiences I had at Commerce had opened the world for me and prepared me well. Perhaps my own experiences offer a model to those who follow.

Dewayne Bethea—Class of 1961—Caddo Mills

Shock, anxiety, curiosity, and sadness were some of the emotions felt by most Americans on that dreadful day November 22, 1963. Jerry Flemmons a graduate of ETSTC and a reporter for the Fort Worth Star Telegram paced the halls of Parkland Hospital anxiously awaiting the life or death message of our thirty-fifth president. The medical official came out the side door of the emergency room, and Jerry asked for the location of a pay phone. While both walked toward the phone, the med asked him do you want a scoop. Jerry nodded with some hesitation as the med whispered they're calling for a death certificate. He nervously dialed the Star Telegram office, and the supervisor answered. **The President is dead** – just like that was the way Jerry broke the news. Jerry told me it was a scary career gamble since it was based on a scoop from an anonymous medical employee. So, the first member of the media to officially report the death of President John F. Kennedy was Tejas brother, junior college All-American quarterback, and ET graduate Jerry Flemmons from Stephenville, Texas.

Public sentiment such as it was, no one stepped forward in the following weeks to act as pallbearers for the burial of Lee Harvey Oswald the accused assassin. Once again Jerry stepped to the front, along with other media counterparts, and saw that Oswald got buried.

Chapter 40
THE INTERN HOUSE

Raylene Partin—Class of 1975—Greenville

During the early 1970s, the Department of Literature and Languages had what I call "three generations" of graduate students moving through the recommended courses of study for their Master's and Doctoral degree programs. The department used a small white framed house one block southwest of the Hall of Languages.

My generation of graduate students, the second, received the privilege of officing in this house with some of the members of the first generation. Most of my group looked up to the first group because of their experience and "knowing the ropes." All of us had a desk and chair, access to the kitchen with a real stove and refrigerator, and access to the one bathroom that was tagged with a hand-made sign that had to be flipped to read "Occupied" or "Vacant."

Laughter, colorful language, class-note-comparing, and jam sessions often filled the house as we prepared for graduate class exams. Rumors even had it that one graduate student had made the house his own for living accommodations.

After that one year in the "Intern House," we advanced to the Hall of Languages, usually by two's, with a couple of professors who were to serve as mentors for us. Somehow, I always thought someone figured out how much mischief graduate students could have in a house all their own.

As an intern from fall, 1970, through spring, 1973, I have to say the bonds made at the English Department's "frat" house and in the Hall of Languages are some that have endured and likewise have been most important throughout life. Fortunately, special programs and conferences held now at Texas A&M University- Commerce allow for a reuniting of some of us from the seventies generations and afford us opportunities to catch up on our own careers and families and to reflect upon some very good years at E.T. when we were all one big family.

Chapter 41
THE GREAT RAID OF '62

Charles Shafer—Class of 1963—Mt. Vernon

Not since John Brown attacked Harper's Ferry had a raid caused such excitement. To have begun as a lark born of boredom in the fall of 1962, the great panty raid at then East Texas State College would ensure that Joe, Frankie, and I became legends (at least in our own minds). As a matter of record, Joe and Frankie are not the real names of my fellow miscreants. I gave them new identities to protect the innocent though, in truth, there wasn't an innocent in our circle. As for me, I was guilty from the get-go. I can only hope that the statute of limitations has expired for me.

Now back to my story of the raid of '62. I was starting my third fall at E.T., and like many of my friends, I was without a girlfriend. Unfortunately, we also had too much time on our hands, and the combination of loneliness and boredom got us into far more trouble than we ever bargained for. In fact, what had begun as a harmless romp landed some students in jail and others suspended from school for the remainder of the semester.

Our behavior even warranted a psychological analysis by Dr. William Truax, Dean of Student Personnel Services, who suggested that our inappropriate conduct, though not planned violence, constituted typical mob behavior nonetheless. What stung us most was his assertion that only those young men who are not normally leaders of worthwhile campus activities become leaders of a mob. Moreover, we had thought that bringing a modicum of excitement to a rather lifeless town was a noble calling for us country boys from such places as Winfield, Pecan Gap, Blossom, Cumby, Campbell, and Como. Of course, Dean Truax was right. Deans usually are. In reality, we could probably be more aptly described as small-town pilgrims who had not yet visited the Promised Land and figured this was probably as close as we'd get.

On that fateful fall evening, Joe, Frankie, and I were sitting on the curb in front of the Chat 'N Chew, a greasy spoon diner and hangout for college kids. The diner was across the street from East Hall, the freshman girls' dormitory. As we watched couples coming and going, Joe asked if we'd ever heard of a panty raid. Of course, we'd heard the term before, but neither Frankie nor I had any real notion of what it involved. I suspect that the only panties Frankie and I had ever studied closely were in the lingerie section of the Sears-Roebuck catalog. I think Joe was a bit more worldly, but we'd never know for sure since he possessed the talent of lying with a straight face.

"We wait until after the girls' curfew," said Joe," when all their dates are gone. Then we'll run up, bang on the doors, and yell 'PANTY RAID.' If we're successful, the girls will throw panties and such out the windows."

"What do I need with panties?" asked Frankie quite innocently. "I'll never wear them."

"Dumb Ass," said Joe with a discernible tone of disgust. "You don't wear them. You take them home and display them and lie about how you came to acquire them." Joe muttered something about needing a better class of friends.

We agreed to meet back at the Chat 'N Chew at 11 p.m. The traffic by then should be light around East Hall. None of us, not even Joe, had the slightest inkling that we were about to embark on a mission which would be talked about for years to come at East Texas State.

When I arrived a little before eleven, Joe and Frankie were talking to a small group of guys I'd seen only in classes or at the pool tables in the Student Union Building. Like us, they were probably eternally dateless and needed a little excitement in their lives as well.

"Here's the plan," said Joe, the self-appointed leader of the motley band. "We'll divide into two groups. One group will run up and bang on the door while the other group chants 'PANTY RAID! PANTY RAID'!"

As soon as the chant for panties began, lights began coming on in the upstairs windows, and we could see girls in their nighties peeking though the blinds and curtains. Suddenly a window opened, and just as Joe had predicted, a pair of panties drifted to the small group anxiously awaiting them below. In an instant, windows opened everywhere, and we were inundated by a blizzard of silk and lace. We began grabbing for lingerie like onlookers at a Mardi Gras parade reaching for trinkets thrown from passing floats.

Suddenly, I noticed that our small group was becoming larger—much larger. Within minutes, college boys, high school kids, and curious spectators covered the lawn around East Hall. Bedlam soon spread to Binnion Hall and spilled into the streets. Dr. Truax and Dean of Men Dough Rollins estimated the crowd to be five hundred, and most of them had picked up our chant for panties.

Joe, Frankie, and I had already retreated to the sidewalk across the street when we heard the sirens. "They've called the cops!" said Joe, and we retreated farther into the darkness. Sure enough, as we looked down Live Oak Street, we could see the flashing lights, and they were coming fast, not one car but probably the entire police department. Close behind followed a fire truck. Campus security officers were already on the scene trying to identify participants.

The large group remaining on the dorm lawn made such a racket that they didn't hear the sirens until it was too late. The police cars had blocked the side streets and cut off their escape routes. I had already decided that if caught, I would tell the police I was a missionary, and I'd come to pray for those dark souls ensnared in the web of lust and debauchery.

The raid resulted in disciplinary action against all those identified as college students. The instigators of the raid, Joe, Frankie, and I, had escaped unscathed, but we lay low for a few days, afraid that some of those taken in for questioning might rat on us. Nobody did. We quietly put away our trophies from the raid though Frankie admitted later that he'd worn a couple of pair, which were particularly comfortable.

The following spring semester found Joe, Frankie, and me back on the curb in front of the Chat 'N Chew. Joe was busy spinning yarns to new students who had not known about the melee the previous semester. Most of them were farm boys like the rest of us and were probably just craving excitement.

"You guys ever hear of a panty raid?" Joe asked the unsuspecting group as he grinned like a pig in a turnip patch. Frankie looked at me as I at him, and we both headed home at a dead run.

Chapter 42

THE FARM FAMILY

William "Bill" E. Daniel—Class of 1958—Simms

I graduated from James Bowie High School in Simms near New Boston, in May 1955. I went to Dallas and stayed with an uncle while trying to find a job. I finally acquired a job as a waiter in a restaurant in Oak Cliff. I think it was located on Illinois Avenue. I worked about two days when I received a call from the Agriculture teacher, Mr. Owen Dorrough from James Bowie High School. He said there was a working scholarship open at the E.T. Farm. The scholarship paid tuition and room and board. He said to think about it over night and then get on the Greyhound bus the next day if I wanted to go to college.

The next day I was on the bus going back to Simms. Very shortly after, Mr. Dorrough and I got in his 1952 Chevy pickup and headed to Commerce with my suitcase. We arrived at the field house at E.T., where students were registering for the first summer term of 1955. Mr. Dorrough stopped his pickup in front of the field house, unloaded my suitcase, wished me success, and drove off heading home. I went inside and met some farm boys. They assisted me in the class registration. We walked back to the college farm, and thus a new life began.

There were approximately thirteen farm boys back then. They were from north, east, and northeast Texas areas mostly. Occasionally a farm boy would come from west Texas. We all quickly bonded as a family. My first job at the farm was milking the cows (low man on the totem pole). During the summer term 1955, the milking crew began at 3:45 a.m. We had to milk, eat at the cafeteria, and be in class at 6:30 a.m. This routine included walking from the farm to the campus. We went to school in the morning and worked at the farm during the afternoon. We were able to go home every six weeks for the weekend if I could get a ride with someone or if I decided to "thumb it" from Commerce to Simms (approximately ninety miles/near Naples).

These were other jobs at the farm such as picking up food scraps from the cafeteria, cooking them at the steam machine at the dairy barn, and feeding them to the college farm swine. Others were working with swine at the brood sow barn, caring for the beef cattle, pasteurizing and bottling the milk for use by the student body at the college cafeteria, and working in the slaughter plant on the farm. The latter assignment included slaughtering the cattle, swine, chickens, and sometimes sheep. We chilled the meat, processed it, placed it in the cold storage area, and delivered it to the college cafeteria as requested by the cafeteria manager, Miss Little.

The farm grew corn and other crops for ensilage to feed the dairy cattle. The college farm had an upright silo and a trench silo for curing and storage of the silage.

One of the more enjoyable jobs was showing the dairy cattle at the various fairs. I was blessed by being able to show and attend the East Texas Fair in Tyler, the Four States Fair in Texarkana, and the State Fair of Texas in Dallas. I enjoyed staying with the cattle for several days. I enjoyed the college rodeo each year. It was there that I decided not to pursue bareback bronc riding professionally.

All of the farm boys came from a rural/agriculture background. Each was interested in agriculture. Most of the farm boys took their college studies very seriously as each was at E.T. by choice and desire. We bonded and enjoyed one another. Many of the farm boys remained friends during the next fifty years.

I would like to thank Dr. A. C. "Buck" Hughes and others for giving me the opportunity to attend college. I could not have attended without this type of scholarship. I feel that we were a respected group on campus.

Along with work and studies, we had our fun as others did. I double dated in a 1941 Ford sedan that belonged to a classmate, Bob King, from Saltillo. The auto would not have won a beauty contest, but we were proud of it! I finally got a 1950 Ford two door in 1957. It cost Mom and Dad $212.00, and I was glad to have it.

I look back on my years at E.T. and feel lucky and proud for having the opportunity. I also remember the day I met Miss Glenda Johnson, whom I ask to marry me and be my wife. We married in 1958 and are still married today in 2010.

My gratitude remains for Mr. Owen Dorrough, my high school Ag teacher, for helping me secure the Farm Boys Scholarship, for Dr. Hughes for all he did for me at E.T., for all the other instructors' help, and for the farm programs the college had. I would also like to thank Dr. Hughes for helping me get the job with the Agricultural Marketing Service, USDA in 1958.

I am proud of TAMU-Commerce.

Audrey Robnett Little—Class of 1939

One incident that I shall always remember was when I took an elementary music course with Miss Katherine Murrie. She could scare her students half to death with her booming, threatening voice. She declared no one would pass her course who could not stand before the class and sing correctly the notes of an unfamiliar song. I knew I was not able to read those notes. When time came for testing, I was the third student called to sing. I asked to be excused due to a store throat. She said that I would be first the next day. After class I reminded her that she had said that everyone who was in the Choral Club would be exempt from singing before the class. She then checked her roll and marked "X" by my name in her roll book.

Now, I had to figure out a way to get in the Choral Club. I just started attending. Miss Murrie said she would add my name to the list when she received my registration slip, but I had never registered. Several weeks later Miss Murrie said, "You know, Audrey, Mr. Windell failed to send me your slip, but I'll just add your name to the roll anyway." Now that was one "A" that I surely did not deserve—in music or Choral Club.

Chapter 43

COLLEGE WAS HOT AT OLD E.T.

Richard Ellison—Class of 1951—Texarkana

On a gray wintery day in January 1949, my train from Texarkana arrived in Commerce during a light snow. The afternoon fading, I stopped into the Railroad Hotel located scarcely a hundred feet from the train depot. I enquired about a room, and the clerk said, "I only have one room left, and it's only rented during an emergency." I took it, even with that warning. Having just completed a three-year hitch in the Navy, substandard or not, that quaint hotel experience was hardly an obstacle.

College registration the next day, meeting a navy shipmate . . . Ray Carr, and a fine group from Naples . . . Lester Slaton, J. Mack Presley, and the queen of Point, Texas, Mary Beth Rabb, all added up to an exciting event. What a campus I discovered? Everyone I passed gave a welcoming hello. It was simply contagious.

After settling in the infamous Biltmore and completing my first year of studies, word spread that the USAF R.O.T.C. was coming to campus. The $37 a month pay with uniforms was as attractive as an addled perch to a hungry river otter. It seemed too good to pass up, so like many veterans on campus, I eagerly signed up.

Scarcely eight weeks passed when we were sitting in the auditorium one day listening to Major William Lindley, resident head of R.O.T.C., read his list of permanent, newly appointed officers to head up the three squadron organization. The first person announced was just a warm-up to ones ears, so when the major said, "Cadet Commander Richard Ellison, Squadron Commander

Bill Engle, Squadron Commander, etc." *Whoa, am I hearing correctly?* I thought. "Lester, did he call my name?"

"He sure did," Lester Slaton said. "You are it, son."

With that announcement, my plans for a fast-track degree hit a major stumbling block amounting to three more hours each day shot to heck and back. Not really. Not all was lost. I could resign at any time my studies warranted it. After a year, I reached that point, and I recommended my squadron commander, Bill Engle, for my replacement.

During my junior year, Ray Carr asked me to pledge the Tejas Club, of which he was the 1950 president. The members were mostly veterans, and we were proud to carry on the fine Tejas tradition founded just a few years earlier. The Tejas Club was made to order for a fine campus social experience. It was a real honor to be part of that group, and even today, thanks to Jace Carrington and his wife Susan, we remain a close-knit organization.

In retrospect, the caring leadership and skills of the administration and faculty deeply enhanced the E.T. experience. My favorites were President James Gilliam Gee, a fine campus builder and administrator who brought the R.O.T.C. unit to our campus; John W. "Dough" Rollins, dean of men; Dr. Cecil Wright, head of the math department; Weldon "Bub" Taylor, instructor in math; Major William Lindley, head of R.O.T.C.; Miss Mary Lou Whitley, English instructor; Dr. C.O. Mitchell, Business Administration, and Mr. E. M. Box, professor of Physics.

In January 1950, we organized an impressive military ball in the Student Union Building and danced to an excellent orchestra of twenty-one pieces furnished by the Air Force. As I escorted Mary Ann Gamble, our ROTC Queen, down the aisle, I realized that college was indeed hot, and that in time I would look back on the E.T. years as the important life-experience that it turned out to be.

In general, the corps prospered, and we were ready to serve our country a second time. At the time of my Air Force commission in 1951, the Korean War commanded our services in the U.S. Air Force. We served well.

Salute!

Chapter 44

SPORTS MEMORIES

John Newman—Class of 1953—Dallas

Most of my blue and gold memories relate to sports. That 1952 football team could have beaten almost any team in the country after winning the Tangerine Bowl 33 to 0. In 1962, we ended Texas A&I's winning streak with a 3 to 3 tie. We did even better when we won 7 to 6 to end their undefeated 46-game streak in 1977. In 1988, we were losing 7 to 30 at halftime but came back to win 41 to 37. In 1991, we ended Pittsburg State's streak of thirty wins 20 to 13. Of course, there was the great 21 to 18 win over Carson Newman for the NAIA national title in 1972.

E.T is the only team to have a player on the two most famous professional defense teams—Dwight White with the Steelers' Steel Curtain and Harvey Martin on the Cowboys' Doomsday Defense.

The men's basketball program has had some outstanding teams. One I remember best was when we had the Grangers and 7' Lee Johnson in the late 1970s. I remember Coach Jim Gudger wearing red socks and throwing chairs.

Back in the 1950s, we had a group called the Madhatters as a pep organization for all games. I believe it lasted only a few years after I graduated.

E.T.'s rivalry with North Texas, which ended in the 1950s, can't be overlooked.

As a student I lived in South Dorms. The buildings had been brought to the E.T. campus from an Army camp.

On campus some of my favorite professors were Dr. Jack Bell, Dr. Paul Street, Dr. Minnie Behrens, Miss Frances Potts, Dr. Pat Pope, and Dr. H. M. Lafferty.

Chapter 45

A Hallmark Moment

Jackie Polson—Class of 1959—Dallas

My first semester at East Texas State College in January 1956 was the most fun time of my life. Like a Hallmark Special movie, it was different, interesting, romantic, and unforgettable. It was a time of few responsibilities and many new experiences.

The first day I arrived on the Commerce campus, my cousin Carol Warren and five of her Marpessa friends took me on a driving tour. An Elvis Presley song played on the radio, and all of the girls, except me, sighed, "Oh, Elvis!" This ignorant little city girl from Dallas asked, "Who's Elvis?" Six shocked faces turned to me at once; however, I soon became an avid Elvis fan myself.

Joining a social club after Pledge Week was one of my first decisions, and I joined the Marpessa Social Club. I played on the intramural teams when I had no athletic ability, but we had a good time. Varsity is not for everyone. The social clubs met on Monday night, and later everyone went to the Student Union Building (SUB) to the dance. Dancing had been my favorite activity for many years. The SUB was also a favorite meeting place for students between classes during the day.

My cousin Carol and I kept a dating calendar in our room to keep track of which night we were dating various boys. At first, we dated a different person almost every night. I had always heard you had to kiss a lot of frogs before you found the prince. We ended up dating a few octopuses too, but we quickly threw those back in the water. Eventually, we began to date two Tejas members named Sam Simpson and Jimmy Chambers and had the most fun of all with them. We went to dances, picnics, church, ballgames, movies, and many other activities.

I had many other new experiences at E.T. I watched my club sisters chase greased pigs in a rodeo during Western Week. The Marpessas performed *The Banana Boat* song in a musical show competition. We adopted a child on Orphans Day and tried to make it a fun time. A big victory came when Dean Margaret Berry allowed girls to wear Bermuda shorts with long socks toward the end of the spring semester. Oh, I almost forgot to mention the big panty raid of 1956 when a girl opened a back door in Binnion Hall to allow boys to enter. Locked in our dorm rooms, I remember recognizing the voice of Robert Stolusky yelling in the hall, "Hand me them drawers!" Dr. James G. Gee, our college president, soon ended the raid.

Social life trumped academic life for this freshman. Unfortunately, academics were on the low end of my priorities. If I could freeze a memory in time as a Hallmark moment, it would be the spring semester of 1956 at East Texas State College in Commerce, Texas. I will never forget that happy time.

Toby McDowell Harty

I cannot think of Old ET without remembering how my mother, May McDowell, spent her lifetime with aspirations of going to school and getting a degree. The opportunity arrived in 1944, when I was in high school and my three brothers were in the U.S. Marines. Upon my graduation in 1945, I joined her in Commerce. She took a teaching position with the Army for one term and then came back to campus as Dorm Mom at Mayo Hall, where I lived.

After the war was over, she had the privilege of having me and my brother, Bill, on campus with her for a period. I married and left the campus, whereupon my brother, Jack, was home and came to join her living in West Dorm. In 1948, my brother Sam completed his enlistment in the Marines and, along with his wife and baby son, came to live in the Quonset hut married student housing. She completed her B.S. in 1949, and her M.S. in 1952. She taught school most of the rest of her lifetime retiring in 1973.

East Texas State Teachers College. East Texas State University, or Texas A&M University at Commerce—each has been a forever influence on the lives of the McDowell family.

Chapter 46

TRIBUTE TO AN "ODDIE" BUT "GOODIE"

Scott Reighard—Class of 1986—Pennsylvania

For those of you who attended ETSU in the 1970s and 1980s, and maybe even into the 90s, you probably remember this diminutive man in the English department who always walked around with a Pittsburgh Pirate hat on and who always seemed to wear high top sneakers. Yep, Dr. Lawrence McNamee. He was quite the character and a pivotal person in getting me to consider English as my major.

I first met Dr. Mac when I took vocabulary building. It was the fall of 1984 upon my return to ETSU after a year roaming the desert. That's a joke, but Dr. Mac would probably appreciate it. He was a quick witted man who had this endearing quality. I don't think he stood an inch over five foot eight, and if he was a boxer (of which was his passion) he would have been a featherweight, but more on the boxing later. He made an immediate impression on me because he would tell these awful jokes in class and then laugh at them. He had this innocent smile that would display almost all his teeth, and he would close his eyes when he laughed. I used to just laugh at his laugh. Maybe he thought I was actually laughing at his jokes. I don't know, but we hit it off pretty quickly.

We first talked about the fact that I was born in Pennsylvania (as was he), but spent my later growing years in Florida. I told him about my uncle who was a golden glove boxer, and we talked repeatedly about our knowledge of boxing. He would even play the little hand held cassette tapes of boxers he interviewed. One day he actually played a tape of when he got to ask Muhammad

Ali a question, and then there was the Don King interview. That was a great one. Dr. Mac would ask these offbeat questions like, "So Don, how long does it take to do your hair up like that?" We would share stories about the Pittsburgh Pirates because I was initially from Pennsylvania.

One day Dr. Mac said, "I can help you with your vocabulary." "Okay, how?" I asked. He told me to come by his house. He gave me his address and told me to be there on an early Saturday spring day. So, I showed up and he said, "Let's take a drive. I want to show you my little farm." Okay, a little odd, but this was Dr. McNamee. So we hopped in his truck, and I saw it was not an automatic, but a manual column shifter. I had never driven a vehicle with that feature, but Dr. Mac was patient as he instructed me in the proper techniques of shifting, etc. When I finally got the hang of this weird driving technique, we headed out to this little place just outside of Commerce. I pulled the truck up to this ranch gate, and he hopped out to open it. I say hopped because this guy had the energy of a young man. He was amazing.

Okay, so we proceeded on this property, and I think I said something like, "Wow, this isn't a small farm."

He said, "I was just kidding, we're actually here to do a little work." Well, the work turned out to be loading manure onto the back of his truck. I think I cussed more that day than I had in a long time, and he coyly said, "You see, I told you I could help you with your vocabulary." So I shoveled crap for what seemed to be hours, and then when we got back to his house he pulled around the side area, and we unloaded it into a "modest" garden he had in the backyard. Notice I said he drove. I think he got tired of me grinding the gears. I think I called him an SOB that day too, in a good way, that is. It would be the only time I helped him shovel something other than his "manure." An English teacher, always trying to teach a metaphor, and he was very good at it.

You know, it's funny that most of the students I talked to always thought he was just this weird little guy, but I had a tremendous amount of respect for him. Two men, Dr. McNamee and Coach Hawkins have had a great impact on my life, but then again, doesn't the Bible refer to the hoary headed man as the wise one we should take council from? Maybe I was a better listener than I can remember.

The only regret I have is that after I left ETSU I never talked with him again. I feel bad about that now. I wish that somehow, say ten years or so after

I graduated, I would have called him, or wrote him a letter. I don't even know if he is still alive. I would imagine he'd be in his 90's, maybe even a centenarian, but I would never put it past him to still walk the grounds wearing that silly black Pittsburgh Pirate hat, briskly striding in his high top sneakers, and faking a jab at someone.

Chapter 47
STUDENT, DAUGHTER, WIFE

Judith Hall Schroeder—1964/1966—Texarkana

STUDENT: Some girls go to college seeking their "Mrs." degree. On the other hand, I sought my B.A. in English, and I did receive it eventually in August 1968 as a transfer to UT-Austin. Although Dr. Lawrence McNamee is not here to verify this tale, I shall tell it anyway. As one of Dr. Lawrence McNamee's Shakespeare students in the mid 1960s, I had a semester examination that was quite different. Doing well in his course and learning that he needed typing assistance of the manuscript for his book on U.S. doctoral dissertations in the field of English, the professor assigned me the job of typing for him. This task was my substitute examination. I later graduated with my B.A. in English and history and taught secondary English for forty years.

DAUGHTER: My mother and father were both E.T. students. Mother (Ann Humphrey Hall) and I had two similar college experiences. We met our spouses at E.T., Mother in the late 1930s and I in the mid-1960s. Also, we were both students of Gertrude Warmack in physical education. Under her tutelage, we both performed in programs, Mother as a Thanksgiving wishbone (picture in 1930 yearbook) and I in an isometric demonstration.

My dad (Clarence Elton Hall) was a lifelong seeker of knowledge, and education meant so very much to him. He went to West Texas to pick cotton to earn money to go to college. In the late 1930s, he entered E.T. and worked his way through by taking a cow to sell its milk, mowing lawns, and doing all kinds of jobs to survive. Putting his lawn mower under a bush outside his classroom building, he sat in an English class, and from the back row he could hear the pleasant voice of my mother at the front. After she stood him up on their first date, thinking he wasn't serious, he became more persistent in efforts to date her. They married in 1931 and raised a teacher, a musician, and a lawyer. Retiring as professor emeritus in Engineering from Louisiana State University, Dad had experienced many years as an educator at the University of Nebraska (Lincoln) and the University of Tennessee (Knoxville), as well as in public schools.

WIFE: I did get my real "MRS." with my marriage to Morton Richard Schroeder forty-two years ago. As a student at E.T., he credits the influence of three professors for his B.S., M.S., and Ed.D. degrees and for his book publications. The professors were Dr. Otha Spencer, Dr. Curtis Pope, and Dr. Jack Bell, all extraordinary in their support, instruction, and inspiration. His books were *Texas Signs On*, a radio and television history; and *Lone Star Picture Shows,* a panorama of the Texas film industry and the historical movie palaces.

My husband's doctoral dissertation was about the origins and the first ten years of WBAP broadcasting (presently Dallas' KXAS Channel 5). He fondly recalls the following caption under pictures in the 1940 E.T. *Locust* yearbook: EAST TEXAS STATE GOES ON THE AIR—over Fort Worth's WBAP. A radio engineer came to the campus of East Texas State once every month and sometimes more often, to set up a branch station of WBAP on the Commerce campus. The programs were under the direction of the music department, and nearly every member of that department was in charge of one of the programs. Head of the department, Dr. Roy J. Johnson, was above watching the Fort Worth technician. President Whitley made one of his talks in behalf of the college. The EasTexans, under the direction of Gilbert Waller, were oftentimes featured on the broadcast.

As student, daughter, and wife, I have many ties binding me to E.T.

Dorothea Sparks Bennett—Class of 1943

Back when women were learning to smoke, I was having a Coke at the Chatterbox Drug Store across the street from the campus on Monroe Street. I was watching a girl get sick trying to learn to smoke. I asked her why she wanted to smoke since it made her sick. Her answer was, "It gives me something to do with my hands." As for me, I used my hands to knit.

Chapter 48
THREE WAYS A BROTHER

Frank Turner—Class of 1961—Tucumcari

It doesn't seem possible that over fifty years ago I departed Tucumcari, New Mexico, for East Texas State College located in Commerce, Texas. The question I was asked then and now: How did a guy from New Mexico Military Institute find East Texas State? The best answer and only real guidance I got was from a NMMI professor. I told him that big schools intimidated me, and I wanted to pursue some sort of degree in agriculture. He recommended E.T. that had an attractive school catalog. So, in the fall of 1959, I headed to East Texas State.

I arrived in Commerce not knowing a soul, but something felt right to me about the E.T. campus. I only had to walk from East Dorm to the Student Union Building to realize what a friendly campus East Texas was. Soon after school began, "rush" started for the social clubs, which would later become fraternities and sororities. Two Tejas members, Burley Denton and Jerry Mills, invited me to the Tejas house for a smoker. I had been to a couple of other men's club's smokers, but after about five minutes, I knew I wanted to be a Tejas. This was one of the best decisions I ever made. So many of the Tejas members and their families remain close friends to my wife Rosalie and me today.

A couple of songs that were popular at that time were "Mack the Knife" and "Ten More Miles to Tucumcari." As a Tejas pledge I sang the latter many times, and I think the members got the worst end of that. The music was different in East Texas; Bob Wills was not the King; Jimmy Reed was. The two-step was not the most popular dance; the push was. Lone Star Beer and

Pearl Beer were more popular than Coors Beer. "Going to the river" took on a whole new meaning.

You had to be in the Ag department only a short time before you knew Buck, Dr. A. C. "Buck" Hughes, a gruff-talking, Camel cigarette smoker with a heart of gold. Passing through Commerce on our honeymoon in November of 1963, I chose Dr. Hughes as the first person to whom I would introduce my new bride, Rosalie. President Kennedy was assassinated the next day.

East Texas State had the reputation of a "suitcase college," which meant a lot of students went home on weekends. This meant I got a lot of invitations to visit in the homes of fellow students (both male and female). I really enjoyed this. I found that most of my friends came from homes much like my own.

Earlier I mentioned how much I thought of Dr. Buck Hughes. I also thought a lot of Dr. Foster Hamlin. Toward the end of my E.T. stay, Dr. Hamlin invited me and two other Tejas members, both of whom were former Marines, to a cook-out at his house. He told us we were brothers three times: Tejas, Marine Corps, and Ag majors.

The faculty member who has meant the most to so many of us was our fraternity sponsor, Dr. Fred Tarpley. He is one of Rosalie's and my dearest friends. He has been such a wonderful mentor to Rosalie in her writing career. Under the guidance of Dr. Tarpley, while doing research for one of her books, Rosalie probably spent more time in the E.T. library than I did while attending E.T.

My last summer semester at E.T. was a bit different from other semesters. My employment with the school required that I live in a dorm that was filled with girls attending cheerleading camp. Life would drastically change once this semester was over, I graduated, and left for Marine Corps Officer Candidate School.

East Texas State College, now Texas A&M University-Commerce, remains an important place in our lives. I am proud to remain active in school affairs. We have so many very dear friends because of that two-year stop in my life.

Chapter 49

E. T. 1930

Denny Darby—Class of 1962—Greenville

My mother, Coy White Darby, and her sister, Loys White Ingram, graduated from Campbell High School in 1930. Loys was the class valedictorian, and my mother was the salutatorian. They both aspired to be school teachers upon graduation from college.

That fall, my granddad, Offie T. White, drove them to Commerce in his Model T Ford and helped them find a room in a school-approved boarding house on Monroe Street.

My wife, Juanita Martin Darby, B.A. 1961, told my mother how the dean of women at E.T. in the early sixties would routinely stop women on campus and tell them they needed to be wearing a girdle. Mother topped her story by relating an experience that illustrated how the administration controlled the lives of female students in 1930.

Two boys had asked Mother and Aunt Loys out on a double date to attend a movie in downtown Commerce. The sisters accepted and told the boys where they lived. The boys told them to be ready at 7 p.m. that evening.

When their dates arrived, Mother and Aunt Loys saw that the boys were in a car. They had expected to walk downtown. The rules for coeds stipulated that *riding in a car with a member of the opposite sex is forbidden*. Since the boys did not want to walk, they had to think of some way around the rule. They really wanted to see the movie. After some thought, she and her sister stepped up on the running boards of the car, grabbed hold of the door handles and told the boys they were ready to go. They rode to downtown Commerce hanging on to the outside of the Ford with its notorious *rumble seat* unoccupied. She said that other than a little windblown hair, the ride there and back was uneventful.

The sisters graduated with teaching certificates in 1932, but because of the Great Depression, neither was able to get a full-time teaching position. They both worked as substitute teachers in rural schools around Hunt County. Mother married in 1934 but continued to sub when the opportunity came along.

One of my earliest memories is when I was four years old and sitting with the first graders at Liberty School, while my Mother worked as a substitute teacher for the six grades taught there.

My mother and Aunt Loys always spoke well of their college. Their youngest sister, Sandra White Oden, started her college education there with a music scholarship in 1952. She enjoyed being the vocalist fronting the E.T. orchestra for two years. Aunt Sandra got degrees from UT Austin and S.F.A. in Nacogdoches.

My wife's dad, Lt. Col. James A. Martin, retired from the Air Force in 1956. He purchased a house on Greenville Street in Commerce. It sat just two doors east of the E.T. Campus and Binnion Hall, a girls' dormitory.

During those times, college panty raids were in vogue all over the country. My wife related that one evening, after her family had all gone to bed, they heard chanting from a large group of boys gathered on the lawn outside the girls' dorm. The boys vocally demanded that the occupants of the dorms throw samples of their lingerie out the windows or they would storm the place. Soon, Dr. James Gee, the president of the college, stepped in front of the group in his pajamas and robe with a .45 Colt automatic pistol in his hand. He stated that he wanted the group to disband in ten seconds or he would start shooting. The stampede started in much less than the allotted ten seconds. My wife recalled that so many boys jumped the fence in their back yard and frightened their family dog so badly that he didn't come out of his house for days.

I enrolled at E.T. in 1958 and received my B.S. and a ROTC commission in the Air Force in 1962.

Chapter 50
BINNION HALL—1959/1962

Dian Fife—Class of 1962—Van

B innion Hall was my new home away from home. The keeper of the hall was Mrs. Ruth Gant. Boy, did she ever patrol, watch, and make us toe the line. I lived in room number 214 the entire time I was at E.T. It was a great location, where you could see the happenings on the campus. It overlooked a green area, which included sidewalks, benches, and the infamous SUB. Sorority houses now occupy this area.

Ruth Gant, the house mother, was a very aristocratic lady. How she ever tolerated us, who came from small East Texas towns and who had not been reared as she had been, is beyond my comprehension. She had such polished manners and poise, and yet she endured our many stunts. We had to be in the dorm by 10:30 p.m. during the week, and 12 midnight on weekends, that is, unless we got special permission to be out later if we went to Dallas. There was a sheet at the desk that we signed "out" on leaving and "in" on returning. She promptly locked the door at the said time and then checked to make sure everyone had signed in. If you were even one minute late, you had to ring the door-bell and answer to her as to why you weren't in on time. It was as bad facing her as facing your family. It wasn't a pleasant experience.

On both ends of the porch, there were swings where we liked to sit and watch the cars, the cafeteria, and the sights when it was warm. The lobby had a piano and many sitting areas to entertain visitors. Students managed the front desk where the sign in/out sheet was located. Visitors came to the lobby to ring for you in your room. The first few years there weren't telephones in our rooms, just a switch on the wall that buzzed to let you know that you had a call or message. To answer, you went to the end of the hall to the one phone for each wing of the dorm. Picking up the phone caused the one downstairs to buzz. You were then told if you had a visitor, phone call, or message. The first thing you checked when returning to your room after class was the switch on the wall. If it was white, that indicated that someone had called while you were out. How exciting it was to run down the hall anticipating whether you had a call or a message waiting for you!

A balcony on the second floor overlooked the front of the dorm. This was a multi-purpose area. When it was warm, we used it for sunbathing; however, most nights we used it to spy on those coming in with dates. The balcony got to be crowded about 10:15 p.m. Since we had already checked with the sign-out sheet to see who were out on dates, the balcony was the perfect place to see who their dates were as they walked to the front door. To avoid detection, we ducked down until they got to the porch. Most couples preferred to avoid the porch lights to say good night, so they sought out areas in full view of the balcony for these last kisses. Alas, most times our giggles gave us away, and we were spotted.

Many couples opted to come in through the back door because it had fewer lights than on the front porch; however, it was closed at 10 p.m. The back door was much better for smooching, but you missed out on thirty minutes if you chose that entrance.

We finally got a television for the lobby and phones installed in our rooms. The phones were still operated downstairs through a switchboard. All phones were shut off at 10:30 p.m.; however, we soon discovered a way to circumvent the system. If you wanted to talk to someone, usually your boyfriend, after the phones were off, you simply dialed them before the switch board shut down and left the phone dangling until you wanted to talk. That prevented the phones from breaking the connection. We also discovered that this was great way to get food after hours. The guys would go to the Dairy Queen, bring it back, and then would throw something at our window to get our attention. We then lowered a bucket on a rope to retrieve the food. Having a phone in our room was great, but for some reason the suspense and excitement of returning to your room to discover the white buzzer indicating that you had a message was lost.

Since community showers and bathroom facilities were located on each wing of the floors, we often had a good distance to go to the bathrooms. We were always trying to be creative and come up with pranks to pull. As there was no place to hang clothes, and since you had to carry your towel and soap with you, most the time we just wrapped the towel around our body. Stealing towels and pouring cold water on someone in the shower were regular antics. One of the more clever and devious tricks was to put Saran Srap on the commodes. This trick was more successful if it occurred at night. Then, during the wee hours when someone stumbled down to the bathroom trying not to fully waken, she would be startled wide awake by a warm, wet feeling all over her feet.

Because there were no "houses" in those days, members of each social club or sorority tried to room as close together in the dorm as possible. One area would be one club, and then in a different area or on another floor, there would be another club. Breaking into an opposing club's room and taking something for display before they realized it was missing was a one up on the first club. Waste paper baskets made excellent containers for water fights with opposing clubs members. Often we filled the baskets with water and crept down the hall to flood their floors. This happened so often that, unbeknownst to us, the water soaked down to Mrs. Gant's ceiling. We had to return to our rooms to refill the baskets. As we rounded the corner armed with containers filled for another round of battle, Mrs. Gant greeted us. For some reason, we quickly lost interest in water fighting.

For weeks there had been rumbling of a panty raid. The guys had told us when they would be over. For days we were so excited anticipating this big event. Mrs. Gant had gotten wind of it and told us that we were to stay in our rooms. You knew that was going to happen! The guys came over to the parking lot behind the dorm. Needless to say, all of us gathered in rooms that overlooked this area. Once they arrived, the guys really didn't know what to do but finally started yelling for us to throw our panties. We all were just yelling and having a great time at the attention this was causing. As the campus cops and Mrs. Gant tried to disperse the men, all of a sudden one pair of lacy panties floated from a third floor window, tossed down by their owner. I don't know who was more shocked. We couldn't believe what we were seeing. One of the quietest, smartest girls on campus had flung her underwear to the raiders below!

Activity period was from 9:30-10:30 a.m. on Monday, Wednesday, and Friday. On those days, the dorm was active as girls were busy "licking and fluffing" getting ready for this hour. No matter if you had skipped earlier classes, you got up and made it to the SUB because this was the best time to hustle. There was music, dancing, socializing, ping-pong, and having your morning coffee. Living in Binnion and attending E.T. was the best time ever!

Chapter 51

A HARLEY TO OLD E.T.

Bobby Harper—Class of 1962—Caddo Mills

It was early September 1955. I had just graduated from Caddo Mills High School, and I was not one of the best students. At graduation, there were only nine students on the stage. Even though I was a below average student, I had a gnawing in my gut to attend college. Most of my classmates had taken jobs in Dallas or had committed to help their families with the farming operations. Now that I think about it, I must have been a little insane. I was not a great student, and I had not heard any of my classmates mention going to college. Why did I think I was college material?

The only college I could consider was East Texas State Teachers College. I had a good friend who had attended SMU, but the tuition at a church school was totally out of my league. If my memory serves me correctly, tuition alone at SMU was five hundred dollars per semester. I did not have a car, but my parents were supportive of this crazy college thing. If I wanted to attend college, they were okay with it, but I knew there would be little, if any, financial support. Mother had told me that my father, who had passed away when I was four, had left me a little money. It turned out to be a total of nine hundred dollars. After that was gone, I would be on my own.

That summer I had worked on a crew moving houses. On the weekend, I also worked at the local City Service gas station. My bank account was somewhere south of five hundred dollars. I had done a little checking and found that freshman registration at ETSTC occurred that very day. I had not made an application, nor had I visited the campus to get advice. This was decision day.

It was early in the morning, and I was at the City Service gas station talking with some of my friends when Tommy Hill pulled up on his Harley. It was one of those stripped down, flat head models.

"Hey Tommy! Where are you headin' so early?"

Tommy replied, "I'm on my way to Commerce. I qualify for the G.I. Bill, and I'm going to go to college."

Tommy, who had just returned from the Army and Korea, was several years older than I was, but he had dated my older sister, Carol. After thinking about that, it may have given me a little bit of an upper hand with Tommy.

"Having given it some thought, I didn't see how I could make it to college without a car."

"Hell fire, hop on the back. You can work out the details later." Tommy replied.

In less than thirty minutes, I was in the Field House on the E.T. campus and feeling about as lost as a snake in a snowstorm. There were hundreds of students standing in expansive lines leading to teachers sitting behind long tables. It was the infamous freshman registration.

As I entered the field house, someone asked me if I needed help. Boy, did I ever need help. After a little guidance and lots of luck, I was standing in one of those lines registering for classes. I signed up for English, algebra, chemistry, history, physical education and student orientation. I had looked at the college catalogue, and I was going to be an engineer like my buddy Frank, who went to SMU and became the president and CEO of Lufkin Industries. I would soon discover that my high school preparation was not sufficient for the engineering program, and math would become my major.

After I completed my class schedule, I arrived at the pay station. The total bill was $42.50, and that included not only tuition, but also a student card good for all ball games, the library, and any other student activity. At that time, it didn't matter how many hours you registered for, it was a flat rate per semester. I believe the tuition was $37.50 and the activity card was five dollars.

I had been told to take no more than four solid courses, and that proved to be excellent advice. Later, I would need to furnish a high school diploma, but they gave me a few days to do that. I was now a freshman at ETSTC, complete with a blue and gold beanie. I wonder if they still have to wear those things.

After registering, I saw Tommy Gavin, another one of my friends from Caddo Mills.

"Hi, Tommy! Would it be possible for me to ride back and forth with you for a few days until I find a place to stay in Commerce?" The Harley did not appeal to me after the ride from Caddo.

"Sure, Bobby. In fact, we need another roommate at the place where I'm staying here in Commerce. Would you be interested?"

"That sounds great. Are you going there when you leave here?"

"Sure, you can check the place out and see what you think," Tommy replied.

I told Tommy Hill that I had arranged with Tommy Gavin, so he could go back home when he finished registration. I would pass on the Harley ride back.

The little cottage on Washington Street was two blocks off campus. It was an easy walk, so a car would not be necessary. The rent was fifteen dollars per month, and that included all utilities. There would be no telephone, radio, or television—and that was a good thing. It was one large room, with a cardboard partition around the bathroom. There were four single beds arranged around the wall, and there was a complete kitchen in one corner. I told Tommy to add me to the list. He told me where the used bookstore was, and I found most of my books for between two and three dollars each.

There must have been some special force at work. There was no way I should have been able to attend college, but here I was, and I now knew that I could handle the financial part. I would later find the academics a little more difficult than the financials.

During that year, there were four or five of us boys in the little cottage. The number varied as some dropped out of school, and others joined us. We were all from Caddo Mills, and all our families had vegetable gardens. As a result, we all brought fresh vegetables from home every week. Tommy Gavin's family had cows and hogs, and they furnished a good deal of our meat. We all took turns cooking and cleaning dishes. We became fair cooks over the next two years, and the Gavin family did its part at providing student assistance in a very direct way. Without their support, the little cottage would have had very little meat on the table.

Tommy gave me a ride to and from Caddo on the weekends, so I could continue working at the City Service gas station. In the summers, I worked on a house moving crew for the Farr and Gavin House Moving operation. Both jobs paid seven dollars per day, so by the end of summer, I would have enough money to pay for my tuition and books. Mother gave me fifty dollars each month from the money my father had left me. That made the financial part of college a little easier. Coke dates at the Student Union Building (SUB) and an occasional Tejas party were well within my financial means. Life was good, and the girls were pretty. The rage at the SUB was the East Texas "push" dance, and over time I became a pretty fair pusher, even if I do say so myself.

I made it through the first two years of college just fine. With my military obligation hanging over me, I dropped out of school after my sophomore year, got my military service out of the way, saved up a little money, purchased a 1955 Super 88 Holiday Oldsmobile, and returned to E.T. three years later. I completed my Bachelor of Science degree in math in 1962, and I did it in four years and one summer semester.

I understand that the registration process, acceptance, and financial situation may be a little different today. I am still curious about the beanie.

Bobby Harper—Class of 1962

It was the fall of 1961 and we were all in high spirits. It was homecoming week, and the entire Tejas membership was about two blocks from the Tejas Club house on Washington Street. We all had on our grubbiest clothes to work on the float. We had a great theme and we did in fact win the best float that year.

As we were working on our Homecoming float, someone yelled that the house was on fire. We did not know which house, but we went into the street and saw fire trucks just down the street. It was our own Tejas House. We ran down the street in hopes of salvaging a few things. The firefighters would not let us close to the house, and they were working feverishly with the water hose. They were connected, but there was no water. My room was on the front, and held all of my belongings except the work clothes I had on.

The house burned to the ground in a matter of a few minutes. All of my clothes, books, drafting supplies etc. were gone. The next day I saw Weldon (Bub) Taylor on campus and he asked me to come to his office. He had a stack of math books all signed by him as a gift to me. He was not only a great teacher, but also a great man. I don't remember any other person showing this simple act of kindness. One of those things you never forget.

Chapter 52
MENTAL MOTION PICTURES

Frances Neidhardt—Class of 1978—Ulaski, TN

Late summer still invited bare arms and sandals when in 1974 I first drove the one hour southeast from Sherman to Commerce on State Highway 11. Beside me on the seat was my 1966 master's thesis from Hardin-Simmons University, *The Influence of Nathaniel Hawthorne on Stephen Crane*. The highway and I became old friends. For three years I commuted to East Texas State University. Adding a semester when studying conversational French at the University of Aix-Provence, I earned a cap and gown by the spring of 1978. On my final drive from Commerce to Sherman, I brought gifts from the University. In my lap lay a large red dissertation with a pompous title in gold, *Verbal-Visual Simultaneity in Faulkner's The Sound and the Fury: A Literary Montage Filmscript for Quentin*. Beside me lay a doctoral degree diploma in the college teaching of English. As I write now, thirty-six years later, the past and present moments overlap with awareness of my life's enrichment, and that of others I've touched, by my walking through the Hall of Languages door. I am indebted to professors, colleagues, and students met and learned from, ideas created and put to use, discoveries made, and errors forgotten or forgiven. I am grateful for perspectives stretched in classrooms and through papers researched, typed at 2 a.m., presented at state, regional, and national professional literary conferences, and by the stimulus gained from notable persons visiting the Department of Literature and Languages.

My motive for choosing East Texas began with its touting by a doctoral alumna and colleague at Grayson County College, where we both taught. At Grayson, Dr. Helen Leatherwood had established the social sciences. I had taught for five years, half-time in art, my second field and second love, and was a faculty wife at Austin College. Though I painted and taught art seriously, my enchantment with the written word rose often in our chats. When talk turned to advanced study in my first field, literature, Helen saw an opening. "How about E.T.? I loved it!" she enthused. "Lots of adults mixing with the farm kids, scads of teachers commuting from as far away as Dallas and Fort Worth—no joke. Virtually a potpourri of ages, life-styles, skin colors. Mostly smart profs, old sensitivities, high graduate standards—but flexible."

"How's the English Department?" I asked.

"Outstanding!" One day she looked me in the eye and made a forecast. "East Texas State University would be exactly right for you. Go for it!" When she added that doctoral students wrote creative dissertations, I was sold. Helen pointed, I enrolled, and thanks mainly to Dr. William "Bill" Jack and Dr. Joanne Cockelreas, Helen's descriptions proved apt and my study a delight. Ten fruitful years of teaching ensued. I commuted to Brookhaven College in Dallas, taught at Austin College in Sherman, returned to East Texas as adjunct and interim, then retired to write and create.

People are cameras whose eyes photograph persons and places around them. Some images are retrievable. While at East Texas State, I, too, was a camera. Extant in memory are shadowy pictures of individuals and ideas met there. Most prominent among them is Dr. Bill Jack, a man of wit, feeling, and an amused sense of absurdity. Dr. Jack recommended me for a teaching assistantship (TA) and fixed a table in his office for my colleague Jeanette Harris and me, which launched the beginning of a long friendship. To get credit for watching silent films that Dr. Jack rolled seemed miraculous—the upshot being inspiration for the creative dissertation I would write. In the darkened room that was his theatre, Dr. Jack's high laugh during scenes shown of Charlie Chaplin trapped by machines in *Modern Times* was infectious. He made no attempt to hide tears when icon Lillian Gish, in a film image he had watched dozens of times, opened the door to welcome her son home from war, the camera's slowing to a close-up of her hand gently touching his shoulder. Hours of black and silver films like *Birth of a Nation, Intolerance, Green,* German expressionism's *Blue Angel*, and especially the Soviet master films *Battleship Potemkin* by Eisenstein and *Mother* by Pudovkin suggested to me parallels between movies and books. I found Soviet montage exciting and useful, montage being an expressive method of cutting and editing a film for metaphorical, tonal, and visual effects. Through the concept of simultaneity, wherein time and space were manipulated for narrative, intellectual, and emotional purposes, Eisenstein linked film and literature. To him, even such subjective modes as the inner *film monologue*, which he equated with fiction's *stream of consciousness* mode, could be filmed.

As I watched Eisenstein's famous *Odessa steps* sequence from *Battleship Potemkin,* I experienced an epiphany. I saw that Faulkner's free-form construction of *The Sound and the Fury's* poetic and verbally erratic Quentin section, famed for its "stream of consciousness" style, might lend itself creatively to montage filming. Under Dr. Jack, my graduate committee approved my writing of a literary filmscirpt designed strictly for reading.

Dr. Cockelreas was mentor for the required theoretical section. The work sits quietly on a shelf, but in its day I presented some of its aspects at the Modern Language Association in New York and at Texas Woman's University's Rhetoric of the Arts symposium starring Jacques Barzun.

My summation with schema I drew for the theory was published in the international journal *Bye Cadmos.* A cutting I titled "Anno Domino June Second 1910," as read by my students and recorded by E.T.'s media department, was played at the South Central Modern Language Association conference in Houston. Leaders in Faulkner's Oxford, Mississippi, at Yoknapatapha read and acclaimed the filmscript.

In my experience, the vibrant and intellectual "you-can-do-it" Dr. Cocklereas was unequaled for one-on-one mentoring in composition at all levels. Co-author of the Barnes and Noble text *Writing Essays About Literature: A Literary Rhetoric,* she stayed informed on trends in literary theory and was resourceful as guide to our inexperienced TA group. Sharing my interest in space/time modernist modes in all the arts, she advanced my thinking with early advice to aim all my papers toward art/lit comparative subjects and submit them to MLA. I credit her and Dr. Jack with the 1980 National Endowment for the Humanities grant awarded me for a summer term at Yale.

Literacy studies were a steady joy and challenge. I recall the magnetism of Dr. Richard Tuerk, whose depth of voice and knowledge on American lit topics could spellbind such classes as Emerson and the transcendentalists with lectures ranging from Darwin to existentialism. Seminars on Faulkner and Gabriel-Marquez, Wordsworth and Coleridge, William Blake, and a review of Greek myth were a treat that has lasted. Dr. Dick Fulkerson's British lit knowledge and expertise in syntax and logic included a flow of red ink seen rather often by the verbose. His close readings and incisive attempts to improve my writing and thinking hit home. He returned my Brontë paper on Jane Eyre's surrealist paintings with small red circles. In the margin was this quiet note: "Eleven prepositional phrases in a forty-four-word sentence." Lesson learned!

Department chair Dr. Fred Tarpley was a dynamic and well published linguist and Texas writer. His collaborative talents connected us TA's with professional scholars across the state. His creative bent and keen ideas continue to benefit English alumni and the university, most recently his support of Dr. Mary Cimarolli's welcomed book, *Man of Grace: A Remembrance of Paul Wells Barrus*, and its launching. His required linguistic classes I tried to elude have improved sound in my ongoing poetry writing, the first one written in memory of E.T.'s Mary Buckley. My *Things Seen and Seen Again* was published by Austin's Sulphur River Literary Review Press (begun at E.T.), edited by E.T. alum Michael Robbins, and picked up by the National Museum of Women in the Arts in Washington, DC.

Notables Dr. Tarpley imported to campus included Gwendolyn Brooks, the tiny Black poet whose powerful poetry wowed us all. I recall graphically the visit by British novelist Anthony Burgess. His youth-oriented best-selling book *A Clockwork Orange* dealt ironically with mind tricks used for political reasons to remove free will. Required reading for all English classes, it stirred discussion campus-wide. Burgess had invented for the book a slang argot, *Nadsat*, by combining forgotten language scraps with rhyming Cockney slang. Students, faculty, and Burgess enjoyed playing around with the crossword puzzle created from *Nadsat* by a student of mine and printed in the campus newspaper.

My students in composition and literature classes earned my respect for their talent, vitality, flexibility, and good nature throughout my sometimes experimental—and not always successful—teaching methods. Arriving before them fresh from drawing and design studio classes where openness was the rule, with every mark made visible for all to see, I viewed the traditional English class as privatized. Early on I began seeking ways my visual arts experiences could complement verbal assignments. Within rhetoric's broad offerings, I wanted to create a visually rich verbal interaction among students, teacher, and the body of knowledge to be studied. Of ideas I initiated, most memorable is the three-week project wherein my students and I, with support by Dr. Cockelreas, linked theory and the visual arts. Here is the project:

Working from the basic composition modes of analysis, description, narration, and argument, I projected slides of paintings in class and asked, "Does Van Gogh analyze his subject, or does he seek motional response?" "Is this cubist painting by Picasso analytical? How so?" "Does Gauguin tell a story with these South East Islanders?" "Do Motherwell's huge black splotches argue something?"

The class composed paragraphs within each mode and chose one favorite from each. Four voices were recorded reading their compositions, and I chose four parallel musical excerpts. All these elements were correlated for us by the media department. Our amateur production, *Variations on a Theme*, was shown to several classes. Eventually, it was chosen for presentation at the Conference on College Composition and Communication in Washington, DC. Here was a sharing of selves and ideas and experience beneficial to the intellect as well as to the enrichment of persons involved.

Two individual students with problems still hover in mind: the very bright girl who shed tears on discovering in her term paper heavy with footnotes that Beethoven's "black brow" did not prove him a Negro; in advanced composition (a last-chance class to pass requirement), the always gentle football hero with a beautiful body and exquisite manners, who was touted as a Dallas Cowboys potential, yet could never learn to write just one coherent paragraph. The failing grade I gave him would terminate his degree and his chance with the Cowboys. Was my decision just? In my mellowed years, I rather suspect it was too hard-line.

In these memories of E.T., I looked at past images. Today's pictures differ. Society's alarming shift from family support to isolated single living has become clear in my current role as a Texas Institute of Letters councilor. As head judge for the award granted to the *Best Book of Poetry* published by a Texan in 2009, and panel judge for the J. Frank Dobie-Paisano fellowship for an emerging writer, I have read writing samples from dozens of the nation's brightest young people. Sadly, the resounding theme that emerges is loneliness and a thread of despair in a heedless society as never before, the fostering of human understanding and individual caring falls to those of us who guide—teachers.

Chapter 53

ENGLISH USAGE TEST

Ken Davis—Class of 1976—Odessa

Of all the things famous and infamous at East Texas, few garnered more attention and angst than the Junior Usage Test. As non-English majors, most students feared this ordeal as much as anything on or off campus. For those who may not know, this was a test given in your junior year to determine if you had accomplished a command of the English composition skills. The test consisted of going into a room, being given a subject, and writing five hundred words about that subject. To pass, you had to demonstrate a command of grammar. That consisted of knowing where to put commas, periods, using a complete sentence, not misspelling words, etc.

Most of us in those very cynical times (the 1970s) took great exception to the logic used for this test. The illogic of it went something like this: Go in. Get your subject. Write the most elementary of sentences; i.e., "See Dick run. See Jane jump." If one was able to keep it incredibly simple or did indeed have a command of grammar, one could pass the test.

I happened to be president of my fraternity and was a member of the Inter-Fraternity Council. As a member of the IFC, we had lunch with Dr. D. Whitney Halladay, ETSU president. One day after our lunch with Dr Halladay, I asked him for a few minutes of his time. I then asked him my burning question. I framed it as follows:

"Why is it that we administer the English Usage Test? It seems to me that we give this test after a student has had fourteen years of school that would have included many years of grammar as well as two years of college English.

"Rather than using this as a test for how well we've been taught the subject and being introspective regarding success in teaching, we use it as a test to determine if people are learning. I believe the failures on the test were more an indictment of teaching failures than learning failures.

"Then, to assume those who failed would learn what they need to know by taking one more semester of English was astounding."

I believe the conversation took him by surprise. He was courteous and receptive to my comments but made no other comments or commitments.

However, it was not many years thereafter that the Junior Usage Test was discontinued. I will forever wonder what impact that conversation had. It did change the way I look at problems. Today, we would call that experience "out of the box." I learned one great skill because of a Junior Usage Test. It did create some good, after all.

Editor's Note: President James G. Gee called Dr. Paul Barrus, head of the English Department, to his office and showed him an illiterate letter telling the president "Me and my wife is very happy to be E.T. graduates," etc. Dr. Gee ordered Dr. Barrus to create a test to be sure that no person with that level of writing skills would "egen" receive an E.T. degree.—FT

Bobbie Fleming Purdy—Class of 1967—Bonham
For this Fannin County country girl of modest means, E.T. was a perfect fit. It wasn't far from home, and it was affordable, yet it was here that a host of excellent teachers challenged me, perhaps for the first time in my life, to really think and encouraged me to form and express my own opinions. E.T. opened the doors to a brave new world. Lifetime-long friendships developed; new and different ideas were explored, and the dream of a college education came true. My husband, Arlan, and I both came to school at E.T. and loved the environment so much that we stayed, he retiring after thirty years employment with the university. It was good then . . . and it is still good (even with a new name).

Chapter 54

PRE-MED EXPERIENCE

Gaynor "Gay" Janes—Class of 1957—Cooper

An old friend from East Texas State Teachers College (NOT Texas A&M-Commerce) and I recently reconnected by accident. He sent a single-spaced, very small print, precisely worded mail-out regarding a two-day meeting of the East Texas Historical Association at Sam Houston State University in Huntsville. At the last minute (my usual), I had to call. It was too late to email or write a response. The final day to respond was December 1, 2007. It had taken many years to realize that procrastination is not only my middle name; it's my full name!

Though I had not seen or spoken to Fred Tarpley for a long time, I laughed out loud when I read his letter. The exactness, precision, and correctness of his writing even in an unofficial document were so typical. Recognizing the author was easy. No one else would or could have done it so well.

Fred and I have been friends since 1957, my senior year in college. I had traveled fifteen miles from Cooper, Texas, (population 2,249) to begin my college career at age sixteen. Fred (really old now at 77 and I'm only 72) had arrived from small-town Leonard, Texas, via Hooks several years before. He ultimately became chair of the English Department, a position which he held for many years. He's a really good guy. We share a mutual family tradition that was (is?) common in the area: being cheap.

My personal history involves traveling to the city of Houston on my own after graduating from E.T. (in three years at age nineteen) in 1957 to begin school at Baylor University College of Medicine. I became a fifth generation physician, yet big changes occurred early in life. I finished medical school in 1961, internship in 1962, OB-GYN residency in 1965, a gyn-oncology fellowship in 1966, and entered a thirty-eight and one-half year extremely successful solo practice before retiring four years ago. My accomplishments include delivering over 5,000 babies and performing over 20,000 major surgical procedures. I was also one of the primary instigators of "natural childbirth" in the United States and made the first movie with the same name.

After reading Fred's letter, I made my typical dingbat guy mistake. Dialing what I thought was his number listed in the letter, I heard "Jim Ainsworth." Shock. Confusion. I was flabbergasted! He was a graduate of Cooper High School, several years behind me. I had dialed the telephone number of Jim's publishing firm printed on the letterhead. When I responded with my name, he said, "Your father was my hero. Dr. Olen saved my dad's life." More shock! One and one-half hours later, our conversation ended. I still hadn't talked with Fred.

My dad and his two physician brothers, in my physician grandfather's five-bed country hospital, had successfully operated on Jim's father, removing 6-8 inches of constricted small intestine. Jim's father was emaciated and dying of malnutrition. Jim and I had never met, but it was like we had grown up together!

Coming of age on a small farm and herding cattle, Jim attended E.T. for his bachelor's and master's. He practiced his acquired art of financial investment adviser in Commerce. This successful CPA from Klondike, Texas, (four miles from Cooper), retired soon after age 50.

Jim thought, "What am I going to do? So I went into professional calf-roping for five years." Shock! When Jim got too old for the rodeo, he again thought, "What do I do now? I began writing and writing, day and night, for seven years." He established his own publishing firm, wrote several well-known books, and now talks about writing all over Texas in boots, jeans, leather jacket, and cowboy hat. No, Jim doesn't play guitar and sing country songs! He is also cheap. I relate to and admire his writing so much that I have given his books to my four daughters and many friends. Fred helped him edit his work from the start.

Fred, Jim, and I have several qualities in common learned from our families and growing up in the same general area. These were certainly encouraged and emphasized by our instructors at E.T.

I learned by example and being told to trust and depend on friends and family but to "do it myself."

Failure was not an option, but failure was okay if you had tried your best. Change is also okay, but dedication counts more.

Lead by example, not words, but writing and speaking and communicating accurately and with honesty are essential.

Hard work is not only counted on but expected. Always do what you say you are going to do.

To paraphrase the Bible, faith, hope, and charity (or love), and the greatest of these is love.

Now to my requested assignment. After the above encounter with Jim, I arranged to meet both Fred and Jim at the history conference. We spent the entire day talking about each other's lives. I took extensive notes which I now cannot find. This is typical for me.

I retired in January 2005 and joined a Retired Physicians Organization Life Writing Group in June 2007. You married women will understand why my loving wife was happy to get me out of the house. One of the OLLI's (Osher Life Learning Institute) founders is the writing instructor for fifteen retired docs in Houston. All are allowed to make comments about the articles we read. It's really great. Both Fred and Jim have been very helpful in improving my writing skills. They know I'm grateful.

In the fall of 2009, Fred said, "You are the perfect author to write why so many E.T. students got into medical school in the 1950s and 1960s." We all know that "flattery" will get you every time. I agreed to write "some little something" for an anthology about E.T. "sometime in the spring." Fred knows just how to handle us procrastinators!

Three women were instrumental in my college training. Margaret Berry was dean of women and taught my first semester history class during a six-week session. We really connected. I made an A. After taking 22-24 hours per semester with all A's, I was registering to sign up for the second year spring semester. I had planned carefully by attending college each summer following high school so that I could apply for medical school in two years and three summers. At the end of the registration line, an old-maid English professor said, "You can't take this many hours." Until then, I had always been so respectful of women and girls. My shocked reply was, "But. But. But. I always make all A's!" Her quiet answer was, "Don't you want to do other things and be well-rounded?" Indignantly I answered, "I'm in the band, on the student council, ping-pong champion, daily basketball player, winner of the dance competition this year, and the one frequently sent for moonshine by my fraternity friends!"

She sternly answered, "Come with me. We're going to Dean Berry's office!" Marching across the small campus to the Administration Building, I silently worried, "What have I done?" The final result of that interminable wait and subsequently long discussion in Dean Berry's office was her saying, "Oh, let him do it. He's so young and innocent." The English professor stormed out. I quietly thanked Dean Berry and quickly left. When I got outside, I jumped in the air and yelled as loud as I could with my upraised fist high above my head. Dealing with my very accomplished and stern mother had been so beneficial! Years later, as I reminisced, I realized that I owed both women.

Dr. Elsie Bodemann was chair of the Biology Department, one of my three majors. She was extremely pleasant, strict in her grading, a good judge of character, and one of the founders of the pre-med recommendation committee. After Baylor Medical accepted me at the end of my second year, she offered me the position of lab instructor of the Microbiology lab. I was so flattered that I blushed and accepted. I didn't know it then, but she knew I was too young and immature for the big city and medical school.

E.T. turned out to be one of the best experiences in my life. Most of the students were older, served in World War II and the Korean Conflict, and used the G.I. bill to finance their education. Sometimes the worst that can happen to you is NOT dying. Those G.I.s understood this well. They knew sacrifice and were grateful for the chance to live their lives as each wished. They could live at home in the small surrounding towns and drive to school so much cheaper. They studied long and hard and taught me well about how to live.

The same happened during and after Viet Nam. Hence, my explanation as to why so many got into medical school during those times.

As for me, I was valedictorian of my 1957 spring graduating class at E.T. and received $25.

All true, as well as I remember!

Chapter 55
THE OGLESBY FAMILY

Ann Oglesby Julian—Class of 1962—Commerce

A family tradition began when our mother, Lucille Woosley Oglesby, attended E.T. for one year.

Our father's father died when he was very young. Therefore, R.J. Oglesby was forced to quit school at a very early age and help support his mother and siblings. Since they chose marriage over a degree, the parents wanted more educational opportunities for their children. They moved to Commerce for that purpose. They were wise in their ways.

All six children earned B.S. degrees, and four of them attained the master's degree. One hundred percent is not a bad ratio.

Brother Bob graduated from Commerce High School on Friday and joined the Navy the next week. Most able-bodied young men were making this patriotic decision for our country. After his Navy hitch, he returned to Commerce to begin his academic work at E.T. While there, he made many friends and joined the Paragon social club. His major was journalism. He worked on the *Locust* yearbook and became the business manager. He was active with his many tasks with the yearbook, his class work, and social obligations. After he earned his B.S., he worked toward the completion of his M.S. He was sidelined when he began work for Proctor and Gamble.

Then he became of age to apply for the F.B.I. He became a special agent and traveled the world. When he was in Puerto Rico, his sister Ann lived with him and taught school at Ramey Air Force Base. His next appointment was in Mexico. He met Tessa Newth, an English nurse and tourist. His next stop was a trip to England for their wedding. Several years later, they moved to Washington, where he did more secretive work. He transferred to Colombia.

That was the time of the Jim Jones suicide fracas. Bob was in the area and was assigned the task of interrogating, investigating, and getting everything in order. No other agent was allowed to help. Their government proclaimed that one was enough. After that event, Bob and family were in Bogota until his retirement. He had several fascinating jobs before returning to earn his M.S. at E.T. He and his family attend many events on campus.

Sister Jean followed her brother's educational program and began her college days three days after high school graduation. She was studious, popular, and dedicated to her work in the library. She took time to pose for the cover of E.T.'s *Varsity* magazine, a school periodical that has long been gone. She completed her degree in three and a half years. She met B.S. Follis, a veteran who had returned to his home in Cumby after the war. She graduated in January, married in February. Mr. and Mrs. Follis moved to West Texas to meet the demands of his work. They returned to Commerce two years later, and Jean worked as Dean Young's secretary until she earned her M.A. They moved to Port Neches and later to Baytown. Jean retired from her teaching career and became a full time homemaker. Her husband died of cancer in 2008. She is now living in Baytown with her son John.

Next, came sister Christine. Friday graduation and Monday college was also her routine.

Christine was involved. She was head majorette, Who's Who in Texas universities, and business manager of the *Locust* yearbook. Her band days kept her busy. That is where she met her husband, Bobby Wickersham, from Cooper. Bobby had been a marine and returned to E.T. for his degree. He was Cooper band director when they married.

She had completed her degree, and he was working on his M.S. His master's was in music and hers was in counseling. They were working and living in Wichita Falls when Bobby had a heart attack and died in 1980. Christine was at her desk in October of 1989 when an aneurysm caused her death. They had three children, Celia, Pat, and James.

Brother Mike attended one year and then served in the Army. After his Army stint, he returned to E.T. and became a marvelous student. He was a Lambda Chi member and president of the student body. He met his wife, Jeanenne Grammar, at E.T. She was a Gamma Phi Beta member and a studious individual. The first year of Dallas Cowboys cheerleaders was fun for Jeanenne. The Cowboys organization chose high school cheerleaders to represent them.

Jeanenne was a Bryan Adams high school cheerleader and one of the chosen few. Mike and Jeanenne were married, completed school, and joined the work force. Mike created and managed several insurance claim companies. Jeanenne taught school for several years. They had three sons, Jason, Dan, and Adam. After Jason's accidental death, Mike and Jeanenne joined forces to form Oglesby and Associates Company. They made a big impact on the university and the town of Commerce with their beautiful construction additions to the community.

Brother Joe was the last of the six Oglesby siblings to enter E.T. He took a different route. He married Kay Talley from Commerce. He served his country before attending E.T. Joe and Kay were studious individuals. The Dean's List and other honors came their way.

Sister Ann was another Commerce High graduate who finished high school on Friday and entered E.T. on Monday.

Joe majored in criminal justice, and Kay became a nurse. They have three boys, Marc, Kevin, and Joe Paul. Joe and Kay moved to Yukon, Oklahoma. Joe worked for the Department of Federal Justice there before retirement. He is now a consultant in justice work. Kay was a nurse and now coordinates programs to match doctors and hospitals in different areas. Both have fond memories of E.T.

Edith Dodson Perham—Class of 1938

As my roommate and I were walking home from class one day, we saw a goat on someone's porch. As soon as the goat saw us, it jumped over the banister and started after us. It jumped and ran with so much speed that it chased us for the two and one-half blocks that we had to go to reach our destination. We lived in a small apartment upstairs, so we crossed the porch and started up. That goat did the exact same thing; however, it got stuck in the stairway steps, and he broke the first two steps. The landlady was quite upset, but with some help, she managed to get the goat out of the stairway. I don't know who paid for the damages, but we never saw that goat again.

Chapter 56

HALF-BLIND DATE

Buddy Kinamon—Class of 1964—Blue Ridge

For this narrative to make any sense, one needs to remember that back in the prehistoric days of E.T., girls and boys lived in separate dorms. Those for girls were veritable bastions of virtue to which girls were required to return by 10:30 p.m. on school nights and by midnight on Fridays and Saturdays—no exceptions. At the witching hour, dorm "mothers" locked and barred the doors. Anyone returning even a minute late won a free visit with the dean of women. After three such visits (assuming no additional damaging circumstances which could significantly reduce the number of allowed visits), one was granted former student status along with an opportunity to try one's fortune elsewhere..

In order to retrieve one of the sequestered females for a date, boys approached the reception desk in the lobby and asked the girl on duty to *buzz down* the intended date. The receptionist pressed the button for the specified room a pre-determined number of times to signal the appropriate girl. Shortly thereafter, the beckoned damsel descended the stairs, met her date, and they commenced their intended mission. With this background information, the remainder of the story might make sense.

Early in my first fall semester of Graduate School, my roommate and I had just returned from an ill-conceived road trip, having avoided any meaningful sleep the night before. Near the crack of noon, a persistent knock disturbed my slumber. Following a futile attempt to motivate my roommate to respond to this incessant knocking, I dragged myself to the door to find a friend with an offer. He suggested that I take a ride with him to nearby Greenville. I declined. He insisted—explaining that he and his date were driving a friend for a doctor's appointment, and they would all feel more comfortable with another person along. I again declined. He again insisted. Finally, I acquiesced—more to stop the noise than from any desire for an activity involving additional travel in a car.

I hastily pulled on some clothes and climbed into the back seat of his convertible. Sitting across from me was a girl with a rather large patch over one eye—and not the exotic black kind worn by pirates and other persons of intrigue but a big honking white gauze patch complete with white tape. This is about the only thing I remember about her—given that I slept most of the time there and back.

Shortly thereafter, my steady girlfriend of two-plus years decided I was a bad risk and issued my walking papers. I learned the value of serious groveling at this time. I finally convinced her to give me one more chance. She informed me that she already had a date for the upcoming football game but that she would break it and resume our relationship afterwards. Drawing upon my limited chivalry, I assured her that would be inappropriate and that I would go to the game with some of the guys. As it turned out, all of my male friends had dates, and that left me with the embarrassing proposition of going to the game alone—a situation that was sure to brand me a social leper. After exhausting my list of possible candidates, I got the bright idea to ask the one-eyed girl. After all, she could not be all that particular, especially in her present condition. Since I couldn't recall her name, I called our mutual friend, the sponsor of the convertible ride, to inquire. Armed with this information, I made the phone call. To my great surprise, she agreed to accompany me to the game.

When the big night rolled around, I made my way to the dorm lobby with her name written on a small piece of paper. I relayed the information to the receptionist with a request to "buzz her down." I took a seat in the lobby strategically positioned to see anyone coming down the steps. A short time later, a girl walked toward me. I stood politely and expectantly and waited. She walked right past me, took her date by the arm, and left. I sat down. Shortly thereafter, the scene was repeated—girl walked toward me, I stood, she walked past, I sat down.

After several more of these disappointments, I looked up and sighted an ethereal vision of loveliness floating lightly toward me. I was not about to repeat my previous embarrassing blunders, so I remained seated and waited to see who the lucky guy might be. To my surprise, she walked up to me, stood there for a minute (sans patch), and asked, "Are we going or not?" Five months later we married—and remain so after almost a half-century.

Chapter 57

LEFT-RIGHT

Bobby Hazlewood—Class of 1955—Commerce

I graduated from Commerce High School in May of 1951, at the age of seventeen. In September of that year, I ventured away from the farm to attend college at East Texas State Teachers College in Commerce, Texas. I joined several fellow "Commerce Tigers" who grew up together out in the country, and we registered at the same time for classes at "The College."

I had two good reasons for going to college. Number one reason was I did not want to look at the rear end of that mule plowing down those cotton rows any more. Number two reason was I wanted to fly airplanes.

My older brother gave me a 1929 model A Ford, and off I went to college, a grand total of four miles. I enrolled in the Air Force ROTC program and signed a contract to go into flight training upon graduation.

In order to pay for college expenses, I got a job, as a "soda jerk," at Cranford's Drug Store. I worked there for all four years of college. My model A did not have an ignition key, just a toggle switch to start the car. While slaving away at the drug store, I often saw my car pass by driven by Bill Hollowell and George Cox who were out for a joy ride. They never did put any gas in the car.

During my first semester at E.T., I took an Algebra class with W. W. Taylor. There were two math instructors named Taylor at this time. One was Bub Taylor, but I can't remember the first name of the one who taught my math class. However, I do remember how he taught the class. He would start on the left-hand side of the long chalkboard, write algebra problems and solutions with his right hand, and erase them with his left hand all the way to the far right-side of the board. Then, he would head back the other direction, write with his left hand and erase with his right. When he finished on the left side of the board, he would look over his shoulder and ask, "Now, did you get this?"

I thought, *this is a little old country boy's welcome to college.* I must have gotten it, because I made a B in that algebra class and went on to graduate in December of 1955. A good number of those other "old country boys" finished their college educations at E.T. also. Some of us still keep in touch and even run in to each other from time to time.

When I graduated from East Texas, I was commissioned as a 2nd Lt. in the United States Air Force. I reported to Malden, Missouri, for basic flight training. I first flew forty hours of training in the T-34 and then sixty hours in the T-28. Both were single engine prop planes.

After completing the basic flight training, I reported to Laredo Air Force Base for jet training. This was six months training in the single jet engine T-33. When I completed the T-33 training, I received my wings, and then was off to Perrin Air Force Base in Sherman, Texas, for combat training in the F-86D super saber, which would break the sound barrier. That was the culmination of my dream come true.

Rex Newsom—Class of 1939

I had just finished high school in Saltillo, when Mrs. Noble Arthur came there to visit friends, one with whom I lived. She asked me what was next on my list, and I told her I wanted to go to college in Commerce, but my funds would not allow that. She told me she needed a hasher to work in her boarding house, and if I had $17 she would help me go to college.

I accepted her offer, and we were off to Commerce. My greatest hour in college was when the student body elected me business manager of the campus newspaper, *The East Texan.* Every month in 1938 and 1939, Bub McDowell gave me a check for selling advertising for the paper. Usually it amounted to about $40—I was rich.

Odell Bowen, Delton Burnett, and I worked for our meals at Mrs. Arthur's. One Saturday she asked us to wash the transoms after dinner. So, with pails, water, mops, and rags, we proceeded to go in the dining room and start our clearing detail. We had scrubbed two walls before Mrs. Arthur came in inquiring as to what we were doing. She quickly realized that we three farm boys did not know what a transom was. We took the tongue lashing with much humility.

Chapter 58

FIRST FEW DAYS

Gilbert Rodriguez—Class of 1983—San Juan

The following story is about my first few days as a freshman at ETSU. It was the summer of 1979 and my first time away from home. It was hard to say goodbye to my mom when I boarded the bus and left South Texas towards the big city of Commerce, but I was excited about college life. I was sad because I didn't own a car, and the only way to get there was by taking the bus.

I took the Greyhound and arrived with just my suitcases. Since it was hot that day, I didn't look forward to the long walk to Hubbell Hall. I had a map of the campus and a map of the city of Commerce. When I looked at the map, it didn't look too far, so I picked up both of my suitcases and started the journey to my dorm. I left the Greyhound bus depot and walked west on Bonham Alley to Washington Street, and then I went down to Live Oak Street. When I got to Live Oak, I took a right and then a left on Monroe Street. I went as far as Chestnut Street, and I knew that I had to come back to this great place, the Commerce Dairy Queen. The reason for the importance of the Dairy Queen is because when I left South Texas, I was working as the assistant district manager, and later on, this particular DQ would become the place where I met my future wife. Since I was carrying two suitcases, I didn't feel like stopping, so I continued my journey to the dorm. When I got to Hunt Street, I knew that I was near campus because I saw the Security Department at the corner. I knew I was on campus, and I decided to continue my walk until I reached Hubbell Hall.

When I arrived at Hubbell Hall, there were many of us ready to check in, and the check-in process was quick. They gave me the key to my room.

I went up to the third floor, and I opened the door. I thought to myself, *Why is the room divided in half?* I thought all of us had separate rooms. I wasn't ready to share my space with anyone. I thought that going to college was going to be a great experience, but it was starting to worry me. I knew that I had my own half room because the other guy I was supposed to share my room with had already unpacked and had all of his stuff tucked away properly. I was afraid that this guy and I weren't going to get along because he was very organized, and I wasn't the organized type.

I started to unpack, and while I was unpacking, in walked this very well built jock. I thought, *Oh no, I'm not going to be able to compete for the ladies against this guy.* He was ready to go out running and asked if I wanted to go. I told him about my walk from the bus station, so he left without me. As I started looking around, I couldn't find the shower, but I did find a tiny restroom between our room and the room on the other side.

I was introduced to the "RA," but I didn't know what that meant. It stood for Residence Assistant. He was just across the hall from us and was the one we needed to go to for any issues or problems. I asked him where the shower was, and he walked me down the hall half way and opened a door. It was a community shower area. There was a tub on the right, and further on, there were about four shower stalls. On the left side were only towel hooks. I said, "Thanks," and he went back to his room. I knew that this was going to be an experience, but why couldn't I have the necessities, just like a normal equipped bathroom?

I went back down the hallway, and I noticed a huge TV (about 25"), a table and chairs in the corner, and an odd-looking sofa in the middle of the room. To the side of the room, there was a small kitchen/laundry area. I opened the fridge, but it didn't look like anyone was using it. I checked out the washer and dryer. It seemed like I needed to take care of those as well, because they were going to be used a lot if I wanted clean clothes.

This was my first day. I was tired, and I didn't want to walk all the way back to the Dairy Queen to eat, so I asked the RA what my options were. He told me the cafeteria (if I followed the sidewalk in front of the building), or if I went back to the Student Union Building, I could get something at that cafeteria or go upstairs to get some junk food. He reminded me to make sure that I used my lunch card. Since it was my first day, I didn't understand about the lunch card, but the RA explained it perfectly. He said that it came with the room but that I had to go to the SUB so the school could make one for me. Since I didn't have enough energy to go to the SUB, I decided to wait. My stomach was growling all night, but I made it.

I noticed after waking up that my roommate wasn't acting as cheerful as he did the day before, and I asked him what was wrong. He said that he probably worked out too much yesterday and wasn't feeling good. We talked about our background, and I found out that he was from Freer, Texas. He was here on a football scholarship. I congratulated him and told him that I hoped he would feel better. He said that he was going to Dallas to visit some friends and that he wouldn't be back until late Sunday. I wished him luck and told him that I'd see him when he got back. He left and I spent the day walking the campus.

I went down the sidewalk past the cafeteria because I didn't have a lunch card. I took the tunnel under Highway 24. According to the campus map, I was in the "West Halls" area, and I thought they were very cool-looking apartments.

I started towards the main campus, and the first place that I noticed was the Zeppa Center. I went in to check it out, and it had a front desk person who asked for my "card." I didn't have one, so I asked him if he could just show me around. I was amazed what was located inside. He showed me a state-of-the-art bowling alley, a very nice swimming pool with a high diving board, and an outside tanning area. At the very end of our tour, he showed me a workout area that included stationary weights.

I left the center and walked towards the administration building. I did notice that in front of that building, there was a sidewalk with a lot of writing on it. I found out later that it was meant for fraternities. This gave me a strong motivation to look into joining a fraternity. Later I would join Pi Kappa Phi, Delta Sigma Pi, and Alpha Phi Omega. I walked to the SUB. It had a huge cafeteria, a bookstore, a barbershop, an ice cream shop, and a very nice "Lion's Lair," which was like a small café. I knew that it couldn't get any better than this, so I kept looking. I took the steps upstairs. I came across a snack area, a large play area that included pool tables, and my favorite hangout place—a video games alcove.

I went up one last floor. It was full of rooms and a big ballroom. After my adventure, I headed back to Hubbell Hall, but this time, I left out the front entrance, University Drive. I knew that I was here to "belong," and I walked out the front entrance with pride, knowing I was now a student here. I was looking towards four years of memories. I got back to my room and went to sleep.

My roommate awakened me making lots of noise—he was packing up. I asked him what was wrong, and he said, "Don't touch me!" I repeated, "What's wrong?" He answered, "I have to leave." Then he got my attention. He told me not to get too close to him and that he was probably contagious. He explained to me that he was diagnosed with having hepatitis. He packed up all of his belongings and left out the door. Now, I went from having a roommate to having no one at all. I started to get lonely, and I thought *this was going to be a very long year without a roommate.*

Golda Lockfoot Loschke—Class of 1939

I was a freshman at ETSTC in 1939. Tuition was $19 per semester. I did light housekeeping at the home of Mrs. Oscar Cutler on Moore Street. My room rent was $14 per month.

I broke out with the measles while taking a final History test in Miss Effie Collier's class. My final English test was taken after the Christmas holidays. Miss Mary Bowman was the teacher, a great instructor, and friend as well.

Due to rainy weather and poor road conditions, my parents had to go by way of Paris to get to Commerce and take me home.

I completed one full year of college and began teaching the primary grades (1, 2, and 3) at Selfs in Fannin County, two miles from my home. I was nineteen. I had a two-year high school certificate. My ambition was to be a high school Math teacher. After a summer Math course with Dr. Bledsoe and a group of seasoned men teachers, I decided to become an elementary teacher.

A few days after school started in the fall of 1931, a fourth grade boy who was in the first grade when I was in the tenth grade at Selfs called me "Golda." His teacher told him he shouldn't do that. He said, "I don't know why not. She ain't nothing but a kid."

Chapter 59

JACK RUBY AND THE
TEJAS GANG

Roy Rhodes—Class of 1959—Royce City

It was a Saturday night. Dwayne "Buffer" Bethea, Larry "Lash" Horton, Bobby Harper, Frank "Tuc" Turner, and John McAlister were Tejas. I was another Tejas, Roy "Preacher" Rhodes. We had no girls, nothing to do, and the campus and the city of Commerce had no form of alcoholic refreshment available. We were bored!

After heavy dialogue some genius suggested that we go to the Vegas Club in Dallas. Four members of the group were experienced in that venue while Tuc and I were rookies from small towns who had never been "clubbing" in the big city of Dallas.

Of the two rookies, Tuc was a transfer from a military school in New Mexico, and I was right off the farm. My mother, a fundamental Baptist, would have made Billy Graham look like a flaming liberal. So, off we went with maybe $40 among the six to "light up the town."

The Vegas Club was a familiar hang-out for the older members of the Tejas Social Club, especially Bobby and Lash. Owned by the infamous Jack Ruby, it was a popular Dallas watering hole where the locals listened to the Joe Johnson band and danced while enjoying a few libations.

After we arrived, finding a booth in that crowded place was a challenge; however, after standing around for a while, we found seats and began sampling the beer, or at least five did while "the Preacher" had a coke. After all my Mom had told me, she had rather see me dead as drunk. I was a bit nervous in this unfamiliar territory and sat there engulfed in fear and trepidation.

Accustomed to beer, Tuc enjoyed himself from the get-go. Bobby and "Lash" were upper classmen and possessed experience with the Vegas Club, beer, and the ladies. They had lived together as roommates on Travis Street in Dallas just a few blocks away. As a result, they knew the owner, Jack Ruby, and the dynamics of the club quite well.

As the evening wore on, the beer began to influence the imbibers. Several girls came in, and two of them made eye contact with Lash. Being a suave and debonair person, he asked one to dance. The couple was having a fine time on the floor when suddenly I saw a "blur" coming from across the room heading straight for Lash. As the situation unfolded, it became obvious that the blur was the boyfriend of the dancing girl.

Lash had a reputation for being a man of temper, and he never backed down from a fight. Out of the blue, the boyfriend hit Lash square in the throat. Stunned, he began to gag; however, he recovered quickly, then proceeded to beat the crap out of the boyfriend. During the fight, the boyfriend's buddy entered the fray and grabed Lash by the neck from behind. Bobby, sitting just a few feet away, saw what had transpired. He immediately went to Lash's aid, and with two quick blows to the head, the boyfriend's buddy hit the deck, out cold.

Two more of the boyfriend's buddies joined in bringing the other Tejas brothers out on the floor. It was "no contest." The bad guys quickly picked up the boyfriend and retreated to the far side of the room. The fight was over.

Jack Ruby knew Lash and Bobby and said to them, "Get the hell out of here. The cops are on the way." The six valiant warriors raced out the back door and hid behind a shopping center until the police left. Five were laughing and joshing each other while the "Preacher" was having hallucinations of being arrested, sent to jail, and having to call his parents.

All was well once we were back on our way to Commerce except for the one who got sick and had to hang his head out the window. It was a great college adventure for six of E.T.'s finest.

Chapter 60

FROM "BIG D" TO E.T.

Derryle G. Peace—Class of 1974—Dallas

While I was attending North Dallas High School, my basketball coach, Larry Drake, encouraged me to look at East Texas State University for my education. He was an alumnus of the school. I wrote a letter to Jim Gudger, the E.T. basketball coach at that time, and he invited me to a basketball tryout in the spring of my senior year. I came to campus on a Friday morning, spent the night in Sikes Hall, ate in Watson Cafeteria, and literally had a wonderful time meeting students and other individuals. I was a decent basketball player at the time but was not spectacular. No scholarship was offered, but I knew by the time I left on Saturday afternoon that this was the place for me.

Like so many of my peers, my family members had limited experience in a college setting. I had uncles who had attended college but none graduated. My uncles (and parents) were college-age in the early 1940s, and opportunities for members of our ethnic group to attend college in Texas at that time were limited to historically Black colleges.

I enrolled as a freshman in the fall of 1970. The university had been desegregated for only a few years and consequently had a small African American enrollment. I found it interesting that I was quite comfortable in this environment and quickly developed friendships that are intact to this day. Those friendships were a source of encouragement and support during difficult days.

The experience in Commerce was a challenging but fun time. I remember taking classes that had no more than three African Americans in them, particularly during my freshman year. I found the instructors to be fair but had no problem expressing my concerns when I felt that they were not.

SILVER LEOS WRITERS GUILD

I quickly found how naive and protected my urban upbringing had been. I met students from DeKalb, Hooks, Marshall, Tyler, Deberry, Gladewater, and other towns who were more worldly and sophisticated than I could ever imagine. What I discovered as well was that most of my peers and I had similar values. Many of us began our formal education attending segregated schools and became pioneers in the era of desegregation. We were God-fearing, church-going, motivated teenagers who recognized the opportunity afforded us to have a better life than our parents. We were a proud lot, and failure was not an option.

I spent five and one-half years on campus and received my B.S. in 1974 and M.S. in 1975. I lived in an apartment, Sikes Hall, Stone Hall, Hubbell Hall, Acker Hall, and even rented a house one summer. I had a host of roommates who included a university football player, a future Distinguished Alumnus, a future minister, a future basketball coach, and a computer expert. I retain a friendship with each of them and cherish the memories that we share.

I attended school every summer in an effort to get finished as quickly as possible. I did so because I never thought that a summer job would allow me to make enough money to make a difference in my economic situation. During the summer sessions, I would run into many of my public school teachers who were attending classes. All of them told me that they had graduated, gotten jobs, had families, and found that they needed to obtain additional certification or degree in order to advance their careers. All of them encouraged me to stay and get a masters degree before going out into the world. I did just that but not without divine intervention. I was to graduate a semester early (even with a dual major) and transfer to the University of Texas at Arlington and work on a masters in social work. When I filed for graduation, I discovered that I lacked two electives. I was devastated! One of my best friends was in the master's counseling program and suggested that I take the electives and two introductory counseling courses. He was convinced that the graduate courses would transfer. I took two electives (Typing and Defensive Driving) along with the counseling courses and fell in love with the program and its faculty. I found them to be a raw, brash, and humorous crew.

I was greatly impressed with the faculty and staff and was drawn to people who exhibited genuine concern for my well-being. I had the joy of attending classes taught by the Dr. J. Mason Brewer, Dr. D. Arlington Talbot, Dr. Mary Preas, Dr. Steve Ball, Dr. Harold Murphy, Dr. Robert Gold, and others. I had the pleasure of being mentored by Ivory Moore. Each one of these individuals, along with others, made an indelible impression on me and poured their gifts of knowledge into me that have made a difference in my life.

I have shared my story and experiences at A&M-Commerce with others over the years. Whatever I have accomplished in life is largely due to my experiences and education at the university. Remember my high school basketball coach mentioned earlier? I talked with him yesterday, and he retired a week ago after teaching forty-four years. If he touched my life in such an amazing fashion, I can only imagine how many more he has touched.

I hope to leave such a legacy!

Go Lions!

Margaret Miller Button—Class of 1939

While attending E.T., I was privileged to work in the office of Mr. John S. Windell, registrar, one of the finest men I ever knew. It was fun working with people like Jeff Woodruff, Student Council president, who provided us with an amusing incident in the office almost daily. Many times Jo Bob, Iva, Imogene, and I would form a circle around Jeff and sneak him into Mr. Windell's outer office when Jeff would show up late and signal us from the hall.

An incident defines the time in which we were living. I spent the day of the big Friar dance in 1938 interviewing for a teaching position in Caddo Mills. Interviews in those days were conducted wherever you could find the school trustee—like in a corn field, etc. After walking for some time in the 100-plus temperature, I found this one trustee on his un-air-conditioned cultivator working on his "back-forty." His questions included, "Can you coach girls' basketball and volleyball? . . . Play the piano for church services? . . . Build fires in the school stove?" My reply to all his questions was, "Of course" or "Oh, yes."

When I finally got home and dressed for the big dance, I noticed that my sun-burned face matched my red dress perfectly. I did get the teaching job at Caddo Mills and was dreading having to coach volleyball, etc. when just before the beginning of school, I was hired to teach my favorite subjects in Bogata High School.

Chapter 61

BOYS WILL BE BOYS

Jimmie Jacobs—Class of 1956—Plano

Two weeks out of high school in Plano, I found myself in the "chicken department" on the farm at East Texas State Teachers College in Commerce in the summer of 1953.

The biggest dose of education we received as Farm Boys was the first week of school, and that was to respect upper classmen and to watch out for tree limbs when Arnold Jordan was driving the old flat bed truck to the cafeteria for our meals. The Farm Boys persuaded the city not to trim the limbs on the way to the campus from the farm. The plan was to run under trees and knock the new boys off the truck. No one told them about the hazards of the tree limbs as we all waited our turn at the wheel of the flatbed truck.

The fearless leader of the chicken departments was none other than Tom Blakey, and my most important job was making sure Tom woke up and made it to his first class. The first morning I woke Tom, he said, "Thank you." That evening I got chewed out because I let him go back to sleep, and he missed his first morning class.

The second morning, I not only woke Tom, I got him out of bed and on his feet. That evening I got a terrible chewing out and was told we will never be able to trust you. (Who trusts whom?)

The third morning I was instructed to use a heavy dirty army floor mop that was wet to wake Tom. He said, "No problem. You have passed our testing program. We didn't think you would make it, but your services will not be needed in the future." What? I am off the hook because of a dirty mop?"

Tom Blakey set a good example for us. He worked hard, made good grades, and never uttered a cuss word that we heard. He would offer to help when anyone needed advice.

When Tom graduated with a master's degree, Preston Curry became our boss. We suffered since all he wanted to do was work, study, and go to church. He had an advantage over us. He knew some of the teachers who went to church with him. We could not figure out if Preston had a handicap or had been around Mr. Alvin Rix too long.

On a hot summer day, Dr. A. C. "Buck" Hughes, director of the farm, let us all have an afternoon off, and sure enough, Preston wanted to stay and work. The "chicken boys" had a meeting and did the proper thing. James Graves, Charles Thompson, and I placed Mr. Curry in a car and gave him the evening off.

Three of us had $2.18 among us, and we decided Preston Curry needed to go to the Dairy Queen. But he only wore an old pair of army shorts. I parked the car under the brightest light next to the sidewalk that went back to the campus, so the students had to pass by there. We stopped all the girls who walked by and told them that Preston was sick and to please go over and say hello. The only thing Preston had to hide his nakedness was an old hot army blanket. Francis told Preston, "You must be sick using that blanket to stay warm."

Preston's reply was, "I am sick of the thugs I rode to town with."

Don't get the wrong idea. We had the utmost respect for Preston, and we would have worked all day and night for him if he had the need. He was and still is a very bright Christian man who is loved by all who know him.

Boys will be boys, and one weekend we went to Lovers Lane and slipped up on a couple pitching woo. About seven of us surrounded the car, and placed a shotgun and rifle on the car and fired them at the same time. We yelled and screamed very loud, and we saw the making of a different kind of haste. After the terrible deed, we were all laughing so hard, but the atmosphere changed abruptly.

A caravan of cars and trucks came our way with spotlights, trying to find us. The only safe passage we had was through a muddy creek bed to make our way to the dairy barn. The creek was not deep, and we crawled with bullets whizzing over our heads. After crawling half way to the dairy barn, James Graves said, "Somebody tell me I am having a good time." We were exhausted as we hosed ourselves off and went quietly to the dorm. These extra-curricular activities were not a required part of our curriculum.

Chapter 62

THE TWO OF US

Lavonne Verner Wells—Class of 1950—Commerce

B eing born, raised, and educated in Commerce was a wonderful experience although many times along the way, I had my doubts.

I have an identical twin, Evonne, who is five minutes older than I am and is the dominant sister. Growing up we were inseparable, thanks to our mother who would never let us be separated in classes. That pattern lasted from first grade through our college graduation. Sometimes that was a real good thing since I talked very little. I know that is hard to believe for those who know me today. We switched seats when it came time for oral reports. The teacher never knew, and it saved me from pretending to be ill and skipping a day of school. If one of us had too many cuts in a class, she just said "Those are not all mine; some of them are my sister's." Then the confused teacher would usually attempt to correct the records.

I was petrified the day we enrolled at East Texas State Teachers College. I had never seen so many people in one place except at a sporting event. We registered in the reading room of the beautiful old library, where instructors seated themselves behind tables in one long line. Their subject and name were on a card on their desk, so a student just went to the desired section and looked for the freshman teacher.

Evonne and I registered with Sarah Garvin for English, and our class was in the Old Main building. History was in the Education (Ferguson) Building. Dr. J. G. Smith was the instructor, and he taught without a textbook.

We failed that class. We got Mother's lecture about ". . . we are not paying for you to go to school to fail. You will make your grades or go to work." Since work was a dirty word to me, I never failed another class. No, Evonne and I did not always make the same grades; she was better in English, I was better in "boys." I played the field, but, after a couple of years, she fell in love with a junior student and married him in August of 1950. It took me another three years to decide that a certain cute airman was the man for me. I insisted that he enroll in East Texas State, where he earned three degrees. All four of us—Evonne and I and our husbands—became proud alums of East Texas State Teachers College.

Typing and shorthand were included in our degree plan as well as science. Since we were physical education majors, we attended a lot of activity classes, which we loved. My life revolved around Whitley Gym.

The campus buildings consisted of the library, the Education Building, Main, Mayo Hall, West Dorm, and the gym. White frame buildings housed the music/band, journalism, home economics, industrial arts departments, and a medical clinic. Other new buildings, added from 1946-50, housed the science department, Student Union Building, field house, football stadium, East Dorm, Binnion Hall, cafeteria, and agriculture department. The addition and removal of buildings over the years caused parts of our history at E.T. to change.

There were so many situations we had to absorb as college students from 1946-1950, but boys headed the list of must-do things. Oh yeah, Evonne and I exchanged dates many times. The poor guys never knew it either.

One instructor in the education department had the unfortunate experience of having three unique couples in the class—a set of girl twins, a set of boy twins, and a married couple. The boys were even more identical than we were. When Dr. Deonier called roll, he would just say Verner and Verner, Chapman and Chapman, and Nations and Nations. Why? Because our names were Evonne and Lavonne, the boys were Avon and Devon, and the couple's names were Yvonne and Bobby. There was no way he could ever keep the names straight.

Evonne and I were accustomed to answering to both our names. It mostly made life easier. We were called "twin" a lot and answered to that name as well. I don't believe Elizabeth Huggins ever called us anything else.

Being hometown girls, we got overlooked a lot when it came to social events. However, that situation had compensations. On holidays, there were guys who lived too far away to go home or were basketball players and had to stay on campus for games. We hometown girls had them all to ourselves. There was a family of Ingrams from Quitman, who made up the starting lineup, and only one of them was married. There were five of us city girls who graduated in 1946 from Commerce High School and continued our friendship through college. So, four basketball players plus one friend and the five girls spent many hours together during the guys' free time.

What does one do on a snowy night in Commerce in 1946? Have snowball fights, make snowmen, cook pop corn, make fudge, play cards, gather around the piano, and have a sing along. The Verners', Dunns', and Days' doors were always open to us. That was the best year of my life in college. Only one of us, Dr. Dorothy (Dunn) Ingram, married a player (Troy Ingram) from that team. We all remained friends.

Chester Smith from Vinita, Oklahoma, was the odd man out; he didn't play basketball. He had been in the Navy with Truitt Ingram, and they were roommates. He was my choice for a date. He was my first love. I have tried to locate him since the computer and internet became available but to no avail. All of the team except one is deceased, and one of our group of ladies, Margaret Day Winton, died in 2008.

Evonne returned to Commerce in 1988 after retiring from teaching. I did not return until 1998 to become a house mom for Gamma Phi Beta (Tooanoowe) sorority. That was a wonderful four-year experience.

Had Evonne and I not lived at home, we would not have been able to attend college. Even at that, $37.50 per semester was a chunk of change times two. We got to live in familiar surroundings, eat home-cooked meals, and share clothes and room with only one person. The only drawback was walking the mile to campus and back twice a day—and sometimes three times if we had to do work at the library. Finally, when we were seniors, Dad would let me drive the car to night activities. Yeah, I picked up the gang of girls and boys too.

This was the era when World War II veterans returned to pursue their education. There were a lot of married couples attending classes, and along with them were babies. My favorite babysitting job was for Jess and Lou Cummings, who just happened to be the directors of Mayo Hall where the athletes were housed. Hey, I would have done that babysitting for free.

I think all of us would say our lives were totally changed by attending East Texas and receiving the quality education that prepared us for our futures.

It will always be E.T. to me.

Chapter 63

REQUIEM FOR A SCHOOL TEACHER

Chuck Armstrong—Class of 1970—Paris

The thump made by a stack of textbooks hitting the battered wooden desk literally jarred me awake. I wasn't the only jock whose sleep that 7 a.m. was disturbed; I was just the only one dense enough to have taken a seat in the front row. Like my colleagues, and our semi-lovely, sorta-fan-club, girl-type friends, I had signed aboard an improbably-early-morning literature class to punch the last, required English ticket toward an unlikely-to-be-achieved B.S. degree at a former state teachers college in Nowhere, Texas. Without having formally discussed it, we decided no one would actually expect a bunch of athletes and their sweethearts to appear each day for a 7 o'clock class (especially English), even one that met Tuesday/Thursday instead of Monday/Wednesday/Friday. It smelled like an easy B+, maybe better. Little did we know . . .?

As my eyes drifted into focus, I saw a pale-faced apparition standing behind the ancient desk, his own piercing, crystal-blue gaze taking visual notes while his skin tightened against high cheekbones and a smooth, receding hairline. He was square, from chiseled jaw to even shoulders to blunt fingertips, which peeked below square sleeve openings of his seersucker jacket and jutted alongside seams of his trousers. Today he would be called "short." In that era—the late '60s—he was "average height."

He had so much disdain for us he didn't bother to look anyone in the eye as he spoke the first words of our spring semester. In a voice vaguely reminiscent of an eagle's claws raking down my grandmother's washboard, he snarled, "I just want you to know, I didn't always make my living teaching school."

For a moment, I could feel hairs on my forearms quiver the way they had a few minutes into the first day of boot camp. I mentally asked myself the same question I had on the grinder at San Diego, "My God, what have I done?"

For standing before us was not "your-father's-English-teacher" but a card-carrying, gold-plated, bad-attitude, don't-give-a-shit United States Marine. The years might have dimmed his vision and thinned his hair, but—as a fellow member of the Brotherhood—I could almost see the Eagle, Globe, and Anchor glowing through his soul. Behind me I heard a wise classmate whine under his breath, "Man, I am so droppin' this son-of-a-bitch before noon!"

In the blur that followed, the square-jawed character gave us the basics—all the info we had a "need-to-know." His name was Lee Dacus; he was stuck with us and vice versa; he would be "on time, every day," and expected the same of us; we would explore meaningful English literature together; and—by the way—he was a World War II combat veteran of the United States Marine Corps. "That fact," he unapologetically explained, "might color a few discussion points in the weeks to come."

I don't remember the rest of that class. Maybe we got a list of textbooks and headed to the weight room. Perhaps we mimed taking notes through the obligatory, first-day class synopsis. Or, we might have sat catatonic, while Lee—or Thurman Lee Dacus as I came to know him—told us why showing up at the appointed hour each Tuesday/Thursday was a splendid, non-negotiable use of our time.

As the semester unfolded, I didn't drop the class. I was on a timetable driven by desire to graduate and a ticking clock by which I foolishly imagined the Vietnam War was passing me by. I got to know Lee well. We were both bound to the Marine Corps, he as an aging combat vet and I as an untried wannabe. As our relationship gained traction, I got bold enough to ask Lee about his combat service.

I knew a good bit about World War II, of course. My father—in 1942 a reluctant, 32-year-old Army draftee—left my infant sister at home, trained for infantry duty, staged in England, waded ashore across a Normandy beachhead on D-Day, walked to Germany, survived four major campaigns, got discharged, and never looked back. Like many boys of my vintage, I grew up in post World War II Texas surrounded and nurtured by relatives and Dutch uncles who spoke—if at all—reluctantly about their heroic service in Europe and the Pacific. When the movie *The Battle of the Bulge* showed in my hometown of Paris, Texas, my father declined to see it with me, stating laconically, "I saw the play."

But, until I became acquainted with Lee Dacus, I never had a frank, unemotional discussion about the brutal, island-hopping, amphibious assault-style combat that was the Marine Corps' trade during the Pacific War. We weren't drinking buddies. His job was getting marginally-interested college students into the graduation queue without compromising standards for passing sophomore English. Mine was checking the necessary academic blocks along the way to graduation and a commission in the Marine Corps so I could help the "other-poor-dumb-bastard" die for *his* country.

The few times we met outside class, we sat in his office chatting about World War II. I learned he fought in the bitter battles of Tarawa and Saipan. The day my father waded ashore at Normandy, Lee survived a direct hit on his landing craft at Saipan, taking command of his peers seconds after his squad leader was killed. Among the academic litter of his office was the framed citation for his Silver Star, lauding former Corporal Dacus for heroic action during which he was seriously wounded in combat. Ironically, the only time my father ever talked about "somebody-else's-war," it was to express sympathy for Marines on Saipan. He said, "We thought it was pretty tough at Normandy 'til we heard about the Marines who hit Saipan. They *really* had it rough!"

The semester rolled along. I showed for class "on time, every day" and made an A. Because of Lee's influence, I decided to add a second major (English) to my history degree. He didn't go overboard persuading me. He said, "You know, Corporal Armstrong, it's just a few more courses . . . who knows, you might even stumble onto a professor who knows what he's doing." I had always liked to read. I just hadn't realized how cool it could be to think—if only occasionally—about *what* I had read. When I met Lee, my only ambition was to be a globe-trotting gunfighter. It never occurred to me I would also become an award-winning author who was asked to review books, articles, and screenplays.

The night I received my degree from East Texas State University I was no longer Corporal Armstrong, but Second Lieutenant Armstrong, wearing the dress uniform of a United States Marine Corps officer. Sharing the stadium with me was Thurman Leo Dacus, receiving his Ph.D.

Before I departed for Southeast Asia and later, subsequent combat deployments, I went to Commerce, Texas, to huddle with my old mentor.

As years passed and deployments stacked up (I have now attended seven shooting wars), Lee became more frail, and I became more negligent about getting fresh insight. I occasionally told him how much I appreciated his friendship and guidance; I just wish I'd told him more often. He died during one of my offshore adventures and was laid to rest, his son told me, proudly, wearing his Silver Star.

There's a simple lesson to this story—one I've repeated frequently to high school and college students rolling their eyes and dissing the seedy-looking characters who wake them up on first class day. *Don't rush to judgment; could be that guy didn't always make his living by teaching school.*

H. Logan Swords—Class of 1939

When I attended ETSTC, I worked in the Library. It was very pleasant work, especially since my supervisor, Miss Opal Williams, was such a nice person. One Friday night, while I was on duty, something happened which changed the direction of my life. A girl whom I had never seen before turned in a book to me, and at the same moment turned my head and my heart. I asked Peter Fannin, with whom I was working, "Who was that?" He answered, "That was Ruth Riley from Fort Worth. She is President and Mrs. Whitley's niece. She lives in the dorm."

I gave Ruth time to get back to the dorm and then called and asked her for a date. She said she didn't know me, and she didn't give dates to strangers. My heart sank, but I suggested that she might know my sister, Lois Swords. Those were the magic words that made her change her mind. She did know Lois and liked her very much. She gave me a tentative date for Sunday night, but she insisted that I call her Sunday afternoon. (She wanted to have the opportunity to break the date in case I didn't check out.)

The page had to have strong lungs and a voice that would carry for blocks. I stood there, and Ruth walked those steps and into my life forever on October 16, 1937. Ruth and I married in 1940.

Chapter 64

THRICE FOUND LOVE

Rebecca Shirley—1959-1961—Honey Grove

E ast Texas State has played a huge part in the life of my family. It is strange that none of the players in these scenes "walked across the stage" of this institution, but we all have roots that go deep into that black Hunt County soil.

In the early 1930s, Maude Bartlett came to East Texas Normal College as a transfer student from Nacogdoches. She lived off campus and shared an apartment with her aunt, Irene Mills. S.L. Todd, a resident of Fannin County, came to E.T. to pursue his studies, and there he met Maude. Although both were teaching in the long term, he in Fannin County and she in Bowie County, and going back to E.T. in the summers, they managed to build a relationship and married in April 1933. That was the beginning of my family. S.L. taught in one-room schools in north Fannin County for about ten years but gave up that profession to become a farmer. Maude also taught for several years in Cass County and in Fannin County. She had the opportunity to complete her degree by correspondence but elected to raise a family instead.

In the mid 1950s, Doris Ann Todd, eldest daughter of S.L. and Maude Todd, came to East Texas State Teachers College to major in elementary education. She lived in Binnion Hall and worked for her room and board by serving food in the college cafeteria. A year earlier, Joel Dotson from Atlanta had come to East Texas and majored in Industrial Arts. They met, dated, and fell in love; and in September 1957, they married.

In 1959, Rebecca Todd, youngest daughter of the Todd family, made her way to East Texas State University to major in Home Economics. She followed in the footsteps of her older sister and worked for Ma Little serving food in the college cafeteria. She also lived in Binnion Hall in the last room on the east wing of the third floor. Standing behind the steam counter provided a good opportunity to size up all the boys who came to eat. She met Buster Jack Wilson, who was from Venus in Johnson County. He was an Agriculture major, and they immediately caught each other's eyes. The courtship took a rapid course, and they married in November 1959. They moved into the old G.I. Village, located a few blocks south of campus, and continued their studies. Buster went on to get both his bachelor's and master's degrees from E.T., but Rebecca found herself in the family way and got no further than junior level.

Doris Ann completed her college work, partly by correspondence, and got her B.S. from East Texas in the mid 1960s. Rebecca transferred to Sam Houston State in Huntsville and received her degree in the mid 1970s. Both Todd girls spent several years teaching elementary school.

I heard my dad, S.L. Todd, make the statement: "If it had not been for East Texas State, none of us would have found a mate!"

Kittye Ruth Lawler Coles—Class of 1938

I had completed registering except for going to the library to receive my books. At the door of the library sat a football player by the name of Scaley Coles. His shirt was unbuttoned half-way, and his hairy chest was exposed. If Scaley liked the looks of a girl, he required them to show their registration papers. He put their name and place of residence on his list.

A few days later, he came over to the dorm flashing around his list of girls. He told me I was thirteenth on the list, and he was going to date each girl and for me not to give up. He would get around to me one day. I told him not to be in a hurry, as it wouldn't do him any good to get to my name on his list.

Time went by, and by the night of November 18, I was so homesick. I was sitting in the dorm office, and Louis Waller and Scaley came into the office. They told me Louis had a model T Ford coupe, and they were having a contest to name the car. The winner would have a date to the show with Louis. They took me for a ride in the car. I submitted a name, but I didn't win. The name "Shasta" won. (She Shasta have gas, and she Shasta have oil to run) I found out Scaley wasn't such a bad guy. He would come over every night, and romance began to bloom. He started going by his name, Earl, as I didn't like Scaley for a name. He also started buttoning up his shirt.

On August 22, 1938, I received two degrees—that morning my B.A. and that night my MRS.

Chapter 65

REMINISCENCES OF ROB
AND E.T.

Alton L. Biggs—Class of 1974—McKinney

While our friends and loved ones are with us, their lives are vivid images in a mirror. The mirror's lively images reflect their best and worst. Sometimes little ripples in the glass distort the images so that we observe the slight imperfections, but they don't detract from the overall view. In death, the same images break into a million shards. We pick up the shards that reflect only parts of the original image—our unchanging memories. Just this weekend I attended the memorial service of my college roommate and best friend. The broken images I share from a few shards of the mirror are sharp now, and the pain of loss directly results from the cutting edges. Perhaps sharing will reduce the pain.

I commuted to Commerce from McKinney in 1970 and 1971. A tall, lanky guy who had a keen sense of humor and a deep-chested laugh and I sat in many of the same classes during those years. While in biology classes during those years, this young man, I soon learned was Robert "Rob" Eric Slingerland. Rob and I sat next to each other on the second row, left corner as one entered the lecture hall. I thought it odd that we sat next to one another, listened to Dr. Robert "Bob" K. Williams present the same lectures, but left with such divergent views. Whereas I loved Bob and those classes, Rob's sentiments were tantamount to hatred. But either way, we both learned a great deal about life and living things. Sitting in those classes began a close friendship and deep kinship between us that lasted the tests of time until God separated us on Monday, April 5, 2010.

In 1972, Rob asked me to share a room with him. After considering the offer for a couple of days—and securing the blessing of my parents—I readily accepted. Ponderosa Apartments became our base of operations. The apartment we shared on the ground floor facing the entrance became home away from home for the last two years of our undergraduate work. There Rob and I studied together, played cards together, ate meals we prepared together, and drank beer together, our friendship growing stronger every day. Although we never spent that much time in deep study, we studied enough to keep our grants and scholarships. We never ceased to be surprised when we occasionally attained the Dean's List. One bit of architecture we devised included a pyramid of beer cans that eventually completely filled the front apartment window. The slivers of our lives haunt me now that Rob can no longer share them with me.

During the summer of 1973, our lives continued to intertwine. As soon as the spring semester concluded, off we drove for our summer adventure. We spent the summer together at Camp Greylock for Boys. The camp, located in the Berkshire Mountains of Western Massachusetts, had never encountered a pair like the two of us Texans. Rob lived on the senior side of the camp and taught tennis on the immaculate clay courts while I lived on the junior side and developed a nature curriculum for six-year-olds through seniors in high school. We spent as much time together as possible playing cards, visiting the nearby girls' camp, and generally having fun. The adolescent boys were not Rob's cup of tea, but I enjoyed caring for the six-year-olds. Rob never went back to Greylock after that summer, but I went another three summers. After my first summer I became the coordinator of hiking and nature for the entire camp. Rob liked camping, and I think he would have enjoyed that aspect if he'd come with me once more.

Rob majored in chemistry and I majored in broad field natural sciences with an emphasis in biology. We both enjoyed the discovery of the mysteries in our fields. In the early 1970s, we didn't have any inkling that carbon nanotubes would be useful in fields like physics and engineering, nor that humans possess only about 30,000 genes instead of 150,000 in our genome. However, the things we learned at East Texas State University (*A.K.A.* Texas A&M University-Commerce) served to prepare both of us well for successful yet divergent careers. We learned one tremendous lesson often lost on students—how to integrate new discoveries into a framework to strengthen and expand our knowledge base. Rob's chemistry bent steered him towards petroleum chemistry and drilling mud, while my love of the intricacies of life led me into the classrooms of Texas public schools for more than three decades.

An undergraduate degree wasn't sufficient for either of us. Rob continued straight on after his B.S. in Chemistry to get his M.S. in Chemistry. During these two years we kept in constant touch. Rob served as Best Man when I married Louise McMahan, a girl we'd coerced into skipping classes to play cards with us on occasion. I received my M.S., entered marriage, and went right to work in the classroom. I was shocked when Rob told me he'd found the light of his life, and I was happy to attend his wedding when the time came. So, armed with his M.S. degree, Rob got married, and got right to work in the oilfields.

Eventually Rob invented patents and special chemistry for drilling mud. In addition to teaching, I took advantage of professional opportunities, and eventually coauthored many textbooks for McGraw-Hill Publishing Companies. Rob and I agreed that it was the institution of East Texas State University that developed and buttressed our innate capabilities. The university's student-centered faculty—then as now—possessed a keen understanding of what was important for a student to know and understand. It empowered us to succeed.

The shards of mirror that reflect bits and pieces of my deep love for Rob Slingerland shine brightly today. I know that they may change as I change, but I vow to keep them as tightly held as I can. Perhaps there'll be less pain a year from now. They say that time heals all wounds. Perhaps. Ask me a year from now.

Irene Goodson Arlington—Class of 1938

When I was a freshman at E.T. and in Mr. Stanley Pugh's typing class, he came by my desk and asked, "Where are your feet?"

I replied, "On the floor."

He said, "That's where they are supposed to be."

Another time Mr. Pugh asked, "Are you visiting or taking this course?" Evidently, he thought my typing partner and I were talking too much.

Dr. J. E. Franklin made a lasting impression on my life with the poem that begins, "A career, did you say? I'm an artist . . . a cook . . . a nurse . . . a seamstress . . . ." and ended with "You see I'm a mother of two." Dr. Franklin thought that being a mother was a very important career for a woman.

Chapter 66

DOWN ON THE FARM

Frank Thorp—Class of 1959—Leonard

M y sojourn at East Texas State Teachers College began in August 1956. I worked and lived on the College Farm, under the direction of A.C. "Buck" Hughes. My work there paid for my tuition, room, and board.

I had an Agriculture Education major and a Science minor for my B.S. degree, which I received in August 1959.

My assignment as a graduate assistant was in the slaughter house for $100 per month, while I worked on my M.S. Degree, with a major in Technical Agriculture and a minor in Biology.

In January 1960, I married Lynda Barnard, also a student at E.T. She graduated in 1961. I taught science at Commerce High School after graduation in 1960; then Uncle Sam called me for duty in the U.S. Army for two years. After my discharge from military duty, I worked for the Texas Department of Corrections for thirty years, retired, and settled in Celeste, Texas, where I currently reside.

Many exciting stories came from my time spent on the College Farm getting my education.

Thirteen to sixteen male students lived in an old Army barracks, doing the everyday operation of the Farm. Each individual performed specific chores in the morning before we went to classes. We arranged our schedule so that we were out of class by 12:20 p.m. and could work uninterrupted all afternoon and evening.

Leaving class, we walked directly to the cafeteria to eat lunch. Afterwards, we walked to the farm, changed into work clothes, and met Buck Hughes at the door at 1 p.m. to receive our assigned work duties until 4 p.m. Then, we received our other chores that lasted from 4 p.m. until finished. After that assignment, we changed clothes again and piled into a panel truck to go to the cafeteria for our evening meal. Sometimes we would be late, and the girls who worked there would have our trays filled for us since they were waiting for us to get finished with our meal so they could clean the cafeteria. This led to many friendships between the girls and Farm Boys, and several developed into marriages.

Prominent in stories told by Farm Boys was A. C. "Buck" Hughes, who was a very firm leader but very thoughtful and fair to each of us.

The Poultry Department, better known as "The Chicken Boys," was the only department not included in the rotation of chore assignments. That was my assignment when I first worked on The Farm.

The Dairy Barn was just across the fence from the poultry yards. We were responsible for placing the eggs in incubators, and when the chicks hatched, there were always some of the eggs that did not hatch that were very rotten.

The Dairy Boys drove the cows into the barn down the lane which was just over the fence from the poultry barns. One afternoon we "Chicken Boys" decided it would be fun if the Dairy Boys were surprised with a shower of rotten eggs as they drove the cows into the barn. So we hid behind the barn until they started up the lane, and the shower of rotten eggs began. It was funny then, but as you know, "pay back" was bound to come.

There is also a story of survival, which is unbelievable but true. Three boys packed silage into an upright metal silo. The silage was chopped in the field and blown into a trailer. We backed up the trailer to an elevator that carried the silage to the top and dropped it into the silo loose. The boys were supposed to walk around and smooth the silage evenly in the silo, packing it to keep out excess air pockets.

This occurred in the summer, inside a metal cylinder where the temperature registered 138 degrees, and it was so hot you could barely breathe. We managed to get out of the silo without collapsing.

There are many, many stories of events that happened during the four years I was at E.T. Some are sad, most are happy, and many are just about boys being boys that cannot be printed for the public.

There were so many people who influenced my life during my years at East Texas, but the two most important were Dr. A.C. "Buck" Hughes and Mr. R.A. Rix.

Thanks, E.T., for all the memories and education I received in your hallowed halls and barns.

Chapter 67

CURFEW

Colleen Lewis Hines—Class of 1956—Hooks

For two years, I was a part of a close-knit group of girls on the second floor of Binnion Hall. Among others, the gang included Nelda Jones, Jane Conlan, Peggy Little, and Anita Luna. Even though we were in different social clubs, some Les Choisites and some Kaidishan, and some independents, we were tight. We gathered in each other's rooms to discuss boys, our classes, what was going on campus . . . any topic that came to mind.

In October 1955, we learned that Elvis Presley was giving a concert at the City Auditorium in Greenville. Borrowing a car from the brother of one of the girls, away we went to see the King. Screaming and crying right along with all the other girls in the audience, we practically swooned as Elvis sang, "That's All Right, Mama," "Blue Moon over Kentucky," and "My Happiness." About half way though the concert, one of the girls glanced at her watch and noticed it was almost time for the lights to blink outside Binnion Hall, signaling that the doors were about to be locked. Rushing to the pay phone in the lobby, we called our dorm mother, Mrs. Ruth Gant, petitioning her to allow us to stay until the finish of the concert, even though we knew it would be past curfew time. She consented.

After the concert ended, Elvis came out and greeted us face to face. With his black hair and dark eyes, he was so handsome in his pale purple suit. He gave me an 8x10 photograph, and then I asked him for the lavender handkerchief spilling out of his coat pocket. He gave it to me.

On August 16, 1977, the day the King of Rock and Roll died, I was on the phone with a student when she mentioned that Elvis had died that day. I had to end our conservation immediately. I needed a moment alone.

Ladies and Gentlemen: Elvis has left the building. Colleen has left Binnion Hall.

Chapter 68

LORAINE'S MOSAIC

Peggy McElrath and Patricia McElrath Collins

> To those people who say
> The past is the past and that's where it should stay,
> I say, "Oh, pshaw!"
> Some might call the following events serendipity,
> Or just simply coincidence, if you will.
> Yet, I believe this true story to be absolutely amazing!

My mother's life became so intertwined with the education she earned from East Texas State Teachers College as to form a beautiful, intricate mosaic spanning some thirty-two years. Loraine Wright's mother, Cordelia, and her stepfather, Samuel Jackson McElrath, provided her with the first opportunity to *be all that she could be*. They placed the centerpiece of the mosaic innocently enough in the fall of 1928, when they drove her from the small farming community of Lannius, Texas, to the big city of Commerce—where they enrolled her as a sub-college student at ETSTC in order to complete her high school education.

At this time, Cordie and Mr. Mc placed Loraine in a boarding house located at 2402 Monroe Street near the campus. Loraine shared the house and many wonderful experiences with several other girls from surrounding communities who had come to enrich their lives through the educational process.

In the summer of 1930, Loraine added another piece of the mosaic when she received her teaching certificate from ETSTC and began teaching seventh grade in Lamasco, Texas. She placed her career temporarily on hiatus in 1932, when, at the age of twenty, she married Samuel Dennis "Doc" McElrath, aged twenty-nine. Over the next ten years, she bore two boys and two girls while continuing her education at ETSTC. She took an extension course in Bonham in the fall of 1943. She took a correspondence course in the fall semester of 1945 and one in the fall semester of 1946.

In 1945, Superintendent Millard Brent of Dodd City, Texas, added another piece to the mosaic when he asked Loraine to teach all grades in a two-room schoolhouse. During the winter months, an important part of her duty was to build a fire in the huge wood stove before the students arrived. Loraine's three- and five-year-old daughters came to school with her each day and loved the warm atmosphere their mother created for her students and them. We can still remember the smell of the wool coats that hung in the cloakroom during cold, damp days.

Students always looked forward to the arrival of the traveling librarian, Kate Estes, who drove the book mobile to each of the rural schools. Loraine allowed them to go inside the fascinating vehicle to check out books.

The friendships made in that tiny school lasted some fifty-eight years as Loraine and her family always attended the *Dodd City Reunion* held on the *Fourth of July* every five years. Mother's Hilger students honored her with speeches and a beautiful flower bouquet at the most recent reunion in 2005.

Loraine's mosaic really began to take shape in 1950 when she shuttered her home in Dodd City in order to move the family to Commerce. She enrolled her eldest son, Sammy, at E.T., and she set out to complete the college degree she had started working on some twenty-two years earlier.

The large rent house sat on Stonewall Street where the Ferguson Social Sciences Building stands today. She rented out extra rooms to college students to help defray expenses. Thankfully, for her young daughter, Peggy, who could play anything by ear just like her mother, there was an upright piano in the house. She probably drove everyone in the house crazy with her incessant playing of "Irene Good Night," yet no one ever complained.

Loraine enrolled her two daughters, Patricia, age ten, and Peggy, age eight, in the A. L. Day elementary school located on Church Street. She enrolled her fifteen-year-old son, Billy Gene, in high school.

We recall hurrying down the street at lunchtime each school day to Mr. Schifflet's house, where he served the biggest, tastiest hamburgers using tomatoes from his own garden for a whopping ten cents each. Students, some even from the college, would form long queues, patiently waiting to get that most delicious meal.

Mother always spoke fondly of two of her professors in particular; her English instructor, Lawrence F. McNamee, and Dr. Minnie Behrens, head of the Department of Elementary Education. Dr. Behrens was mother's advisor. Loraine belonged to the Association for Childhood Education in 1952, a club for Elementary Education majors. A good student, she made the Dean's List on more than one occasion. She became good friends with classmates with whom she continued to correspond for years.

Loraine spent a great deal of time studying and doing research in the college library so her daughters also spent many enjoyable hours in the children's library upstairs.

The wonderful, two-story Student Union Building, built to resemble an English Hunting Lodge and furnished in maple with hardwood floors, contained a large ballroom, and several other rooms. We enjoyed "family night" there every Tuesday and watched free movies on sixteen-millimeter film. One particular movie was entitled *Mother is a Freshman* starring Loretta Young and Van Johnson. It made a huge impression on us, in spite of the predictable plot because Loretta's wardrobe was comprised of all sorts of mesmerizing colors, sometimes in ethereal shades, fur things, and dazzling ensembles! One of the college plays we attended with mother in 1952 was entitled *The Gentle People*.

Oh, yes, and let's not forget the ping-pong games we played in the recreation room. In order to play, one had to rent the ping-pong ball for ten cents, which was refundable—if returned in good condition at the end of play. Amazingly, we played right next to college students—mostly guys who never fussed at us for being there.

Another great memory of E.T. was when we would often strap on our shoe-skates and spend hours gliding *round and round* on the seemingly unending, smooth-as-glass concrete square, directly behind Binnion Hall. Not once did any girl ever fling open a window to tell the young skaters to *go away* or to *stop bothering her* because of the sound created from the rhythmic, nearly hypnotic melding of the ball-bearing skates onto the concrete surface.

By far, the most significant memory about E.T. was Leo, the concrete lion, who sat perched so regally in the median across from the Education Building. In retrospect, it's hard to imagine that the lion exuded such an imposing yet intriguing presence to us in 1950.

Leo journeyed to the back of the president's house for a while but thankfully returned to his proper place, keeping a watchful eye over the campus and its students. Ironically, the inscription etched below the lion's feet is E.T.S.T.C. Seniors Summer 29. Leo always and shall continue to hold a special place in our hearts as Loraine was a sub-college student on the campus the very year the seniors donated the lion.

On August 17, 1952, after two years of dedicated, hard work, Loraine earned her Bachelor of Science degree in elementary education from ETSTC. Shortly thereafter, she put that new degree to good use by securing a contract to teach first grade in the windy, dusty, friendly West Texas town of Dumas.

Loraine set the next piece of the mosaic in place when she first began working on her master's degree at E.T. by attending both semesters in the summer of 1954. Two years later, in the summer of 1956, Dennis, her husband of twenty-four years, died in Bonham, Texas. She found herself a widow at the age of forty-five. Mother taught one more year in Dumas but moved the family to Dallas in the fall of 1957, so she could complete her master's degree at Commerce while teaching first grade in the Dallas Independent School District.

Loraine's odyssey, which started in the fall of 1928, as a seventeen-year-old girl enrolled in sub-college at ETSTC, followed a meandering path spanning many years and finally reaching its destination back in the place *where it all began*. Now a mature forty-nine year-old woman, Loraine Wright Howell McElrath, proudly received her Master of Science degree on August 26, 1960, from East Texas State College.

Loraine moved out West to teach first grade in Indian Springs, Nevada; then in Las Vegas, where she continued to teach until her retirement in 1975. She left her daughter in charge of her house in Las Vegas, so she could move back to her *real roots* in historic Bonham, where she renovated an historic house located on what was *Silk Stocking Row* in the early days. Her house is now 105 years old and quite a beauty.

The lifelong love of learning that this precocious child exhibited early on blossomed into her unfailing determination, despite unbelievable odds, to be all that she could be. Loraine never forgot to visit her alma mater through the years and kept abreast of the happenings at E.T. as an alumni member. How fitting that she took a seat with her beloved Leo in August 2009 at the very young age of ninety-eight.

Hugh C. (Tommy) Tomlinson—Class of 1940

Many pleasant memories linger of time spent with Mr. R. A. Rix, head of the Ag Department and members of the "Kernel Club." I also enjoyed and profited by my trips with Mr. Rix to his "extension classes," which met in the courthouse in Quitman, Texas.

My first day in Commerce as a senior, I was fortunate to meet a freshman (freshlady) whom I married and have lived with these last forty-seven years.

Ruth Riley Swords—Class of 1938

Our graduation day was a wonderful experience. Nothing quite matches getting that first college degree in your hands— especially after you see (as many of us did) one of the would-be graduates, who was standing in line near us, being pulled out of line (cap, gown, and all) because he had not qualified for graduation. All of us gasped and whispered inaudibly to ourselves. "But for the grace of God . . . ."

Something else unusual happened that day. Our commencement speaker, who came from another college to Commerce by train, left his speech in his brief case on the train. Officials of ETSTC sent a car speeding to the next stop of the train, but they were unable to arrive in time to retrieve the briefcase. Our speaker apologized to us, and then he gave us a much shorter speech—from his heart rather than from his notes.

In spite of these and other mishaps, nothing could spoil the exhilaration of our graduation since it was from such a special school.

Chapter 69

A LATE START

Sarah Roach Swindell—Class of 1967—Celeste

When I started to college, I was six years older than other incoming freshmen. I thought that I was a very old woman. I was also married with an infant son. This was during the days of college-draft deferments, so the registration lines were long, all the way down in front of the gym and even in front of women's gym. However, the lines did move rapidly. Once inside, we found tables set up for class registration. Sometimes the class times you needed would not be available to finish out the fifteen-hour schedule . . . and you'd have to scramble around to find a course that would fit your time frame and your degree plan. Instead of teachers' names, "staff" was the only designation for English and history teachers. You never knew whom you had until the teacher showed up!

Back then in the mid-to-late 1960s, we were still wearing the freshman beanie. It wasn't very flattering, and before I had finished my undergraduate years, it had disappeared. We were not allowed to wear our high school letter jackets either. The different sororities and fraternities were in competition for spirit awards during games. Attending home games was required by the social organizations, and the support of the large crowds gave E.T. an advantage.

Of the thousands of students who attended E.T., many were commuters. Those of us from Celeste usually made up two full carloads. We had great fun meeting others in the parking lot next to the old science building on the southeast corner from the women's gym. As I recall, there wasn't a parking fee, but we did get a sticker to show that we were enrolled for the semester. We had fun riding back and forth, too. I guess you would say that we made the most of our situation. All of us had first period classes, and most had to be on our jobs by noon.

There was a free period on A days for Forum Arts and other activities. During this time, different programs and speakers came from all over the country—maybe even from around the world. We heard a famous jazz band from New Orleans and Hal Holbrooks' award-winning one-man Mark Twain show to name a couple. When there wasn't a program, we had an extra few minutes to study or to talk to friends on the parking lot. We became better acquainted with our high school rivals from Leonard, Wolfe City, and Ladonia. Romances blossomed on the parking lot. Sometimes there were programs in the new Student Center and during the cultural-arts-break period. It was difficult to find a seat in the Lions' Den there.

The largest class that I attended was biology with Dr. Edward Fox. We met in the auditorium of the Social Studies building. I couldn't count the number of students, but the room was full. Dr. Steve Razniak had a large number for our general studies science class, as well. The big football players were perched high on the last seats.

Elizabeth Huggins had us in tournaments in tennis and badminton. We rotated partners and won "paper drinking cup" trophies. We left our white tops and blue shorts in baskets at the end of each class. During one summer session, swimming class was first period; so Mrs. Pauline Emerson (from Greenville) and I went around the rest of the morning with wet heads!

Another thing I remember was Western Week. Almost everyone dressed in boots, hats, and cowboy fringe. I wore borrowed clothes during this week. I had a dress or two for "A" days and likewise for B days . . . all from the same pattern. I rotated those around.

Chapter 70

ALL IN THE CARDS

Mick Trusty—Class of 1972—Leonard

As a student at East Texas State University, I was like many others. I came from a small town in northeast Texas and was a first generation college student. Commerce, and the activity surrounding the university, was like a large city to me. There were only nineteen people in my high school graduating class, and I will have you know that I graduated in the top ten! Every first year class I had at the university held more people than I had ever seen in one classroom. As I had attended school only with people I had known since childhood, all of these folks in Commerce were strangers. It was an exciting time for me in Commerce if for no other reason than I met new people.

During the late 1960s and early 1970s, there was a strong culture of serious card playing at the Sam Rayburn Memorial Student Center in the Lions' Den, or Lair, I cannot remember. Instead of wasting our time studying in the library, we normally played Spades while waiting for our next class. Sometimes we played Spades instead of going to the next class—or the class after that. This pastime was another exotic thing I learned in college; how to play cards. I had played only dominoes before landing at Old E.T.

In any event, my regular card partner was a young lady named Kandy Curtis. She has been Mrs. Randy Joe Hulsey for the past many years, and both she and he are both Old E.T. graduates and still very good personal friends. I met Kandy the first day of my freshman year when I checked into the old Sikes Hall men's dorm. My freshman roommate, Bruce Sprinkle, had met her and introduced us. We were in some common classes early on and became friends.

Well, in 1971 Kandy brought a new card player to our table one day during the summer session. She was a former majorette from Sulphur Springs High

School, and I must admit her beautiful smile struck me. Now you know where this story is headed, but if you do not know me, you may get confused along the remainder of the way. Her name was Wanda Mae Oxford. She had long dark wavy hair, dark eyes, dark complexion, a radiant smile, and dimples. It did not hurt that she dressed very nicely, had exceptional majorette legs, and curves in all the places where I liked to see curves. Unfortunately, at least at the time, I had been married the previous year, and she was engaged to her high school sweetheart. As you may know, we married young in the country in those days. So, for two long, and I mean very long, semesters we played cards, joked, laughed and never made a move toward one another. Playing cards with Wanda way back then was, as Charles Dickens wrote, "It was the best of times, it was the worst of times."

In the spring semester of 1972, the lovely Miss Wanda left school to be married to the previously mentioned high school sweetheart. For the next thirty-one years, life went on for both of us without any knowledge of the other. Wanda married, had children, and divorced. I married, had children, and divorced, married and divorced, and yes, again married and divorced.

Oddly, Wanda continued to spend her life in Sulphur Springs. I lived in various cities in Texas and Oklahoma, pursuing my banking and legal career. Eventually I landed back in the Dallas-Fort Worth area and was asked to serve on the Alumni Association Board of Directors. During my board tenure, my photo was in some publication, and Wanda saw it. She looked me up in a lawyers' directory and sent me a nice card asking if I remember the card games at Old ET. I called her. Some months later, we had dinner. Some more months later, I met her family, and she met my family. Almost a year later, we married, and not so oddly, we live in Sulphur Springs.

So here we are, thirty-nine years after we first met, together, and looking forward to retirement. Wanda and I are active in philanthropic efforts for our university, attend most of the football games, and I am now on the Foundation Board of Directors. Two of our children are also graduates of our university. We have been married for six years, and it seems like forever but in a great way. She still has those wonderful majorette legs, can still twirl a baton, and when I look at her today, I still see that lovely, smiling, dimple-cheeked former majorette sitting across the card table at Old E.T. in 1971.

Chapter 71

THE PLAYOFFS

Jan Vowell—Coach's Wife—Beaver, OK

It was an incredible afternoon for the Lions and their fans. About 250 people—ETSU coaches, football team, and their fans watched the NCAA Division II press conference on a big-screen television at Binnion Hall. When they announced East Texas State University would play Grand Valley State University in Allendale, Michigan, the cheering crowd expressed an elation that we had not experienced before. The noisy fans gave Coach Vowell a standing ovation as he went to the podium.

"We are glad to be here," Vowell said. "We are glad to play anybody, anywhere in America. Wherever we play, we're going to represent East Texas State well." He talked about not letting Michigan's cold weather affect the Lions' play. "I expect this bunch to play hard."

Grand Valley State University: While the ETSU team prepared to make the two and a half hour plane ride, we wives had to decide what to take. After all, everyone was invited to a reception and dinner at the Kent Country Club in Allendale. I must say that Grand Valley State University was so warm and welcoming—such hospitality and class.

While we were at the reception, two of our players were making news. Mick Still and Dusty Corner were busy saving Allison Mark, a young Michigan woman. Ms. Mark was walking to her car, which was in an area where there had been several attacks on women in the past year. So when a man approached and made several comments to her, she showed him her can of mace. He told her that the spray wouldn't hurt him, as he'd been sprayed with mace several times.

She then saw Mick and Dusty, and ran toward them. She was acting like they were long lost friends. Motioning with her head, she alerted Mick and Dusty of her impending danger. Mick and Dusty continued walking with her, and when they got to the man, they told him to leave. After the man left, Dusty and Mick walked the young lady to her car.

The next morning Coach Vowell received a letter from Allison Mark. She wrote that two of our players had saved her from probable harm and that she wanted to thank them for being such fine gentlemen. "I was so scared at the time that I didn't think to get their names," said Mark. "All I could think about was getting in my car and getting out of there."

Coach Vowell was proud of the young men. "They were literally heroes," he said. "It shows that our players are gentlemen, good citizens, and great ambassadors for East Texas State University." A nice footnote: Mick Still earned National Defensive Player of the Week honors from Dan Hansen's Football Gazette and USA Today for his play against Grand Valley State University.

The next morning, there was a light dusting of snow on the ground, and we knew it was going to be cold at the game. The cheerleaders held a pep rally before the team got on the bus to go to the stadium. Everyone was buzzing with excitement. Parents of the players and our faithful fans gathered to send the team off for a victory.

The two teams were evenly matched, and the Grand Valley Lakers scored first. They missed the extra point, and went ahead 6-0. The Lions scored 5:05 minutes later on an eighty-three yard, 13-play drive. Bob Bounds threw completions of seven and sixteen yards to wide receiver Brian Harp, and a thirteen yarder to tailback Gary Perry on a bootleg. Perry later ran it in for a touchdown, when left guard David Gaskamp opened the way with a key block. The score was 7-6 Lions.

After two Lakers fumbles in the first half, the Lions were able to get Billy Watkins close enough for a field goal. The score at halftime was 10-6 Lions. In the third quarter, Bounds threw a touchdown pass to wide receiver Gary Compton for a 17-6 score. The fourth quarter found the Lakers scoring after a Lion fumble. The Lakers scored on a five yard option keeper, and passed for the two point conversion with 9:09 left in the game. The score was 17-14 Lions.

Billy Watkins scored a second field goal, a 35-yarder with 4:02 remaining. The Lakers kept the ball on the ground, as they moved from their twenty-five to midfield. They were running out of time, and they needed to score, so they attempted a pass. The biggest break of the game was when Terry Bagsby, known for harassing quarterbacks, went on a blitz and got knocked backwards. The quarterback didn't see Bagsby in the middle and threw it right to him. Bagsby wasn't known for his catching ability, so when he intercepted the ball, everyone was jubilant. There was 1:08 left in the game, and we ran out the clock.

We won our first playoff game 20-14. After much celebration, we got on the plane and headed for Commerce. Our next playoff game would be with the Pittsburg Gorillas in Pittsburg, Kansas.

Pittsburg State University: The Lions chartered a flight from Majors Field in Greenville, Texas, to Joplin, Missouri. After a thirty-mile bus ride, we arrived in Pittsburg, Kansas. The cold wind was whipping the Pittsburg State flags that lined the main thoroughfare of town. That might have given us inkling as to what would be in store. There was not a warm and welcoming feeling in Pittsburg. We went to the reception that evening, which was held in a very small room. We wondered about the size, but as it turned out, we didn't need a bigger room, because we were the only ones there . . . so much for camaraderie.

When we walked to the stadium the next day, we saw this large, black, blow-up gorilla. Our fans were so impressed, and Rheba Icenhower decided right then that ETSU should have a gigantic, gold, blow-up lion. As everyone knows, with Rheba's and others' hard work and fundraising, the Lions had one for the 1991 football season.

Our seats were in the upper section of Brandenburg Field/Carnie Smith Stadium. Gorilla fans were seated among us. We really didn't have a Lion section. Our cheerleaders were way down in front of us on the stadium floor. Just as we were told, Gorilla fans were rabid fans. They shouted rude comments to us and the team. Grown men spit on our players as they were going to the dressing room.

That environment, and the fact that our running game was limited because of all the injuries, made us very nervous. Gary Perry left the Grand Valley game in the second quarter due to someone rolling up on his leg. Jarrod Owens and Willie Mozeke were both hurt earlier in the season. It was going to be up to Bounds to make up for the injuries.

The Lions scored first by moving the ball down the field eighty yards in twelve plays. Receivers Compton, Chapman, and Owens caught short passes, and Bounds scrambled for thirty and twelve yards. They converted three third downs to continue the drive to the end zone. Owens was headed for a touchdown after a four yard reception, when he fumbled into the end zone. But not to worry...Gary Compton recovered the fumble for one of his three touchdowns of the day.

The Gorillas returned a short, "popover" kick and scored in two plays. The score was 7-7. Then the turnovers happened . . . eight turnovers in all. We lost three lost fumbles and five interceptions. The Gorillas took advantage and scored the next thirty-two points before Compton scored with a twenty-yard catch from Bounds. The Gorillas came back with an eight-yard touchdown, making the half-time score 39-14.

The Lions' defense stopped the Gorillas in the third quarter, then the offense scored late with Compton's eight yard reverse and Owens' one yard run. Score was 39-28 Gorillas. We might still have a chance.

After the Lions stopped the Gorillas at their 34-yard line, David Chapman fumbled the ball. The Gorillas recovered and scored three plays later. Bounds threw an interception, and the Gorillas went forty-nine yards for a touchdown. The Lions failed to score again. The final score was 60-28 Pittsburg State University.

Asked if the "popover" kick was the turning point of the game, or if it was the fumble after closing the gap to 39-28, Coach Vowell remarked. "Either then or when we got off the plane yesterday." Incidentally, the next year we beat Pittsburg State in Memorial Stadium and broke their regular season record of fifty-six consecutive wins. We won 20-13.

The plane ride home wasn't a joyous occasion like last week, but we knew deep-down that we had accomplished something that we would never forget. On the way home, President Morris addressed the team. "I want to tell you all how very grateful we are for what you've done for East Texas State. E.T. is better off because of the 1990 Lions."

"While you hate to end the season with a loss, you have to see we had a great year," said Coach Eddie Vowell. "I'm certainly proud of this football team." He went on to talk about how proud he was of the players off the field. "Our kids are student/athletes, not just athletes. They are fine young men."

"I could say something about them all. Most of them have tasted the 2-9 seasons, as well as the NCAA quarterfinals. I'm going to miss them," Coach Vowell said.

Except for a few unfortunate breaks, our young athletes could have been national champions. We remember, though, the season was as it was supposed to be. We were blessed to be associated with such a group of amazing young men . . . the 1990 football team.

Chapter 72
MEMOIR OF A DINNER DANCE

Lee McCasland—Class of 1956—Greenville

I n the springtime a young man's fancy lightly turns to thoughts of—what else but the Paragon spring dinner dance.

The year was 1955; our club president, John Foster, and the men of the Paragon Social Club were developing plans for their annual spring dinner dance. Spring dinner dances were a long-held tradition for all the social clubs at East Texas State Teachers College. About the same time, the several members who were residents of the Paragon House had recently completed a fund-raising drive, spearheaded by Bill "T-Bone" Timmons. The purpose of this activity was to purchase a large, console television for the living room of our residence, large by 1955 standards. Of course, the television was a black and white unit, but we thought it was terrific. Jerry McGowan, who was voted the 1955 Outstanding Paragon, was one of the residents who enjoyed the new attraction, as did Dana Ransom, who was to become president of the student body. Other members that I remember living in the Paragon House were Jerry Chandler, John Foster, Herby Hobbs, J. C McDowell, Bill "T-Bone" Timmons, Jack Thornton, Mike Waller, and me. Many club members who were not residents of the house would stop by to view their favorite programs because in 1955 not everyone had such an up-to-date means of entertainment in his dorm room. The women's main dormitory was Binnion Hall, followed by East Dorm. The residents had curfew on week nights at 10:30 p.m. Many Paragons would say goodnight to their dates on the front porch of Binnion Hall and then hustle over to the Paragon House to watch the "Steve Allen Show," forerunner of the Tonight Show. It was in this setting that plans for the dinner dance were formed.

John Foster had obtained a donation of some venison at no cost to the club, and this gift was a welcomed happenstance. We arranged for a local man known for his flavorful barbecue to cook the meat and have it ready the evening of the dance. Being ever resourceful and looking for a bargain, the men of the Paragon Club thought they would save additional money by preparing one of the side dishes for the dinner. Who could not do potato salad? On the day of the dance, the potato salad preparers assembled at the Paragon House's pristine, or maybe nearly pristine, kitchen. There I viewed the largest industrial food preparation dish I had ever seen, and it was in our little kitchen. The aluminum container was about the size of a number two washtub. Hopefully, this unit of measure is helpful to you in visualizing its size.

The dinner dance was to take place at the Majors Field recreation facility, located at the former World War II Army Air Corps training base, a few miles south of Greenville, Texas. The band, the food, and the dancing were all wonderful, and it was indeed a night to remember. The men and women attending the affair bragged about the wonderful flavor of the venison barbecue, the outstanding potato salad, the baked beans, and the cole slaw. The Paragon Club rules did not allow the serving of alcohol at any of its functions, so what comes next cannot be attributed to an over abundance of that type of beverage.

At the end of the evening, all the participants returned to their places of residence. About one or two o'clock the next morning, after a couple of hours of sleep, the occupants of the Paragon House began to awaken one by one to an awful disturbance in the middle of their bodies. It seemed that there was almost a simultaneous and urgent need for the some twelve residents of the Paragon House to evacuate the contents of the prior night's dinner. There were only two bathrooms. Please know that one visit to the facility was not sufficient. As the sleepless night wore on, it occurred to us that we might not be the only ones so afflicted. What about our dates and others who had attended? What should we do? Is this a learning experience? At about 8 a.m. we felt compelled to contact the college dispensary to report this incident. The nurse told us that they had been wondering when they would be hearing from the residents of the Paragon House. It seems that most of the women who had attended the dance reported to the dispensary during the early morning hours.

Then the surprise came when the nurse told us not to come to the health facility because they were full. The nurse would come to the Paragon House!

This announcement caused an additional level of concern because the housekeeping skills of twelve college-age men would not withstand a white glove inspection. So, the sick and wounded set about a spring cleaning with the haste and motivation that heretofore had never been exhibited. In due course, the nurse arrived bringing a magic elixir that saved the day. There was no lasting damage except for a number of scholars who did not attend classes the following morning.

The incident of food poisoning points out a classical difference between then and now. So far as I know, there was no talk of a lawsuit and no demand for reimbursement of medical expenses, not even a reprimand from the East Texas State Teachers College administration. It was viewed as an unfortunate incident, and we all went on with our college lives. Indeed, it was a simpler time.

What could have caused such a perfectly wonderful dinner party and dance to become so toxic? One story helps point out the source. Ruth Ann Wright White, president of the Marpessa Social Club, was among several people who did not particularly like potato salad. Naturally, she did not have a helping. Ruth Ann slept like a baby through the night and learned about the excitement only when she awoke the next morning with memories of a wonderful evening. Not so for her date, J. C. McDowell, who suffered along with the majority of us. Additional investigation squarely put the blame on the potato salad as the culprit. but it really did taste good . . . the first time.

Audrey Robnett Little—1939

Another incident, which plagues my memory, is the one when my sister enrolled in Miss Emma Creagh's art course. She had attended class only a few days when she became ill. Not wanting to take any cuts so early in the semester, she asked me to sit in the class for her, answer roll call, and get her assignments. I managed to sneak in, unnoticed by the instructor, and sit down behind several other students. On the third day, after I answered roll call, Miss Creagh suspiciously raised her voice and said, "Miss Robnett, where are you?"

Then she arose from her chair and walked back where I was sitting and asked if I were Miss Robnett, and I said, "Yes, Ma'am." She replied, "That's funny; the Miss Robnett in class yesterday was a blonde."

Chapter 73

LIFE IN MAYO HALL

Phillip R. Rutherford—Class of 1962—Roxton

I moved into Mayo Hall when I was a junior, and it was a relief. I had been in East Dormitory for two years, and Miss Crump, the dorm mother, and I did not exactly see eye to eye. We got off on the wrong foot when I was a freshman, and she threatened to kick me out of the dorm for various piddling offenses I won't go into here. Suffice it to say, after fifty years of rumination on the events and a bit of maturity, I admit she may have been partially—only partially, mind you—in the right.

But to me, Mayo was paradise although it was old, and bricks sometimes fell from the parapets. Each two-room suite had a bath between the rooms, an arrangement much more convenient and civilized than the big communal bathrooms in East Dorm, where you could stand in line for seeming hours to take care of essentials.

And our dorm mother, whose name I cannot remember, through fear, intimidation, or good judgment, stayed in her room and left everyone alone. A Miss Crump she was not.

There were occasional beer parties on the roof, complete with lawn chairs and binoculars to spy on the girls who left their shades up across the way in Binnion Hall. From some of the strip teases we saw, I could believe the rumors that many of the girls we watched knew they were being observed. Regardless, it was teenage heaven.

To give you an example of how loosely things were supervised in Mayo, I ran a gun shop out of my room. I sold Japanese Arisakas, Mauser 98s, German Lugers, and a variety of Browning automatic pistols, not to mention Colts, Remingtons, and P-38s. Every time I had a new gun, I'd post a "For Sale" sign on my door, sit back, and wait for customers. If a student did such today, the campus cops, the Commerce police, the Hunt County sheriff, and probably the ATF would throw him under the jail.

Like me, my roommate, Larry Barnes, came from Roxton. Being a freshman, he was less sophisticated than I. For example, when instructed to get mixes for a party for our fraternity, Delta Tau Delta, he bought Dr Peppers, grape sodas, root beers, and big oranges, but I valued Barnes as a roommate.

Sometime in the early fall, Larry showed up with a tow-sack stuffed full of peanuts his family had grown on their farm south of Roxton. We started eating them, and instead of throwing the shells in the waste basket like civilized people, we threw them on the floor. That was so gross and so much fun we vowed we would not sweep until we had eaten the entire fifty-pound bag. And, that was exactly what we did. Our room was a horrible mess. I do not exaggerate when I say peanut hulls were almost ankle deep. You might say we were living in hog heaven.

Then one morning about 5:30, I jumped from the top bunk to the floor in preparation for my job in the cafeteria. The second I hit the floor I began sneezing and sneezed uncontrollably for what seemed like the next half hour. Never before had I ever had a hint of a nasal allergy, but I have had one ever since.

We still did not sweep out the room until we began tracking the shells into the hall and down and stairs, and the janitor began complaining. When a note from the dorm mother appeared next to my gun sale notice that we were to clean up the room or else, we figured that our little experiment in hygiene, or lack thereof, had run its course.

I am somewhat fearful of revealing the best dorm joke I ever played while at E.T. since my dorm mates might read this confession, but assuming that bygones are bygones, I will take the chance.

My suitemates had been playing little tricks of various kinds on us, and I decided to get even. One day while they were in class, I sneaked into their room with a baby giant firecracker and a box of cocoa. I removed the glass cover from the light in the middle of the ceiling and unscrewed the bulb. Then I broke the glass of the bulb, being careful not to break the filament. I twisted the filament carefully around the fuse on the firecracker and buried it in the box of cocoa. Next, I screwed the base of the bulb back into the socket and suspended the cocoa box with a wire. Finished, I returned to my room, eagerly awaiting the return of my suitemates.

Fortunately or unfortunately, they returned together, opened the door, and switched on the light. As it should have, the filament became white hot and started the firecracker fuse burning. All I heard was a loud but muffled "Whunff!" and then a fair amount (actually quite a lot) of coughing and cussing.

I stuck my head into their room from the bathroom to view my handiwork. It was like nothing I had ever seen before. Powdered cocoa was everywhere. It was on the bunks, the desk, the dresser, the chest; it covered the floor, and chocolate remained suspended in the air so thick you could hardly see. It was in the closets, in the sheets, on the walls. As I had not quite expected this result, I disavowed any knowledge of the cocoa bomb.

A haze of cocoa dust hung in the air for weeks. I'll bet that when they demolished Mayo years later, you could still smell cocoa in that room.

Of my old suitemates, I ask forgiveness.

I married my wife, Lou Carolyn May, the last week I lived in Mayo.

By this time my suitemates had changed. One, a quite good friend I'll call Bill, I liked a lot, but the boy was a thief, a real honest-to-goodness kleptomaniac. Barnes and I had stuff disappear all the time. You brought in a new stick of deodorant, and it would be gone in a day. A bar of candy on the desk wouldn't last till you returned from class. Trust me. This was incessant. And when we hunted the purloined items, we always found whatever we were looking for in Bill's room in his chest. For some reason, Barnes and I never confronted him. We'd just take back, when he wasn't there, whatever he had stolen.

At the end of the second semester, the leather strap of my girl-watching binoculars disappeared. I knew where to look. Guess what? I found it in a drawer in Bill's chest. I suppose that pushed me over the edge.

Lou and I had decided to elope during the last week of classes. The only thing we lacked was money for the license and preacher. Pooling all we had, we still didn't have enough. I knew where to find some though

Don't jump to conclusions. As much as my suitemate had stolen from me, he never stole money. I guess somehow it was against his twisted principles. Likewise, I would never have stolen money from him, even if he had had any. But, I got supremely even and made money to boot.

Instead—remember now, this was finals week—I took all his textbooks, every last one, and sold them at Ig-Noble's Non-Profit Bookstore. Now I had enough money to get married.

Bill nearly went nuts. He searched frantically in his room and in ours for his books. He went to the cafeteria to see if he had left them there. He retraced his steps to his classrooms to see if he had left them under the desks. He didn't find them.

I guess everything worked out all right for old Bill, as I saw him frequently the next semester. He didn't flunk out.

Let me make one thing clear. To this day some fifty years later, I don't feel one bit guilty about selling his books. He deserved it.

I wonder if the good Dr. Mayo, the founder of E.T., could ever have envisioned all the antics that transpired in his namesake hall.

Charles J. Muller—Class of 1939

My principal memories of my many years spent on campus from kindergarten to the eleventh grade in the training School and then three years in college gave me nearly all the friendships that have lasted and that I have cherished for the balance of my life. The depression of dime burgers and quarter picture shows remain. The many professors prepared me for my career in spite of my wanting to have a good time. I delivered ice during my summers and made a decision that a t-square was a better way to make a living than the use of my back.

I transferred to Massachusetts Institute of Technology in the fall of 1938 to begin the study of architecture based on the foundations provided me by Mr. Keaton, Dr. LaGrone, Mr. Baker, Mr. Cowling, and Dr. Bledsoe of the E.T. Math department. After graduating from MIT in 1941, I returned to Commerce and was awarded a B.S. degree from E.T. for the work completed at MIT. I entered the Army as a second lieutenant and was discharged as a major in November 1945.

Chapter 74

CAMPUS LIFE

Mary Beth Rabb Tuck—Class of 1951—Point

It was a cool day in the spring of 1950 as I stepped out of the library door in my red rubber boots. It had been raining all morning, and the grass and sidewalks were still wet from the downpour. I started down the steep steps and looked across the green campus. I saw a young man with a thatch of carefully combed red hair coming up the sidewalk toward me. As I descended the steps, the young man briskly stepped forward, extended his hand, and introduced himself.

"I'm Kenneth Tuck from Naples, Texas. My best friend, Gary, thought it would be a good idea to meet you. He told me you were at the library, so I came to find you," he said.

The sun was out by now, so we stood by the old leaning tree beside the library and chatted. He suggested we go to the Student Union Building for coffee. I agreed, and we strolled down the sidewalk toward the small building. As we walked inside the coffee shop, there were many familiar faces. One of them was Gary McNatt, Ken's best friend from the same hometown. We sat down in a booth with another couple we both knew, and that began a friendship and a romance that would last for many years. We became a *couple* in a short time. Ken was popular on campus. The voters elected him vice president of the student body, with Alex Kibler as president.

The fun times we had included Western Week, where we all dressed in western clothes, complete with pants, boots, a cowboy hat, and belt. Some of the females wore western skirts, but during this special time, the administration relaxed the rules to allow pants. Special activities included a western dance, parties, and a lot of fun, including a *spitting* contest. Otha Spencer,

Journalism professor, got a photo of a group of students dressed in western attire during the great *tobacco-spitting* contest, with Ken Tuck, reared back to make the winning *tobacco spit*.

Each year, the college had a homecoming parade with wonderful floats that each organization would put together. The Les Choisites' float was always in the parade with members aboard. Several of the members were Home Economics majors, so I remember one year that we decorated our float with a large pot and spoon. Each member wore a chef hat and carried a spoon, with the slogan. *Let's Cook the Cougars*. We did not win the award for best float. Ken was in the Tejas Club, and their float had a giant bronze football player high atop the float. He was Gary McNatt, painted with gold paint. The Tejas won the award, and his picture came out in the E.T. annual, *The Locust*.

To earn extra money, Ken worked at Mrs. Sherrill's florist, located at her home on Washington Street. Ken was great at selling flowers, such as mums, in the fall and corsages for the formal events during the year. Well-known on campus, he sold to nearly every person who attended the college events or her date. Often, I would ride with Ken in Mrs. Sherrill's van to a Greenville florist to transport flowers back to add to Mrs. Sherrill's floral selection. We both loved Mrs. Sherrill and enjoyed visiting with her at her home and florist.

In the fall, the E.T. women's clubs conducted *rush* week to add members to their club rosters. Around the town of Commerce, each club would have a rush tea in the nicest homes, where they invited those they wished to join their organization. For this event, the ladies would wear their *dressiest dress*, with heels and hose, a fine hat on her head, and nice gloves on her hands holding a small handbag. They would attend these fine teas and return home to wait for the *bid*. I was not too worried about my bid. I knew the Les Choisites Club would choose me.

Presentation dances were in the spring, when clubs would introduce their new members. The *EasTexans* played our favorite *big band* music so we could dance. These events lasted until nearly twelve midnight, so we didn't have to be in our dorm until then.

During the spring, the clubs always had a dinner dance in Dallas at one of the well-known dinner clubs. We would all dress to the *nines* in semi-formals, carpool to Dallas, and return to the dorm by 1 a.m. for the special curfew.

In the fall of 1948, I attended the first football game at the new Memorial Stadium for the dedication ceremony. My brother, Harold, was one of the many

E.T. men lost in World War II, and his name is on the memorial plaque, still displayed on the wall outside the stadium. When a pep club was organized, we gladly joined, cheering our Lions on.

We often walked to downtown Commerce to shop at Freezia and Steger or to go to a movie because we didn't have a car. Few people had cars to drive. We had several nice places to eat in Commerce, but the favorite hangout for students on campus besides the Student Union Building, was the Chatterbox across the street from East Dorm. In our third floor corner room, my room-mate and I had a sand bucket with a heavy cord attached that we could let down for someone we summoned from the front of the Chatterbox. We always got hungry after the dorm doors locked at night!

They would come over, stand below the window to take the bucket, remove our money, and then get our burgers from the Chatterbox. They placed the burgers in the bucket for lifting through the window into our room. By this means, we ladies could feast after curfew hours.

I shall always treasure the memories of Old E.T. as I studied with a caring faculty and enjoyed many friends. It began my life as a teacher. In 1970, right after I received my Ph.D. degree, Wathena Temple, head of the Home Economics Department, summoned me back to teach Food and Nutrition courses at East Texas State University.

Gretchen Howell Colehour—Class of 1939

I spent most of my time at E.T. in the Library, where I was a full-time member of a small staff. "Full-time" meant more than 8 to 5. I was there from 1933 until 1950. Beginning salary was $125 a month! I had a room at the only dormitory during the first years. Board and room were $25 a month. Later I rented an apartment from Dr. and Mrs. E. N. Saucier for $12 a month. Those were happy years. Opal Williams was head librarian. She was an exceptional person in many ways. My M.A. degree in 1939 was among the first granted.

As for memorable experiences, there were many, some very dear to me as I met a wonderful faculty and student body. I cherish those memories. Most of the faculty of my time is no longer there. I still correspond with several and with some of the students who helped me in my department (cataloging and processing books).

Logan Swords was at the loan desk, and I did not know him as well as the ones in my office. I remember Logan as being handsome and a good worker.

Chapter 75

WALKING ON THE EDGE

Dewayne Bethea—Class of 1961—Caddo Mills

In early October, 1957 I met Earlene "Pepper "Granger in the Student Union Building on the campus of East Texas State Teachers College. Our meeting was by accident in the pen, pencil, and paper aisle. She was very attractive with that little blue and gold freshman beanie sitting on her stylish mid-1950s duck-tailed dark brown hair. Later in 1958 and 1960, she was selected as a "Locust" Beauty.

I was happy to be back in school after spending the summer in Winchester, Kentucky, working seven days a week and twelve hot hours a day on the pipeline. Trust me; most of the girls I met in Winchester were not pretty college freshman cuties.

On our first date a week later, Pepper and I were sitting in the Education Building watching an old black and white film of a Shakespeare play fulfilling our English assignment. After Shakespeare we headed for Chigs, a popular short order restaurant located west of Commerce on the old Greenville highway. We heard a song on the juke box, "You Send Me," by Sam Cooke; it became our song. Two cokes and one order of French fries later, we jumped into a borrowed 1950 Chevrolet Deluxe and motored straight to the rodeo arena to watch the collegiate rodeo. My date was one of the nominees for rodeo queen 1957. Shakespeare, Chigs, and an East Texas rodeo, all in one night. How's that for a broad range of college culture? Pep and I have reminisced many times through the years about that night long ago.

I knew them as Mrs. Stolph and Bertha, a mother and daughter team, who ran a boarding house on Live Oak Street. They served two meals per day—dinner and supper as they were called in the fifties. Dinner was fresh cooked, but supper was primarily leftovers. When I first started eating there, it cost twenty dollars per month. Her small living room provided a nice place for chit-chat and small-talk after meals. The students who ate there were a mixture from all social clubs and some independents. In addition to the college cafeteria and boarding houses, Commerce had several short order restaurants. My favorites were Chigs on the Greenville highway, City Cafe downtown Commerce, and Chat and Chew, also downtown. Truthfully, I seldom dined in restaurants for financial reasons, but these were my favorites when I did.

My blind date had us pick her up, on the street, in front of the Student Union Building; she was waiting in the dark expecting us. Jace Carrington, the match maker, slowed his 1953 Pontiac Indian to a gentle stop. I opened the back door, and she quickly slid into the back seat beside me. Once inside the car, though dimly lit, I could see she was a looker, and I loved the way she smelled. Introductions and small talk circulated within the Pontiac as the driver pointed it in a northerly direction toward Delta County. Somewhere north of Cooper, perhaps near Enloe, the Pontiac slowly ground to an easy halt in the edge of a cotton field. By the light of the moon, the four of us could see each other in a shadowy sort of way as we talked. As time slipped away, I continued to wonder; who was this alluring perplexing girl beside me, but the answers never came. I had a name, but I'm not sure, even to this day, if it was really hers. All too soon, it was time to get the girls back to the dorm, so my friend Jace fired up the Indian and maneuvered our party of four back to the highway and south toward Commerce. Back on campus parked in front of Mayo Hall, she and I got out, stepped to the curb, hugged, said our farewells, and she vanished into the dark. The spring semester of 1958 ended two weeks later, and I never saw her again. That clandestine date with the gorgeous mysterious girl puzzles me even now. Was she someone's steady girl— fiancée—wife—or just a fantasy in a young man's world?

We arrived at the old building located on the corner of Mayo Street and Lee Street; the brick and glass store front was painted midnight black. A sign on the door read, "Coffee House, open from 4 p.m. until 11 a.m. daily." Our group consisted of Larry "Lash" Horton, Tommy "TK" Kelly, Bobby "Bob" Harper, and me, four Tejas Brothers. The first wise crack came from Lash, "Who in thunderation drinks coffee at night?" Bob Harper replied, "Maybe there's more to this place than just coffee." TK kicked in, "I've heard they sit on floor cushions, wear black turtlenecks, and recite poetry."

MEMORIES OF OLD E.T.

I responded by saying, "Jerry Flemmons told me they call themselves Beatniks, and they're trying to find themselves."

Lash quickly countered, "Sounds like a bunch of bullshit to me, but let's go see for ourselves."

Once inside it took only a few minutes to realize all we had heard was true; some twenty-five students, dressed in black, most wearing dark glasses, sat on the floor. A young lady was standing on a slightly elevated platform reading poetry. The room smelled of incense, second hand cigarette smoke, and a sweet odor I had never smelled before. Once my rowdy friends and I realized there was no rocking music, no Jax beer, and no babes for dancing, it was time to haul ass. We made a quick exit, and like a pack of coyotes, were soon looking for new excitement. Little did I know we probably witnessed the forerunners of the next generation's counterculture movement.

Some of the non-school sponsored activities during the fifties decade were swimming in the sand pits and picnicking swimming or fishing in the North Sulphur River Channel. Additionally, "tonkin" at the Texoma Club across the Red River, or hanging out at the infamous Jack Ruby's Vegas Club on Oak Lawn Avenue in Dallas was part of the fifties scene.

A group of about thirty gathered in front of the Tejas house at 1322 Chestnut Street one mid-week night during the spring semester of 1958. Most were Tejas, but the group had a scattering of Artemas, Paragons, and Independents. Some members of the group were actually survivors of the great panty raid of 1956, so the rebel rousers had experienced leadership. Organizers reviewed former Tejas President Earl Stubbs' plan of 1956, for flaws, but there were none. The new plan was to march down Monroe Street to the courtyard behind Binnion Hall. As the assault on the great campus fortress began, my brother-in-law, Robert "Stoz" Stolusky stepped to the front, raised his trumpet, and for the next five blocks played "When The Saints Go Marching In." The rebels bellowed the words as best they could. As you can see, this was no sneak attack. The campus cops were positioned on the courtyard when we arrived; no one, including us, was surprised. The next day Pepper Granger, my future wife, told me that President Jimmy G. Gee was guarding the front. As we passed East Dorm on our approach to Binnion, about twenty additional curious students joined us. The scene was chaotic, but the coeds were very willing participants as the panties came raining down. Our goal accomplished, the crowd dispersed, the retreat back to 1322 Chestnut began as the trumpeter led the rebels back to their lair. The whole affair was simple: tease the girls, and prank with the establishment.

Fortunately, somewhere along the way I began to realize the danger of walking on the edge as a lifestyle. I gradually improved my grade point average, and little by little, I began to focus on getting through school. From the beginning I had always known that I did not want to continue picking cotton, hauling hay, scooping grain, moving houses, pipe lining, driving a belly dump and the list goes on. The problem was I had no direction or focus on what to pursue as a career. Perseverance, gumption, and the inability to quit will do wonders

Pepper and I married in 1960 . . . fifty (Did I say fifty?) years ago, and share two wonderful children. We were always friends, but we soon became lifelong soul mates. She reminded me again just a few days ago how as a teenager at old E.T. she prayed for the Tejas and our safety every night, and trust me we needed it.

I received a B.S. Degree in 1961 and a M.Ed. Degree in 1970. Public Education was my career. I was a teacher, football coach, athletic director, high school counselor, vocational counselor/director, assistant superintendent, and superintendent. I am proud to say I attended East Texas State Teachers College and East Texas State College, and received a B.S. and M.E. Degree from East Texas State University and was a student at Texas A&M University Commerce during the spring semester of 2009 in Dr. Fred Tarpley's English 697 memoir writing class. Pepper taught American history most of her career, specializing in World War 11.

To Dr. Fred Tarpley, Dr. Ruth Ann White, Dr. Harold Murphy, Dr. John McQuary, Coach Earnest Hawkins, Dr. Welcome Wright, Dean Margaret Berry, and Dr. Lawrence W. McNamee, thanks for getting me out of the hay field and off the edge.

E.T. What a great ride while making fond memories! I feel so sorry for those who missed the trip.

Chapter 76

UNIVERSITY LIFE FROM 1965-1969

Karen Marshall—Class of 1969—Dallas

It was 1965, and my parents took me to East Texas State University to begin my freshman year of college. I chose ETSU, as each student affectionately knew it, because the ratio of girls to boys was in my favor. Not a particularly scholastic reason, but mine nonetheless. I went to high school in Dallas and was used to all of the activities that a large metropolitan city offered. This was going to be quite a change, but I was excited.

Assigned to live in Binnion Hall, my roommate was a girl I had known from Highland Park. The room was small for two people, with two metal desks and two metal beds. Anything else to help it feel like home had to be added by the occupants. The lobby had a large sitting room complete with several TVs, but as I quickly learned, the boys could not occupy it until 4 p.m. Until that time, they were required to call for us on a phone at the check-in area and wait in the entry. Batman was the new "hot" show on TV, and at 7 p.m., when it was showing, the sitting room was full of students singing, "Batman, dadadadada. Batman."

The rules were simple . . . no boys in our room at any time. If we left the campus overnight, we had to sign out, stating our destination and telephone number. They periodically checked for accuracy. Curfew was 10 p.m., Sunday through Thursday, with Friday and Saturday extended to 12 p.m. Five minutes before we had to be in the dorm, a light would blink. If we didn't make it in on time, we encountered discipline. We wore dresses to class. The rules forbade slacks and jeans until late afternoon—even in snowy weather. The dress of the day was wild colors, mini skirts, go-go boots, dresses with loafers, and hair teased to resemble a basketball. The dorm mother was Mrs. Hemdon. She seemed elderly when I was eighteen, but she probably wasn't more than sixty. She had a sweet, grandmotherly smile, but still she could crack that whip. Even though I thought she was fair, I knew better than to cross her. A dorm monitor was on each floor to handle smaller problems.

There was a large community bathroom and shower on each floor. We also had one bathtub, which was our only source of privacy in the bathroom. I was always aware, though, that someone was waiting right outside the door to relish in the privacy that I was now enjoying.

The boys would sometimes have panty raids on the girls' dorms, much to the chagrin of the dorm mothers.

Across the street was the cafeteria, and behind that were the ROTC and Literature and Language buildings. The cafeteria and dorms across the highway were built a few years later along with the high rise apartments.

Registration for class was in the Field House. Long lines snaked inside and out as we walked station to station to sign up for each class, praying the whole time that the class was not already full. The cost for a class load of fifteen to eighteen hours was about $95.00, with another hundred dollars for books. Dorm fees for the semester were around $250.00. That left me with around $55.00 to have fun.

Many people commuted, and most of the others went home for the weekend. Gasoline was twenty-five cents a gallon, and if we were lucky, a gas war would be going on which could cut that in half. If we played our cards right, the cost to commute from Dallas was about twenty-five dollars a month.

Fall was a fun time. It always began with football games, pep rallies, and cooler weather. One exceptional activity was Western Week. Every student had to wear western clothes the entire week or face the fraternity boy sheriff. The penalty was going to jail for thirty minutes or pay a small fee. Western activities went on all week and culminated in a rodeo put on by the Agriculture department.

Another fun, fall activity was "adopting" children from Buckner Orphans Home who were bussed in to our campus for an entire day. We adopted one or more children and spent the entire day entertaining them and providing gifts. Normally, we did this right before the Christmas holidays.

It usually snowed at least once in January. Students borrowed the cafeteria trays and slid down the hills. Broken bones excluded, it was lots of fun. Finals were at the end of January. If we had kept up with our classes, we could enjoy the holidays. Otherwise, we spent that time studying so that we could come back the next semester and do it all again.

Computer science was just beginning to be a course of study. Students would have hours of assignments in the computer labs writing and executing programs. Each computer was six to seven feet tall and three feet wide. The circular disk that housed the programs was the size of a dinner plate. We punched three-feet-long trays of computer cards along with program information and inserted them in the correct order for the computer to read and execute. We used hundreds of cards to execute even the simplest of instructions.

Dr. Clyde Arnspiger, as director of General Studies, established "the Social Process" as the framework for the core curriculum for freshmen and sophomores. Everyone took a Personalities Foundation course, and every required course during the first two years did an analysis of each discipline with applications of "Man seeks values through institutions using resources." In a required English course with Dr. Fred Tarpley, I recall putting literature through that social process. Every student can recite the foundation to this day.

I was an English and business major. Dr. Paul Barrus was one of my favorite professors. It was difficult to get into his classes because he was so popular. He was a hard professor but fair and fun. He was a gentleman in his sixties with a very distinguished look about him. He came into class the first day in "hippie" clothes and jumped up on the table at the front of the room. Everyone looked around in disbelief. He then said, "You have, because of my looks, age, or stature, assumed that I would talk and act in a certain way. You have labeled me. If you are ever going to succeed, get out of the box. Expect the unexpected. Look for the unusual. If you are going to succeed in my class, you will do this, or everything you write will be mediocre." I have never forgotten that. He made a lasting impression on my life.

Dr. Shaw was in the Business Department. He and his wife frequently had entire classes of students over for dinner.

The old Sam Rayburn Memorial Student Center, recently demolished, was new then and a place for students to relax and visit. The Vietnam War was going on, and many students marched in protest, experimented with drugs, and experimented somewhat with their morals. Fortunately, while this seemed to be the norm in many parts of the country, ETSU students seemed to remember their roots. I remember a student who had just returned from Vietnam. As he was walking to the student center, a car backfired. He literally jumped into the bushes in fear.

In the spring, we got suntans the old fashioned way by invading a small lake on the right side of the highway heading to Dallas. It was just before the entrance to Interstate 30. No one really swam, but we each took a towel and headed for the lake to enjoy the companionship of other students and to sunbathe.

E.T. held graduation at the football stadium. I've never been quite sure what we would have done if it had rained. By that time, I was married, and my husband went early just to make sure his name was in the program.

It was, and still is, an exceptionally wonderful place to go to college. The friendships made there have lasted a lifetime. I met my husband there, and our life, including two boys and three grandchildren, all started at old ETSU.

W. Garland Button—Class of 1938

While the lives of all of us in the Class of '38 were in varying degrees touched by the Great Depression, we were able to have our share of fun. I was a member of a famous or infamous men's social club known as the Artema Club. It was the forerunner of the Lambda Chi Alpha fraternity. It would require the writing of a book just to summarize our experiences. We had an almost indescribable amount of fun, but we also developed lifelong friendships which over a half century later means more to us than we could have ever imagined during our student days. All of us in the class of '38 owe a debt of gratitude to our Alma Mater, which we can never repay. In the spirit of the founder of E.T., Prof. W. L. Mayo, we were afforded the opportunity to secure an education regardless of our financial means.

Chapter 77
Remembering E.T.

Mike Oglesby—Class of 1964—Commerce

As I think back on the summer of 1958 when I first enrolled in classes at East Texas State, all I can see is this immature seventeen-year-old who was unprepared for college. I was a Commerce boy, born in the old Lieberman Hospital, who had remained close to home, being the fifth of six kids. There had never been any doubt that my younger brother and I would follow in the footsteps of the eldest brother and three sisters who had all graduated from East Texas. I just took this for granted. I thought college life would just be an extension of high school—playing the drums, riding around in cars, dating girls, and reading the books that I *wanted* to read.

It didn't take me long to pledge a social club, the Artemas, which was probably not the best thing for me to do. If you saw the movie "Animal House" with John Belushi, then you know what the fraternity house was like. After a fair GPA in the summer, I proceeded to fail most of my subjects in the fall and spring and ended up on scholastic probation.

One bright spot in all of this happened during the fall of '58 came about because of my affinity for the drums. I was called to play with a group was backing up J. P. Richardson, "the Big Bopper." He performed at the theater in Sulphur Springs. I had played with a number of bands throughout my senior year of high school and was really into rock and roll; this was quite a thrill for me since "Chantilly Lace," his single was such a big success. In the spring of 1959, Richardson, Buddy Holly, and Richie Valens lost their lives in a plane crash. "It was the day the music died."

In the summer of 1959, a fraternity brother, Jerry White, convinced me to sign up for the Army Draft for a two-year stint. With my failing grades and my lagging interest in school, it seemed like the best thing for me to do. It was an impulsive act, but one that changed the direction of a life for the better. I was sent to Ft. Riley, Kansas, for heavy weapon infantry for eleven months and then on to Korea for thirteen months, where I spent many cold hours guarding the DMZ line. It's amazing how quickly one grows up when workdays begin at 5 a.m., and duties must be performed efficiently and accurately for the good of all. I certainly began to value the educational opportunities that I had let slip through my fingers.

Honorably discharged in 1961, I returned to Commerce and enrolled at E.T. I was twenty-one and coming from an entirely different perspective than that seventeen-year-old. I took full advantage of the history and political science courses, leadership positions in the fraternity, Inter-fraternity Council, and student senate. I eventually became vice-president of the student body and then president in 1963. The Sam Rayburn Student Center near the stadium opened this year. It was also the year of the Kennedy assassination, and I remember how we sat glued to the television set in the new ballroom and watched Walter Cronkite cover this heart-breaking story. In addition, 1963 was the year that I met and married my wife, Jeanenne Grammer, from Dallas. She worked in the old Student Union Building for the director, and that is where we met. It seems like the name Sam Rayburn played a very significant part in our lives, for which I am grateful.

From scholastic probation to a campus leader delivering a speech to incoming freshmen in the spring of 1964 was a big journey. The topic of the speech was "How Much a College Education is Worth." I had learned it the hard way.

Elizabeth Cowser Chitsey—Class of 1939

In one of my art classes, Miss Emma Creagh had the class make a characterization of someone on campus. At the time, John Hart was teaching my English class in a classroom in the new Library building. I chose him, thinking he would never see it. Later Miss Creagh put them all on display, of all places, in the Library foyer just outside the English classroom. I thought I was doomed, but he must have had a good sense of humor. I made an "A" in his class.

Chapter 78

Ford's Theatre

Jerry S. Phillips—Class of 1962—Carizzo Springs

My affiliation with E.T. began in the fall semester of 1960 as a drama major under Dr. Curtis L. "Pat" Pope. I stayed in close contact with the drama department through 1978, when I earned my third degree from E.T.

In addition to being a student in the drama department, I was employed as an instructor for a number of years. Over the years I worked with many exceptional talents.

While there is no shortage of fond memories, my greatest experience was being in the show that went to Washington, D.C. The play was "The Time of Your Life" by William Saroyan. The production under the direction of Dr. Pope was selected to represent the Southwestern United States in the American College Theatre Festival at Ford's Theatre in Washington. On March 23 and 24, 1971, East Texas State University students gave three performances in Ford's Theatre. Of course it was quite an honor for E.T. and everyone involved in the production.

There were many unforgettable occurrences. Approximately thirty cast and crew members flew to Washington. A good number having never flown before shared their flight food with those with hearty appetites. On the same flight was a piano used as a major stage prop. The weight of the plane caused more anxiety among the novice passengers.

The cast had plenty of fun in the capital city. One young actor wanted to make the same leap to the stage that John Wilkes Booth had made after shooting Mr. Lincoln. The actor, who will go unnamed, made the historic jump while others stood watch for security officers. The stage floor of Ford's Theatre was raked, or slanted downward toward the audience. Walking on such a stage was a new experience for all of us, and even the piano had to be "blocked up" so the casters would not roll.

'The two evening performances are well remembered, but the matinee performance was difficult as the cast had "over partied" the previous evening. In fact, my good friend Dr. Pope and his wife moved to a different floor of the hotel because of the loud celebration. I cannot deny my contribution.

I only hope that after almost forty years, the rest of the cast and crew remember the Washington trip as fondly as I do. We can all say, "We played Ford's Theatre."

Chapter 79
THE GOOD, THE ECCENTRIC. . .
AND THE
JUST PLAIN WEIRD

Bobbie Fleming Purdy—Class of 1967—Bonham

For the most part, all the teachers I had at E.T. were superb educators. However, a few were eccentric, to say the least. For some unknown reason, I met several of the unusual ones in the English Department.

My very first college class . . . the first Monday. . . was Honors English 101. As the song goes, "We were all in our places with sunshiny faces," when in strolled a slightly built, dark- haired, dark-eyed gentleman who introduced himself.

"I'm your instructor for this course. My name is Who I Shot Two," he stated. In actuality, he was Dr. Hugh I. Shott, II.

Continuing his introduction, he said, "I speak three languages . . . English, French . . . and West Virginian."

He checked the roll and assigned a paper . . . title of which I do not recall . . . to be handed in next class day. He dismissed us as he left the room, class lasting only minutes.

Come Wednesday, Dr. Shott appeared, collected our papers, and once more dismissed us, this class being shorter than Monday's.

The rest of the class seemed to be just as puzzled as I.

On Friday, Dr. Shott strode in and returned our work as he commented, "These are excellent papers . . . for high school seniors. You're in college now.

I think my marks and remarks on your papers are self-explanatory. Take them home, rewrite them, and I'll see you Monday morning."

He made his exit as quickly as he had arrived, leaving the entire class somewhat stunned. In our hands were papers fairly bleeding red ink, and I don't think there was a grade above a C.

What had happened here? Most of us were either valedictorians or salutatorians in high school, were pretty full of ourselves. Where were our A's?

In one week, with one assignment, Dr. Shott deflated those smug egos, got our attention, and paved the way for a semester of real learning. I should never have had misgivings about this professor. He was one of the best teachers I had at Old E.T., and I give him a great deal of credit for my ability to write.

For Honors English 102, my instructor was one of the just plain weird ones. Class met in one of the long, narrow rooms in the Hall of Languages with barely enough room for the teacher's desk and two rows of student desks. The twenty-five or so of us seated ourselves, men and women interspersed.

The professor arrived, pointed to the first man sitting on the front row, and said, "You there . . . move to the back." To a woman on the back row he said, "Move up here, right in front."

This continued until the front row consisted of women only . . . and the men sat behind.

"That's more like it. Now, I'll have something to do while you're taking tests," he commented, pointedly staring at the row of feminine legs, all crossed at the knees. You must remember, slacks for women were taboo in those days, so we were all appropriately clad in skirts. Right up our skirts is where his eyes crept.

Almost in unison, feet hit the floor. For the rest of the semester, knees remained glued together, feet stayed planted firmly on the floor, and skirts tucked securely around legs.

Naïve as we were, none of us considered complaining to the dean. This was 1963, and he was a professor. His class *was* quite interesting; however, he seemed to find sexual innuendoes where I doubted any existed. I thought he took pride in being the dirty old man on campus.

Some sort of cloud must have followed me, though, because for English 201, I drew another weirdo, this time a lady.

A few weeks into the semester, while the class was taking a test, she jumped from her chair and said, "Well, would you look at that?" Someone put in a new pencil sharpener . . . but it's a little high, don't you think?"

She reached over her head and grabbed the crank . . . the crank for opening and closing the window. I wondered if she ever tried to sharpen a pencil there.

Next semester, my English 202 classroom was next door to this same lady's classroom. One day, she rushed into our room and proceeded to unload items from her tote, painstakingly aligning them precisely on the desk top. When she finally looked up, she froze and stared at us, eyes wide with panic.

"Where is my class? What have you done with my class? You're not my students. Where are my students?" she asked. Ever so slowly she began gathering her things and putting them back in the tote, scrutinizing us as if we were Martian aliens.

Finally, someone gathered his wits and said, "Miss ____, I think they're next door. You're in the wrong room."

Clutching her tote to her chest, she fled the room . . . backward, her eyes never leaving ours until she had cleared the door and was safely in the hall, at which time our classroom erupted in hysterical laughter.

English 202 brought Shakespeare. . .and Dr. Lawrence McNamee. His initial "Heil Hitler!" was a bit disconcerting and shocking, but he had a genius for making Shakespeare come alive . . . and alive one must stay in his class. From the front of a tiered classroom to the highest level, his aim was remarkable when throwing chalk or an eraser at a sleepy student's nodding head.

Going into the 202 final, I had a solid B+, but needed an A on the final to earn an A for the semester. At the end of the two-hour exam, Dr. McNamee lifted the trash can from under the desk and said, "On your way out, file those papers right here."

I knew I had aced the exam, but when my grades arrived, there it was . . . a B. It was, and still is, my belief that those papers were never graded. After graduation and for years before his death, on more than one occasion I asked Dr. McNamee if he indeed trashed the exam. He would never tell me.

The English Department did not have a monopoly on intriguing teachers. There was the history teacher who assigned papers on topics for which we were to take a side and defend it. Initially, he returned mine with no marks other than a C. Finally, it dawned on me that I had disagreed with him on every paper. From then on, whether I believed it or not, I took "his side" and made A's, and an A in the course.

There was the anatomy and physiology teacher who had all his jokes written in his lecture notes; the genetics teacher sporting the bushy mustache who, according to upper classmen, frequently pursed his lips to "flush the fruit flies;" and the physiology professor who was appalled when I carried a sack of bullfrogs across campus, which, according to him, was most inappropriate behavior for a young woman in that day and time. He needed bull frogs for a project; our farm pool was abundantly populated with them; with my husband Arlan's help, I caught them and took them to class. Shocking, wasn't it?

Though I never liked P.E., Elizabeth Huggins introduced me to one of my favorite pastimes, golf. No matter how awful the shot, she would smile and say, "Now that wasn't too bad, but we can make it better. Let me show you."

Then there was George Nixon. His organic chemistry classes were grueling, and his exams were marathons, always given at night so we had time to finish. Additionally, organic lab met twice a week, also at night. Mr. Nixon got permission from the dean of women for his female students to stay in lab later than 10:30 p.m. Often, experiments ran way past curfew time. George Nixon was one of my favorite instructors, though, right along with Steve Razniak, Charles Rohrer, Daude Griffin, Zeno Bailey, Bub Taylor, and Bobby Wilson, all characters in their own right . . . and all among the good ones.

Helen Ratliff Dickson—Class of 1941

At the age of fifteen, I entered E.T. in 1935. My parents and seven-year-old brother moved to Commerce from Memphis, Texas, so I could attend college. After two years I received a permanent Elementary Certificate and started teaching at Cross Roads, a two-teacher school in Hopkins County. On Saturdays I continued my work at E.T. until I received my B.A. Degree in August 1941.

My memories of E.T. are very dear; the teachers were so dedicated, loyal, and interested in their students. I must mention Miss Effie Taylor, my English teacher, with whom I studied more than with anyone else. She gave me such challenges and fulfilled my goals.

Chapter 80

TIME MARCHES ON

Fred Tarpley—Class of 1951—Hooks

Even though the stentorian voice at the end of each short movie documentary, "The March of Time," admonished me several times about the transience of world affairs, I didn't heed the truism. Nor did I really internalize what my professors at E.T. often alluded to as *sic transit mundi* as I approached graduation in May 1951. In two years and nine months (six long semesters and two summer terms), I would sail forth from Commerce at age nineteen with my bachelor's degree.

Recently I opened my 1951 *Locust* for another review of that year, and as memories gushed from the pages, I realized all too clearly the essence of "time marches on." There before me in brilliant photographs by Dr. Otha Spencer, *Locust* sponsor, and his students were provocative images of that year. Turning the *Locust* pages evoked delicious nostalgia and sobering reality.

Dr. Spencer's always innovative "annuals," as they were sometimes called, began with a section on "Life at East Texas State, 1951." The effects of the Korean conflict on Commerce became evident, especially in the commissioning of the initial class of first lieutenants from the Air ROTC unit. Western Week, when everyone looked like Gene Autry's sidekicks, had coverage from the selection of Dot Ann Reynolds as Western Week Queen to the jailing of many students and faculty for breaking laws of the annual celebration, to the full execution of a few offenders with a dousing in a watering trough.

Homecoming then took the spotlight with Queen Rita Jennings riding regally in a sleek convertible in the parade. Other parade components attracted throngs to downtown Commerce, where elaborate floats had napkins woven into chicken wire with colorful designs and eye-dazzling contours. Tejas Social

Club took first place for the second consecutive year, this time depicting a "Friendship" theme. Fourteen visiting bands marched in the parade from Binnion Hall right down Commerce's main street and back to the campus. Other entries, simple but clever and effective, avoided time-consuming labor and the opulence of napkin-stuffed chicken wire. An Air ROTC cadet in uniform patriotically pushed a gurney carrying Mary Ann Gamble, a *Locust* beauty, with her broad smile enchanting the crowd as she lay under the medic's sheet.

Photographic scenes from the annual Christmas Party for Orphans showed campus couples with their adopted children for a day. The students presented gifts to 187 orphans from three homes in the region. Engagements and marriages often followed the vicarious domestic joy stimulated by the event.

Intimate scenes of student life in dormitories revealed what transpired after classes ended each day. Cameras clicked at the French Club Mardi Gras Ball when the Student Union Building ballroom became the famous Paris bistro where existentialist intellectuals met at that time. Students turned out in costume to compete for king and queen of Mardi Gras. Maria Tamayo, dressed as a Spanish lady, won the queen's crown, and Fred Tarpley, wearing a devil's mask and some of Lucifer's accessories, served as king.

Glimpses of Sadie Hawkins Day appeared, with Li'l Abners and Daisy Maes in costume staging a Dogpatch race allowing women to pursue men. Student Association officers smooth-talked teachers into starring roles in the Faculty Frolics and caused them to risk losing their classroom reputations. The most startling surprise was Dr. Paul W. Barrus, head of the English department, singing "She's More to Be Pitied Than Censored," "She's Only a Bird in a Gilded Cage," and other Victorian barroom ballads. His bartender costume and Irish tenor voice presented another side of the Emerson/Twain/Milton scholar. Dr. L. D. Parsons of Chemistry and Miss Pauline Rogers of English as singing hillbillies exposed a new facet of their usual personalities.

The preservation of campus events was comprehensive and amazing. It was clear that E.T. lived up to its slogans of "The South's Most Democratic College" and "Where Everybody Is Somebody." Most students had class photographs in the *Locust*, and various college activities highlighted several more. Campus enrollment was 2,400, and the *Locust* index listed 1,500 students appearing in class sections plus all the other pages containing named students. Some students showed up on only one page, but most had listings on multiple pages, sometimes as many as twelve. The student body of 2,400 filled the 2,200-seat college auditorium to overflowing for pep rallies and stage events.

The professional qualities of major productions of the Speech and Drama Department during 1950-1951 were obvious in scenes with rich costuming and animated performers.

By student vote, Margaret "Gussie" Flesher of Greenville was "Most Popular Girl," and Bill Atchley of DeKalb was "Most Popular Boy." A. Lane Lewis was president of the Student Association.

Victors of student elections smiled on page after page. Popular vote selected eighteen college beauties, whose designation would now be politically incorrect. The 1951 beauty judge, Ed Miley, Dallas commercial photographer, chose Peggy Pressley, Marilyn Smith, Midge Lowrey, Mary Ann Gamble, Shirley Riley, and Stella Eubanks as *Locust* beauties entitled to full-page portraits by Otha Spencer. The *Locust* editor made it clear that they were all first place winners presented in no special order. Presented in no special order, the other twelve college beauties each decorated one-fourth of a page and were Rita Jennings, Winona Kolander, Margie Castles, Mable Irons, Shirley Strickland, Margie Ashburn, Barbara Seaman, Peggy Teague, Dot Stubbs, Louise Nance, Dot Ann Reynolds, and Jane Jenkins. Three of the twelve college beauties were from Naples, and three were from Greenville.

Each undergraduate class had a full-page photograph of its officers, who planned meetings and specific activities. Presidents in 1951 were Thurman Dale, freshman from Groves; Peggy Teague, sophomore from Texarkana; Wayne Austin, junior from DeKalb and Hooks; and Charles Dexter, senior from Sulphur Springs.

Before local social clubs began affiliating with national sororities and fraternities in 1959, each social organization was unique on campus. Women were members of groups with exotic names: Caramica, Kaidishan, Kalir, Les Choisites, Marpessa, and Tooanoowe. Men were members of social clubs whose names radiated friendship and superiority: Artema, Cavaliers, Friar, Ogima (*amigo* spelled backwards), Paragon, and Tejas. When clubs, with memberships ranging from nine to forty-six, posed for their individual member photographs, they wore short, neat hairstyles, and distinctive but uniform attire.

Many other departmental, honorary, athletic, religious, or service organizations were active, each with pages in the *Locust*. Some were local, and others were regional or national. In 1951 twenty different organizations, not counting social clubs, had montages of individual members. The EasTexans dance band played at all college dances, at social club annual dances, and for radio shows and other occasions.

Twenty students chosen by faculty members for Who's Who in American Colleges and Universities had details of the activities qualifying each for his or her selection beside quarter-page photographs.

Before baccalaureate services became another victim of social change, the college administration invited the pastors of member churches of the Commerce Ministerial Alliance to speak under a rotation plan. On Sunday afternoon Texas Sen. A. M. Aiken, a dynamic leader in state education reform, spoke on "We Want People Who Are Willing to Do a Day's Work."

In 1951 Peggy Masters, Commerce, edited the *Locust*, and Fred Tarpley, Hooks, edited the weekly *East Texan*. The Gee Library at Texas A&M University-Commerce contains complete files of those publications.

Since 1973 no student attending the Commerce college has had the opportunity to find a comprehensive record of his or her collegiate experience. Like handwritten letters, the yearbook has practically disappeared. Gone are the files of personal communication in non-digital letters tied with ribbons and filed for posterity. The 304 pages of the 1951 *Locust* presented the college community. The yearbook is an excursion into the past and offered the realization that time has indeed marched on.

Students in the technological age have cell phones, computers, texting, FaceBooks, and Twitters for communicating ephemeral and often abbreviated missives. Death messages made up the bulk of long distance phone calls in 1951, and most students brought no automobile with them to college. When students decided that they had grown too sophisticated for "high schoolish activities" in college, they abandoned traditional collegiate life in favor of individualism, apartment living, marriage, grownup habits, cohabiting with significant others, commuting, and fulltime jobs. If there were a college yearbook today, it would preserve an entirely different culture.

Yes, time marches on, and the clock could not be turned back because of shifts in society, behavior, values, economics, and all the other factors that define the present. Nevertheless, college-age generations before 1973 can meander through the past in their yearbooks and savor the formative years of their lives. In my personal library, the *Locust* collection ranks at the top of my most treasured volumes.

Chapter 81

A DECADE OF FUN
1968 – 1978

Gregory V Cole—Class of 1969—El Paso, "Inherit the Wind Kudos"

The cast members of "Inherit the Wind" had the privilege of performing for Mr. John Scopes at the old University Playhouse. He gave us a "well-done"—what a treat. Mr. Scopes, was a young biology teacher in Tennessee, was the defendant at the famous Monkey Trial because he had taught evolution. The great Clarence Darrow was his defense attorney. Mr. Scopes came to Commerce from Shreveport, where he had retired, to see the play.

Gregory V Cole, "No Place at the Inn"

In about 1968 or 69, Al Hirt and band, the famous jazz group from New Orleans, came to the E.T. campus for a concert through the efforts of Forum Arts. After the show, there was no place to go to wind down in Commerce, so the drama students arranged an impromptu party for the band. Wow, was it fun to hang out with Al Hirt and his band!

Pati Mayer Milligan—Class of 1972—Gladewater, "Living in Smith Hall 1970"

The summer of 1970 was not very restful for the women living in Smith Hall Dormitory but it was one of the best summers of my life. I had just entered ETSU as a senior and I moved into Smith Hall with my old friend from Kilgore College, Kay Dudley Fouchet. The biggest problem was that the air conditioner in the dorm was broken but at least the windows opened, and we bought a fan. I remember going down the hall to shower in only cold water to cool off, but I was sweating again before I got back to my room.

The fire alarm woke us at least ten times in the middle of the night, and we all had to go downstairs to the inner courtyard. Some "guys" had called in a bomb scare, and we always thought it was some fraternity guys who wanted to see that many girls in their pajamas. Each bomb scare took at least an hour, and we weren't particularly thrilled, but at least it was cool out there. It was such an innocent time.

I had to take a sweater to a 7:30 a.m. Calculus III class because it was so cold in that room. Even being so cold, I still had trouble staying awake during class, and I sat on the front row. When I walked back to the dorm around noon the wind was blowing hard as it always did, and I remember it burning my skin.

Kay and I qualified for the honors dorm in the fall, but we lived there less than a week because it was so boring. Thank goodness they still had a room available on our hallway and we moved back to Smith Hall where it was so much fun. There was a small racial incident when the common TV room had a heated discussion about whether to watch "Alias Smith and Jones" or "Flip Wilson." We finally agreed to share the two common TV rooms on the floor with one showing Flip and the other Smith & Jones.

Another life lesson was when Kay and I dated Mexican-American brothers, George and Ed Garcia. Our dorm friends from Arizona couldn't understand how we could date these fun, good looking guys. Being from East Texas we hadn't known anyone of Mexican descent and had no prejudices against them. It was such a great year, and my friends at Smith Hall were the reason.

Pati Mayer Milligan and Donna Hutcheson, Goin' to the Potty

It was the first day of the semester 1972 when Bernie Hill a fellow computer science teacher came up to Pati and Donna asking if they were "goin' to the potty." Pati and Donna looked at each other and thought, "Is this guy crazy." Bernie went on to add, "Are you goin' to the potty tonight?" The next thought was "What business is it of yours?" Rather than be rude, Pati and Donna said nothing. Thank goodness, Bernie did not realize what the ladies heard. His next comment was "Didn't Doctah Goddad let you know about the potty at his house tonight? Ah you two going." Little did the ladies know until that point that Bernie was from Boston and hence did not pronounce the " r's " the same as we Texans do. Between all of the laughs, they told Bernie yes, they were planning on attending Dr. Goddard's party that night!

Pati Mayer Milligan, "Token Female of 1972"

I had just finished my master's degree from Texas A&M and could not find a job in my specialty. I had one interview that told me they were hiring only if they got the space shuttle, but they did not get the contract. My first grade teacher, Virginia Baker from Gladewater, was working on her doctorate and was taking Computer Science 126 during the summer of 72. She had been ill and made an appointment with Dr. Alton Goddard, department chair, when she couldn't get in touch with her teacher. He told her that she wasn't behind because her teacher was also ill, and he could not come back to teach. He asked her if she knew anyone who could teach computer science. She said she did, and he did too. Dr. Goddard did remember me as one of his students and gave me a call. At the interview he said they were required to hire a woman as an instructor in the department and did that bother me. I told him that being a computer science major, I was often the only woman in my classes and I would be happy to be his "token female." That is how I got the job, and I enjoyed it for the next six years. I received tenure and could have stayed at E.T. working for Dr. Goddard forever, but I got married and had to move.

Pati Mayer Milligan, "The CS group has fun."

There were six of us around the same age plus spouses. We played softball, pool and foos ball, partied, and had group dinners. At the softball games, the ladies would admire James Hobbs' shapely legs peeking out of the short shorts he wore at the ball games. At the dinners we learned how to make a Persian dish of eggplant and beef that was/is absolutely delicious! Dr. Ed Rodriguez had parties for faculty, students, and visitors—we had fun! One night at a downtown establishment, the police came upstairs where we were playing foos ball and attempted to arrest Dr. Larry Satterwhite for sleeping in public. We all rallied to his defense but had to leave the establishment anyway.

The current head of the IT Services Department for TAMU-Commerce was just a hippy nerd with long hair in 1972-78. Mike Cagle developed the Cagle's Operating System for the University data center computer—a whopping 512 K memory with tape drives and all. Cagle's operating system was the precursor for Windows operating system at the university.

Pati Mayer Milligan and Donna Hutcheson, "Calling"

In 1976, we moved to new Computer Science Department offices. Even though our offices were across the hall from each other, we could not see or hear normal volumes of speech. Besides, in our 20s we had too many secrets to discuss that all the men in the department could hear. So, anytime we were not teaching class or with students, we would call each other on the phone to whisper.

Donna Hutcheson—Class of 1974—Rossville, GA, "Teaching in High Schools"

In 1976-78, I taught a course entitled "Teaching Computer Science in Secondary Schools." At that time, the female students wore skirts so short that when they wrote on the blackboard, the boys in the class had a front row view of underwear. To help get past that tendency, I cautioned the females to stand in front of the mirror every morning before leaving home, raise both hands as far above the head as possible. If any underwear was visible upon arriving at class, the class grade was docked 5 points.

Donna Hutcheson, "Skating the Halls"

The computer science classes were taught in the Business Administration Building between 1972 and 1978. I was always in a hurry, so I would not be late for classes. In 1975, the ACM student organization bought me a set of roller skates to make going from class to class easier and faster. I used the skates until Dr. Goddard told me to stop—I was jeopardizing the rest of the students and faculty!

Pati Mayer Milligan, "The Red Stamp"

When I graded exams, I seemed to use a lot of red ink with -1s all over their papers. One semester my class got together and bought me a rubber stamp with red ink that said -1. I used it from then on. We really had fun with our students.

Donna Hutcheson, "Watch that Step!"

One year, I don't remember which, I was giving an exam in one of the rooms with the podium on a step above where the student chairs were. Just before handing out the exam, I reached out with my left hand to close the door (holding the test papers in my right hand), and promptly fell off the step. The fall broke my elbow and scattered the tests everywhere. Needless to say, no test that day! I had to make out a new test because surprisingly enough, some of the copies went missing!

Chapter 82

WEEKEND

Charles Bailey—Class of 1967—Cooper

S omeone in the restaurant's kitchen played a radio, but we heard only a murmuring static under the buzz of talk and laughter and the clatter of dishes and glasses. The doors of the kitchen flew open, and Mrs. Evans, the owner made a beeline right to our table.

"Charles," she said, "the President's been shot."

"What?"

"Shot."

One of my friends covered her face. Another muttered, "Goddamn."

We sat for several minutes, as did the rest of the patrons. Mrs. Evans continued to pour coffee because she had to, but, moving between the tables, her eyes never met anyone else's, and she said nothing beyond what was necessary.

We remained silent for quite some time until I grew fidgety and finally said, "I've got to find out what's going on." I left and started up Hunt Street toward the main quad. About halfway there I did an uncharacteristic thing: I turned right into a building, which sat next to the Charquette, the place where I usually ate lunch—the Baptist Student Union. Not that I had suffered some stroke of piety. I had never gone to the BSU before, but, through the window in the lounge, I saw a television set. When I walked in, I knew it was true. The President had been shot. The newsmen wept.

I watched the drama: the ambulance at Parkland Hospital, the body being rolled inside. I couldn't stand waiting to hear the final news. The year before, I had joined the Young Democrats and worked doggedly for John Kennedy, and I thought my own virtue somehow lay in his cause. So, unnerved and shaken, I went outside again and wandered to the circular drive in front of the old

Administration Building. The coeds had spilled out of Binnion Hall and the sorority houses on that street. Some stood around, frozen in their distress; others wandered from group to group trying to glean any new information. Soon the boys showed up too. It was everybody, groups that normally kept their distance from one another: the frat guys in madras shirts, the nerdy math and science majors, the ag boys in jeans and boots. They all milled around, half-talking, half-listening, all disoriented. Still not knowing the outcome, in desperation, I drove home to watch my own TV, and the rest of the horrible story unfolded that afternoon and over the weekend.

The interminable Saturday and Sunday dragged by. Then, the weekend finally over, word came out that Congress had designated that day, Monday—the day of the funeral—an official day of mourning. Colleges and universities all over the country shut down—all over the country, that is, except in Commerce and at East Texas State. The school's president, Dr. James Gee, a dyed-in-the-wool Republican, thought cancelling classes amounted to students and faculty trying to get a day off. Teachers and students alike met his position, of course, with strident opposition. As a result, he cancelled classes for one period—an hour of "official mourning"—for a slain president. The academics again objected. I suppose some teachers followed Dr. Gee's pronouncement. Most did not. I suppose some students attended classes. Most did not.

By the time I had watched the funeral and come to the campus, students had gathered on the lawn of the President's mansion, in that same area where they had congregated the Friday before, addled and heart-broken by that day's events. Pensive now, they sat in a crowd on the grass and the sidewalk that led up to the white columns that spanned the president's red-brick house. All the types I had seen earlier leaned together or stretched their legs in front of them: the frat boys, the science majors, the sorority girls, the Ag boys. They all were singing. A few played guitars. The music majors led the harmony, and everybody sang: first, patriotic songs—"America, the Beautiful" and "My Country 'Tis of Thee"—then, folk songs with a vague gospel flavor because the folk movement still dominated the radio—"Michael, Row the Boat Ashore," "Kumbaya," sort of dirges. Word got around from administrator types that the students "sat down" before the President's residence to sing protest songs. Protest? The only song that suggested any action was "If I Had a Hammer":

"It's the hammer of justice.

It's the bell of freedom.

It's a song about love between my brothers and my sisters all over this land."

Protest? The gavel, the Liberty Bell, a song of unity rather than division? We did sing one song about war, by Pete Seeger:

"Last Night I Had the Strangest Dream
I never dreamed before.
I dreamed the world had all agreed
To put an end to war."

It wasn't an anti-war song at all—at least not for us. We didn't think we could end the Vietnam War singing about it. We knew things were more complex than that. But we were in mourning, and needed simplicity and comfort. We sang that song because the word "dream" ran through it like a litany. That's what we mourned, the loss of our dream. When people mourn, they need comfort, dreams, and most of all they need lots of music. Funerals in the South prove that. Nobody rose up against anything. We simply hung out with friends who had lost the same thing—the dream. As the day faded to evening, some of us went to the Charquette for bags of hamburgers that we passed around. People ate. A protest? It was something different from a protest. A protest happened in the cities of the East and the West. In Commerce, directly out of the tradition of East Texas, the students had staged an "all-day 'singin' and supper on the ground." What could have been more appropriate or more meaningful?

The doors of the mansion remained shut all day. This peaceful civil disobedience went unacknowledged.

Although I sensed something at the time, this dichotomy between the urban and the rural became clearer to me a few years later. S. I Hayakawa, the noted semanticist, spoke at East Texas State. Shortly thereafter, as president of San Francisco State University, he rose to prominence when he confronted the Students for a Democratic Society, jerking the wires from their speakers as they addressed the student body. Following that incident, the national press quoted him as saying that such an event would "never occur at an East Texas State," implying that only dynamic, urban institutions like his had students capable of the independent thought necessary to stage elaborate protest. Dr. Hayakawa was right—although not for his reasons. The protest at San Francisco State, violent on both sides, would never happen at East Texas State. Indeed, it had not happened. Our protest was hardly a protest at all—not in the sense that

Hayakawa used the word. In fact, we protested only insofar as truth protests what those in power mistakenly believe, that they can maintain their power in the face of change. Our protest exposed the self-righteous complacency that wanted to hold onto its own power indefinitely. Our protest showed that the establishment finally crumbles and is replaced by a new order, true for a while but inexorably doomed to pass also.

The next day the students on the lawn went back to class because, as Frost put it, "they, since they were not the one dead, turned to their affairs." Just so. Four years later, James Gee retired, and a new president was hired. A new mansion was built. In addition, things were great—for awhile. Hayakawa resigned from San Francisco State seven months later to run for the senate as a Republican. He served one term. The SDS dissolved, faced with apathy. Mrs. Evans served more coffee. The Charquette sold more hamburgers. East Texas State College became East Texas State University. And education endured.

Marjorie Lynch Jackson—Class of 1939

My most memorable experience at E.T. was receiving the information from Government Professor Claude V. Hall that my being valedictorian of the class of 1939 would enable him to secure for me a three-year full tuition scholarship to Tulane Law School. My goal upon entering college had been to prepare myself for law school. Without his interest and effort on my behalf, I could not have afforded to go to law school and would have missed the pleasure and satisfaction of getting a legal education and working in the legal field until my retirement in 1987.

A memorable amusing incident was my dilemma when Bob Varley swallowed goldfish on campus. I was a commuter student from Greenville at the time, and the Varleys were our next-door neighbors. Should I tell his parents about this extraordinary demonstration? As it turned out, the event was too sensational to be kept under wraps which resolved my dilemma.

Chapter 83

COMMUTE

Hoyle Julian—Class of 1962—Sulphur Springs

C ollege was not in my immediate plans when I graduated from high school. Instead, I was off to the pipeline construction business to make money. One day as I was standing in knee deep mud with a cast on my right arm due to a fractured metacarpal in my right wrist, I decided this job was not a good career choice. I headed home to Sulphur Springs to go to E.T. I arose early, milked the cows, caught the commuter car, and attended E.T. By living on a dairy farm, I was up at 4:30 a.m. for daily chores. Cows had to be milked twice daily. There was not too much time for other activities. I joined the Ogima Social Club (no fraternities in those days). Freshman pledging chores were tame when compared to present ones. Being left on a country road with few or no clothes and having to get back to campus on our own was the most embarrassing one.

Once, the weather was so bad that we had to spend the night in Commerce. Stanley Garvin's aunt was Sarah Gavin, an English teacher at the university. We stayed with her. Wow, did she spoil us in one night. She placed hot water bottles in bed with us to warm our feet.

When Dad had a stroke, I had to drop one of my classes to have more time to help on the farm. With no counseling, I dropped my ROTC. That was probably the wrong course to drop. But at twenty, I was not as smart as I thought I was. I became aware of that fact later in life.

We had adventures with the four or five commuters. Never a dull moment with that group. We stopped for tamales at a house on the highway outside of Commerce. I think the operators opened a can and handed them to us, cold, on a paper plate. About three weeks later, we passed that house. Police cars surrounded it. We found out that the tamales sign was a front for the local bootlegger. Commerce was dry at that time. Imagine their surprise when we stopped for tamales.

My major was Math. Many interesting professors taught that subject. Dr. Cecil B. Wright, head of the department at that time, was a stickler for perfection. I gave it my all and passed with pride. I would encounter him later when I earned my master's degree.

I was taking my last course in the summer of 1960. When invited to complete a bridge group, I met my wife, Ann Oglesby. She was teaching in Puerto Rico and was home for the summer. I completed my course, received my degree, and was ready for the next step. Ann returned to Puerto Rico in the fall, came home at Christmas, and we were married February 11. 1961.

We returned to campus, and I earned my M.S. in l965. My next encounter with Dr. Wright came during this time. There were five students in Theory of Numbers. During the first test, one at a time, three students got up and left. One at a time, each went to acquire a drop slip, return to class and have Dr. Wright sign it. There were two of us left in class. Les Green and I had to have that class for our degrees. We hung in and made it.

My company, ARCO Oil and Gas was reorganizing. Offered an early retirement package, my last assignment was a three-week trip to Jakarta. Ann decided that she could retire early, and we came to Klondike. We had bought land there many years earlier and thought the atmosphere and environment would fit our needs.

Since that time, we have worked for the university and have attended all events possible. There are athletics, music, theater and the planetarium to enjoy. We are living the university life without taking tests and attending classes. One of the more satisfying things I do at this time is my math tutoring. I have been able to save a few students and keep them in school. This is still our E.T.

Chapter 84

BUCK HUGHES

Jerry Lockhart—Class of 1961—Tyler

My family dropped me off at the Farm dorm in the summer of 1957. After they left to return home, I stretched out on the bed in my room, looked at the ceiling and felt homesick already. I told myself that I'd better get used to looking at that old ceiling because I had at least three more years of it ahead of me.

About that time, a slightly-built, red-haired man came down the hall and noticed me in my room. He introduced himself as Curtis Richardson, a dairy professor in the Ag Department. He asked if I would like to go across the street to the dairy barn and watch the evening milking. We did, and that pretty much ended my spare time for the next three years.

The dozen or so boys on the Farm soon became like family to me, and we became as close as brothers. They were the hardest working people that I was ever around. Billy Bob "Bloodhound" McWhorter helped me through registration for the summer semester. At some point during the process, we came to a table staffed by upper classmen selling freshman beanies. My friend said, "Keep walking. Farm Boys don't wear beanies." That was my first indication that I was now a part of a group that was not your run-of-the-mill students.

Dr. A.C. "Buck" Hughes was a dominant figure in the Ag Department and on the Farm. Although not yet head of the department when I first came to the Farm, he was, nevertheless, a force to be reckoned with. I learned later that he was a man with a gruff exterior but a very kind heart. My second year in school he became department Head, replacing Mr. Alvin Rix.

One of my favorite recollections of Buck concerns an incident during silage harvest my first year on the Farm. A four-wheel trailer loaded with silage had blown out a tire on the way from the field to the silo. Alton Neal, an Ag instructor and farm supervisor, was talking to Pete, the shop mechanic, about mounting a new tire on the wheel that lay on the shop floor. As it turned out, Pete didn't have a sixteen-inch tire on hand, and he told Neal he'd have to pick one up in town.

About that time, Buck arrived and wanted to know what was holding up the work at the silo. They explained the tire problem to him. He looked around and said, "I don't understand the problem. You've got lots of tires on the rack." They patiently explained that those were fifteen-inch tires and the wheel was sixteen inches. "Hell, stretch it," he demanded. They pointed out that it was impossible to do so. He stormed out telling them, they could make it fit if they wanted to badly enough.

Buck and his wife, Lucy, were childless, but Buck considered every one of his students like one of his own kids. Upon graduation, we were assured of a job because of his vast network of friends throughout the state. You might not get the job you wanted or the location you desired, but you sure as heck got a job, thanks to Buck!

For years following my graduation, while visiting with Buck in his office, I would ask him about various boys. He would tell me exactly where they were and what they were doing.

I met Buck's baby sister when she was a freshman and I was a sophomore. We married after a six-month courtship. Before the wedding, Buck called me and his younger brother Charles, also a Farm Boy, to his office. He explained in great detail that he would see to it that no one would have grounds to accuse him of going easy on his kinfolks. He kept his promise.

I knew without a doubt that these were friends I could count on. The College Farm was instrumental in shaping my life in ways too numerous to explain. After fifty years, I still feel the same way.

Chapter 85

CHANGING LADIES FASHION TRENDS

Raylene Partin—Class of 1970—Greenville

Recently I received a postcard from the Alumni Association with a picture of the Ferguson Social Sciences Building in the background and a panorama of the entire student body, faculty, and administration of 1927, in the foreground with an inset picture of the same building as it appeared in 2009. As I noted the dress styles of the women, emphasis on "dresses, skirts," I was reminded of my undergraduate days from June 1967 through August 1970.

Females on campus wore dresses, skirts and blouses; slacks and pant suits were not to be seen. Having a few friends who lived in Binnion Hall, I remember their rules for slacks and curlers in hair: confined to dorm rooms and certainly not past the front door of Binnion.

My worst memories of the fashion trend for ladies in the mid to late sixties were the dresses and skirts I had to wear on cold, windy days when I would walk across campus going from class to class, or to the Sam Rayburn Student Center for lunch, or to work at the James Gee Library. To keep the legs warm, most of us young women wore hose with fishnet hose over those. We armored our bodies with heavy coats, secured our necks and heads with scarves tied securely, and kept our fingers flexible for note-taking in the next class with warm gloves and mittens.

On the really cold, windy days when there was sufficient snow, many students would "borrow" cafeteria trays from the Student Center cafeteria and take them to the top of the hill east of the Student Center, sit down on them, and then hold on tight trying to guide them down the hillside to the east entrance doors. Of course, there were many spills and a few crashes into the Student Union building's glass doors. This was the E.T. version of sledding and was not to be deterred by fashion restrictions.

While umbrellas were standard fashion accessories for males and females on campus, most learned to keep spares and backups handy. We never knew when wind would reverse the Mary Poppins act or when rain would saturate the umbrella cover to the point of dripping through on us as we trekked across campus. Some of the most colorful days at Ferguson Social Science Building were the "heavy drencher" days because umbrellas of all sizes and hues lined the hallways where students hoped they would dry out some before the trek outside began again after class. I even remember a few students who took wet socks off and draped them over the radiators in the building to dry while class was in session.

By the early seventies women faculty and female students alike "hailed" the arrival and permission to wear tailored matching pant suits on campus. I remember Dr. Johnye Sturcken laughing about the "matching pant suits" years later and commenting upon what an "innovation" that was for the faculty women. I have to admit that I have two or three such suits in one of my closets which I have kept as mementos of that fashion era at E.T. For female students and ladies on the faculty, the matching pant suits—most of them polyester—were a welcome change to ladies' on-campus fashion.

John L. Wortham—Class of 1940

As has often been said, "A university is its faculty." It was my good fortune to associate with outstanding professors, both in and outside of the classroom. I shall identify only a few and say a belated "thanks."

To Professor Claude Hall, who provided students with some unique and interesting illustrations in his political science classes; to Dr. Maude Noyes Johnson, whose patience and endurance were frequently challenged in trying to teach students to sing in Spanish who couldn't carry a tune in any language.

To Dr. R. L. Jones, who spent his limited funds and time to provide transportation to a small group who traveled to Paris each Sunday to produce a radio talk show; to the J. G. Smiths, who were counselors, resource providers, and friends.

Chapter 86
FOREWARNED IS FOREARMED

DeLois Bethea Stolusky—Class of 1957—Caddo Mills

I f you're old enough, you will identify with the following statement: The ugliest, most repulsive item of clothing that a female can wear is a hairnet. Worse than wearing a hairnet, however, is being caught wearing one. Brace yourself; it gets worse.

In 1956, I returned to Binnion Hall from a date by way of the back courtyard. I distinctly remember that the mood was light, and the two of us were trying to be cute and witty. The goodbye ritual was sweet but not very romantic. I was interested in a repeat performance as soon as I could manipulate it. With that plan in mind, I went upstairs to my room and joined the usual gathering of club sisters to discuss every single aspect of my evening.

After visiting various rooms up and down the hall, I took a shower, put bobbie pins in strategic places to secure my duck tail hair style and turned out the light. Under the protection of darkness, I took a hairnet from the dresser and put the ugly thing on my head. You know, protection for my ducks.

Since king sized beds hadn't appeared at that time, my roommate, Joyce Taylor, and I created our own. We put our twin beds together and pushed the contemporary, short metal headboards under the sills of the double windows. We could turn off our lights, look down from the third floor and watch everyone kissing goodnight. At 10:25, the outside lights blinked hysterically to send a fair warning. that 10:30 was lurking. This night was no exception.

Oh, but it did become an exception after all. As Joyce and I began chatting and hooking our chins over the window sills for a bird's eye view, I noticed something slinking in and out of the shrubbery below. The freaky-looking creatures began to multiply. They were skulking around in dark corners of the courtyard and under all of the shrubs.

At the very moment my brain suspected something was amiss down there, I heard girls screaming and squealing out in our halls. Before I could react, one of those freaky-looking creatures appeared at our second floor door demanding our panties. These demands came from pin-headed, stocking-covered mouths of the opposite sex who had invaded our domain and with lots of help from traitors. They yelled, "Gimme some skivvies! Gimme some skivvies, right now!"

"Oh, dear Lord. Oh, good heavens. Let me get rid of this blasted hairnet," I said to myself. It was too late. On came the light and there we were in our cute little baby doll pajamas, but I, with that hideous hairnet, was not concerned about the demand for panties. In fact, he probably wanted to withdraw his demand the minute he flipped on that light. I'll never know, because he fled before Joyce and I could feel flattered. Just think how sweetsy-cute I would have been if I had been forewarned. But, no, I'm sure I've been at the forefront of everyone's memory for the last fifty-three years as the dud with the hairnet. Others had more exotic experiences.

It just so happened that my light-hearted date had been a part of the plot but didn't want to tell me and risk my tipping off my girlfriends. He also attempted to convince me that he didn't want me to be accused of knowing about the plan.

I later married that carefree character and continued to chide him for many years for his choice not to warn me before that little panty raid experience. He had no idea that my choosing to give up some skivvies was really a lesser evil than being caught wearing a you-know-what.

Marcella Wortham Prehler—Class of 1938
1934-38 were years during the height of the Depression. My sister, Alyne (who graduated in 1937), and I shared one meager wardrobe; yet, frequently I would see several of our dresses coming and going to class worn by girls who stayed at the same house. I also wore their dresses. Today I wonder how my parents did it. We never received a delinquent tuition notice.

Chapter 87
AN INFLUENTIAL VISIT

Robert G. Cowser—Class of 1953—Saltillo

Feeling somewhat anxious as I stepped off the shuttle bus that gray January day, my lightweight jacket did little to protect me from the damp chill that permeated the atmosphere. The bus I had boarded just a few minutes before made a run each weekday taking college students from East Texas State Teachers College to and from Commerce High School. During my junior year, I was enrolled in an education course required to earn a teaching certificate. Observing classes at the high school that day would be my first such experience. I arrived after the last class period of the day had already begun.

It was forty-nine years before Homeland Security legislation; I was not even required to register at the principal's office as a visitor. I had been given a room number, and it was my responsibility to find the room on the first floor where Mrs. Tula Milford was conducting a ninth-grade English class. I entered the room with trepidation and took a seat near the door, which was located at the back of the room.

When I enrolled at East Texas State Teachers College two years before, I was considering journalism as a major. In our rural community, my only previous contact with a reporter was with a neighbor who submitted a column to the *Hopkins County Echo*, a weekly published in Sulphur Springs. Her report consisted of references to out-of-town visitors who attended funeral services and other items of local interest. Occasionally a student from the high school would give her a list of the names of the officers elected by a certain class for that year. This information would appear in the following issue of the *Echo*.

My parents, who had no formal education, expected me to earn a teacher's certificate. Almost all the people my parents knew who had gone to college had become teachers in public elementary or secondary schools. Exceptions were the Sparks brothers, who earned Ph.D.'s and taught college classes—one in history at Texas Woman's University, the other in English at Duke. These brothers were considered so eccentric by the people of the community that they were hardly role models. For my parents, the concept that anyone who grew up in Saltillo, where I graduated from high school, would or could become an attorney, a medical doctor, or a dentist was remote. Besides, no one had the money to finance a student in the schools that educated professionals. Because of their expectations, I never told my parents that I was considering a major in journalism. They would never have related to my glamorized idea of news gathering and reporting, which was based primarily on radio drama and the movies. Although in my sophomore year I began to follow the curriculum required for teacher certification, I still was not convinced that I wanted to become a teacher. As a junior, I found myself on the teacher-certification track, preparing to observe classes at the only high school in Commerce.

The nervousness I had experienced earlier that morning began to subside once I took a seat in Mrs. Milford's classroom. Neither she nor the students appeared to notice that I had entered. Tula Milford was a woman in her early sixties. She wore rimmed glasses, and her gray hair, which appeared to be rather long, was pulled into a bun. She wore a gray dress with a broad white collar. When I entered the room, she was sitting behind her desk. Because her glance never met mine, I assumed that she was accustomed to observers entering the room after she had begun class.

Except for the sound of Mrs. Milford's voice and the soft, intermittent hissing sound of the steam radiators, the room was quiet. It felt comfortably warm in contrast to the chill I experienced immediately upon stepping off the bus. The windows of the classroom looked out on an enclosed space surfaced with asphalt. The view of a red brick wall appeared stark in its plainness; I soon realized, however, the business of that particular classroom did not depend on accouterments.

Open before her was a textbook from which Mrs. Milford was reading Edwin Arlington Robinson's "Miniver Cheevy." When she finished reading the poem, she chuckled about the folly of Cheevy's wishing he had been born in another century. She pointed out the unappealing sounds of the first syllable of Cheevy's name and commented on the effort required to pronounce "Miniver Cheevy" as opposed to the relatively less effort required to pronounce a name like Allen, for example. Mrs. Milford pointed out that Robinson must have equated that difficulty with the difficulty Cheevy faced in coping with his life.

These fourteen-year-olds were attentive while Mrs. Milford read "Richard Cory," a second poem by Edwin Arlington Robinson. One student questioned why a man with wealth and good looks would ever take his own life. Most of the students were attentive, and several participated in the discussion. In my mind, I contrasted the behavior of these students with the disruptive behavior of some of my former classmates just a few years before when I was in the ninth grade.

After Mrs. Milford called a halt to the class discussion, she allowed the students to work independently on reading and writing assignments for the week. I observed that most of them opened notebooks and began to write. Others were reading library books. One by one, several of the students raised their hands. Mrs. Milford motioned for each to come to her desk at intervals. Each took a sheet of paper or a notebook with him/her. The class period ran its course in a most orderly fashion.

As I noted the faded navy blue skirt of the girl seated across the aisle from me and the scuffed brown loafers of a boy in the desk in front of the girl, I experienced a feeling of appreciation for the concept of public education. I suspected the skirt the girl wore had belonged to an older sister or to a cousin and that the boy's loafers were the only pair of shoes he owned. Yet these students, whose parents probably paid less in school taxes than the majority of citizens in the state, had an opportunity to learn from a teacher as qualified and as dedicated as a teacher in a private school. The parents of these two students probably could not have afforded the tuition charged at a private school.

I left Mrs. Milford's classroom that day with the feeling that I wanted to continue my pursuit of a teaching certificate. Perhaps, after all, I could find personal satisfaction as a classroom teacher. As I boarded the bus that would take me back to the campus, I realized that the goal of becoming a teacher was no longer influenced only by what my parents expected, but one that I myself was now engaged in.

Chapter 88

Track Meet

Ron Mcneill—Class of 1964—Kemp

I t was the end of May 1964. Final exams were over, and Commerce would be a ghost town in a matter of hours. The roads out of town were crowded with cars eagerly headed toward Dallas and all points away from East Texas State. This was the "norm" each year for thousands of students.

However, this year the situation was a little different for a few student-athletes who made up part of the East Texas track team. We had recently won the Lone Star Conference track and field championship, and some of us had qualified to run at the National Track and Field Meet.

This is where the good news-bad news began to work on the "lucky' few. The good news was that we had an opportunity to run at the prestigious National Track Meet. The bad news is that the track meet this year was in Sioux Falls, South Dakota, and Dr. Jesse Hawthorne and the East Texas administration, in their wisdom to save money, decided we would drive, rather than fly.

We spent the end of May and the first part of June on the E.T. campus. However, most of the campus facilities closed down. All of the cafeterias closed. No food service of any kind was available. So, three times a day we made a trek to downtown Commerce, to have breakfast, lunch and dinner at the City Café. The college picked up the tab for the meals, but after a week of eating this kind of food, we were ready for something different.

The time finally arrived for us to "hit the road" for the two-day drive to Sioux Falls. We took two station wagons, and we alternated driving to make the trip a little less traumatic. Mr. Delmar Brown was our head coach. He made the motel arrangements in a town in Kansas for our over-night stop.

He had asked someone at the motel about his team using a local track facility so we could run some of the kinks out after the long drive. We went to the motel and changed into our running attire. Coach Brown got the directions to the track, and we were off for our daily workout.

After driving around for some time and getting more directions, we finally came to the track. It was not a high school running track, but rather, a dirt track that the locals used to race cars on the week-ends. It was a wonder we did not break an ankle. We jogged around the oval avoiding the deepest ruts as best we could.

The next morning we began the final leg of our journey to Sioux Falls, where we found the hotel and all of the accommodations to be extremely nice. The athletic stadium and track were in excellent condition.

The track meet took two days to complete, and our team represented E.T. very well. Several individuals won medals, and the mile relay team won first place at the National Track and Field Meet.

With some success and a lot of fun memories, we said good bye to Sioux Falls and headed back to Commerce, Texas. Our long drive back was uneventful.

I would like to note that Dr. Jesse Hawthorne and his entourage did arrive at the track meet very well rested, after their flight from Dallas.

I think I remember his saying, "Rank has its privilege."

And, so it does!

L. J. Fite—Class of 1940

In 1938-1940 very few students had cars. Our dates were mostly trips to the Library, the Goulash Wednesday night dances, and an occasional movie. One memorable evening, soon after we met, I asked Margaret to go to the movies. I had not a penny to my name. I counted on seeing one of my friends on the walk to town.

When we arrived, I allowed Margaret to cool her heels in front of the theater while I talked to my buddy about a twenty-five cent loan. The friend emptied his pockets—only two dimes—then he pulled out his handkerchief, and a nickel fell out. The loan was made, and Margaret and I enjoyed the two-for-twenty-five cent movie.

Chapter 89
MUSIC, MUSIC, MUSIC

Patricia West Root—Class of 1972—Mesquite

I spent much of my time on the ETSU campus in the Music Building. I made many great friends there. Most of the music majors were like a happy family. We were together in band, choir, classes, and so forth. The band was great, and I enjoyed watching the marching musicians at the football games. I spent time every night in the music rooms practicing for voice or piano lessons. I performed in several operas, which were also time consuming. I loved every minute of it. Well, maybe not 7:30 a.m. music theory classes. I decided not to get into the social sorority life because I just didn't have the time. Instead, I joined the music sorority, Mu Phi Epsilon.

Joy McDaniel was my roommate in good old Smith Hall. We remain best friends and still do things together. Our first summer at ETSU, we decided to go to the patio in the middle of the dorm and get a tan like the other girls. I still remember the Black girls at the dorm laughing at us and saying that they didn't have to roast in the sun because they already had a tan. We went every day for several weeks. As the summer went by, we noticed that the other girls turned a golden brown. However, we only got redder and redder. That was the end of our tanning episode.

One of my fun memories is of the big hill across from the Music Building. When it snowed, we got huge pieces of cardboard and slid down the hill. Now, a large building has replaced the hill.

Joy and Rodney Vike married, forcing me to find a new roommate. It is hard to replace your best friend. I moved on campus to Binnion Hall. Of course, it is no longer a dorm, but I had so much fun being in the middle of everything. The rooms were large, and my classes were close. Integration was just beginning to take hold in most universities. I remember that I had never really been around Black people before. I had a Black suite mate and found her to be very sweet.

My true love from high school and life is Randy Root. He was in the Air Force my freshman year, and I wrote him every day. Each day I got a letter back from Grand Forks AFB. I still remember how exciting it was to look into my mailbox and find those precious letters. We decided to get married on his next leave (nine months later). We've been married for forty years now. I went to North Dakota with him for a year; then he got orders for Viet Nam.

I went back to ETSU and moved into Smith Hall because I couldn't afford an apartment by myself. We had curfews. Randy came home on leave and wanted to get a hotel room for a couple of nights before he had to go to Viet Nam. I remember the house moms weren't going to let me go without permission from my parents or guardian. I explained that he was my husband and could be considered my guardian. He came back to the dorm with a letter he had signed giving me permission to leave the dorm for two nights. Finally, they let me go with him without any problems. We can laugh about it now, but at the time, I thought I would die if they didn't let me sign out. I was so young and in love.

When I left E.T. to get married, everybody was wearing dresses or pant-suits to class. When I came back a year later, the Viet Nam era had arrived. Students were in protest mode. Students wore torn jeans and tie-dyed shirts with holes in them. Of course, the hair was long, straight, and parted down the middle. I remember getting so angry at the callous remarks of the protest-type students who referred to our Viet Nam soldiers as baby killers along with other horrible remarks. My husband was one of them. I tried to tell them that if he had not enlisted, he would have been drafted. Many soldiers didn't have a choice unless they went to Canada. My husband was too patriotic and honorable for that.

Randy sent me his allotment check, and I managed to pay tuition and live on it. I saved enough money for his tuition in the fall. When he got out of the Air Force, we lived in Mitchell Hall married housing and existed on the G.I. Bill. Later, we moved to Mesquite, and I finished college by commuting. I graduated with a teaching degree in music education. I feel that I got a wonderful education.

I taught for twenty-five years, took out some years to be a mom to our son, and retired six years ago. I loved teaching music.

Chapter 90

ONE LION SAID TO ANOTHER LION

Nelma Dodd—Class of 1970—Commerce

Note: This is a recap of the interview of Tommie Dodd and the subsequent story written by Kenneth King and Jim Steely, which appeared in the November 1974 edition of *ETSU Special*.

In 1971, some individuals at East Texas State University became fed up with the apathetic attitude displayed by more and more members of the student body. A campus fraternity decided it was time to do something. They adopted the idea of putting a real live lion on the field during a football game scheduled for that upcoming Saturday afternoon. Thus, Tommie Dodd would debut as the first Lion mascot at ETSU.

News of the feature began to spread. Tommie visited with his grandmother and shared with her the idea of his showing up at the next game dressed as a lion. It didn't take long to convince *Mammaw* that, with her help, some of the apathy among ETSU students could vanish. Tommie and his grandmother went shopping to purchase a pattern, some lion-colored fabric, yarn for the mane, and other necessities they might need. Within a short time, his idea came to fruition. The idea went over so well that after his first appearance, several people asked Tommie to reappear. For the remainder of the 1971 football season, and seasons to come. Tommie helped the apathy disappear.

The Klondike student attended all ETSU home football games—and most of the out-of-town games—after beginning his lion career as a freshman. Youngsters often tried to pull on his tail, which needed replacing several times. Tommie carried a bag of candy to home games for the children.

This new venture also had some hazards. The cheerleaders brought a live lion cub to the last two homecoming games during Tommie's college career. He carried the eighty pounds of fighting, clawing, and biting lion around the stadium. "Cats love fur and yarn," Tommie said, explaining that his costume hair consisted of yarn. The cubs would chew on this hair, and they even nicked his nose a few times.

"Little girls, especially, liked the cheerleaders. Many parents come to the games just to let their children see the cheerleaders and the lion mascot." Considered by many fans as one of the cheerleaders, Tommie undertook the part entirely on his own. "I hope the university will adopt the idea of the mascot and give it support," Tommie said. He gave the lion suit to his fraternity following his last performance. He said they could choose the next lion.

Tommie Joe Dodd graduated from ETSU in August of 1974 with a bachelor's degree in Agriculture Education. He ended the interview with this statement: "I've loved every minute of it."

Coy P. Stewart—Class of 1939

My favorite story about my college days was one of the assignments I had to do as a Friars Club pledge. On a dark, rainy, and stormy night, several of the pledges were driven to a country cemetery. We were given a flashlight, a list of names, and instructions to find these names on the tombstones and record when they were born and when they died. Then we had to walk the two or three miles back to the dorm!

Chapter 91

WORLD WAR II GRADUATION
PROTOCOL

Morton Richard Schroeder—Class of 1964

B ill Morris was a first semester senior majoring in pre-med at East Texas
State Teachers College in the fall of 1941.

When Bill heard about the attack on Pearl Harbor on December 7, 1941,
he immediately volunteered for the armed services. Before he left school,
he met with officials of the college and informed them that he would not be
returning to finish his senior year.

Morris went on active duty with the Army, becoming an aviation cadet.
Sometime during the next year while he was in flight school, he received a
notice from the college that because of how much coursework he had passed
and how close he had been to graduating, the college had decided to grant
him his Bachelor of Science degree, 1942, even though he had never actually
finished.

It is not known if this were a common policy at the college, which graduated many students who had entered service during the war when they had
not finished their coursework, or if this procedure was done only for Bill
Morris. Whether other colleges and universities had a similar policy is also
not known. After the war when Morris was no longer in active service, he
went by the college and picked up his diploma.

Bill Morris was accepted into medical school and became John William
Morris, M.D. Dr. Morris practiced medicine and lived in Greenville, Texas,
with his wife Mary Lou for over fifty years.

Chapter 92
SALAD DAYS

Earl Stubbs—Class of 1957—Naples

*A*ll work and no play makes Jack a dull boy is an old axiom best deleted from academic circles for the simple reason that some students take it a smidgeon too far. As an example, take the incident that occurred during the fifties as I neared graduation.

The Tejas Club elected me president that year. The Paragon Club chose Bill Jacobs, who was by then my brother-in-law, as their president. We were friends and former roommates before we were relatives. To complicate matters even more, another close friend, Ray Ransom, was president of the student body.

So there we were, two social club presidents and the president of the E.T. student body, finding ourselves in a weary state due to excessive study and the responsibilities attendant with our roles in college affairs. To reduce our fatigue and prepare for the final sprint to the end of the semester, we decided to *make a run*.

Unlike the Commerce of recent years, finding a cool beer for medicinal purposes meant driving across the state line north of Paris to purchase beer with 3.2% alcohol content or driving twice the distance to Red Coleman's in Dallas to get the real deal. Since I had a hot-looking 1950 Ford, we chose the leisurely drive to Dallas, even though Bill and Ray belonged to the social club that forbade imbibing alcohol at any of their functions.

After completing the drive, making our purchase, and starting therapy on the way back, we found ourselves in Commerce near the witching hour of midnight. While cruising the downtown area, we noticed a dedicated student going about his job of delivering produce to the grocery stores. We will call him Artis. Upon witnessing this revelation, Ray pointed out that we needed some produce. Bill and I steadfastly attempted to dissuade him, but Ray was very persuasive. When Artis made a delivery and drove on to the next stop, we grabbed a couple of wooden crates of vegetables and sped away.

We drove to Bill's and Ray's clubhouse, where we had a gay old time dumping lettuce and carrots into the beds of sleeping students. After we tired of our revelry, we called it a night, having no idea what happened to the veggies.

Nothing further came of the incident until I walked out of the downtown barbershop a few days later. Waiting for me was an officious appearing man wearing a gun and a badge. He asked me if the car belonged to me. I answered in the affirmative. Then he invited me to his office for a visit and once more, I acquiesced. When we arrived, I was surprised to find my good friends Bill and Ray waiting for me to join them. A strange man with a serious demeanor was in the room along with Artis.

The police officer opened the discussion by relating that a witness saw my car near the theft of some produce from a grocery store. Since my car was a special model, black and white Ford, there could be little doubt as to the owner. By this time, my confidence level had plummeted.

After explaining who we were and how close to graduation I was, it occurred to me that some serious diverting was required to salvage my four years of college. I explained to the policeman and the grocery wholesaler, "Sirs, I am in no way denying ownership of the car. I am not denying the involvement of my car in the theft; however, we were all asleep at the clubhouse when the theft occurred."

The two men glanced at each other. I continued, "As you know, this is essentially a crime-free city. Not only do we not lock our cars, we often leave the keys in the ignition. Those of us who have cars make them available to other students for trips to Chig's, the City Café, or the library. Any one of a dozen students could have used my car to pick up the produce as a joke."

Observing the demeanor of our accusers, I could see light at the end of the tunnel. The police officer said, "Now boys, we don't want you to take the blame if someone else is responsible."

Seeing a narrow opening, I quickly answered, "Sirs, we do not expect this gentleman to shoulder the loss of his produce. May I make a suggestion? We will gladly pay for the produce at this time and handle the theft internally."

The owner of the grocery wholesaler spoke, "Boys, I don't want you to be out any money if you didn't take the produce."

"Not to worry," said Bill. "It will be a simple matter for us to find out who took the produce and recoup our money. Is this plan satisfactory with you gentlemen?"

The policeman and the owner put their heads together and agreed to our proposal. We quickly pooled our resources and came up with the $15 needed to buy our salvation. As we prepared to leave, the owner, with a tear in his eye, said, "Boys, you were willing to take the blame for something you didn't do for the sake of your friends. It is a pleasure for me to know you. If any of you find yourselves in need of funds before you graduate, please let me know."

We all assured him that we would and casually strolled away.

John R. Willingham—Class of 1940

One of my many part-time jobs at E.T. was grading freshman themes for Tom McNeal, and a consequent vow was that, though I liked literature well enough, I would never teach composition, like those poor profs at E.T. Famous last words, for throughout my long career in the classroom, I always had some involvement with composition—including a term as director of freshman-sophomore English at the University of Kansas and the authorship of two books on compositions.

Chapter 93

ON THE COLLEGE FARM

Eddy Lynn Hamilton—Class of 1985—Tom Bean

My high school Ag teacher, Jim Rodgers, helped me make my way to E.T. in 1971. I had always worked with hogs in high school and had champion and grand champion livestock. How did I end up in dairy?

I lived in the Dairy Dorm and had duties of milking and tending to the calves. Dr. Horton was in charge of the dairy, and Shorty took care of the rest of the duty assignments. Mr. Neal had a son-in-law who helped sometimes in the dairy. He was mean to the cows, and they hated him. When I had to milk with him, the cows became uneasy and would not give much milk.

Shorty took care of us, and we took care of him. We brought him beer and kept it in the dorm so his mother would not see him drinking. Dr. Horton did not like our having beer in the dorm.

Johnnie and I were clean freaks. We repainted the dorm, put up some girly posters, and kept the barn spotless. One time my girlfriend came to visit while I was milking and went into the dorm to wait. Dr. Horton came in. My girlfriend was drinking a beer and reading a *Playboy* magazine.

Needless to say, we got in trouble for that and had to go see Buck to keep our jobs. A. C. "Buck" Hughes was the MAN in the Ag Department. Fortunately, he was absent at the time. When Buck returned, he sent Mr. Neal to tell us to shape up. He took all the beer we had and told us we could have no more girls in the dorm. Shorty left and Butch Schneider took his place at the dairy. He and I had gone to Howe High School together.

There used to be a bookshelf in the Dairy Barn Dorm with all the Farm Boys' names written on it. I am sure it went the way all the buildings that comprised the farm—bulldozed and hauled off.

Dale Bullock and Robert Winters lived in the Chicken Barn Dorm. Dr. Wolf was their Manager, and Robert Flusche was a graduate assistant. Their duties were the hardest. We had to help with the eggs. The worst part was cleaning out the houses. Robert was working on a process to turn chicken manure into feed. I am not sure how that turned out.

In the Beef Barn Dorm were Joe Stokes, Rayford Gibson, and Calhoun. Mr. Neal was the manager, and Jackie Lunsford took care of the rest of the chore assignments. Joe spent a lot of time with us at the dairy. Joe was our father figure. He was a great friend.

Mr. Duckworth had general duties over all the rest of the Farm. Duck was the greatest. He was always singing and whistling. He had a great sense of humor. Once we had a Holstein bred to a Brahma bull, and the calf was huge. We had it in the Horse Barn, and it tore up two stalls the morning it was born. Duck was trying to get a rope on it so we could get it moved, and it almost beat him to death.

We helped with all the chores on the farm also. We built fences, hauled hay, cut silage, and performed other related chores. The silage pit was a tough job, not so much when we put the silage in but when we took it out to feed. We had to fork the silage out by hand to feed all the cows at the dairy. We milked 120 cows on a regular basis every day.

The farm had an old 1956 Chevy hay truck. Johnnie and I would take the truck down to the college motor pool every Saturday morning to fill it up with gas for the week's chores. We did everything out of that old truck. Saturday after chores, we would take the truck to the back of the Dairy Barn. Everyone who had a car would come and siphon enough gas to get to town for the night.

At some point in time, the farm furnished the milk, eggs, chicken, and beef for the college cafeteria. We processed chickens for one of the classes with Dr. Wolf. Some of the football team would come out to get milk and eggs from us.

We ate downtown during the times when the chow halls closed. One of the places was named the Chat N Chew. The owners were good to the Farm Boys.

A group of us rode in the local rodeos. We all traveled together most of the time. We usually took a group to help with the All Girl Rodeo in Paris, Texas. The college had a rodeo every year. That was a lot of fun.

I left E.T. after my first year because I was having too much fun to keep up with my grades. The E.T. Farm was my first work experience away from home. I missed a great opportunity by not sticking it out, and it took me a long time to start back. I came back to E.T. after serving in the Air Force and graduated with a degree in Marketing.

Working for Texas Instruments, I received a promotion as soon as I got my degree. I worked there for twenty-five years. The training and experience that I received at T.I. helped me to involve myself in the community where I grew up. I spent many years as a coach and administrator for the youth sports association. I served a term as mayor and two terms on the City Council of Howe. My wife; son, James; and two brothers are also graduates of E.T. All are doing well in their chosen professions. I always wanted to be a ranch foreman. I never got there, but when I go by some of the big ranches near Denton, I still get the itch.

Herbert L. LaGrone—Class of 1939

My most vivid memory of E.T. and Commerce is truly a *community,* defined by Webster as "a unified body of individuals. We were together as a group guided by purpose, hope, and a future. The Depression may have produced some amount of humility and egalitarianism. Excesses for show or pretense was non-existent.

There was an openness and optimism. A camaraderie bonded by diversity and adversity.

We experienced freedom and trust. We enjoyed respect and recognition. We had help when needed and caring always. We shared development at a good age and time.

There were many memorable experiences and amusing incidents at E.T. I remember during the scarf dance at Mayfete when the wind sent the scarves high into the air. The dancers thought they were exposed. Times have surely changed, and I have no idea why I remember such silly events fifty years later.

Chapter 94
THE FIRST GOLD BLAZER

Sherman K. Burns—Class of 1976—Mesquite

Citation

"Sherman K. Burns, in recognition of your contribution to the East Texas State University as a member of the Alumni Association's Board of Directors, and as membership chairman and first vice president of the Dallas County Chapter of the East Texas State University Alumni Association, and in respect for your professional accomplishments and the honour you have reflected upon your Alma Mater, by the virtue of the authority vested in the President of the East Texas State University Alumni Association, and upon the recommendation of the Board of Directors of the East Texas State University Alumni Association, you are cited with the Gold Blazer Award for alumni who have graduated from East Texas State University within the last 10 years and who have made significant contribution to the University, its programs and Alumni Association."

Signed
Joe Mark McKenzie, Ph.D.
Executive Director
ETSU Alumni Association

Signed
John R. Armstrong
President
ETSU Alumni Association

. . . and so started the Gold Blazer Award of the East Texas State University Alumni Association. Joe Mark's original intent for the award was to inspire younger alumni to get involved in the alumni association and to recognize their accomplishments along with their professional undertakings. Joe Mark commented to me that he wanted it to be an outstanding alumni award for those who graduated fewer than ten years previously. He desired that it be given during the homecoming luncheon alongside the traditional Outstanding Alumnus award.

The honor evolved over the years. Its less than ten years' criteria has gone by the wayside, and the award now has its own dinner held separately from the homecoming festivities. Fortunately, it has retained the most important objective to honor and recognize people who have made significant contributions to the now Texas A&M University-Commerce Alumni Association.

My story of the Gold Blazer started back in the early 80s when Joe Mark was trying to organize and revitalize some local chapters of the ETSU alumni association and sent out letters to alumni soliciting interest.

I attended a couple of meetings, and the next thing I knew I was not only the membership chairman and first vice president of the Dallas County Chapter but also on the Board of Directors of the Alumni Association.

We accomplished much by setting up committees to update records of alumni located in the Dallas area. Joe Mark asked members of the Dallas Chapter to help provide him with phone books from the Dallas area so that students working in the alumni office in Commerce could help as well (no internet back then).

Joe Mark was going to teach a class at the Dallas campus of ETSU a week later, so we could drop them off at that time. I decided to stop by the ATT phone store located in North Park Mall and pick up one phone book. When I stopped by the store and told them what I wanted and why, they let me have as many as I wanted. I decided to take thirty-six phone books. Wrapped in bundles of twelve, they had to be carried one bundle at a time to my car.

When I stopped by the Dallas campus and found Joe Mark, he could not believe that I had actually picked up thirty-six phone books. When we put them in the trunk of his car, they weighed it down so much he said that he had always wanted a "low rider."

One of the programs I was most proud of was in the spring of 1984. With assistance from Sandra Crane, we helped place almost one hundred undergraduate students into summer jobs in the Dallas Metroplex area.

I feel honored to have been one of the first two recipients, along with Sandra Crane, of the Gold Blazer award.

Chapter 95
IN, OUT, AND ALL ABOUT

John M. Elkins—1949/1950—Commerce

At ten years of age, twins Homer Earl and John Merl Elkins spent a lot of time on campus at East Texas State Teachers College.

During World War II, there were special governmental programs teaching administration, supply, and accounting to members of the Women's Army Corps (WACs) on the E.T. campus. There were almost one hundred WAC's registered for classes.

The WACs were housed in East Dormitory on Monroe Street. We twins set up a shoeshine stand in front of the Chatter Box eatery across from East Dorm. After school on Fridays and Saturdays, we spent many hours shining the ladies shoes for their Saturday Military Inspection.

We sold *Saturday Evening Post* and *Ladies Home Journal* magazines, as well as *GRIT* newspapers, to the WACs, college students, and faculty. One of the benefits was the boarding houses around campus which fed super lunches. Once in a while the two little boys, usually with dirty bare feet, were invited in for a free meal.

Many times when we went to the President's home selling magazines, President Whitley's wife would invite us in their home for a coke and cookies. As a young little boy, I vividly remember meeting the Honorable Sam Rayburn, United States Representative of the Fourth District of Texas when he visited the ETSTC campus in 1941. In 1961, I had the honor to participate at a meeting with Speaker of the House Sam Rayburn at the Georgia Bar Association Convention at Savannah, Georgia that occurred on May 30, 1961, twenty years after my first meeting with "Mr. Sam."

In 1949 when I returned from my first stint in the military, I lived with my parents south of Commerce on our farm. It was located a tad south of the Sterling Hart Hobby Farm. I had a 1948 Harley Davidson motorcycle, which I drove to and from ET. I passed the G.I. Village everyday as I went to and from class and/or any other place from the farm while attending my first college courses at East Texas State Teachers College.

I met my sweetheart in Cooper, Texas. We set our marriage for June 1950 after she graduated from Cooper High School. The G.I. Bill and part time jobs in and around Commerce were little to none, and I knew it would not support a wife. I withdrew from E.T. and accepted employment with Dallas Power and Light Company as a substation operator in the Oak Cliff section of Dallas, Texas.

Meanwhile, I was a Technical Sergeant in the United States Air Force Reserve and assigned to the 443rd Troop Carrier Group at Hensley Field, Grand Prairie, Texas, as an aircraft flight engineer. My unit was called to active duty on May 1, 1951. Within nine months I found myself in the war flying over Korea.

After retirement with twenty-six years in the United States Air Force, at Perrin Air Force Base, Denison, Texas, I enrolled at Grayson County College. While enrolled, I was offered a position as Director of Veterans Affairs. I completed an Associate of Fine Arts degree at Grayson County College 1974. My work schedule was adjusted, and I was able to continue my higher education goals.

I immediately enrolled at Southeastern Oklahoma State University and completed a Bachelor of Arts in Education. I was certified as a high school teacher in Oklahoma and Texas. I enrolled in graduate school and earned a Master of Behavioral Studies degree. I was certified as a professional and educational counselor in the States of Texas and Oklahoma. Meanwhile, I was employed at Grayson County College as counselor during evening classes.

I returned to ETSU in the spring semester of 1981, and I enrolled in graduate courses offered on campus at Grayson County College, Denison, Texas. I continued employment on the faculty of Grayson County College faculty where I was promoted on the college faculty as a Counselor and Director of Testing. In 1988 I retired from Grayson County College.

In 1972 I volunteered and became commissioned as an officer in the Texas Military Forces. I served in Military Police duties from Company,

Battalion, and Group staff levels. Upon retirement in 2005, I transferred to the Texas Military Forces Honorary Reserves. On June 5, 2005, Governor Rick Perry, promoted me to the rank of brevet Brigadier General in the National Guard of the State of Texas.

The many experiences and quality education I received and training in the R.O.T.C. program at East Texas State was a pivotal point in my life, one I am proud to have been able to do.

Betty Lancaster—Class of 1974

The year was 1955. I had just graduated high school from a rural school in Fannin County and began my academic career at ET the following month. I signed up for a Freshman English class with Dr. Butler, who had been a Presbyterian missionary in China. From the moment of the beginning of the first class things moved rapidly, and I found myself attempting to learn things I had never heard of before about verbs, adverbs, adjectives, and diagramming sentences. Dr. Butler was all business, never cracking a smile and from the moment he entered the classroom, he began his rapid-fire lectures, pausing occasionally to question a student about the assignment for that day. I always made sure I was in my seat well before the time class was scheduled to begin as those coming in late were orally reprimanded.

One morning Dr. Butler entered the classroom carrying his briefcase as usual with the never changing, "all business" look on his face. He laid his briefcase on the desk, opened it, and took out a file of papers. Then he looked out over the class, letting his gaze fall on a girl sitting in the front row and said, "Miss, if you will close the gates of hell, we will begin class." A shocked silence fell over the class, and apparently, the female student sitting in the front row complied with his request, as the class then began. With much hard work, I managed to make a "C" in the class.

I later took time out from school when I married a fellow student. The "C" from Dr. Butler's freshman English class was the only "C" on my transcript when I graduated with honors in May of 1974 with a Bachelor of Arts Degree.

Chapter 96

FALL, 1948

Mary Beth Rabb Tuck—Class of 1951—Point

I t was September 1948, and time to put summer behind and register for E.T. courses. In addition to classes, other exciting things were in the wind. Women's social clubs would have "rush." So, I needed new dresses, a fancy hat, and high heel shoes for teas and other events. Rush teas were most often held in the beautiful homes of prominent Commerce women. Freshman girls lucky enough to receive an invitation were thrilled when they discovered one of the sought-after invitations in their mailboxes.

My sister Bobbye had preceded me to E.T., had lived in East Dorm, and had pledged Les Choisites, better known as "Lacys." When I arrived, the Lacys living in East Dorm were happy to welcome the younger sister of their Lacy sister, so they took me under their wing. I already knew which club I would join, the Les Choisites, but I dressed up and visited other clubs who sent me an invitation. Finally, the time came, and we waited for the "bid." Of course I got one from the Lacys and accepted.

Hazing was permitted, but it was very light and fun. One day, I got caught in the ballroom of the Student Union Building, and a Lacy sister handed me a peanut and told me to push it across the floor of the room with my nose. I did as told and pushed it a few feet before attracting a crowd. It all ended with much laughter and my having a brown nose.

In addition to the social scene, there were classes to attend that fall. When I walked into my first course in chemistry with Dr. B. L. Williams, I didn't recognize anyone among the fifty or so other students in the class. Dr. Williams briefly greeted us, picked up a piece of chalk, and began to write on the board as he lectured. I took notes as fast as I could, but none of it made sense. I was totally lost in chemistry class. And, I was lethal in the lab, saved only by my partner and lab instructor. My high school in Point did not offer chemistry and scheduled only a little math. Convinced I couldn't make it, I went to Dr. Williams' office and begged him to let me drop the class.

He said, "Stay in the class and learn what you can. Then, it will be easier to pass next semester if you have to take it over."

So, I stuck it out. Thanks to Dr. Williams, a wonderful and caring professor, I finally made it through all the four chemistry courses I needed to satisfy the requirements for my degree.

On the first class day in the fall 1948, I met the Home Economics Department faculty, Miss Mary Booth, Miss Orpa Dennis, and Miss Anna Maxwell. At first we were all afraid of Miss Booth, the department head, who also taught the foods classes. Often one of the students would get sternly corrected by her and end up crying. Miss Booth was strict but made sure we learned what we needed to know about food preparation.

On one occasion plans were being made to prepare dinner for the graduating home economics students, and she asked who would make ten pie crusts. I held up my hand.

Why? Why in the world had I held up my hand to volunteer to make ten pie crusts? I wondered. *The only one I ever made in class was a disaster. I must have lost my mind.*

Anyway, I was selected to make pie crusts. Arriving in the kitchen on the appointed day, I lit all the ovens, mixed the dough, rolled it out, put it in pans, and baked the ten pie crusts in five gas range ovens. When they were done, I removed them and stored them safely away. By then, I was exhausted but made sure the kitchen was clean before I returned to East Dorm from the Science Building. The next morning, Miss Booth met me at door of the kitchen lab.

She said, "Did you know that you left two pie crusts in the oven all night long? I came in early this morning to find smoke and pie crusts burnt to a crisp."

It's a wonder I didn't burn the building down! Scared out of my wits, I turned white as a sheet. I expected her to fly into me with rage, but, surprisingly, she was calm. She said that the rest of the pie crusts were very nice, so I felt better about my carelessness; however, I'll never forget that incident. Miss Booth always seemed to like me, and I liked her, but I always "walked a straight line'" in her classroom and lab.

Miss Dennis's classes were enjoyable because she encouraged me to do my best. In one of her classes, I designed a Christmas poster, a picture of which appeared in the *East Texan,* the campus newspaper. Later, when I was a senior, Miss Dennis let my roommate and me bring our laundry to the department to wash and dry. While we washed, we did chores for Miss Dennis around the department.

The professor of my literature class, Miss Adelle Clark, was another favorite teacher of mine. She loved teaching and cared for her students, encouraging each and every one of them. On several occasions, she invited us into her home for a party. I can still quote parts of the *Canterbury Tales*, especially when I have had a couple of drinks!

Every semester, including two summer semesters, I took a full course load. The work and study were hard, but in addition to classes, there were so many fun things to do on campus. We enjoyed Western week in the fall, hay rides, dancing in the Student Union Building between classes, homecoming, and football games in Memorial Stadium, so named for the many E.T. alumni killed in World War II, and the names listed on the plaque that is still there. Listed on that plaque is my brother, Harold Rabb.

Charles Paul Sheppard—Class of 1940

Recollections of my days at E.T. are somewhat like a collage in which experiences and events blend in incongruous relationships suggestive of that period of my life. Recalled impressions include playing for college dances along with Jim Clark and his dance orchestra called "The Southern Gentlemen" and later with Dr. Gilbert Waller and his "East Texas Dance Orchestra."

The beautiful and gracious formal dances were held in the magnificent setting offered by the reading room of the Library. Members of the Friars Club, of which I was one, the Ogima, Artema, Kalir, Toowanoowe, Les Choisites, and Marpesa clubs were always well represented at these functions.

My memories include the exciting football games (and championships won) during the 1936-40 period, playing in Professor Carl Doenier's E.T. Marching Band at the halves, and the commanding presence of Robert Cox who stood tall as the drum major of that band.

Chapter 97
AS THE WORLD TURNED IN
SOUTH APARTMENTS

Lou Carol May Rutherford—Class of 1962—Paris

W e moved to South Apartments in the fall of 1961, our senior years
at East Texas State University. That was also our first year of
married life.

Important events, such as JFK making his mark on history and John Glenn's
space flight, occurred during that year, but I, being a newlywed, was much
more interested in daily happenings. Little did I know that our stay in South
Apartments would leave me with some of my fondest memories.

South Apartments lay about a half mile south of the main campus, off
Culver Street. The ten brick buildings, old World War II Army barracks
moved from Camp Maxey near Paris were lined up in military formation.
Phillip and I lived in Building eight.

Our apartment rented for a whopping $37.50 per month, all utilities, even
a telephone, included. The unit consisted of three equal-sized rooms, one of
which was the bathroom. Had we not been such poor, financially-struggling
college seniors, we could have had a much larger apartment for only five dollars more per month. That would have to wait.

Sharing an entrance with a couple who were fortunate enough to have one
of the larger units, we entered our apartment from a side door,

Living on the end of our building was one of Phillip's Delta Tau Delta fraternity brothers and his wife, Tom and Penny. He was already in grad school;
she worked as a departmental secretary. They, too, were fortunate enough to
have one of the larger units.

Tom and Penny were *As the World Turns* fanatics, always eating lunch in their apartment so they would not miss an episode. Nothing, nothing, was to disturb them during the program.

In those days, we college students, if lucky, had secondhand black and white televisions. The slightest atmospheric changes played havoc with the already snowy reception. My husband, being the handyman he was and still is, had a small electric skill saw that he experimented with in his spare time. Knowing what turning on the saw did to our TV reception, Phillip decided it would be great fun if, during *As the World Turns*, he tested his skills. At first, Tom had no idea what was happening and even showed up at our door to see if our TV was working. By the time he ran out his door and around the corner to ours, Phillip always managed to hide the saw. It took Tom quite some time, and then only after hearing the saw on a lunch period, to discover the cause of his TV problems.

Why he had not heard the saw sounds before I never could figure out. Even those lucky people with the larger apartment had walls like tissue paper.

As you might expect, Tom's discovery did not deter Phillip. He would wait until the program began and then switch on his saw. Tom would come running around the end of the dorm, screaming and banging on our door. When he returned to his apartment, Phillip would flip the switch again.

South Apartments had structural problems other than thin walls. The pine floors in South Apartments had wide spaces between each plank. It was impossible to sweep them, and a vacuum cleaner was not a luxury we could afford. One warm March day right before we were to move to Paris, Texas, to do our student teaching, I came home for lunch and found that termites had swarmed and had oozed out of the spaces between the pine floorboards. We spent hours sweeping up at least two dozen dustpans full of them. The termites must have been holding hands to support the building.

Plumbing presented another structural problem. Our bathtub drained into the same pipe as the tub of the adjoining apartment, which was one of the larger units, maybe having even two bedrooms! I didn't resent the neighbors, however, as they had a couple of children, one being a little boy about five or six years old. Remember, I mentioned that our bathroom was of equal size to the bedroom/sitting room and kitchen. I think the size of the bathroom resulted in Phillip's taking leisurely baths, giving him time to think up silly pranks.

While soaking in the bathtub, he would hear the little boy behind the wall playing in the water and singing. Knowing the child could hear him, Phillip decided it would be great fun to growl as if he were a monster or squeak like a rubber ducky or whatever came to his mean mind. I hope that little boy grew up to be a kind man who would never scare a child. Better yet, maybe he enjoyed every minute he soaked in the tub and knew exactly who was making all the noises. I doubt it, though, since his father seemed to look at us with suspicion.

South Apartments were torn down a few years after we left Commerce. I guess a housing development took over the spot where we lived. I just hope the termites and the monsters and the pranksters didn't remain to invade one of the new houses.

By the way, when we moved back for our first year of graduate school, we were fortunate enough to live in one of the larger units. We were rich as we both had graduate assistantships and brought home $333.00 each month. We even had linoleum on the floors to block the termites, and we didn't have to share our bathtub drain. Today, we still refer to that year as our "wealthy" one.

I'd do it all over again.

Note: Nothing has ever been built on the site of South Apartments. The remaining trees and grassy acres make the park-like tract an attractive part of Commerce. If the termites still reside there, no one ever mentions them. FT

Chapter 98

FRESHMAN YEAR

Robert G. Cowser—Class of 1953—Saltillo

In far eastern Hopkins County during the late 1930s and the early 1940s, the place name *Commerce* was a college and the college was *Commerce*. As far as I knew, it was a place where a few men and women from our community went to in order to earn teaching certificates. Those students took the Cotton Belt train from either the Mt. Vernon or the Saltillo station.

When I attended the High School Senior Day at E.T. in 1949, I learned that Commerce was more than a college campus. People were living in the town who were neither professors nor students. I learned that Commerce had a business district with two movie theaters, a news stand, and two banks.

Enrolling in E.T. later that fall, I shared a room in a private home with another freshman, Billy Hill of Alba. The house belonged to Mr. and Mrs. Stevens and was located on Monroe Street, a few yards from the Library Building, now the Hall of Languages.

Although many World War II vets had graduated by the time I entered college, a few were still studying there. Their superior study habits impressed me. Shacks that had served as temporary quarters at Camp Maxey during World War II were moved to the campus to accommodate veterans and their families. By the time I enrolled, the college had begun to rent these tar-paper dwellings to non-veterans. In 1954 my younger brother and a roommate lived in what was called G. I. Village.

The Student Union Building was a building that had been used as an officers' lounge at Camp Maxey, a World War II training camp near Paris. I spent many hours there playing ping pong with my roommate or sitting in one of the comfortable chairs that lined the walls of the main room, listening to the recorded popular music.

The year I began college was the first year that an entire week had been set aside for orientation of beginning freshmen. There were approximately six hundred of us, most of us coming from within a fifty-mile radius of Commerce. We took proficiency tests, intelligence tests, and career preference tests and met with an adviser who helped us plan a schedule. My adviser was Orpa Dennis of the Home Economics Department.

My mother encouraged me to avoid Saturday classes since she planned to wash my clothes each week. If I could come home on Fridays, then she would have more time to wash and iron the clothes. At the beginning, I was scheduled to meet my American history class on Tuesdays, Thursdays, and Saturdays. At the first class meeting, Miss Martha Hankins, our teacher, distributed the mimeographed textbooks, written by members of the History Department. The sheets were loosely bound with staples. Miss Hankins told the class she would fail anyone who lost a single sheet of the book. "This is ridiculous," I thought and decided that I would change my history class to a Monday-Wednesday-Friday class. First, I had to get permission. Dr. R. L. Jones of the History Department was reluctant to approve my changing my schedule. I did not tell him that I wanted out of Miss Hankins' class because of my objection to her ultimatum but instead told him that I needed to leave on Fridays so that I could do my laundry at home. "Doesn't Commerce have sufficient water for laundering clothes?" he asked.

When I consider how timid I was in most situations, it amazes me that I persisted with my request. After Dr. Jones presented his objections to granting my request, I simply stood there in his office. I was determined not to have my fate in a class determined by whether I lost one page of a mimeographed book bound only by a couple of staples. Eventually Dr. Jones approved my change to Miss Catherine Neal's history class, where I found a niche so comfortable I took the follow-up course the next semester. Miss Neal was stern; she hardly smiled, if ever, but she was a thorough, competent teacher.

Ever since my younger brother studied Spanish in the fifth grade, I had wanted to learn to speak Spanish. Saltillo High School offered no courses in Spanish, but as a freshman at E.T., I could enroll in elementary Spanish. My teacher was Dr. Maude Noyes, an energetic woman who loved teaching. She was married to a professor in the Business Administration School, but because of a law of nepotism in effect at the time, they kept the marriage secret until the year after I took the Spanish class.

I joined the Spanish Club (El Club Hispanico), sponsored by Maude Noyes. As a fund-raising venture, the club planned a Mexican dinner featuring tamales. The dinner was served during a Halloween celebration that took place in the Education Building. Professor Noyes supervised us waiters, making sure that we washed our hands thoroughly with a strong soap and water.

The composition class I took as a freshman was taught by Miss Adelle Clark on the third floor of the Library Building. The class began at 7:40 a.m. so that five class periods could be scheduled before lunch. Miss Clark smiled often, even at such an early hour and was the ideal teacher for an anxious freshman like me.

Mrs. Mike O'Neill taught botany to a class of approximately thirty-five students. She also supervised the weekly labs for the class. Our class met in the laboratory for three hours each Tuesday afternoon. Having had no experience in a laboratory of any kind, I felt as if I were underwater gasping for air and trying to make it to the surface.

I had difficulty memorizing the names of the parts of the various plants and was happy to earn a C in the course. Zoology with Dr. Paul Street the next semester was less difficult for me, maybe because my father owned a team of mules, a few horses, and approximately thirty head of cattle, not to mention the chickens.

Almost every Friday my father drove to Commerce to collect my dirty laundry and me. Then on Sunday he and my mother would drive me back to Commerce. On the first Sunday in December of my freshman year, I returned to the campus early enough to hear members of the Music Department and a local chorus present the Christmas portion of Handel's *Messiah*. It was a memorable experience. Twelve years later, in Durant, Oklahoma, I had an opportunity to sing in a church choir that presented the work.

During the second semester of my freshman year, I continued with the sequential English, Spanish, history, biology courses. I decided to add a course in Business Mathematics taught by Weldon "Bub" Taylor. When I had to make a choice between preparing for the math course or one of the others, I neglected the math. As a result, I earned an F on one of the unit exams. Clearly, Mr. Taylor was disappointed. Once earlier in the course, he told me that I had a "good" math mind; sometimes he would send me to the blackboard to solve a problem. After having failed one of the exams, I became determined that I would be prepared for the final exam, which counted 1/3 of the term mark. As soon as I turned in the final exam, Mr. Taylor motioned for me to sit down. He quickly checked the answers and told me I had earned a grade of 100. He also told me I would earn a B in the course.

Before I began the first-year courses at E.T., I doubted whether I could perform adequately as a college student. At the end of the year, I was confident that with hard work and determination, I could earn the degree I very much wanted.

Louise Dunn Faires—Class of 1943

Arriving at ETSTC in the summer of 1941 was the beginning of a whole new educational life experience. For the first time in my life, I was living away from home and within walking distance of classes. Having grown up on a farm in Henderson County, I had quite a shock during my transition to Commerce's infamous black land following the first measurable rainfall. In 1941 sidewalks were not overly plentiful, and shortcuts between buildings proved to be a slick and sticky encounter.

It was that summer that I met a young man on a blind date arranged by a former junior college classmate. Little did we know that a Sunday date in early December to check the progress of Denison Dam would impact all our lives so significantly.

Chapter 99
The Final Differential

Bobby Harper—Class of 1962—Caddo Mills

I t all came down to this one final exam. I had interviewed with TEMCO in Greenville and had been offered a job starting June 1, 1962. I would be working in the engineering department as an aerospace draftsman. Mobil Oil Company in Dallas had also offered me a job as a computer programmer. I had no idea what a programmer was. There were no computer courses offered in college, so I was not even sure what a computer was. I had dropped out of college in 1957 after my sophomore year and worked for Mobil for three years. In 1960, I returned to college to finish my degree. I felt good that Mobil had offered me a job on my first interview. I had worked for Mobil in Shreveport as a geophysical draftsman, so they had some advanced knowledge of my abilities.

If all went well, I would have my B.S. in Math with a minor in Industrial Education (IE). The IE courses gave me a good background in mechanical drafting. My preparation in mathematics and drafting seemed to be an ideal fit for the engineering job. The pay was better with TEMCO, $450 per month as opposed to $420 per month, and I would be working in Greenville rather than commuting to Mobil in Dallas. I accepted the job with TEMCO and informed Mobil of my decision. There was a little irony in this decision, as I would later retire with thirty-two years in the computer field.

I was taking six courses my final senior semester with two accelerated. As a result of the accelerated format, I had completed two of the six courses in March. Of the remaining four courses, I had completed three and been told by my professors that I had passed. That left only Differential Equations (DE). This was one of the defining senior math courses.

Dr. Cecil B. Wright was the chair of the math department, and I had taken six math courses from him. We knew each other very well, and he was the professor of my DE class. I actually felt good about this course and had a solid "B" going into the final. Dr. Wright had a standard method for determining your final grade. The course grade would consist of three equal parts: the average of daily assignments, the average of minor tests, and the final exam. It was that simple. Dr. Wright would vary from this method only if he had major doubts that a student was properly prepared. If I really busted the final, I could fail and not have my degree. I knew that he would not cut me any slack, nor should he.

One of my accelerated courses that semester was Theory of Equations, and after the final exam, I had a low "C" average. Dr. Wright dropped my grade to a "D," which was one of only two "Ds" that I made in college. The other was in Dr. Bill Dunn's government class, and a "D" was a common grade with Dr. William Dunn. I had really done poorly on the final exam in Theory of Equations, and Dr. Wright was not happy with my background in that class. When I asked him why my grade had been lowered, he just looked at me with a frown and said. "It could have been worse Mr. Harper." That was enough said. I never mentioned it again.

It was my final senior semester. My future job was based on my successful graduation. I was broke and in debt to my grandfather who had loaned me $670 to finish my senior year. My wedding date had been set for August 5 of that summer. I had one more course to finish, and it was well known that this course was Dr. Wright's favorite. He had told us at the beginning of the class that he very seldom gave an "A" in DE. He also told us, "I can teach my dog to do Calculus, but it takes a little brains to do DE."

It was one of those stormy, rainy May days as I walked up the steps of the old Education Building. I had climbed these steps many times in my four years at ETSC, but never with such concern and doubt. Dr. Wright normally held all of his classes on the second floor in the north end of the Education Building. His office was on the third floor. I think he had had polio when he was younger as he walked with a noticeable limp. He came into the classroom and greeted us in his usual manner. "Good morning, gentlemen. Today is your final exam, and it consists of four questions. Please put all of your notes and books away."

This was not good news. With only four questions, I could miss two of them and end up dropping from a strong "B" to a flat "F." This did not do anything to lessen the pressure I was feeling. I could handle a "D" as my GPA was sufficient, but an "F" would leave me one course short of graduation.

He passed out the one-page test, and on his command, I turned the test paper over. I scanned the four questions very carefully. I was in total shock. Was the good Doctor trying to play tricks on us, or was I missing something? I scanned the four questions again.

There is a special form of an equation in DE, which can be solved by inspection. This means that if you recognize the special format, you can just write the solution down with little or no calculations or translations. If I was not wrong, all four of these questions were of one of those special forms. I had spent the last several days studying these special cases, and I was almost sure that they all fell into the special format.

It took me less than twenty minutes to complete the test. I checked my answers, and then started to have second thoughts. Was I wrong? Had I misinterpreted the formats? Were all of my solutions simply garbage? This was not good. I finally decided to go with my initial gut feeling. I folded the paper, put my name on the outside, and walked to Dr. Wright's desk.

I laid the completed test on his desk and started out the door. Dr. Wright stopped me as he said, "Wait just a minute, Mr. Harper." He took out his red pen, and opened the test paper. After scanning it twice, he closed the paper and with his red pen wrote a big 100% on the front. He then looked up at me with a smile, and said softly, "Good job young man."

I left the class feeling as if I could fly. The weight of the world had just been lifted off my shoulders. I would have my B.S. I would have the job. Even though I was not sure of it at the time, I even had that elusive "A" in DE. I am not sure to what I should attribute this success. Was it my study habits, or just blind luck? No matter. The world, and all that was in it, was good.

Chapter 100

THE WRIGHT WAY

Buddy Kinamon—Class of 1964—Blue Ridge

C oming from a small rural high school, I did my best to find the "easy" instructors during my first two years at E.T. It was the second semester of my junior year that I ended up in the class of Dr. Cecil B. Wright. Within the first few weeks I discovered that he was the ultimate instructor. After that, I took all my math courses under him whenever possible.

Those who knew him will remember that he suffered from polio as a child and walked with a pronounced limp—practically dragging one leg. This physical handicap did not affect his teaching. When the opening bell rang, he stepped to the board, cocked his bad leg, and began his lecture. When he drew freehand diagrams on the board, they appeared printed from the book. The only tools he used were a yardstick for straight lines and his handkerchief for circles. Again, it was near perfect.

He had a very dry sense of humor—meaning that one never knew whether to laugh or retain the game face. He never told jokes but said things in a humorous way. He was also a man of great character. I never knew anyone who spoke ill of him. I could relate several events where he employed his dry humor to make an ever-lasting impression of some great mathematical principle; however, I will defer that in order to relate events that highlighted his great character.

I received a teaching assistantship for graduate school; otherwise, I would not have been able to continue my education. I was married in March of my first calendar year of graduate school, and we had our first child in January of the following year. As the proud father, I sent Dr. Wright a birth announcement—not expecting a gift. To my great surprise, he and his wife sent a much-needed little suit.

During the following academic year, I took a job teaching Math and Physics at Greenville High School while I completed my M.S. Dr. Wright allowed me to teach a night course under the teaching assistantship program—which added much needed financial resources. Following completion of my M.S., I completed the school year at Greenville and moved on to Aerospace—first at LTV, then NASA Houston, then back to LTV. After almost six years, we had our second child. I again sent Dr. Wright a birth announcement—strictly out of respect for him. Again, to my amazement, he sent a gift.

Over the ensuing years, I have taken courses at U of Houston, SMU, and UT-Dallas. I measured all subsequent instructors using him as the standard and found them wanting. I have taught several night courses at colleges and tried my best to emulate his teaching style—knowing that I fell far short but was better for the attempt.

Among the lessons I learned from him beyond subject matter was a profound concept of fairness. I was typically a B student in my early days as a Math major but strived for the coveted A. At the beginning of each semester, he presented the grading standard—1/3 homework, 1/3 periodic quizzes, and 1/3 final exam. He graded each homework paper and returned it at the following class.

One knew exactly where he stood. I was close to an A in Integral Calculus and had high hopes. When the semester ended, my average was 89 2/5—not quite the required 90. I went to see him to discuss the matter. I said, "Dr. Wright, that is very close to an A." He replied "Yes, but not close enough. If you had 89 3/5, I would round it off to 90." No further explanation was required. I knew the required standard and knew equally well that I did not achieve it. I never forgot his sense of fairness and attempted to use it throughout my teaching. It has also been useful in all aspects of my life to put a face on the abstract concept of fairness.

Chapter 101

TRADING COTTON FOR COLLEGE

Jerold D. Moore—Class of 1964—Commerce

Had East Texas State Teachers College been located any place else but Commerce, I probably would never have gone to college. But since it was practically in the backyard of the cotton farm north of Commerce where I was raised, and since it was especially friendly to the local school graduates, I found myself enrolled in college at the ripe old age of sixteen.

It would be a mistake to assume that I was one of those child-prodigies who aced all of the high school work and tests and therefore was bumped into college at an early age. In 1939 it was no different than 2010—kids had to be six to start school. My birthday is in the middle of November, which meant that ordinarily I would have been almost seven when I could start the first grade. However, my granddad was a trustee of the country school I was to attend, and with his influence, I was able to start school at five. The next year the State of Texas changed the number of years needed to graduate from high school from eleven to twelve, and to accommodate this change, every student was simply bumped up a year. That meant that I was in the third grade at age six and therefore graduated at age sixteen.

So, there I was—sixteen years old with a mother who was determined that I would go to college, and there was a college practically in our backyard. The tuition at that time was $35.00 a semester, including books, with no extra fees. Not only was I young, I looked younger, and that seemed to baffle the instructors when I came into a classroom. I didn't know exactly what to expect or how to cope with the demands of college life.

I made a low score in English on the entrance exam and was quickly dispatched to English 101X. Luckily, or maybe unluckily, my friend Bob was in the same class which started at 1 p.m. right after lunch, during the warmest part of the day and without air conditioning. You can guess the rest. Not exactly sterling English students and not finding the instructor (who, by the way, never checked roll) particularly stimulating, every afternoon Bob and I found ourselves facing the same hard decision—go to class or not go to class. In addition, it was hard for our young ears to ignore the beckoning siren's call of the Student Union Building, where students were laughing and chatting, smokers were smoking, and the black jack game was in full swing upstairs.

The classes I did enjoy at E.T. were shop and drafting. I benefitted from the hands-on opportunities, especially under the guidance of Mr. Kibler. I think my wife is saving some of my handiwork, but I'm not sure where. The skills I learned in the drafting classes helped me get a drafting job at Rockwell Valves in Sulphur Springs in 1956 when I still lacked six hours completing my degree. From there I used those skills and training to move on to TEMCO in Greenville and while working there I was able to complete the course hours to graduate from the college, which by then was East Texas State University, in 1964. I wasn't so young anymore, but they tell me I still looked young for my age.

Many of my memories of Old E.T. revolved around the fun times and the fun people who gathered in the SUB, the dorms, and at ball games. It was a simpler time full of simple pleasures. It startles me when I think of some of the antics we pulled in those years, things that if done today would result in severe and long-lasting penalties being levied on us.

One particularly exciting time was when East Texas State and North Texas State were big football rivals. One Friday night before a Saturday game, rumor had it that some of those North Texas students were driving a spanking new Oldsmobile past the E.T. athletic dorm yelling trash out the window and blowing the horn. The rumor continued that one of the E.T. football players grabbed a shotgun and stuck it out the window of that old converted army barrack and fired at that car. The North Texas students made a hasty retreat away from the campus. Rumor did not say whether the shotgun hit its target, but it's more exciting to think of that new Oldsmobile with E.T. shot in its fenders.

I have many other memories about the colorful friends and characters who rambled around on the campus while I was there but the telling of them would require naming names. At this stage of my life, I feel the need to protect the few years I have left.

I can, however, tell one more that was told to me by a friend about the night he woke up in his second floor room above the College Inn on the north side of the campus and found himself choking on smoke. As he explained it, he got out of bed to see what the problem was and found that a mattress in another room had been burning. Upon investigation, he discovered that the occupant of that room had returned from a fun evening, lay down on his bed to smoke a cigarette, and fell asleep. When he woke up, he found that a small fire had started in his mattress. He got up, wet a washcloth, put it on the burning spot, and went back to bed. Shortly, he woke up again to find that the fire had gotten bigger, so he got up, wet a towel, put it on the burning spot, and went back to bed. Later, another tenant woke up because of all the smoke and discovered that the entire mattress was on fire. He pulled the sleeping party-goer out of bed and threw the mattress out of the window. And—that's my memory of the true story my friend told me.

Dr. James G. Gee was president of ETSTC while I was enrolled, and he clearly was the man in charge of the campus and a man of strong views. I particularly remember his attitude toward integration of the college which he announced by saying there would never be any Blacks at East Texas State Teachers College. However, to his credit, when the time came for that inevitable change, he oversaw a smooth end of segregation on the campus.

There aren't many cotton fields around the campus these days, and those young freshmen of 1951 have watched many changes in the world, the region, the town of Commerce, and the college we knew as East Texas State Teachers College. Many of us have seen our children, grandchildren, and even great-grandchildren pursue their education at the same campus. The name may be different—but the roots firmly in place are from Old E.T.

Chapter 102
CROSSING THE RIVER

Phil Pemberton—Class of 1964—Caddo Mills

In the late 1950s, most of the East Texas State College students were from small towns and cities of populations under twenty thousand people. My high school graduating class of eighteen had eight students entering E.T. in September of 1959. All five of the boys pledged the Tejas social club.

The town of Caddo Mills, Texas, boasting a population of 512, had no stoplights on Highway 67. Some ten years prior, on a summer day, you might find any or all of these five boys, Jimmy Bost, Gerald Castle, Jere Kelly, Glenn Newman, and me standing around Conard Bethea's mechanics garage watching the work. As we were usually in the way, Mr. Bethea would ask if we would go find a pair of "skyhooks" he needed. He might say, "Boys, I think they may be at the Gulf gas station." We would hurry to the station only to be informed the skyhooks might be at the blacksmith's shop. After this stop, the conspiring grownups sent us on this goose chase to the lumberyard, cotton gins, and other locations. An hour later, we reported our failed quest. The next search might be for a *left-handed monkey wrench* or a *nut and bolt reducer*. We were as gullible as eight-to ten-year-old boys usually are. Being gullible didn't end in Caddo Mills.

At E.T., several of the Tejas social club brothers ate at a boarding house owned by Mrs. Stolph located on Live Oak Street. The twenty-five dollars was for twenty meals a month, including lunch and dinner. Several of the fraternity brothers worked serving and washing dishes. After eating, we returned to the fraternity house called the Hoss House located on Washington Street. This two-story wooden structure built in the 1920s had room for up to twenty people at fifteen dollars per month.

On a typical Thursday evening from six to eight o'clock, some of the brothers in the house might study in their rooms; others got ready for a "coke date," or took a date to the library. It was safe to go to the library since B.E. "Burley" Denton, the flatulent phantom of the halls of knowledge, had already graduated. By 8 p.m., all the others remaining in the house had settled into their routines. Some brothers living elsewhere would drop by to visit and watch the black and white television.

The voice of Larry "Lash" Horton would shout, "Who would like to go across the Red River for a beer?" Pencils or pens dropped on desks. First out of a room might be Dewayne "Buffer" Bethea, son of Conard Bethea, with his arms folded in a stoic position and a pencil behind his ear asking, "When will we be back?" Someone might inquire, "Why not go to Dallas?" At this time, Hunt County was a dry county with no alcohol sold except by a plentiful number of bootleggers. A debate might start as to whether to go north or west for suds. If one of the mathematics majors was in the house such as Greg "Toad" LeMaster, Tony Gavin, Billy Halbert, or Bobby Harper, they might argue for crossing the river. They would give a logical convincing reason. It is sixty-six miles to Dallas and only forty-four miles across the river to Oklahoma. This is a ratio in mileage of 66:44 or 3:2. The beer in Oklahoma is 3.2 percent with less alcohol by volume than Texas beer. The 3:2 ratios versus 3.2 beer with less alcohol intake and less distance to travel must be more than a coincidence. The travel direction was settled. To get more riders, Lash would cup his hands and say, "Free catfish and nickel beer at the lounge." Books snapped shut, and the television expired. Jerry "Hog Jaw" Norman with great enthusiasm would state, "I'll drive the "Green Gnat." This was his 1950 four-door green Dodge. Perhaps Jim Hammock would drive his "Campus Cruiser." The last effort to fill the second car would be to bring your books and study for your Friday test going to and coming back from Oklahoma.

Once we had acquired enough twenty cents per gallon gasoline, we were on our way to the north bank of the Red River. The first stop would be a place called the TV Lounge. This establishment had typical low lighting, a spacious dance floor, and no free catfish or nickel beer. After the initial quenching of our thirst, some would remain at this enterprise looking for the love of their life while a carload of other voyagers went to the next bar down the road.

The next stop was a tavern called Pop's Place with much less ambiance, much more noise, and cheaper beer. The beer was cheaper although the price was more than a nickel, and the only free catfish were swimming in the Red River. There was a shuffleboard table at the rear of the bar usually commanded by two ladies who could certainly hold up their end of the table. In fact, they could hold up each end of the twenty-five foot table with one hand while quaffing a mug of beer in the other hand. Each woman was a steady player and would field dress at about 230 pounds. Playing for a beer a game, we paid a great deal of tuition over the years to become competent commanders of the chrome disks.

Eventually, we all gathered at one of the two places and caravanned back to E.T. If one was riding in the car with Milton "Little Mouse" Mallory, you heard the story about Henry "Big Mouse" Davis and others who once drove a car with slightly deflated tires across the railroad bridge over the Red River. No matter what time we returned to the fraternity house, it was our duty to wake all who declined the trip of brotherly bonding. Gullibility was insured to live another day. As boys looking for *skyhooks* or young men looking for free catfish and nickel beer, life was still in the chase.

John Allen—Class of 1939

My Aunt Annie's phone rang at 1:40 a.m. I answered, sleepily. An officious-sounding voice said, "Mr. Allen, this is James A. Byron of WBAP. Not one single piece of music you submitted for the College Choir broadcast tomorrow is cleared. Sorry I couldn't reach you earlier, but you'll have to make substitutions that comply with our BMI license." The E.T. choir had a broadcast from the campus every other Saturday.

I hot-footed it across campus and got Roy Johnson out of bed. Mr. Johnson was the head of E.T.'s Music department. The two of us were down in the floor studying about four square yards of sheet music, trying to pick a program the choir could sing without rehearsal when Hiram Goad dropped by. He said he saw the light on and wondered what was up. For several minutes we ignored Hiram until he began to stifle snickers and guffaws. It was then we realized we'd been had. The snake gleefully admitted he was the caller who got us out of bed—not James A. Byron!

Months later we got revenge. I went by Dean Ferguson's office and liberated an E.T. letterhead and envelope. I typed a letter expelling Hiram. When he opened it at Mrs. Alexander's boarding house, he turned ashen. He suffered trying to decide which of his many infractions resulted in his expulsion. With justifiable pleasure, I told him I was the author of the letter.

Chapter 103
TWO TIMES—60S AND 70S

Dolores Meyers—Class of 1978—Kilgore

My time at Old E.T. was divided, the first time being a newly wed and necessarily employed. I lived in South Dorm with my husband, Woodie Meyers. Fast forward to late 70s. I was an adult student with two children in school. Our best friends, Mary Jane and Carroll Lakey, also attended E.T. Mary Jane enrolled as a student somewhat later. She was the inspiration for an old lady like me to start to E.T. at the age of thirty-three.

I enjoyed getting an education like nothing else. I transferred from Eastfield Community College in Mesquite and started to E.T. as a junior. With a family and my husband's income, this was hard for us economically. Woodie taught and coached at Seagoville High School, and one of his college friends, Jim Williams, was working on his administrative degree at E.T. Jim and I rode the bus together from Seagoville to Commerce each day for summer classes. He made me get on first so I could save him an aisle seat to accommodate his long legs.

Looking back at the first time I lived at E.T, I'm amazed at how little we lived on. I worked at Cranford's Drug for fifty cents an hour. We spent no more than a dollar a week on gas and five dollars a week for groceries. We had a hand-me-down Pontiac sedan. A lot of mornings it wouldn't crank, so I walked the mile to work.

Looking back, it's unbelievable that ladies wore high-heeled shoes and stockings to football games, even in freezing temperature.

In closing, let me say that I had some very interesting classes with good instructors. I'm very fortunate to be educated, and I believe a good education teaches you how to learn. I've never stopped being curious about everything and everyone and deem it a pleasure to know how to find answers to questions. Last, but not least, I can thank Old E.T. for providing me a way out of poverty.

Chapter 104
AN UNFORGETTABLE
EXPERIENCE

James Jeffcoat—Class of 1957—Commerce

I t was late in the day, and the change of the tide had caused the sea breeze to turn inland, cooling Savannah to a comfortable temperature. I was a happy and very proud new father, as my wife, Mary, had just given birth to our daughter, Rosalind.

The date was April 21, 1954, and we were still living in Savannah, Georgia. It was decision time following my discharge from the U.S. Navy. Get a good job to make a living for our family or go back to college under the World War II G.I. Bill.

Having grown up in Commerce and attended the Training School on the campus of ETSTC, the decision was easy. Go back home and get an education.

I made several calls to the college to coordinate everything necessary to get started. The director of housing said that we could move into G.I. Village. The timing was almost perfect to start to school during the first term summer semester.

In May 1954, we moved into our assigned apartment in G.I. Village. Things went well with signing up for the G.I. Bill and entering the freshman class. However, it did not take long to find out what living in GI Village was like. As a child, I watched the construction of these apartment units following World War II, and I was not dispelled by the fact that they were made of plywood and sat about three feet off the ground on bois d'arc stumps. At the time that seemed very acceptable to me.

As I recall, the rent was $30 per month and $10 more for a telephone. Though we had to adjust to a few things out of the ordinary while living there, we were happy to have a place to live with our new daughter. Our apartment was on the east end of a four apartment building. Every time the wind blew, we felt our rooms move slightly. None of the apartments had air conditioning. In fact the Science Building was the only building on campus that did have air conditioning.

Also, we had to be careful of our conversations as the partition between the apartments had an opening at the top of the wall about two inches down from the ceiling. Sometimes we enjoyed the conversation of the couple next door, and likewise I am sure they often tuned in to ours.

With the apartments being off the ground, our plumbing froze in the winter when the temperature dropped to freezing. There was no heat except from the kitchen stove. It is amazing how you learn to adjust when you really have the desire to get an education.

Having lived in Commerce most of my life, and virtually growing up on campus, I had many opportunities to interact with professors and personnel. I knew everyone working on campus.

The Ag farm boys let me ride with them on the garbage wagon, and sometimes even let me drive. It never mattered to me that we were hauling garbage. One of my favorite hangouts was the campus dairy barn where they made ice cream.

No one believes this, but there was a "burning pit" located about where the parking lot for the Field House is now. They burned the old books there. I don't know if there is anyone alive who can verify this, but I have in my library a few of the books that I "rescued" from the burning pit.

My buddies and I enjoyed hunting by the creek that ran through the campus, about where the football field is now located. That was a favorite courting place for the WACs when they were on campus. We used to shoot our guns in the air just to see the couples scrambling out of the bushes and trees. For twelve-year-olds, that was great fun.

I have many memories of football games, dances, and other events that happened on campus before, during, and following World War II. The U.S. Army and WAC organizations were on campus, and they played an important role with me. We used to watch the Army Engineers drill and run their obstacle courses. Then, on days when they were not around, we ran the obstacle courses to prove that we could do many of the same physical things that the Army guys could do.

In 1944 most of our Training School class transferred to Commerce High School. The remaining students became the last class to graduate from Training School when it closed in 1948.

As a football player at Commerce High School, I received a four year scholarship to play football at ETSTC. I was just a young skinny kid, but I thought I could hold my own, even though most of the college football team consisted of grown men from World War II. What a misjudgment that was. I started working out with the team in August of 1948, and three weeks into practice, I had to make another decision. Do something else or prepare to die on the practice field. I was about six feet tall, weighed 160 lbs., and could not outrun anyone. Every play I expected one of two things to happen: to be carried to the hospital or die from the collisions I endured. So, I gave up all of this fun and joined the U.S. Navy.

This story actually begins five years later when I returned to ETSTC to continue my education. I enjoyed serving in the U.S. Navy, but having grown up around aircraft, I decided that I wanted to complete the last two years of college in the USAF ROTC Program, then return to the military as a commissioned officer, and make a career of flying aircraft.

All of this occurred as I had planned. Having gone straight through school, I managed to graduate in the summer of 1957. I was commissioned in the USAF Reserves, but due to the fact that I had graduated as a "Distinguished Military Graduate," I also received an appointment as a commissioned officer in the regular US Air Force.

After completing all of the required flying schools and initial flight training in the C-124 Globemaster, I settled into making a career out of the USAF. However, in 1961 I had an opportunity to apply for and received permission to return to ETSTC to finish graduate school. This happened in 1962, and I completed my required courses and graduated with a Masters Degree before returning to active duty.

The education I received at Old E.T. was invaluable during my USAF career. Looking back, I was a proud inductee into the Kappa Delta Pi Zeta Mu Chapter in graduate school. I am grateful that I had the opportunity to attend ETSTC; it has always been an important part of my life.

Today's modern school at Texas A&M University-Commerce is a far cry from the old ETSTC campus. Walking through campus looking at the new and modern buildings and hearing about all the technology that is now the leading major subject is a wonderful experience.

However, nothing can ever take the place of the memories I have carried all of my life of the Old E.T., and the campus life that existed back then.

Chapter 105

High Drama on
November 23, 1963

Morton Richard Schroeder—Class of 1964—Garland

In the spring of 1963, Dr. Curtis L. Pope, Professor and Head of the Drama Department at East Texas State University, arranged with city officials of Jefferson, Texas, to present plays in that time capsule of the Old South. That spring Dr. Pope and his students presented two performances in the courtyard of the historic Excelsior Hotel.

Dr. Pope's first presentation on campus in the fall semester of 1963 was *Mister Roberts*. When casting that comedy, he notified the cast members that two weeks after the run on campus, we would take the play to Jefferson and present it at the Jefferson Playhouse.

On a Friday morning in November, the cast and crew, and trucks and personnel from college maintenance left for Jefferson. We arrived at the playhouse just after lunch and started unloading scenery and props. Then the crew went inside and started setting up for the opening night's performance.

Just as the crew started arranging the scenery, Midge Pope, Dr. Pope's wife, rushed in the front door and down the center aisle. She ran up to her husband and said, "They just shot Kennedy. They just killed the President."

Dr. Pope sat down on the front row of seats. Midge added, "I knew something bad would happen if he went to Dallas. I just knew it."

Dr. Pope sat quietly for a few minutes and then called the cast and crew together. He announced the events in Dallas to those who had not heard and then added that he had decided to go ahead with the production that night despite this national tragedy. The hit comedy was presented to a small audience who were not disposed toward laughter.

The next week in *Stage Craft and Scenic Design*, Dr. Pope spoke about another event which happened that weekend in Jefferson. On Sunday, when he and Midge were in the lobby of the Excelsior Hotel preparing to return to Commerce, they heard some local citizens of Jefferson laughing and joking about the assassination of President Kennedy. They were delighted about the events of the weekend. Dr. Pope was devastated. He never took another theatrical production to Jefferson!

Chapter 106
TIME TO OPEN THE TIME CAPSULE

Scott Reighard—Class of 1986—Pennsylvania

T here was a phone call during the summer of 1981. I spoke with Coach Ernest Hawkins about my prospects of playing football for him. Florida wasn't exactly within the recruiting zone of then ETSU although there were three of us from Florida who happened to arrive that year, the most notable being Alan Veingrad. However, despite my lack of high school football, coach told me, "Son, if you're willing to drive 1,300 miles to come to school, then you are welcome to come tryout." I was a three-sport athlete in high school who hadn't played football since ninth grade recreation football. To say this was a tall task was to say the sun was insignificant.

How did I end up at ETSU, all the way from Florida? Well, it's a funny story. I was, and continue to be, a huge Minnesota Vikings fan, and they happened to draft this guy by the name of Wade Wilson. When I read about him in subsequent days of the draft, I saw that he came from a pro style offensive system at East Texas State University. I figured, if a quarterback from a small school like ETSU could get drafted, it was worth considering. When you're seventeen, you think you can do anything. We've all been there, right? Anyhow, I wanted to be a receiver, and a pro style system was the best place for me to ply my desire. Weird yes, odd yes, but it happened that way.

On Friday, July 31· my mom and dad waved goodbye as I pulled out of the driveway. I was seventeen years old and had never driven farther than thirty miles away from home by myself, let alone the nearly 1,300 it would take to get to Commerce. My father said the following before I hopped into the driver's seat, "Don't speed; don't pick up hitch hikers, especially girls—they'll give you something you don't want anything to do with; and mind your money." A tearful hug from my mom made me feel as though I was going on that *Journey to the Center of the Earth* not knowing if I would return in one piece.

Without any major mishaps, other than hitting an owl about halfway between Hattiesburg and Jackson, Mississippi, I arrived safely in Commerce on Saturday, August 1, only to find out that I was the only football person there. Everyone else was arriving on Sunday. I found Coach Hawkins in his office. I'm sure he looked at me and thought, "Kid, you're not off to a good start."

Coach called over to Hubbell Hall, which was preparing for all freshman players to arrive, and they were nice enough to set me up in Room 303 a day before everyone else. Thus began a truly roller coaster ride over the course of the next five years.

Ego and reality are sometimes a hurtful combination. By the spring of 1983, I was completely frustrated with myself and the lack of opportunities, mostly due to the fact that not playing high school football was now catching up to me. I felt I was behind the learning curve, plus the fact that these guys were a heckuva lot faster than I was, and stronger as well. I left ETSU thinking I would never return.

A sense *of déjà vu* occurred in the summer of 1984. Once again, I was on the phone with Coach Hawkins. I think he was more skeptical than the first time. I had quit before. Why would this attempt be any different? I had taken a year off from school, and that decision allowed me a lot of time to think about what I wanted to do. I kept working out, running and lifting. I was tossing the ball around almost everyday, plus I had gained ten pounds, muscle weight that is. It was another early August day, and I was on my way back to Commerce.

Other than our school winning the Florida state lacrosse championship my senior year, one of the greatest days of my young life occurred in the summer of 1985. Coach Hawkins summoned me to his office. I was nervous. When coach calls you in, a lot of bad stuff starts swirling in your head. I sat across from the enigmatic hoary headed legend, and he said, "Son, I have to give you a lot of credit. Most boys would have never returned. They would have tucked their tails between their legs and run away for good. You not only came back, but you have made substantial progress, and for that I am going to reward you."

I worked extremely hard and even worked into getting some game action. I knew all the routes, could finally read most defenses, and made some gains with my speed. Because of this, coach gave me a partial scholarship, either that or he just felt sorry for me. Either way, I couldn't believe what I was hearing. He could have given me a dollar, and I would have been ecstatic. In retrospect, leaving ETSU was the best thing I could have ever done although my timing was terrible. The year I was away, they won the Lone Star Conference.

In December of 1986, I had answered most of the questions I had about myself. I graduated having played four full seasons as an ETSU Lion. For a kid who didn't play high school football, to earn a partial scholarship, and to get some playing time behind some great receivers like Wes Smith and Winfred Essix is a pretty fulfilling accomplishment.

One of the worst days there was when Coach Hawkins announced his retirement. I was going into my senior season, and the coach who gave me a shot, the one who took a chance on a marginal guy, was leaving. I think I was the saddest guy on the field that day when he made his announcement.

My senior year was not exactly a bell weather year for me. In fact, it was rather anti-climatic. What was to be a year of hope and opportunity all hinged on one man, Eddie Vowell. I had a few nagging injuries, and even tore my quadriceps muscle because I went back to practice too early. Now, this excuse may sound like sour grapes, but you had to be there. He actually attempted to get me to quit my senior year. He called me into his office and said, "You have no chance of playing for me; why don't you just quit." Can you imagine? All the hard work I put into this, busting my you know what day after day, getting bigger, stronger, faster, smarter, etc, and he says I have no shot?

Anyhow, I soon developed a motto: Never allow anyone to talk you out of, or keep you from, your dream. Every day I went to practice and gave one hundred percent. Every day was just another day he would have to look at me. The only compliment he ever gave me was, "I admire your intestinal fortitude because others would have quit." I guess that was a compliment. So, I soldiered on and completed an improbable dream. I played college football, and no one, no one, can take that away. Because of those days, both good and terrible, I am the man I am today and grateful for those trying times that asked the question, "How bad do you want this?"

So, coach, am I still on your Christmas card list?

Chapter 107

THE BEST OF TIMES

Evonne Verner Richardson—Class of 1950—Commerce

M y college years were the best experience of my life. Of course that meant staying at home four more years. However, home was a good place to be if you lived in Commerce, Texas, and had wonderful parents and a brother, plus the joy of being an identical twin. Had we not lived here, we could never have attended ETSTC.

Five Commerce High School graduates who were friends all through high school entered E.T. in the fall of 1946. Most of us did not have classes together, except for Lavonne and me, but we stayed closely connected. Our common class was Physical Education, and our free time seemed to be spent at Whitley Gym. We hung around the gym after class so we could watch the boys basketball team practice.

This era was during the Ingram dynasty, when the starting five players were from Quitman, Texas, and were all related. Only one of our five married one of them; that was Dorothy Dunn, who married Troy and moved away for him to coach.

By the time we left the gym each day, there were about eight or ten guys and gals in a group, and it did not take a lot to entertain us, just a bowl of popped corn or fudge seemed to do the trick with the boys.

Elizabeth Huggins, Gertrude Warmack, and Dr. Everettt Shepperd were my favorites instructors. They all became lifetime friends of our family. By our senior year, we had to do some serious studying, and we spent a lot of hours in the beautiful old library with all the chandeliers, brass fittings, and rich oak tables. The reading room was a huge two-story open space which accommodated the military balls held by the ROTC units and other social events.

I remember the "T" bench that was sacred and positioned just southeast of the Student Union Building, and I was fond of the romantic "leaning tree," which was finally cut down. Many students became engaged at that leaning tree.

I married in the summer of 1950, and all our high school group of girls had married also, except for Lavonne. She taught one semester, and then decided Dallas was the place for her. Dorothy, Lavonne, and I still live in Commerce. Things seemed to have come full circle with us.

I have always appreciated the sacrifices my parents made for me to receive a quality education. Thirty years later I retired from teaching physical education, sponsoring cheerleaders and drill teams, coaching math, English, and even one disastrous semester of high school math. I warned them. Well, I did have good discipline in my classes.

I am enjoying my retirement as Lavonne and I live in the house where we grew up in Commerce. I always have a best friend, just across the hall. I maintain a small clothing alteration business, but most of my time is spent in volunteering, mostly on the E.T. campus for projects with the Alumni Center and athletics.

Yes, E.T. was the best of times.

Charlene Munn Acker—Class of 1944

Sam H. Whitley was president while I was at E.T. I'll always be thankful for President Whitley. He was willing to help a country girl get a job on campus. I worked in the typing bureau on the same floor as his office. I remember a girl, Iris, who worked the same hours. President Whitley would come in for a short visit. He would look at me and say, "Hi, Iris." Then he would look at Iris and say, "Hi, Charlene." We all would have a good laugh. He knew which name belonged to each girl. He was a kind and courteous gentleman.

Chapter 108

THE BIRTH OF
TEXAS A&M UNIVERSITY -
COMMERCE

Sherman K. Burns—Class of 1976—Mesquite

I really enjoyed my years as a member of the East Texas State University Endowment Foundation Board. It wasn't so much the prestige of being on the board; it was the people with whom I was able to interact. It was also nice to be out of the office for a day with the feeling that I was giving back to the university that had meant so much to me.

The Endowment Board met twice a year, once during the fall semester and once in the spring. In 1995, during the fall meeting, I found myself at the President's home for the cocktail reception that typically followed a full day of meetings.

I always looked forward to this event because most of the faculty attended, and it was a great time to visit and catch up with some of my former professors. Some of my favorites from the business school included Mr. Jack Ingram, Dr. Sue McCall, Dr. Robert Noe, Dr. Manton, and Dr. Tressie Presley.

The real buzz on campus at that time was the pending merger of East Texas with Texas A&M. During the party I happened to end up standing next to President Jerry Morris and asked him about the merger and name change. I also asked Jerry about the results of the survey that had gone out to the alumni regarding the name change.

To be honest I was really hoping the name would be changed to East Texas A&M, and not Texas A&M Commerce. I felt strongly that the "East

Texas" portion should survive in some fashion, so it was a great time for me to "politic" for my choice. Jerry informed me that not only had a survey gone out to the alumni and students but local residents and businesses in Commerce were polled.

He told me that the results were almost evenly divided between the two names. The local residences and business people had overwhelmingly wanted Texas A&M University-Commerce (for obvious reasons), but the alumni and students were leaning more to the East Texas A&M University name. Of course I immediately jumped on the rationale that current and former students should carry more weight than the "locals."

Interestingly enough, Jerry then shared some conversations he had with some other university presidents who had merged into Texas A&M. He gave examples of West Texas A&M and Tarleton State versus Texas A&M – Kingsville. He mentioned that those that had not used the Texas A&M (with the city) had regretted not doing so, mostly due to the prestige of having the "A&M" as part of the name.

I did remind Jerry that East Texas A&M, like West Texas A&M had the "A&M" part. I guess we all know how that turned out, and Texas A&M University-Commerce was born.

Otha Spencer—Class of 1942

A memorable E.T. episode was my being called to President Sam Whitley's office when I wrote an editorial against a faculty member who, I thought, was exerting too much influence in a social club. I wasn't kind in my words. The president said he probably agreed with me, but he reminded me that "things aren't done that way on the campus," and that I must apologize. I did, in print, and found that the faculty member didn't care about what I thought. I was crushed that I had not been a great editorial influence on the campus.

Chapter 109

HOMAGE

Ann Oglesby Julian—Class of 1962—Commerce

Our last homecoming was a sad event.
With tears, we sang our last lament.
Once we had lost our good name,
Loyalty and pride were not the same.
East Texas A&M Commerce
Would have been a good name.
Or, East Texas A&M
Would have caused no shame.
After one hundred years of proud tradition,
Why were we consumed by another's ambition?
Is it too late to reconsider our name
One more time?
East Texas' many virtues are on the line.
If not,
Goodbye East Texas, my dear old friend,
We were with you until the very end.
Can anyone not see why it will be?
ALWAYS, ALWAYS E. T. TO ME!

INDEX

Clark, Jim, 280
Clark, Miss Adelle, 79, 280, 286
Clements, Robert, 37, 42
Clemmer, Miss, 46
Clemmons, John, 42
Clovers, The, 35
Cochran, Dr. Sam, 3, 5
Cockelreas, Dr. Joanne, 147
Cole, Gregory V., 240
Colehour, Miss Gretchen Howell, 216
Coles, Kittye Ruth Lawler, 186
Coles, Scaley, 186
Collins, Patricia McElrath, 195
Commerce High School, 20, 79, 157, 163,
    180, 191, 257, 303, 310
Compton, Gary, 71, 205, 207
Conlan, Jane, 193
Cooper High School, 154, 276
Cooper, 1, 153, 154, 158, 221, 245, 276
Cooper, Larry, 80
Corner, Dusty, 205
Cory, Richard, 259
Costner, Kevin, 70
Cowley, Malcolm, 113
Cowling, Mr., 215
Cowser, Robert, 257, 284
Cox, Bill, 85
Cox, Ellen "Tweet," 85
Cox, George B., 85, 163
Cox, Homer, 85
Cox, Robert, 280
Cox, Zelma Barlett, 85
Crader, Helen, 15
Craig, Shelby, 102, 103
Crane, Sandra, 274
Cranford, Jean, 45

Crawford, Coach C. W. "Boley," 73
Creagh, Miss Emma, 211
Crump, Miss, 212
Cummings, Jess, 180
Cummings, Lou, 180
Curry, Preston, 177
Curtis, Kandy, 202

Dacus, Dr. Lee, 182, 183
Dale, Thurman, 238
Daniel, William "Bill" E., 120
Darby, Coy White, 136
Darby, Denny, 136
Darby, Juanita Martin, 136
Darrow, Clarence, 240
Davis, Henry "Big Mouse," 298
Davis, Ken, 151
DeGenaro, Jennie Jennings, 95
DeKalb, 173, 238
Delta Chi, 63
Delta Sigma Pi, 168
Delta Tau Delta, 213, 281
Dennis, Miss Orpa, 26, 279
Denton, Burley, 35, 36, 37, 42, 134, 297
Dewberry, Morris Lee, 91
Dexter, Charles, 238
Dickson, Helen Ratliff, 235
Dodd, Nelma, 38, 264
Dodd, Tommie, 264
Doenier, Dr. Carl, 280
Dorries, Dr., 98
Dorrough, Owen, 120, 122
Dotson, Joel, 185
Doty, Mrs., 46
Dowell, Dr. Bob, 32
Doyle, Carolyn Andrews, 69